OTHER BOOKS BY CHRIS GRABENSTEIN

THE HAUNTED MYSTERY SERIES
The Crossroads
Winner of the Agatha Award and the Anthony Award

The Hanging Hill
Winner of the Agatha Award

The Smoky Corridor

The Black Heart Crypt
Winner of the Agatha Award

CHRIS GRABENSTEIN

RANDOM HOUSE 🏠 NEW YORK

Text copyright © 2013 by Chris Grabenstein
Jacket art copyright © 2013 by Gilbert Ford

All rights reserved. Published in the United States by
Random House Children's Books, a division of Random House, Inc., New York.

Random House and the colophon are registered trademarks of
Random House, Inc.

Visit us on the Web! randomhouse.com/kids

Educators and librarians, for a variety of teaching tools, visit us at
RHTeachersLibrarians.com

Library of Congress Cataloging-in-Publication Data
Grabenstein, Chris.
Escape from Mr. Lemoncello's library / Chris Grabenstein. — 1st ed.
pages cm.
Summary: "Twelve-year-old Kyle gets to stay overnight in the new
town library, designed by his hero (the famous gamemaker Luigi Lemoncello),
with other students but finds that come morning he must work with friends
to solve puzzles in order to escape." —Provided by publisher.
ISBN 978-0-375-87089-7 (trade) — ISBN 978-0-375-97089-4 (lib. bdg.) —
ISBN 978-0-307-97496-9 (ebook)
[1. Libraries—Fiction. 2. Books and reading—Fiction. 3. Games—Fiction.]
I. Title. II. Title: Escape from Mister Lemoncello's library.
PZ7.G7487Es 2013 [Fic]—dc23 2012048122

Printed in the United States of America

20 19 18 17 16

First Edition

For the late Jeanette P. Myers,
and all the other librarians who help us find
whatever we're looking for

1

This is how Kyle Keeley got grounded for a week.

First he took a shortcut through his mother's favorite rosebush.

Yes, the thorns hurt, but having crashed through the brambles and trampled a few petunias, he had a five-second jump on his oldest brother, Mike.

Both Kyle and his big brother knew exactly where to find what they needed to win the game: inside the house!

Kyle had already found the pinecone to complete his "outdoors" round. And he was pretty sure Mike had snagged his "yellow flower." Hey, it was June. Dandelions were everywhere.

"Give it up, Kyle!" shouted Mike as the brothers dashed up the driveway. "You don't stand a chance."

Mike zoomed past Kyle and headed for the front door, wiping out Kyle's temporary lead.

Of course he did.

Seventeen-year-old Mike Keeley was a total jock, a high school superstar. Football, basketball, baseball. If it had a ball, Mike Keeley was good at it.

Kyle, who was twelve, wasn't the star of anything.

Kyle's other brother, Curtis, who was fifteen, was still trapped over in the neighbor's yard, dealing with their dog. Curtis was the smartest Keeley. But for *his* "outdoors" round, he had pulled the always unfortunate Your Neighbor's Dog's Toy card. Any "dog" card was basically the same as a Lose a Turn.

As for why the three Keeley brothers were running around their neighborhood on a Sunday afternoon like crazed lunatics, grabbing all sorts of wacky stuff, well, it was their mother's fault.

She was the one who had suggested, "If you boys are bored, play a board game!"

So Kyle had gone down into the basement and dug up one of his all-time favorites: Mr. Lemoncello's Indoor-Outdoor Scavenger Hunt. It had been a huge hit for Mr. Lemoncello, the master game maker. Kyle and his brothers had played it so much when they were younger, Mrs. Keeley wrote to Mr. Lemoncello's company for a refresher pack of clue cards. The new cards listed all sorts of different bizarro stuff you needed to find, like "an adult's droopy underpants," "one dirty dish," and "a rotten banana peel."

(At the end of the game, the losers had to put everything back exactly where the items had been found. It was an official rule, printed inside the top of the box, and made winning the game that much more important!)

While Curtis was stranded next door, trying to talk the neighbor's Doberman, Twinky, out of his favorite tug toy, Kyle and Mike were both searching for the same two items, because for the final round, all the players were given the same Riddle Card.

That day's riddle, even though it was a card Kyle had never seen before, had been extra easy.

FIND TWO COINS FROM 1982 THAT ADD UP TO THIRTY CENTS AND ONE OF THEM CANNOT BE A NICKEL.

Duh. The answer was a quarter and a nickel because the riddle said only *one* of them couldn't be a nickel.

So to win, Kyle had to find a 1982 quarter *and* a 1982 nickel.

Also easy.

Their dad kept an apple cider jug filled with loose change down in his basement workshop.

That's why Kyle and Mike were racing to get there first.

Mike bolted through the front door.

Kyle grinned.

He loved playing games against his big brothers. As the youngest, it was just about the only chance he ever got to beat them fair and square. Board games leveled the playing field. You needed a good roll of the dice, a lucky draw of the cards, and some smarts, but if things went your way and you gave it your all, anyone could win.

Especially today, since Mike had blown his lead by choosing the standard route down to the basement. He'd go through the front door, tear to the back of the house, bound down the steps, and then run to their dad's workshop.

Kyle, on the other hand, would take a shortcut.

He hopped over a couple of boxy shrubs and kicked open the low-to-the-ground casement window. He heard something crackle when his tennis shoe hit the windowpane, but he couldn't worry about it. He had to beat his big brother.

He crawled through the narrow opening, dropped to the floor, and scrabbled over to the workbench, where he found the jug, dumped out the coins, and started sifting through the sea of pennies, nickels, dimes, and quarters.

Score!

Kyle quickly uncovered a 1982 nickel. He tucked it into his shirt pocket and sent pennies, nickels, and dimes skidding across the floor as he concentrated on quarters. 2010. 2003. 1986.

"Come on, come on," he muttered.

The workshop door swung open.

"What the . . . ?" Mike was surprised to see that Kyle had beaten him to the coin jar.

Mike fell to his knees and started searching for his own

coins just as Kyle shouted, "Got it!" and plucked a 1982 quarter out of the pile.

"What about the nickel?" demanded Mike.

Kyle pulled it out of his shirt pocket.

"You went through the window?" said a voice from outside.

It was Curtis. Kneeling in the flower beds.

"Yeah," said Kyle.

"I was going to do that. The shortest distance between two points is a straight line."

"I can't believe you won!" moaned Mike, who wasn't used to losing *anything*.

"Well," said Kyle, standing up and strutting a little, "believe it, brother. Because now you two *losers* have to put all the junk back."

"I am *not* taking this back to Twinky!" said Curtis. He held up a very slimy, knotted rope.

"Oh, yes you are," said Kyle. "Because you *lost*. Oh sure, you *thought* about using the window. . . ."

"Um, Kyle?" mumbled Curtis. "You might want to shut up. . . ."

"What? C'mon, Curtis. Don't be such a sore loser. Just because I was the one who took the shortcut and kicked open the window and—"

"You did this, Kyle?"

A new face appeared in the window.

Their dad's.

"Heh, heh, heh," chuckled Mike behind Kyle.

"You broke the glass?" Their father sounded ticked off. "Well, guess who's going to pay to have this window replaced."

That's why Kyle Keeley had fifty cents deducted from his allowance for the rest of the year.

And got grounded for a week.

2

Halfway across town, Dr. Yanina Zinchenko, the world-famous librarian, was walking briskly through the cavernous building that was only days away from its gala grand opening.

Alexandriaville's new public library had been under construction for five years. All work had been done with the utmost secrecy under the tightest possible security. One crew did the exterior renovations on what had once been the small Ohio city's most magnificent building, the Gold Leaf Bank. Other crews—carpenters, masons, electricians, and plumbers—worked on the interior.

No single construction crew stayed on the job longer than six weeks.

No crew knew what any of the other crews had done (or would be doing).

And when all those crews were finished, several

super-secret covert crews (highly paid workers who would deny ever having been near the library, Alexandriaville, *or* the state of Ohio) stealthily applied the final touches.

Dr. Zinchenko had supervised the construction project for her employer—a very eccentric (some would say loony) billionaire. Only she knew all the marvels and wonders the incredible new library would hold (and hide) within its walls.

Dr. Zinchenko was a tall woman with blazing-red hair. She wore an expensive, custom-tailored business suit, jazzy high-heeled shoes, a Bluetooth earpiece, and glasses with thick red frames.

Heels clicking on the marble floor, fingers tapping on the glass of her very advanced tablet computer, Dr. Zinchenko strode past the control center's red door, under an arch, and into the breathtakingly large circular reading room beneath the library's three-story-tall rotunda.

The bank building, which provided the shell for the new library, had been built in 1931. With towering Corinthian columns, an arched entryway, lots of fancy trim, and a mammoth shimmering gold dome, the building looked like it belonged next door to the triumphant memorials in Washington, D.C.—not on this small Ohio town's quaint streets.

Dr. Zinchenko paused to stare up at the library's most stunning visual effect: the Wonder Dome. Ten wedge-shaped, high-definition video screens—as brilliant as those in Times Square—lined the underbelly of the dome like so many orange slices. Each screen could operate independently or as part of a spectacular whole. The Wonder Dome could become the constellations of the night sky; a flight through the clouds that made viewers below sense that the whole building had somehow lifted off the ground; or, in Dewey decimal mode, ten sections depicting vibrant and constantly changing images associated with each category in the library cataloging system.

"I have the final numbers for the fourth sector of the Wonder Dome in Dewey mode," Dr. Zinchenko said into her Bluetooth earpiece. "364 point 1092." She carefully over-enunciated each word to make certain the video artist knew what specific numbers should occasionally drift across the fourth wedge amid the swirling social-sciences montage featuring a floating judge's gavel, a tumbling teacher's apple, and a gentle snowfall of holiday icons. "The numbers, however, should not appear until eleven a.m. Sunday. Is that clear?"

"Yes, Dr. Zinchenko," replied the tinny voice in her ear.

Next Dr. Zinchenko studied the holographic statues projected into black crepe-lined recesses cut into the massive stone piers that supported the arched windows from which the Wonder Dome rose.

"Why are Shakespeare and Dickens still here? They're not on the list for opening night."

"Sorry," replied the library's director of holographic imagery, who was also on the conference call. "I'll fix it."

9

"Thank you."

Exiting the rotunda, the librarian entered the Children's Room.

It was dim, with only a few work lights glowing, but Dr. Zinchenko had memorized the layout of the miniature tables and was able to march, without bumping her shins, to the Story Corner for a final check on her recently installed geese.

The flock of six audio-animatronic goslings—fluffy robots with ping-pongish eyeballs (created for the new library by imagineers who used to work at Disney World)—stood perched atop an angled bookcase in the corner. Mother Goose, in her bonnet and granny glasses, was frozen in the center.

"This is librarian One," said Dr. Zinchenko, loud enough for the microphones hidden in the ceiling to pick up her voice. "Initiate story-time sequence."

The geese sprang to mechanical life.

"Nursery rhyme."

The geese honked out "Baa-Baa Black Sheep" in six-part harmony.

"Treasure Island?"

The birds yo-ho-ho'ed their way through "Fifteen Men on a Dead Man's Chest."

Dr. Zinchenko clapped her hands. The rollicking geese stopped singing and swaying.

"One more," she said. Squinting, she saw a book sitting on a nearby table. *"Walter the Farting Dog."*

The six geese spun around and farted, their tail feathers flipping up in sync with the noisy blasts.

"Excellent. End story time."

The geese slumped back into their sleep mode. Dr. Zinchenko made one more tick on her computer tablet. Her final punch list was growing shorter and shorter, which was a very good thing. The library's grand opening was set for Friday night. Dr. Z and her army of associates had only a few days left to smooth out any kinks in the library's complex operating system.

Suddenly, Dr. Zinchenko heard a low, rumbling growl.

Turning around, she was eyeball to icy-blue eyeball with a very rare white tiger.

Dr. Zinchenko sighed and touched her Bluetooth earpiece.

"Ms. G? This is Dr. Z. What is our white Bengal tiger doing in the children's department? . . . I see. Apparently, there was a slight misunderstanding. We do not want him permanently positioned near *The Jungle Book*. Check the call number. 599 point 757. . . . Right. He should be in Zoology. . . . Yes, please. Right away. Thank you, Ms. G."

And like a vanishing mirage, the tiger disappeared.

Of course, even though he was grounded, Kyle Keeley still had to go to school.

"Mike, Curtis, Kyle, time to wake up!" his mother called from down in the kitchen.

Kyle plopped his feet on the floor, rubbed his eyes, and sleepily looked around his room.

The computer handed down from his brother Curtis was sitting on the desk that used to belong to his other brother, Mike. The rug on the floor, with its Cincinnati Reds logo, had also been Mike's when *he* was twelve years old. The books lined up in his bookcase had been lined up on Mike's and Curtis's shelves, except for the ones Kyle got each year for Christmas from his grandmother. He still hadn't read last year's addition.

Kyle wasn't big on books.

Unless they were the instruction manual or hint guide to a video game. He had a Sony PlayStation set up in the family room. It wasn't the high-def, Blu-ray PS3. It was the one Santa had brought Mike maybe four years earlier. (Mike kept the brand-new Blu-ray model locked up in his bedroom.)

But still, clunker that it was, the four-year-old gaming console in the family room worked.

Except this week.

Well, it *worked*, but Kyle's dad had taken away his TV and computer privileges, so unless he just wanted to hear the hard drive hum, there was really no point in firing up the PlayStation until the next Sunday, when his sentence ended.

"When you're grounded in this house," his father had said, "you're *grounded*."

If Kyle needed a computer for homework during this last week of school, he could use his mom's, the one in the kitchen.

His mom had no games on her computer.

Okay, she had Diner Dash, but that didn't really count.

Being grounded in the Keeley household meant you couldn't do anything except, as his dad put it, "think about what you did that caused you to be grounded."

Kyle knew what he had done: He'd broken a window.

But hey—I also beat my big brothers!

* * *

13

"Good morning, Kyle," his mom said when he hit the kitchen. She was sitting at her computer desk, sipping coffee and tapping keys. "Grab a Toaster Tart for breakfast."

Curtis and Mike were already in the kitchen, chowing down on the last of the good Toaster Tarts—the frosted cupcake swirls. They'd left Kyle the unfrosted brown sugar cinnamon. The ones that tasted like the box they came in.

"New library opens Friday, just in time for summer vacation," Kyle's mom mumbled, reading her computer screen. "Been twelve years since they tore down the old one. Listen to this, boys: Dr. Yanina Zinchenko, the new public library's head librarian, promises that 'patrons will be surprised' by what they find inside."

"Really?" said Kyle, who always liked a good surprise. "I wonder what they'll have in there."

"Um, books maybe?" said Mike. "It's a *library*, Kyle."

"Still," said Curtis, "I can't wait to get my new library card!"

"Because you're a nerd," said Mike.

"I prefer the term 'geek,' " said Curtis.

"Well, I gotta go," said Kyle, grabbing his backpack. "Don't want to miss the bus."

He hurried out the door. What Kyle really didn't want to miss were his friends. A lot of them had Sony PSPs and Nintendo 3DSs.

Loaded with lots and lots of games!

* * *

Kyle fist-bumped and knuckle-knocked his way up the bus aisle to his usual seat. Almost everybody wanted to say "Hey" to him, except, of course, Sierra Russell.

Like always, Sierra, who was also a seventh grader, was sitting in the back of the bus, her nose buried in a book—probably one of those about girls who lived in tiny homes on the prairie or something.

Ever since her parents divorced and her dad moved out of town, Sierra Russell had been incredibly quiet and spent all her free time reading.

"Nice shirt," said Akimi Hughes as Kyle slid into the seat beside her.

"Thanks. It used to be Mike's."

"Doesn't matter. It's still cool."

Akimi's mother was Asian, her dad Irish. She had very long jet-black hair, extremely blue eyes, and a ton of freckles.

"What're you playing?" Kyle asked, because Akimi was frantically working the controls on her PSP 3000.

"Squirrel Squad," said Akimi.

"One of Mr. Lemoncello's best," said Kyle, who had the same game on his PlayStation.

The one he couldn't play with for a week.

"You need a hand?"

"Nah."

"Watch out for the beehives. . . ."

"I know about the beehives, Kyle."

"I'm just saying . . ."

"Yes!"

"What?"

"I cleared level six! Finally."

"Awesome." Kyle did not mention that he was up to level twenty-seven. Akimi was his best friend. Friends don't gloat to friends.

"When I shot the squirrels at the falcons," said Akimi, "the pilots parachuted. If a squirrel bit the pilot in the butt, I got a fifty-point bonus."

Yes, in Mr. Lemoncello's catapulting critters game, there were all sorts of wacky jokes. The falcons weren't birds; they were F-16 Falcon Fighter Jets. And the squirrels? They were nuts. Totally bonkers. With swirly whirlpool eyes. They flew through the air jabbering gibberish. They bit butts.

This was one of the main reasons why Kyle thought everything that came out of Mr. Lemoncello's Imagination Factory—board games, puzzles, video games—was amazingly awesome. For Mr. Lemoncello, a game just wasn't a game if it wasn't a little goofy around the edges.

"So, did you pick up the bonus code?" asked Kyle.

"Huh?"

"In the freeze-frame there."

Akimi studied the screen.

"Turn it over."

Akimi did.

"See that number tucked into the corner? Type that in the next time the home screen asks you for your password."

16

"Why? What happens?"

"You'll see."

Akimi slugged him in the arm. "What?"

"Well, don't be surprised if you start flinging *flaming* squirrels on level seven."

"Get. Out!"

"Try it. You'll see."

"I will. This afternoon. So, did you write your extra-credit essay?"

"Huh? What essay?"

"Um, the one that's due today. About the new public library?"

"Refresh my memory."

Akimi sighed. "Because the old library was torn down twelve years ago, the twelve twelve-year-olds who write the best essays on 'Why I'm Excited About the New Public Library' will get to go to the library lock-in this Friday night."

"Huh?"

"The winners will spend the night in the new library before anybody else even gets to see the place!"

"Is this like that movie *Night at the Museum*? Will the books come alive and chase people around and junk?"

"No. But there will probably be free movies, and food, and prizes, and *games*."

All of a sudden, Kyle was interested.

4

"So, exactly what kind of games are we talking about?"

"I don't know," said Akimi. "Fun book stuff, I guess."

"And do you think this new library will have equally new computers?"

"Definitely."

"Wi-Fi?"

"Probably."

Kyle nodded slowly. "And this all takes place Friday night?"

"Yep."

"Akimi, I think you just discovered a way for me to shorten my most recent groundation."

"Your what?"

"My game-deprived parental punishment."

Kyle figured being locked in a library with computers

on Friday night would be better than being stuck at home without any gaming gear at all.

"Can I borrow a pen and a sheet of paper?"

"What? You're going to write your essay now? On the bus?"

"Better late than never."

"They're due in homeroom, Kyle. First thing."

"Fine. I'll keep it brief."

Akimi shook her head and handed Kyle a notebook and a pen. The bus bounced over a speed bump into the school driveway.

He would need to make his essay really, really short.

He was hoping the twelve winners would be randomly pulled out of a hat or something and, like the lottery people always said in their TV commercials, you just had to "be in it to win it."

Meanwhile, in another part of town, Charles Chiltington was sitting in his father's library, working with the college student who'd been hired to help him polish up his extra-credit essay.

He was dressed in his typical school uniform: khaki slacks, blue blazer, button-down shirt, and tastefully striped tie. He was the only student at Alexandriaville Middle School who dressed that way.

"What's a big word for 'library'?" Charles asked his tutor. "Teachers love big words."

" 'Book repository.' "

"Bigger, please."

"Um, 'athenaeum.' "

"Perfect! It's such a weird word, they'll have to look it up."

Charles made the change, saved the file, and sent the document off to the printer.

"Your dad sure reads a lot," said his ELA tutor, admiring the leather-bound books lining the walls of Mr. Chiltington's home library.

"Knowledge is power," said Charles. "It's one of our fundamental family philosophies."

Another was *We eat losers for breakfast.*

Kyle and Akimi climbed off the bus and headed into the school.

"You know," said Akimi, "my dad told me the library people had like a bazillion different architects doing drawings and blueprints that they couldn't share with each other."

"How come?"

"To keep everything super secret. My dad and his firm did the front door and that was it."

The second they stepped into Mrs. Cameron's classroom for homeroom period, Miguel Fernandez shouted, "Hey, Kyle! Check it out, bro." He held up a clear plastic binder maybe two inches thick. "I totally aced my essay, man!"

"The library dealio?"

"Yeah! I put in pictures and charts, plus a whole section about the Ancient Library of Alexandria, Egypt, since this is *Alexandria*ville, Ohio!"

"Cool," said Kyle.

Miguel Fernandez was super enthusiastic about everything. He was also president of the school's Library Aide Society. "Hey, Kyle—you know what they say about libraries?"

"Uh, not really."

"They have something for every chapter of your life!"

While Kyle groaned, the second bell rang.

"All right, everybody," said Mrs. Dana Cameron, Kyle's homeroom teacher. "Time to turn in your extra-credit essays." She started walking up and down the rows of desks. "The judges will be meeting in the faculty lounge this morning to make the preliminary cut. . . ."

Crap, thought Kyle. There were *judges.* This was not going to be a bingo-ball drawing like the lottery.

"Mr. Keeley?" The teacher hovered over his desk. "Did you write an essay?"

"Yeah. Sort of."

"I'm sorry. I don't understand. Either you wrote an essay or you didn't."

Kyle halfheartedly handed her his hastily scribbled sheet of paper.

And unfortunately, Mrs. Cameron read it. Out loud.

" 'Balloons. There might be balloons.' "

The classroom erupted with laughter.

Until Mrs. Cameron did that tilt-down-her-glasses-and-glare-over-them thing she did to terrify everybody into total silence.

"This is your essay, Kyle?"

"Yes, ma'am. We were supposed to write why we're excited about the grand opening and, well, balloons are always my favorite part."

"I see," said Mrs. Cameron. "You know, Kyle, your brother Curtis wrote excellent essays when he was in my class."

"Yes, Mrs. Cameron," mumbled Kyle.

Mrs. Cameron sighed contentedly. "Please give him my regards."

"Yes, ma'am."

Mrs. Cameron moved on to the next desk. Miguel eagerly handed her his thick booklet.

"Very well done, Miguel."

"Thank you, Mrs. Cameron!"

Kyle heard an odd noise out in the parking lot. A puttering, clunking, clanking sound.

"Oh, my," said Mrs. Cameron, "I wonder if that's *him*!"

She hurried to the window and pulled up the blinds. All the kids in the classroom followed her.

And then they saw it.

Out in the visitor parking lot. A car that looked like a giant red boot on wheels. It had a strip of notched black boot sole for its bumper. Thick shoelaces crisscrossed their way up from the windshield to the top of a ten-foot-tall boot collar.

"It looks just like the red boot from that game," said Miguel. "Family Frenzy."

Kyle nodded. Family Frenzy was Mr. Lemoncello's first and probably most famous game. The red boot was one of ten tokens you could pick to move around the board.

A tall, gangly man stepped out of the boot car.

"It's Mr. Lemoncello!" gasped Kyle, his heart racing. "What's *he* doing here?"

"It was just announced," said Mrs. Cameron. "This evening, Mr. Luigi Lemoncello himself will be the final judge."

"Of what?"

"Your library essays."

5

Eating lunch in the cafeteria, Kyle stared at his wilted fish sticks, wishing he could pull a magic Take Another Turn card out of thin air.

"I blew it," he mumbled.

"Yep," Akimi agreed. "You basically did."

"Can you imagine how awesome that new library's gonna be if Mr. Lemoncello and his Imagination Factory guys had anything to do with it?"

"Yes. I can. And I'm kind of hoping I get to see it, too. After all, I wrote a real essay, not one sentence about balloons."

"Thanks. Rub it in."

Akimi eased up a little. "Hey, Kyle—when you're playing a game like Sorry and you get bumped back three spaces, do you usually quit?"

"No. If I get bumped, I play harder because I know I

need to find a way to get back those three spaces *and* pull ahead of the pack."

"Hey, guys!" Miguel Fernandez carried his tray over to join Kyle and Akimi.

He was being followed by a kid with spiky hair and glasses the size of welders' goggles.

"You two know Andrew Peckleman, right?"

"Hey," said Kyle and Akimi.

"Hello."

"Andrew is one of my top library aides," said Miguel.

"Cool," said Akimi.

"Mrs. Yunghans, the librarian, just confirmed that Mr. Lemoncello is the top-secret benefactor who donated all the money to build the new public library. Five hundred million dollars!"

"She heard it on NPR," added Peckleman, who more or less talked through his nose. "So we did some primary source research on Mr. Lemoncello and his connection to Alexandriaville."

"What'd you find out?" asked Kyle.

"First off," said Miguel, "he was born here."

"He had nine brothers and sisters," added Andrew.

"All of 'em crammed into a tiny apartment with only one bathroom over in Little Italy," said Miguel.

"And," said Peckleman, sounding like he wanted to one-up Miguel, "he *loved* the old public library down on Market Street. He used to go there when he was a kid and needed a quiet place to think and doodle his ideas."

25

"And get this," said Miguel eagerly. "Mrs. Tobin, the librarian back then, took an interest in little Luigi, even though he was just, you know, a kid like us. She kept the library open late some nights and let him borrow junk from her desk or her purse—thimbles and thumbtacks and glue bottles, even red Barbie doll boots—stuff he used for game pieces so he could map out his first ideas on a library table. Then . . ."

Andrew jumped in. "Then Mrs. Tobin took Mr. Lemoncello's sketch for Family Frenzy home to her husband, who ran a print shop. They signed some papers, created a company, and within a couple of years they were all millionaires."

But Miguel had the last word: "Now, of course, Mr. Lemoncello is a bazillionaire!"

"What are you four nerds so excited about?" said Haley Daley as she waltzed past with the gaggle of popular girls in her royal court. Haley was the princess of the seventh grade. Blond hair, blue eyes, blazingly bright smile. She looked like a walking toothpaste commercial.

"We're pumped about Mr. Lemoncello!" said Miguel.

"And the new library!" said Andrew.

"And," said Kyle melodramatically, "just seeing you, Haley."

"You are *so* immature. Come on, girls." Haley and her friends flounced away to the "cool kids" table.

"Check it out," said Akimi, gesturing toward the

cafeteria's food line, where Charles Chiltington was balancing two trays: his own and one for Mrs. Cameron.

"I'm so glad you have lunchroom duty today, Mrs. Cameron," Kyle heard Chiltington say. "If you don't mind, I have a few questions about how conventions within genres—such as poetry, drama, or essays—can affect meaning."

"Well, Charles, I'd be happy to discuss that with you."

"Thank you, Mrs. Cameron. And, may I say, that sweater certainly complements your eye color."

"What a suck-up," mumbled Akimi. "Chiltington's trying to use his weaselly charm to make sure Mrs. C sends his essay up the line to Mr. Lemoncello."

"Don't worry," said Kyle. "Mrs. Cameron isn't the final judge. Mr. Lemoncello is. And since he's a genius, he will definitely pick the essays you guys all wrote."

"Undoubtedly," said Peckleman.

"Thanks, Kyle," said Miguel.

"I just wish you could win with us," said Akimi.

"Well, maybe I can. Like you said, this is just a Move Back Three Spaces card. A Take a Walk on the Boardwalk when someone else owns it. It's a chute in Chutes and Ladders. A detour to the Molasses Swamp in Candy Land!"

"Yo, Kyle," said Miguel. "Exactly how many board games have you played?"

"Enough to know that you don't ever quit until

somebody else actually wins." He picked up his lunch and headed for the dirty-tray window.

Akimi called after him. "Where are you going?"

"I have the rest of lunch and all of study hall to work on a new essay."

"But Mrs. Cameron won't take it."

"Maybe. But I've got to roll the dice one more time. Maybe I'll get lucky."

"I hope so," said Akimi.

"Me too! See you guys on the bus!"

6

Working on his library essay like he'd never worked on any essay in his whole essay-writing life, Kyle crafted a killer thesis sentence that compared libraries to his favorite games.

"Using a library can make learning about anything (and everything) fun," he wrote. "When you're in a library, researching a topic, you're on a scavenger hunt, looking for clues and prizes in books instead of your attic or back-yard."

He put in points and sub-points.

He wrapped everything up with a tidy conclusion.

He even checked his spelling (twice).

But Akimi had been right.

"I'm sorry, Kyle," Mrs. Cameron said when he handed her his new paper at the end of the day. "This is very good and I am impressed by your extra effort. However, the deadline was this morning. Rules are rules. The same as they are in all the board games you mentioned in your essay."

She'd basically handed Kyle a Go Back Five Hundred Spaces card.

But Kyle refused to give up.

He remembered how his mother had written to Mr. Lemoncello's Imagination Factory when he and his brothers needed a fresh set of clue cards for the Indoor-Outdoor Scavenger Hunt.

Maybe he could send his essay directly to Mr. Lemoncello via email.

Maybe, if the game maker wasn't judging the essays until later that night, Kyle still had a shot. A long shot, but, hey, sometimes the long ones were the only shots you got.

The second he hit home he sat down at his mother's kitchen computer. He attached his essay file to a "high priority" email addressed to Mr. Lemoncello at the Imagination Factory.

"What are you doing, Kyle?" his mom asked when she came into the room and found him typing on her computer.

"Some extra-credit homework."

"Extra credit? School's out at the end of the week."

"So?"

"You're not playing my Diner Dash game, are you?"

"No, Mom. It's an essay. About Mr. Lemoncello's amazing new library downtown."

"Oh. Sounds interesting. I heard on the radio that there's going to be a gala grand opening reception this Friday night at the Parker House Hotel, right across the street from the old bank building. I mean, the *new* library."

Kyle typed in a P.S. to his email: "I hope at the party on Friday you have balloons."

He hit send.

"Who did you send your essay to?" his mother asked. "Your teacher?"

"No. Mr. Lemoncello himself. It took some digging, but I found his email address on his game company's website."

"Really? I'm impressed." His mom rubbed his hair. "You know, this morning, I said to your dad: 'Kyle can be just as smart as Curtis and just as focused as Mike—*when* he puts his mind to it.' "

Kyle smiled. "Thanks, Mom."

But his smile quickly disappeared when a *BONG!* alerted him to an incoming email.

From Mr. Lemoncello.

It was an auto-response form letter.

Dear Lemoncello Game Lover:

This is a no-reply mailbox. Your message did not go through. Do not try to resend it or you'll just hear another *BONG!* But thank you for playing our games.

7

Heading back to school on Tuesday, Kyle knew he had to put on a brave face.

He smiled as he walked with his class toward the auditorium for a special early-morning assembly. The one where Mr. Luigi L. Lemoncello himself would announce the winners of the Library Lock-In Essay Contest.

"I hope he picked yours," Kyle whispered to Akimi.

"Thanks. I do, too. But the lock-in won't be as much fun without you."

"Well, when it's over, and the library is officially open, you can take me on a tour."

"That's exactly what I'm going to do! *If* I win."

"If you don't, I'm sending a flaming squirrel after Mrs. Cameron."

For this assembly, the seventh graders, most of whom were twelve years old, were told to sit in the front rows, close to the stage. That made Kyle feel a little better. At least he'd get a chance to see Mr. Lemoncello up close and personal.

But his hero wasn't even onstage.

Just the principal; the school librarian, Mrs. Yunghans; and a redheaded woman in high-heeled shoes who Kyle didn't recognize. She sat up straight, like someone had slipped a yardstick down the back of her bright red business suit. Her glasses were bright red, too.

"That's Dr. Yanina Zinchenko!" gushed Miguel Fernandez, who was sitting on Kyle's right.

"Who's she?" asked Akimi, seated to Kyle's left.

"Just the most famous librarian in the whole wide world!"

"All right, boys and girls," said the principal at the podium. "Settle down. Quiet, please. It is my great honor to introduce the head librarian for the new Alexandriaville public library, Dr. Yanina Zinchenko."

Everybody clapped. The tall lady in the red outfit strode to the microphone.

"Good morning."

Her voice was breathy with just a hint of a Russian accent.

"Twelve years ago, this town lost its one and only public library when it was torn down to make room for an elevated parking garage. Back then, many said the Internet had rendered the 'old-fashioned' library obsolete, that a new parking garage would attract shoppers to the

33

boutiques and dress shops near the old bank building. But the library's demolition also meant that those of you who are now twelve years old have lived your entire lives *without* a public library."

She looked down at the front rows.

"This is why, to kick off our summer reading program, twelve twelve-year-olds will be selected to be the very first to explore the wonders awaiting inside Mr. Lemoncello's extraordinary new library. You will, of course, need your parents' permission. We have slips for you to take home. You will also need a sleeping bag, a toothbrush, and, if you please, a change of clothes."

She smiled mysteriously.

"You might consider packing *two* pairs of underwear."

Oh-kay, thought Kyle. *That's bizarre.* Did the librarian really think seventh graders weren't toilet trained?

"There will be movies, food, fun, games, and prizes. Also, each of our twelve winners will receive a five-hundred-dollar gift card good toward the purchase of Lemoncello games and gizmos."

Oh, man. Five hundred bucks' worth of free games and gear? Kyle sank a little lower in his seat. The next time someone gave him an extra-credit essay assignment, he'd turn it in *early*!

"And now, here to announce our winners, the man behind the new library, the master gamester himself—Mr. Luigi Lemoncello!"

Dr. Zinchenko gestured to her left.

The whole auditorium swung their heads.

People were clapping and whistling and cheering.

But nobody came onstage.

The applause petered out.

And then, on the opposite side of the stage, Kyle heard a very peculiar sound.

It was a cross between a burp and the squeak from a squeeze toy.

8

Over on the side of the stage, a shoe that looked like a peeled-open banana appeared from behind a curtain.

When it landed, the shoe burp-squeaked.

As a second banana shoe burp-squeaked onto the floor, Kyle looked up and there he was—Mr. Lemoncello! He had loose and floppy limbs and was dressed in a three-piece black suit with a bright red tie. His black broad-brimmed hat was cocked at a crooked angle atop his curly white hair. Kyle was so close he could see a sly twinkle sparkling in Mr. Lemoncello's coal-black eyes.

Treading very carefully, Mr. Lemoncello walked toward the podium. The burp-squeaks in his shoes seemed to change pitch depending on how hard he landed on his heels. He added a couple of little jig steps, a quick hop and a stutter-step skip, and yes—his shoes were squeaking out a song.

"Pop Goes the Weasel."

On the *Pop!* Mr. Lemoncello popped behind the podium.

The crowd went wild.

Mr. Lemoncello politely bowed and said, very softly, "Tank you. Tank you. *Grazie. Grazie.*"

He bent forward so his mouth was maybe an inch away from the microphone.

"*Buon giorno,* boise and-uh girls-a." He spoke very timidly, very slowly. "Tees ees how my-uh momma and my-uh poppa teach-uh me to speak-eh de English."

He wiggled his ears. Straightened his back.

"But then," he said in a crisp, clear voice, "I went to the Alexandriaville Public Library, where a wonderful librarian named Mrs. Gail Tobin helped me learn how to speak like this: 'If two witches were watching two watches, which witch would watch which watch?' I can also speak while upside down and underwater, but not today because I just had this suit dry-cleaned and do *not* want to get it wet."

Mr. Lemoncello bounced across the stage like a happy grasshopper.

"Now then, children, if I may call you that—which I must because I have not yet memorized all of your names, even though I *am* working on it—what do you think is the most amazingly incredible thing you'll find inside your wondrous new library, besides, of course, all the knowledge you need to do anything and everything you ever want or need to do?"

No one said anything. They were too mesmerized by Mr. Lemoncello's rat-a-tat words.

"Would it be: A) robots silently whizzing their way through the library, restocking the shelves, B) the Electronic Learning Center, with three dozen plasma-screen TVs all connected to flight simulators and educational video games, or C) the Wonder Dome? Lined with ten giant video screens, it can make the whole building feel like a rocket ship blasting off into outer space!"

"The game room!" someone shouted.

"The robots!"

"The video dome!"

Mr. Lemoncello raced back to the podium and made a buzzing noise into the microphone.

"Sorry. The correct answer is—and not just because of Winn-Dixie—D) all of the above!"

The crowd went wild.

Mr. Lemoncello whirled around to face his head librarian.

"Dr. Zinchenko? Will you kindly help me pass out our first twelve library cards?"

It was time to announce the essay contest winners.

Dr. Zinchenko placed a stack of twelve shiny cards on the podium in front of Mr. Lemoncello.

"Please," he said, "as I call your name, come join me onstage. Miguel Fernandez."

"Yes!" Miguel jumped up out of his seat.

"Akimi Hughes."

"Whoo-hoo."

Kyle was thrilled to see his two friends be the first ones called to the stage.

"Andrew Peckleman, Bridgette Wadge, Sierra Russell, Yasmeen Smith-Snyder."

Yasmeen squealed when her name was called.

"Sean Keegan, Haley Daley, Rose Vermette, and Kayla Corson."

Ten kids, all the same age as Kyle, were up onstage with his idol, Mr. Lemoncello. He was not. Only two more chances.

As if reading his mind, Mr. Lemoncello said, "Only two more," and tapped a pair of library cards on the podium. "Charles Chiltington."

"Gosh, really?" He dashed up to the podium and started pumping Mr. Lemoncello's hand. "Thank you, sir. This is such an honor. Truly. I mean that."

"Thank you, Charles. May I have my hand back? I need it to flip over this final card."

"Of course, sir. But I cannot wait to spend the night in your library, or, as I like to call it, your athenaeum. Because, as I said in my essay, when you open a book, you open your mind!"

Finally, Charles the brownnoser let go of Mr. Lemoncello's hand and went over to line up with the other winners.

"And last but not least," said Mr. Lemoncello, "Kyle Keeley."

Kyle could not believe his ears. He thought he was dreaming.

But then Akimi started waving for him to come on up!

Dazed, Kyle made his way up the steps to join the others onstage. Mr. Lemoncello handed Kyle a library card. His name and the number twelve were printed on the front. Two book covers—*I Love You, Stinky Face* and *The Napping House*—were on the back.

"Let's all pose for a picture, please," said the principal.

When everybody moved into position for the photographer, Kyle found himself standing *right next to* Mr. Lemoncello.

He swallowed hard. "I'm a big fan, sir," he said, his voice kind of shaky.

"Why, thank you. And remind me—you are?"

"I'm Kyle, sir. Kyle Keeley."

"Ah, yes. The boy who proved what I've always known to be true: The game is never over till it's over. *BONG!*"

9

Kyle couldn't wait to tell his family the good news.

"I won the essay contest!" He showed them his shiny new library card.

"Congratulations!" said his mom.

"Way to go!" said his dad.

His brothers, Curtis and Mike, were more interested in Kyle's other card: his five-hundred-dollar Lemoncello gift card.

"It's good for twelve months," said Kyle.

"But you need to use it *now*," said Mike. "We need to go to the store tonight so you can buy me Mr. Lemoncello's Kooky-Wacky Hockey."

"I can't."

"Why not?"

"I have to show my library card at the store to cash it in."

"And?"

"Um, I'm grounded, remember?"

"You know, Kyle," said his dad, looking at his mother, who nodded, "since you worked extra hard and did such a bang-up job on your essay, I think we might consider suspending your punishment."

"Really?"

"Really."

Kyle's mom and dad smiled at him.

The way they smiled whenever Mike won a football game or Curtis won the science fair.

After supper, all five Keeleys piled into the family van and headed off to the local toy store.

"Lemoncello's hockey game is awesome," said Mike as they drove to the store. "Especially when the penguins play the polar bears."

"I'm hoping to find a classic board game," mused Curtis. "Mr. Lemoncello's Bewilderingly Baffling Bibliomania."

"Is that about the Bible?" asked their dad from behind the wheel.

"Not exactly," said Curtis, "although the Bible, especially a rare Gutenberg edition, may be one of the treasures you must find and collect, because the object of the game is to collect rare and valuable books by—"

"The penguins in Kooky-Wacky Hockey aren't from Pittsburgh like in the NHL," said Mike, cutting off Curtis.

"They're from Antarctica. And the polar bears? They're from Alaska."

Kyle had decided to divvy up his gift card five ways. To give everybody—including his mom and dad—one hundred dollars to play with.

As soon as they entered the toy store, the family split up, cruising the aisles with their own shopping carts. His mom was going to upgrade to Mr. Lemoncello's Restaurant Rush. His dad was looking for one of Mr. Lemoncello's complicated What If? historical games: What If the Romans Had Won the American Civil War?

Kyle hung with Curtis and Mike for a while. Being the one with the gift card made him feel like he was suddenly *their* big brother.

Mike quickly found his PlayStation hockey game and Curtis was in geek heaven when he finally found Bibliomania.

"They only have one left!" he gushed, tearing off the cellophane shrink-wrap and prying open the lid. He sat down right in the middle of the store and unfolded the game board on his lap. "You see, you start under the rotunda in this circular reading room. Then you go upstairs and enter each of these ten chambers, where you have to answer a question about a book. . . ."

"Um, I think I hear Mom calling me," said Kyle. "She must need the gift card. Enjoy!"

And Kyle took off.

"The store will close in fifteen minutes," announced a voice from the ceiling speakers.

Kyle flew up and down the aisles and grabbed a couple of board games he didn't own yet, including Mr. Lemoncello's Absolutely Incredible Iron Horse—a game where you build your own transcontinental railroad, complete with locomotive game pieces that actually puff steam.

As Kyle was doing some quick math to see if he'd spent his one hundred dollars, Charles Chiltington rolled up the aisle with a cart crammed full with *five* hundred dollars' worth of loot. Games stacked on top of games were practically spilling over the sides. Mr. Lemoncello's Phenomenal Picture Word Puzzler, one of Kyle's favorites, was teetering on the top.

"Hello, Keeley," said Chiltington with a smirk. He looked down at the three games sitting in the bottom of Kyle's shopping cart. "Just getting started?"

"No. I shared my gift card with my family."

"Really? Well, that was a mistake, wasn't it?"

Kyle was about to answer when Chiltington said, "So long. See you on Friday." Kyle wasn't 100 percent sure but Charles might've also muttered, "Loser."

Since the store was about to close, Kyle headed toward the checkout lanes. When he passed the customer service department, he saw Haley Daley.

"No," Kyle heard Haley say in a hushed tone to the clerk working the Returns window. "I do not want to return these items for *store credit*. I would prefer cash."

44

Kyle finally found his family, showed the cashier his library card, and paid for everything with a single swipe of his gift card.

"You know, Kyle," said his dad as the family walked across the parking lot, "your mother and I are extremely proud of you. Writing a good essay isn't easy."

"Maybe you'll be an author someday," added his mom. "Then you could write books that'll be on the shelves of the new library."

"Thanks, little brother," said Curtis, practically hugging his Bibliomania box.

"Yeah," said Mike. "This was awesome. Way to win one for the team!"

"Best 'family game night' ever," joked their dad.

Kyle was enjoying his rare moment of glory, playing Santa Claus for his whole family. As the week dragged on, Friday night and the library lock-in started to remind Kyle of Christmas, too: It felt like they would never come.

Then, finally, they did.

10

"Now this is what I call a party," said Kyle's mother as she helped herself to a bacon-wrapped shrimp from a tray being carried by a waiter in a tuxedo.

Kyle and his parents were in the crowded ballroom of the Parker House Hotel for the Lemoncello Library's Gala Grand Opening Reception. The Parker House was located right across the street from the old Gold Leaf Bank building and the cluster of office buildings, craft shops, clothing stores, and restaurants called Old Town.

"I'm going to see if I can find Akimi," Kyle said to his mom and dad.

"Give her our congratulations!" said his mom.

"We're proud of *her,* too," added his dad.

Kyle made his way through the glittering sea of dressed-up adults.

Even though his parents had put on fancy clothes for

the reception, Kyle was wearing "something comfortable to go exploring in," as instructed by the Lock-In Guide he'd received on Wednesday. He'd packed a sleeping bag and a small suitcase with a change of clothes, toiletries, and yes, as requested, an extra pair of underpants.

Kyle saw Sierra Russell all alone in a corner near a clump of curtains. It didn't look like her mother had come to the party with her. Sierra, of course, had her nose buried in a book. Kyle shook his head. The girl was about to spend the night in a building filled with books and she was skipping all the free food and pop so she could read? That was just nutty.

Haley Daley, wearing a sparkly blouse, was posing for a wall of photographers who wanted to snap her picture. Her mother was at the party, too. While the cameras were focused on Haley's smile, Mrs. Daley wrapped up a couple of chicken kebabs in a napkin and slipped them inside her purse.

Now Kyle saw Charles Chiltington. Poor guy must not have read the memo about comfortable clothes. He was still wearing his khakis and blazer, just like his dad. Kyle figured the Chiltington family must own like three hundred pairs of pleated tan pants.

"Hey, Kyle!" Akimi waved at him from near a fake shrub curled to look like a Silly Straw.

"Hey," said Kyle.

"Did you remember to bring your library card?"

"Yep." Kyle pulled it out of his pocket.

"Huh," said Akimi. "I got different books on the back of mine. *One Fish Two Fish Red Fish Blue Fish* by Dr. Seuss and *Nine Stories* by J. D. Salinger."

"Guess they're like baseball cards," said Kyle. "They're all different."

"Hey, you guys!" Miguel Fernandez, more excited than usual (which was saying something), pushed through the mob to join them. "Did you try these puffy cheesy things?"

"Nah," said Kyle. "I'm sticking to food I recognize."

"The 'puffy cheesy things' are called fromage tartlets," said Andrew Peckleman, coming over to join the group.

"Huh," said Kyle. "Good to know."

A waiter passed by with a tray loaded down with small boxes of Mr. Lemoncello's Anagraham Cracker cookies.

"Oh, I love these," said Kyle, taking a box off the platter and opening it. "The cookies are in the shapes of letters. You have to see how many words you can spell."

"Cool," said Miguel, snagging a fistful of cookies out of Kyle's box. "Taste good, too!"

"Yep," said Kyle. "But the more you eat, the harder the game gets."

"Why?" asked Andrew Peckleman.

"Less letters," said Akimi, snatching two "B's" and a "Q" and wolfing them down. "Mmm. Barbecue-flavored."

Kyle spread out the remaining cookies in his palm: U N F E H A V. He grinned as he deciphered an easy anagram. "HAVE FUN. Sweet."

"Ladies and gentlemen? Boys and girls?" Dr. Zinchenko,

48

dressed in a bright red suit, strode to the center of the ballroom. "May I have your attention, please? Mr. Lemoncello will be arriving shortly to say a few brief words. After that, I will escort the twelve essay contest winners across the street to the library. Therefore, children, might I suggest that you eat up? Food and drink are not permitted anywhere in the library except in the Book Nook Café, conveniently located on the first floor."

Miguel grabbed a few more puffy cheesy things.

When she thought no one was looking, Mrs. Daley shoved a napkined bundle of bacon-wrapped shrimp into her purse.

Akimi nibbled a couple of chocolate-dipped pretzel sticks.

"Aren't you gonna grab some more grub?" she said to Kyle.

"No thanks. I only like food I can play with."

"One last thing," announced Dr. Zinchenko. "We, of course, want our winners to have fun tonight. However, I must insist that each of you respect my number one rule: Be gentle. With each other and, most especially, the library's books and exhibits. Can you do that for me?"

"Yes!" shouted all the winners except Charles Chiltington. He said, "Indubitably."

"Good thing the library has dictionaries," muttered Akimi. "Half the time, it's the only way to figure out what Chiltington's saying."

Suddenly, all the adults in the ballroom started clapping.

Mr. Lemoncello, looking like a beanpole wearing a tailcoat and a tiny birthday-party fireman's hat, strode into the room through a side door.

"Thank you, thank you," he said, stretching the elastic band to raise his kid-sized hat and tipping it toward the crowd. "You are too kind."

When he let go of the hat, it snapped back with a sharp *THWACK!*

"As Dr. Zinchenko informed you, I'd like to say a few brief words. Here they are: 'short,' 'memorandum,' and 'underpants.' And let us pause to remember the immortal words of Dr. Seuss: 'The more that you read, the more things you will know. The more that you learn, the more places you'll go.' Children? . . ."

Mr. Lemoncello flourished his arm toward the ballroom doors.

"It's time to go across the street. Your amazingly spectacular new public library awaits!"

11

Eager to see what was inside the new library, the twelve essay contest winners quickly gathered behind Dr. Zinchenko.

"This way, children," said the head librarian. "Follow me."

The crowd cheered as they marched out of the ballroom, all toting their sleeping bags and suitcases. There was more cheering (plus some hooting and hollering) when they reached the hotel lobby and went out the revolving doors into the street.

The new public library, with its glistening gold dome, took up half a downtown block, its back butting up against an old-fashioned office tower. The building was a boxy fortress, three stories tall, with stately columns that acted like bookends, because the windowless walls had been painted to resemble a row of giant books lined up on a shelf.

"It's like a majestic Greek temple," gushed Miguel.

"And the world's biggest bookcase," added Sierra Russell, who had finally put away her paperback.

Velvet ropes lined a path across Main Street that led to a red carpet leading up a flight of steps to the arched entryway and seriously steel (not to mention *round*) front door.

Kyle had to smile when he saw what was tethered to the railings on either side of the steps: balloons!

A big bruiser—maybe six four, 250 pounds—in sunglasses and a black sports coat stood in front of the library's circular door, which had several large valve wheels like you'd see on a submarine hatch. The burly guard wore his hair in long, ropy dreadlocks.

"What's with that door?" asked Haley Daley, who, of course, had pushed her way to the front. "It looks like it came from a bank vault or something."

"It is the door from the old Gold Leaf Bank's walk-in vault," said Dr. Zinchenko. "It weighs twenty tons."

Akimi turned around and whispered, "My dad designed the support structure for that thing. Check out the hinges."

Kyle nodded. He was impressed.

"Why a vault door?" asked Kayla Corson.

"Because," said Dr. Zinchenko, "one sleepy Saturday, when Mr. Lemoncello was your age, he was working in the old public library over on Market Street. He was so lost in his thoughts, he did not hear the sirens as police cars raced past the library to the bank, where a burglar alarm had just been activated. This door serves as a reminder to us all: Our thoughts are safe when they are inside a library. Not even a bank robbery can disturb them."

Miguel was nodding like crazy. He could relate.

"It also helps us keep our most valuable treasures secure."

"There aren't any windows," observed Andrew Peckleman. "Probably to stop bank robbers from busting in. But shouldn't you people have added windows when you turned it into a library?"

"A library doesn't need windows, Andrew. We have books, which are windows into worlds we never even dreamed possible."

"An open book is an open mind," added Charles Chiltington. "That's what I always say."

Dr. Zinchenko pulled out a bright red note card. "Before we enter, please listen very carefully. 'Your library cards are the keys to everything you will need,'" she read. "'The library staff is here to help you find whatever it is you are looking for.'"

She smiled slightly, tucked the card back into her pocket, turned to the security guard, and said, "Clarence? Will you do the honors?"

"With pleasure, Dr. Z."

Clarence turned one giant wheel, spun another, and cranked a third.

Noiselessly, the twenty-ton door swung open.

*   *   *

The first thing Kyle could see inside was a trickling fountain in a grand foyer of brilliant white marble. The fountain featured a life-size statue of Mr. Lemoncello standing on a lily pad in the middle of a shallow reflecting pool ten feet wide. His head was tilted back so water could spurt up from his mouth in an arc.

Kyle noticed a quote chiseled into the statue's pedestal: KNOWLEDGE NOT SHARED REMAINS UNKNOWN. —LUIGI L. LEMONCELLO

Beyond the fountain, through an arched walkway, was a huge room filled with desks.

When everybody had shuffled into the entrance hall, Dr. Zinchenko turned to the security guard.

"Clarence?"

Clarence hauled the heavy steel door shut. Kyle heard the whir of spinning wheels, the clink of grinding gears, and a reverberating clunk.

"Wow!" said Miguel. "Talk about a lock-in!"

"I'll be in the control center, Dr. Z," said the security guard.

"Very well, Clarence."

Clarence disappeared behind a red door.

"Now then, children," said the librarian, "if you will all follow me into the Rotunda Reading Room."

As the rest of the group started filing into the gigantic circular room, Kyle checked out a display case beside the red door. A sign over it read "Staff Picks: Our Most

Memorable Reads." A dozen books were lined up on four shelves.

One cover in the middle of the bottom row caught Kyle's eye. It showed a football player wearing a number nineteen jersey dropping back to hurl a pass. Kyle made a mental note of the title: *In the Pocket: Johnny Unitas and Me.* Tomorrow morning, when the lock-in was over, he might use his library card to check it out for his big brother, Mike.

"Wow!"

Everybody gasped as they stepped into the Rotunda Reading Room and looked up. The entire underside of the dome looked like space as seen from the Hubble telescope: A dusty spiral nebula billowed up, a galaxy of stars twinkled, and meteorites whizzed across the ceiling.

"Ooh!"

The space imagery on the ceiling dissolved into ten distinct panels, each one becoming a display of swirling graphics.

"Those are the ten categories of the Dewey decimal system," whispered Miguel, sounding awestruck. "See the panel with Cleopatra, the guy mountain climbing, and the Viking ship sailing across it? That's for 900 to 999. History and Geography."

"Cool," said Kyle.

Tucked beneath the ten screens in arched niches were incredible 3-D statues glowing a ghostly green.

"I believe those are holographic projections," said Andrew Peckleman, waving up at a statue that was waving down at him.

The room under the dome was huge. It was circular, with a round desk at the center that was surrounded by four rings of reading desks.

Kyle saw that half of the rotunda was filled with floor-to-ceiling bookshelves. The other half had balconies on the second and third floors that reminded him of the open atrium of a hotel he and his family had stayed at once.

While everybody was gawking at the architecture, Dr. Zinchenko said the words Kyle had been waiting to hear all day:

"Now then, who's ready for our first game?"

12

"Will everybody please line up behind that far desk in front of the Children's Room?" said Dr. Zinchenko, gesturing toward one of the wooden tables in the outermost ring of the room.

"How many of you are familiar with Mr. Lemoncello's classic board game Hurry to the Top of the Heap?"

Twelve hands shot up.

"Very good," said Dr. Zinchenko.

Overhead, the Wonder Dome dissolved into a gigantic, curved Heap box top.

"This will be a live, three-dimensional version of that game. Each of you will be asked a trivia question. If you are able to answer it correctly, you will roll the dice and advance the equivalent number of desks. When you return to the starting point, you will move into the next concentric circle of desks. When you complete that ring, you will

57

move into the next, and so on. If one of you makes it all the way to my desk at the center, you will be declared the winner."

"But we don't have any dice," said Yasmeen Smith-Snyder.

"Yes you do. See that smoky glass panel in the center of the desk? It is actually a touch-screen computer, currently running Mr. Lemoncello's dice-rolling app. Simply swipe and flick your fingers across the glass to toss and tumble the animated dice."

Dr. Zinchenko placed a stack of red cards on her desk. She looked like the host of a TV game show. "Before we begin, are there any other questions?"

Charles Chiltington raised his hand.

"Yes, Mr. Chiltington?"

"What will the winner win? After all, the prize is the most important part of any game."

Kyle didn't totally agree, but he was too excited about playing the game to say anything.

"Tonight's first prize," said Dr. Zinchenko, "is this golden key granting the winner access to Mr. Lemoncello's private and very posh bedroom suite up on the library's third floor. Instead of spending the night on the floor in a sleeping bag, you will be relaxing in luxury with a feather bed, a seventy-two-inch television screen and a state-of-the-art gaming console."

Okay. Kyle was definitely interested in this particular prize.

Judging from the wide-open eyes and chorus of "oohs" and "wows" all around him, so was everybody else.

Dr. Zinchenko flipped over the first question card.

"What major-league pitcher was the last to win at least thirty games in one season?"

Six players got it wrong before Kyle got it right.

"Denny McLain."

"Correct."

He swiped the glass panel, rolled a ten, and advanced ten desks around the room.

"What United States Navy ship was once captured by the North Koreans?"

Miguel nailed that one: "The USS *Pueblo*." He flew twelve spaces around the room.

"What did *Apollo 8* accomplish that had never been done before?"

Akimi, Andrew Peckleman, and Kayla Corson struck out on that one.

But Charles Chiltington knew the answer: "It was the first spacecraft to orbit the moon."

"Correct."

Chiltington rolled a five, landing him in last place.

Kyle's next question was tougher:

"Who was famous for saying, 'Book 'em, Danno'?"

"Um, that guy on *Hawaii Five-0*?"

"Please be more specific."

"Uh, the one with the shiny hair. Jack Lord?"

"That is correct."

Kyle breathed a sigh of relief. Thank goodness he and his dad sometimes watched reruns of old TV shows from the 1960s.

But when he flicked the computerized dice, his luck hit a brick wall. He rolled snake eyes and moved up two measly desks.

Meanwhile, Miguel went down with a question about Barbra Streisand. (Kyle wasn't exactly sure who she was.)

And Charles Chiltington surged ahead with a correct answer about the Beatles' "Hey Jude" and a double-sixes roll.

As the game went on, Kyle and Chiltington, the only players still standing, kept answering correctly and moving around the room, until they were both seated at a desk in the innermost ring—only six spaces away from Dr. Zinchenko's desk and victory. Kyle was seriously glad he and his mom had played so many games of Trivial Pursuit—with the original, extremely *old* cards.

"Kyle, here is your next question: What song in the movie *Doctor Dolittle* won an Academy Award?"

Kyle squinted. He had that movie. An old VHS cassette tape that his mom had bought at a garage sale. Too bad they didn't have a VCR to watch it on. But even though he'd never seen the movie, he had read the front and back of the box a couple of times.

"Um, 'Talk to the Animals'?"

"Correct."

He started breathing again.

"Roll the dice, please, Mr. Keeley."

Kyle did.

Another pair of ones. He moved up two spaces. Now he was only four desks away from winning.

"Mr. Chiltington, here is your next question: Who was elected president in 1968?"

"I believe that was Richard Milhous Nixon."

"You are also correct."

Chiltington didn't wait for the librarian to tell him to roll the dice. He flicked his fingers across the glass pad.

"Yes! Double sixes. Again." He moved around the last ring of desks, tapping their tops, counting them off even though everybody knew his twelve was more than good enough to carry him to the finish line.

"Congratulations, Mr. Chiltington," Dr. Zinchenko said as she handed him the key to the private suite. "You are this evening's first winner."

"Thank you, Dr. Zinchenko. I am truly and sincerely honored."

"Congratulations, Charles," said Kyle. "Way to win."

"Get used to it, Keeley," he answered in a voice only the other kids could hear. "I'm a Chiltington. We never lose."

What happened next was extremely cool.

A holographic image of a second librarian appeared beside Dr. Zinchenko at the center desk. She looked a little like Princess Leia being beamed out of R2-D2 in *Star Wars*. Except she had an old-fashioned bubble-top hairdo, cat's-eye glasses, and a tweed jacket with patches on the elbows.

"Here to present our official library lock-in rules," said Dr. Zinchenko, "is Mrs. Gail Tobin, head librarian of the Alexandriaville Public Library back in the 1960s, when Mr. Lemoncello was your age."

Overhead, the Wonder Dome had shifted back to its ten Dewey decimal displays.

"How old is she?" asked Sean Keegan.

"She'd be a hundred and ten if she were still alive."

"But she's dead and working here?"

"Let's just say her spirit lives on in this hologram."

"Mrs. Tobin's the one who helped Mr. Lemoncello so much," Kyle whispered to Akimi. "When he was a kid."

"I know. Her hair looks like a beehive."

Kyle shrugged. "From what I've seen on TV, the 1960s were generally weird."

"Welcome, children, to the library of the future," said the flickering projection. "Dr. Zinchenko will now pass out Lemoncello Library floor plans—your map and guide to all that this extraordinary building has to offer. Your new library cards will grant you access to all rooms except the master control center—the red door you passed on your way in—and, of course, Mr. Lemoncello's private suite on the third floor."

Charles Chiltington dangled his golden key in front of his face. "I believe you need *this* to enter that."

Mrs. Tobin ignored him. She was a hologram. That made it easier.

"Security personnel are on duty twenty-four hours a day," she continued. "During your stay, all of your actions will be recorded by video cameras, as outlined in the consent agreements you and your parents signed earlier."

"Are we going to be on a reality TV show?" asked Haley, smiling up at a tiny camera with a blinking red light.

"It is a distinct possibility," said Dr. Zinchenko.

"I like television," said the ghostly image of Mrs. Tobin. "*Rowan and Martin's Laugh-In* is my favorite program. Returning to the rules. The use of personal electronic devices is strictly prohibited at all times during the lock-in."

The security guard, Clarence, and a guy who looked like his identical twin brother entered the rotunda, each of them carrying an aluminum attaché case.

"Kindly deposit all cell phones, iPods, and iPads in the receptacles provided by our security guards, Clarence and Clement. Your devices will be safely stored for the duration of your stay and will be returned to you at the conclusion of our activities. Also, you may use the desktop pad computers in this room to comb through our card catalog and conduct Internet research. However, these devices cannot send or receive email or text messages—whatever those might be. Remember, I retired in 1973. We still used carbon paper. And now Dr. Zinchenko will walk you through the floor plan."

Everybody unfolded their map pamphlets.

"As you can see," said Dr. Zinchenko, "fiction titles are located here in the reading room. The Children's Enrichment Room, with soundproof walls, is over there. Two fully equipped community meeting rooms as well as the Book Nook Café—behind those windows where the curtains are drawn—are also located on this floor. Upstairs on two, you will find ten numbered doors, each leading into a chamber filled with books, information, and, well, *displays* related to its corresponding Dewey decimal category."

Kyle raised his hand.

"Yes?"

"Where's the Electronic Learning Center?"

Dr. Zinchenko grinned. "Upstairs on the third floor, where you will also find the Board Room, the Art and Artifacts Room, the IMAX theater, the Lemoncello-abilia Room, the—"

"Can we go upstairs and play?" asked Bridgette Wadge. "I want to try out the space shuttle simulator."

"I want to learn how to drive a car!" said Sean Keegan. "A race car!"

"I want to conquer the world with Alexander the Great!" said Yasmeen Smith-Snyder.

Apparently, everybody was doing what Kyle had already done: checking out the "Available Educational Gameware" listed on the back of the floor plan.

"Early access to the Electronic Learning Center will be tonight's second prize," said Dr. Zinchenko. "To win it, you must use the library's resources to find dessert, which we have hidden somewhere in the building. Whoever does the research and locates the goodies first will also be the first one allowed into the Electronic Learning Center. So use your wits and use your library. Go find dessert!"

Everybody raced around the room and sat down at separate desks to start tapping on the glass computer pads.

Well, everybody except Sierra Russell. She spent like two seconds swiping her fingers across a screen, wrote something down with a stubby pencil on a slip of paper, then wandered off to inspect the three-story-tall curved bookcases lining the walls at the back half of the rotunda. Kyle watched as she stepped onto a slightly elevated platform with handles like you'd see on your grand-mother's walker. It even had a basket attached to the front.

"Dr. Zinchenko?"

"Yes, Ms. Russell?"

"Is this safe? Because the book I want is all the way up at the top."

"Yes. Just make sure your feet are securely locked in."

Sierra wiggled her leg. Kyle heard a metallic snap.

"It's like a ski boot," said Sierra.

"That's right. Now use the keypad to tell the hover ladder the call number for the book you are interested in and hang on tight."

Sierra consulted the slip of paper and tapped some keys.

"The bottom of that platform you are standing on is a magnet," said Dr. Zinchenko. "There are ribbons of electromagnetic material in the lining of the bookcases. The strength of those magnets will be modulated by our maglev computer based on the call number you input."

Two seconds later, Sierra Russell was floating in the air, drifting up and to the left. It was absolutely awesome.

"The hover ladder must use advanced magnetic levita-tion technology," said Miguel, seated at the desk to Kyle's right. "Just like the maglev bullet trains in Japan."

"Cool," mumbled Kyle.

And for the first time in his life, Kyle Keeley wanted to check out a library book more than anything in the world.

14

"How about we work together?" said Akimi when she sat down at Kyle's table.

"Hmmm?"

Kyle couldn't take his eyes off Sierra Russell. She had drifted up about twenty-five feet and was leaning against the railings of her floating platform, completely lost in a new book.

"Hello? Earth to Kyle? Do you want somebody else to get first dibs on the Electronic Learning Center?"

"No."

"Then focus."

"Okay. So how do we use our wits and the library to find dessert?"

Akimi nodded toward Miguel, whose fingers were dancing across the screen of his desktop's tablet computer.

"I think he's doing a search in the card catalog," whispered Akimi.

"Why?"

"It's how you find stuff in a library, Kyle."

"I know that. But we're not looking for *books* about dessert. We need to find actual food."

Andrew Peckleman stood up from his desk and sprinted up a wrought-iron spiral staircase leading to the second floor. Two seconds later, Charles Chiltington was sprinting up the staircase behind him.

All the other players soon followed. Everybody was headed to the second floor and the Dewey decimal rooms. Miguel finally popped up from his desk and made a mad dash for the nearest staircase.

"It's got to be up in the six hundreds, you guys," he called out to Kyle and Akimi.

"Thanks," said Kyle. But he still didn't budge from his seat.

"I guess the six hundreds is the Dewey decimal category where you find books about desserts," said Akimi. "Maybe we should . . ."

"Wait a second," said Kyle.

"Um, Kyle, in case you haven't noticed, you, me, and glider girl Sierra are the only ones still on this floor, and Sierra isn't really *on* the floor because she's floating."

"Hang on, Akimi. I have an idea." Kyle pulled out his floor plan. "Dessert is probably hiding in plain sight. Just like the bonus codes in Squirrel Squad. Follow me."

"Where to?"

"The Book Nook Café. The one room in the library where, according to what Dr. Zinchenko told us back at the hotel, food and drinks are actually allowed."

They strolled into the cozy café.

"Whoo-hoo!" shouted Akimi.

The walls were decorated with shelves of cookbooks but several tables were loaded down with trays of cookies, cakes, ice cream, and fruit!

"That's why the curtains were closed behind the windows into the rotunda," said Akimi. "So we couldn't see all this food. Way to go, Kyle."

Kyle did his best imitation of Charles Chiltington: "I'm a Keeley, Akimi. We never lose. Except, of course, when we don't win."

After everyone had dessert, Kyle and Akimi were the first ones allowed to enter the Electronic Learning Center.

Kyle flew the space shuttle, making an excellent landing on Mars before crashing into one of Saturn's moons. Akimi rode a horse with Paul Revere. Then Kyle learned how to drive a stick-shift stock car on the Talladega racetrack while Akimi climbed into a tiny submarine to swim with sharks, dolphins, and sea turtles—all of which were projected on the glass walls of her undersea simulator.

All the educational video games had 3-D visuals, digital surround sound, and something new that Mr. Lemoncello was developing for his video games: smell-a-vision. When you sacked Rome with the Visigoths, you could smell the smoky scent of the burning city as well as the barbarians' b.o.

After an hour, Dr. Zinchenko ushered everybody else into the Electronic Learning Center. They'd been watching George Washington debate George W. Bush (both were audio-animatronic dummies) in the "town square" at the center of the 900s room.

At ten p.m. they all tromped into the IMAX theater, also on the third floor, to see a jukebox concert. 3-D images of the world's best musicians (living and dead) performed their hits "live." The best part was Mozart jamming with Metallica.

Finally, around three in the morning, Clarence and his twin brother, Clement, came to escort the kids to their sleeping quarters. The boys would roll out their sleeping bags in the Children's Room, just off the rotunda; the girls would be upstairs on the third floor in the Board Room. Charles Chiltington would be luxuriating all alone in Mr. Lemoncello's private suite.

Exhausted from the excitement of the day—and crashing after eating way too much sugar—Kyle slept like a baby.

He only woke up because he heard music.

Loud, blaring music.

The theme song from that boxing movie *Rocky,* his brother Mike's favorite.

"Whazzat?" he mumbled, crawling out of his sleeping bag.

Kyle glanced at his watch. It was eleven a.m. He figured the library lock-in was officially over and this was the group's wake-up call.

The music kept blaring.

"This is how they wake up astronauts," groaned Miguel.

"Turn it off!" moaned Andrew Peckleman.

Kyle slipped on his jeans and sneakers and staggered out into the giant reading room.

"Dr. Zinchenko?"

His voice echoed off the dome. No answer.

"Clarence? Clement?"

Nothing.

The *Rocky* music got louder.

Akimi leaned in from the third-floor balcony.

"What's going on down there?"

"I think they're trying to wake up astronauts," said Kyle. "On the moon."

He made his way to the front door and reached for the handle.

It wouldn't budge.

He jiggled it.

Nothing.

He jiggled harder.

Still nothing.

Kyle realized that the library lock-in might be over but they were still locked in the library.

15

"Everybody, please take your seats," Dr. Zinchenko said to the parents gathered in a conference room at the Parker House Hotel.

"When do our kids come home?" asked one of the mothers.

"Rose has soccer at two," said another.

The librarian nodded. "Mr. Lemoncello will—"

Just then, an accordion-panel door at the far end of the room flew open, revealing the eccentric billionaire dressed in a bright purple tracksuit and a plumed pirate hat. He was eating a slice of seven-layer birthday cake.

"Good morning or, as they're currently saying in Reykjavik, *gott síðdegi,* which means 'good afternoon,' because there is a four-hour time difference between Ohio and Iceland, a fact I first learned spinning a globe in my local library."

Mr. Lemoncello, his banana shoes burp-squeaking, stepped out of a room filled with dozens of black-and-white television monitors—the kind security guards watch at their workstations.

"Ladies and gentlemen, thank you for joining us on this grand and auspicious day. Today I am pleased to announce the most marvelously stupendous game ever created: Escape from Mr. Lemoncello's Library! The entire library will be the game board. Your children will be the game pieces. The winner will become famous all over the world."

"How?" asked one of the fathers.

"By starring in all of my commercials this holiday season. TV. Radio. Print. Billboards. Cardboard cutouts in toy stores. His or her face will be everywhere."

Mrs. Daley raised her hand. "Will they get paid?"

"Oh, yes. In fact, you'll probably want to call me The Giver."

"And what exactly does Haley have to do to win?"

"Escape! From the library. I thought the game's title more or less gave that bit away." Mr. Lemoncello tapped a button in his pirate hat and an animated version of the library's floor plan was instantly displayed on the conference room's plasma-screen TVs.

"Whoever is the first to use what they find *in* the library to find their way *out* of the library will be crowned the winner. Now then, the children cannot use the front door or the fire exits or set off any alarms. They cannot go out the way they went in. They can only use their wits, cunning, and intelligence to decipher clues and solve riddles that will eventually lead them to the location of the library's supersecret alternate exit. And, ladies and gentlemen, I assure you, such an alternate exit does indeed exist."

The parents around the table started buzzing with excitement.

"Participation, of course, will be purely optional and voluntary," said Mr. Lemoncello, clasping his hands behind his back and stalking around the room.

Several parents pulled out cell phones.

"And please—do *not* attempt to phone, email, text, fax, or send smoke signals to your children, encouraging them to enter the competition. We have blocked all communication into and out of the library. Only those who truly wish to stay and play shall stay and play. Anyone who chooses to leave the library will go home with lovely parting gifts and a souvenir pirate hat very similar to mine. They'll also be invited to my birthday party tomorrow afternoon." He held up his crumb-filled plate. "I've been sampling potential cake candidates for breakfast."

Mrs. Keegan crossed her arms over her chest. "Will this game be dangerous?"

"No," said Mr. Lemoncello. "Your children will be under constant video surveillance by security personnel in the library's control center. Dr. Zinchenko and I will also be monitoring their progress here in my private video-viewing suite. Should anything go wrong, we have paramedics, firefighters, and a team of former Navy SEALs—each with the heart of a samurai—standing by to swoop in and rescue your children. It'll be like *The Hunger Games* but with lots of food and no bows or arrows."

"Why not just have the kids play one of your other games?" a parent suggested. "Why all this fuss?"

"Because, my dear friends, these twelve children have lived their entire lives without a public library. As a result, they have no idea how extraordinarily useful, helpful, and funful—a word I recently invented—a library can be. This is their chance to discover that a library is more than a collection of dusty old books. It is a place to learn, explore, and grow!"

"Mr. Lemoncello, I think what you're doing is fantastic," said one of the mothers.

"Thank you," said Mr. Lemoncello, bowing and clicking his heels (which made them *bruck* like a chicken).

"If any of you would like to check up on your children," announced Dr. Zinchenko, "please join us in the adjoining room."

"Oh, they're a lot of fun to watch," said Mr. Lemoncello. "However, Mr. and Mrs. Keeley, I'm afraid your son Kyle does not enjoy the theme song from *Rocky* quite as much as I do!"

16

Rocky had done its job.

Kyle—and everybody else locked inside the library—was definitely awake.

Even Charles Chiltington had come down to the Rotunda Reading Room from Mr. Lemoncello's private suite. The only essay writer not with the group was Sierra Russell, who, Kyle figured, was off looking for another book to read.

"We're still locked in?" squealed Haley Daley.

"This is so lame," added Sean Keegan. "It's like eleven-thirty. I've got things to do. Places to be."

"Look, you guys," said Kyle, "they'll probably open the front door right after we eat or something."

"Well, where's that ridiculous librarian?" said Charles Chiltington, who was never very nice when there weren't any adults in the room.

"Yeah," said Rose Vermette. "I can't stay in here all day. I have a soccer game at two."

"And, dudes," said Sean Keegan, "*I* have a life."

"Do you children require assistance?" said a soft, motherly voice.

It was the semi-transparent holographic image of Mrs. Tobin, the librarian from the 1960s. She was hovering a few inches off the ground in front of the center desk.

"Yes," said Kayla Corson. "How do we get out of here?"

The librarian blinked, the way a secondhand calculator (the one your oldest brother dropped on the floor a billion times) does when it's figuring out a square root.

"I'm sorry," said the robotic librarian. "I have not been provided with the answer to that question."

"Will we be doing brunch here this morning?" Chiltington asked politely. "I'm not hungry, but some of my chums sure are. After all, it is eleven-thirty."

"The kitchen staff recently placed fresh food in the Book Nook Café."

"Thank you, Mrs. Tobin," said Chiltington. "Would you like anything? A bowl of oatmeal, perhaps."

"No. Thank you, CHARLES. I am a hologram. I do not eat food."

"I guess that's how you stay so super skinny."

Kyle shook his head. The smarmy guy was oilier than a soggy sack of fries. He was even sucking up to a hologram.

Chiltington and the others traipsed off to have

breakfast, but Kyle and Akimi stayed with the holographic librarian.

"Um, I have a question," said Kyle.

"I'm listening."

"Is the library lock-in over? Are we supposed to go home now?"

"Mr. Lemoncello will be addressing that issue shortly."

"Okay. Thanks, Mrs. Tobin."

"You are welcome, KYLE."

After the librarian faded to a flicker, Akimi said, "By the way, Kyle, before we leave, you need to check out that room I slept in last night."

"The Board Room?"

"Yeah. They call it that because, guess what? It's filled with board games!"

"All Lemoncellos?"

"Nuh-uh. Stuff from other companies. Some of it goes way back to the 1890s. I think it's Mr. Lemoncello's personal collection. It's like a museum up there."

Kyle's eyes went wide. "You hungry?" he asked.

"Not really. We ate so much last night."

"You think we have time to check out this game museum?"

"Follow me."

The two friends bounded up a spiral staircase to the second floor, where they found another set of steps to take them up to the third.

When he entered the Board Room, Kyle was blown away. "Wow!"

The walls were lined with bookcases filled with antique games, tin toys, and card games.

"This is incredible."

"I guess," said Akimi. "If, you know, you like games."

Kyle smiled. "Which, you know, I do."

They spent several quiet minutes wandering around the room, taking in all the wacky games that people used to play. There was one display case featuring eight games with amazingly illustrated box tops. A tiny spotlight illuminated each one.

"Wonder what's so special about these games," said Kyle.

"Maybe those were Mr. Lemoncello's favorites when he was a kid."

"Maybe." But the slogan etched into the glass case confused Kyle: "Luigi Lemoncello: the first and last word in games."

"But these aren't Lemoncello games," he mumbled.

The first spotlighted game in the case was Howdy Doody's TV Game. After that came Hüsker Dü?, You Don't Say!, Like Minds, Fun City, Big 6 Sports Games, Get the Message, and Ruff and Reddy.

"It's a puzzle," Kyle said with a grin.

"I thought they were games."

"They are. But if you string together the first or last

word of each game title . . ." He tapped the glass in front of the first box on the bottom shelf. "You *get the message.*"

"Really?" said Akimi, sounding extremely skeptical. "You're sure it's not just a bunch of junk somebody picked up for like fifty cents at a yard sale?"

"Positive." Kyle pointed to each box top as he cracked the code. "Howdy. Dü you like fun games? Get Reddy."

Miguel Fernandez barged into the Board Room.

"Here you are! We need you guys in the Electronic Learning Center. Now."

"Why?"

"Charles Chiltington wolfed down his breakfast, then raced up here to finish the game he started last night so he can enter his name as the first high scorer."

"So?"

"The game he's playing is all about medieval castles and dungeons!"

This time Akimi said it: "So?"

"He's escaping through the sewers. The game has smell-a-vision. You ever smell a medieval sewer? Trust me, it is foul *and* disgusting."

The three of them dashed up the hall and entered the stinky room where Charles was sitting in a vibrating pedestal chair, thumbing his controller. As his avatar sloshed through a sewer pipe, the subwoofers built into his seat made every *SQUISH!* and *SPLAT!* rumble across the floor.

80

"Whoa!" said Kyle. "Knock it off, Charles. You're pumping out total tear gas."

"Because I'm in the sewers underneath the horse stables. It's the secret way out of the castle. I'm going to win another game. That's two for me, Keeley. How many for you?"

"Yo," said Miguel. "This room is two stories above the café. The ductwork is connected."

"What's your point?"

"You're making everybody's food downstairs smell like horse manure!"

"Who cares? I'm winning."

Charles's chair went *FLUMP!* again.

But this time, Kyle smelled . . . pine trees?

Like one of those evergreen air fresheners people hang inside their cars.

"Aw, this stupid thing is broken." Charles jumped out of the chair and reared back to kick it.

"Um, I wouldn't do that if I were you," said Kyle.

"Why not?"

"Because there's a security camera over there and it's aimed right at you."

"What? Where?"

"See the blinking red light?"

Suddenly, an image of Kyle pointing up at the camera lens appeared on every video screen in the Electronic Learning Center.

Until he was replaced by Mr. Lemoncello.

17

"Excellent escape plan, Charles," said Mr. Lemoncello on the video screens.

"Thank you, sir," said Chiltington, smoothing out his khaki pants. "And just so you know, I saw an ant crawling up the side of this seat. That's why I almost kicked it."

"How very thoughtful of you, Charles."

"Mr. Lemoncello?" said Akimi.

"Yes?"

"How come the sewer started smelling like a pine tree?"

"Because I enjoy the odor of pine trees much more than the stench of horse poop. How about you?"

"Definitely."

"Now then, will everybody else please join us upstairs in the Electronic Learning Center? I have a very important announcement to make."

Kyle heard feet clomping up the stairs and soon Andrew, Bridgette, Yasmeen, Sean, Haley, Rose, and Kayla hurried into the room.

"Are we all here?" said Mr. Lemoncello.

"Everybody except Sierra Russell," said Kyle.

"Ah, yes. I saw her downstairs reading *When You Reach Me* by Rebecca Stead. We'll reach her later. It's nearly noon and I'm eager to move on to the next round of our competition."

"What competition?" asked Yasmeen Smith-Snyder.

"The one we are about to begin."

"Sir?" said Sean Keegan. "I have stuff to do today."

"That's fine, Sean. You are, of course, free to leave. If any of the rest of you do not wish to stay and play, kindly deposit your library cards in the discard pile."

A tile in the floor popped open and an empty goldfish bowl atop an ornate column rose up about three feet.

"Just drop it in the bowl there, Sean. Attaboy. Follow the flashing red arrows in the floor to the nearest exit, where you will receive a lovely parting gift along with my everlasting admiration for your essay-writing abilities."

Bright red arrows danced across the floor. Sean followed them.

"What happens if we decide to stay?" asked Akimi.

"You will be given the chance to play a brand-new, exciting game!"

"Is there a prize for the winner?" demanded Haley Daley.

"Oh, yes."

Now Miguel shot up his hand. "Mr. Lemoncello? What do we have to do to win?"

"Simple: Find your way *out* of the library using only what's *in* the library."

"Awesome!"

"Lame," mumbled Kayla Corson. "I'm outta here."

She plunked her library card into the fishbowl and followed the blinking arrows out the door.

"Does anyone else want or need to leave?"

"Sorry, sir. I have soccer at two," said Rose Vermette. "See you guys later." She dropped her card into the discard bowl.

The instant she did, bells rang, confetti fell from the ceiling, and every electronic console in the game room started *ding-ding-ding*ing.

"Congratulations, Rose!" cried Mr. Lemoncello, who had put on a pointy party hat. "For sticking to your prior commitments, you will receive our special Prior Commitment Sticker prize: a complete set of Lemoncello Sticker Picture Games and a laptop computer to play them on! Enjoy."

Charles Chiltington stepped a little closer to the security camera as Rose Vermette skipped out of the room.

"Sir, might we assume that the prize for winning your brand-new game will be even better than a laptop computer?"

"Yes," said Mr. Lemoncello, taking off his party hat. "You may so assume."

"I'm in," said Chiltington.

"Me too," said Kyle.

"Me too," added Akimi, Miguel, Andrew, Bridgette, Yasmeen, and Haley.

Sierra Russell wandered into the room. Her nose was buried so deep in her book she didn't even notice Mr. Lemoncello's gigantic face on all the video screens.

"Is something going on?" she said, mostly to her book pages.

"You bet!" boomed Mr. Lemoncello.

Sierra's head snapped up.

"Oh. Hello, sir."

"Greetings, Sierra. Sorry to interrupt your reading. Just have a quick question: Will you be staying or leaving?"

"Well, sir, I'd like to stay. If that's okay?"

"Okay? It is *wondermous*, another word I just made up. Now then, to read you the rules of the game—because every game needs rules—here is your friend and mine, Dr. Yanina Zinchenko!"

The video screens switched to a close-up of the librarian with the red hair and glasses.

"Your exit from the library must be completed between noon today and noon tomorrow," said Dr. Zinchenko.

Mr. Lemoncello's head popped into a corner of her screen.

"Tomorrow's my birthday, by the way. Mark your calendars."

And he ducked back out of the frame.

"Our security guards will continue holding your cell phones," said Dr. Zinchenko. "You may not use the library computers to contact anyone outside the building. You may, however, use them to conduct research.

"You may also request three different types of outside assistance: one 'Ask an Expert,' one 'Librarian Consultation,' and one 'Extreme Challenge.' Please be advised: The Extreme Challenges are, as the name implies, extremely difficult. If you pass the challenge, your reward will be great. However, if you fail, you will be eliminated from the competition."

Kyle figured he'd avoid asking for one of those—unless he extremely needed to.

"To use any of these 'lifelines,'" Dr. Zinchenko continued, "simply summon Mrs. Tobin."

Chiltington raised his hand.

"Yes, Charles?"

"Would you mind telling us what the prize will be for the winner?"

The video screen switched to an image of Mr. Lemoncello, who had done some sort of quick change. Now he was wearing sunglasses and had a silk ascot tucked into his shirt collar. He looked like a flashy Hollywood movie star. From 1939.

"Fame and glory! The winner will become my new spokesperson and will star in all of my holiday promotions."

"We'll be famous?" gushed Yasmeen, fluffing up her hair and smiling at the security camera.

Haley stepped in front of Yasmeen. "I've done some modeling work. For Sherman's Shoes in Old Town."

Yasmeen stepped in front of Haley. "I was an extra in a hot dog commercial once. . . ."

"Well, I'm a cheerleader; Yasmeen isn't. . . ."

While the two girls continued primping and posing for the camera, Dr. Zinchenko came back on-screen to quickly rattle off some final words.

"Your library cards are the keys to everything you will need. The library staff is here to help you find whatever it is you are looking for. The way out is not the way you came in. You may *not* use any of the fire exits. If you do, an alarm will sound and you will be immediately eliminated from the game. For safety purposes, you will be under constant video surveillance and you will be recorded. In the unlikely event of an emergency, you will be evacuated from the building. Creating an incident that requires evacuation will not count as having discovered a way to exit the library. Any questions?"

"Just one," said Andrew Peckleman, adjusting his goggle-sized glasses with his fingertip. "When exactly will the game begin?"

Mr. Lemoncello's face reappeared on the screens.

"Good question, Andrew! Oh, my. It's noon! How about . . . let's say . . . oh, I don't know . . . *now*!"

18

The contestants raced down the stairs to the Rotunda Reading Room.

Kyle saw Haley Daley dash down another set of steps into the basement, to what the floor plan called the Stacks.

Miguel and Andrew, the two library experts, grabbed separate tables and started working the touch-screen computers. Bridgette Wadge did the same thing.

Charles Chiltington strolled out the arched doorway and into the foyer with the fountain.

Yasmeen Smith-Snyder was running around the circular room with her floor plan in front of her face, like someone frantically checking their text messages while racing down a crowded sidewalk.

Sierra Russell found a comfy chair and sat down.

To finish her book.

The girl definitely wasn't into the whole spirit of The Game.

"So, Kyle," said Akimi, "you want to form an alliance?"

"What do you mean?"

"It's what people do on reality shows like *Survivor*. We help each other until, you know, everybody else is eliminated and we have to stab each other in the back."

"Um, I don't remember hearing anything about 'eliminations.'"

"Oh. Right."

"But, hey, there was nothing in the rules that said we couldn't share the top prize. I just want to *win*!"

"Cool. So, we're a team?"

"Sure."

"Great," said Akimi. "I nominate you to be our captain. All in favor raise their hands."

Kyle and Akimi both raised their hands.

"It's unanimous," said Akimi. "Okay. Let's go ask that antique librarian a question."

"What?"

"We both get to ask one question, right?"

"Right."

"Okay, here's mine: 'Hey, lady—how do we get out of here?'"

"And you think she'll tell you?"

"No. Not really. So, what's your plan?"

"Well, I was thinking—"

Suddenly, Yasmeen shouted, "I win!"

The rest of them stopped whatever they were doing.

"It's just like last night when Kyle found dessert in the most obvious place. To get out of the library, all we have to do is use one of the fire exits. Duh."

She headed toward a hallway between the Book Nook Café and Community Meeting Room A.

Kyle stood up. "Um, Yasmeen? I think maybe you missed some of what . . ."

Charles Chiltington dashed into the room and shouted, "You're not going to win, Yasmeen. Not unless you beat me to that fire exit!"

He bolted toward the corridor.

Yasmeen bolted toward it, too.

"You guys?" said Kyle.

Kyle could see a red Exit light glowing at the far end of the hallway Charles and Yasmeen were sprinting down. Charles stumbled and fell. Yasmeen kept running. Harder. Faster. She slammed into the exit bar on the metal door.

Alarms sounded. Flashing red lights swirled. Somewhere, a tiger roared. Mr. Lemoncello's voice rang out of the overhead speakers. "Sorry, Yasmeen. That's where your sidewalk ends. You broke the rules. You are out of the game. Your library card will be placed in the discard bowl and you will be going home."

As the fire exit door slowly swung shut and Yasmeen disappeared into the bright sunshine outside the library,

Kyle checked out Charles Chiltington, who would've been sent home if he hadn't stumbled and had reached the exit first.

The guy was smirking.

That was when it hit Kyle: Chiltington had faked Yasmeen out. He knew she couldn't win by going out a fire exit. But he ran down the hall to fool her into thinking she was doing the right thing.

Oh, yeah. Chiltington was definitely in it to win it.

No matter who he had to trample.

Whistling casually, Charles strolled back to the lobby.

"What's Chiltington doing out in the entrance hall?" said Akimi. "They told us the way out isn't the way in."

Before Kyle could answer, Andrew Peckleman started shouting at Miguel, who had wandered over to Peckleman's table.

"Get away! You're trying to steal my idea!"

"No, man," said Miguel. "I just happened to see your screen and I don't think that particular periodical—"

"You know what, Miguel? I don't really care what you think! This isn't school. This is the *public* library and you're not the boss in here, so just leave me alone!"

Miguel tossed up his hands. "No problem, bro. I was just trying to help."

"Ha! You mean help me lose." Andrew stormed up the closest spiral staircase to the second floor and the Dewey decimal rooms. Miguel, looking sort of sad, headed up a separate spiral staircase. Bridgette Wadge trailed after them.

"Want to follow those guys like Bridgette did?" whispered Akimi. "I'll take Peckleman, you take Miguel."

"No thanks," said Kyle, looking up at the domed ceiling. "I'm much more interested in the windows up there."

Three stories above the rotunda floor, just below the Wonder Dome, there was a series of ten arched windows set between the recessed statue nooks. The windows acted like skylights at the base of the dome, allowing sunshine to flood into the room below.

"Do you think those windows open?" asked Akimi.

"Maybe. Maybe not. But I've never let a closed or locked window stand between me and winning a game. Just ask my dad."

"What?"

"Never mind. Come on." Kyle trotted over to the cushy chair where Sierra Russell was peacefully reading her book.

"Um, excuse me, hate to interrupt . . ."

Sierra raised her head. She had a very dreamy look in her eyes.

"I need a book."

"Really?" said Sierra. "What kind?"

"Like the one you found. Up there." He gestured to the curving bookcases climbing up the back half of the rotunda.

"Fiction," said Sierra.

"Right," said Kyle. "Love me some fiction."

"Well, what sort of story do you like?"

"Something way up high," said Kyle. "The higher the better."

"Really?"

"Yep."

"Well, that's an interesting way to put together a reading list, basing it on bookcase elevation. . . ."

"I'd like something on the top shelf. Maybe right under the hologram statue of that guy hanging out with the Cat in the Hat."

"That's Dr. Seuss," said Sierra. "He wrote *The Cat in the Hat*."

"Sweet," said Kyle. "But I just like how close he is to that window."

19

"Oh, Mrs. Tobin?" Akimi called out. "I need to use my Librarian Consultation."

"You sure about this?" said Kyle.

"That's the beauty of being a team. After we burn through mine, we'll still have yours."

The hologram librarian appeared and advised Akimi that *Huckleberry Finn* by Mark Twain was the book located right underneath the holographic image of Dr. Seuss and the Cat in the Hat.

After Mrs. Tobin vanished, Kyle and Akimi used their desktop computer to find the call number for *Huckleberry Finn*. Kyle grabbed a pen and scribbled it down on his palm.

"Are you going to do what I think you're going to do?" said Akimi.

"Yep. I'm going to float up there, hoist myself into that nook where the hologram is, reach over to the window, push it open, and stick out my hand. Technically, I will have found my way *out* of the library. Nothing in the rules said anything about how *far* outside we had to go to win."

"You could fall."

"I don't think so. I'm wiry, like a monkey."

"Seriously, Kyle. It isn't worth it."

"Um, yes it is. Did I mention I want to *win*?"

"You should improvise a safety harness," suggested Sierra Russell.

"Huh?"

"Well, in this adventure book I read once, the hero was in a very similar predicament. So he removed the curled handset wires from several telephones, bundled them together, and made a safety rope."

Ten minutes later, Kyle, Akimi, and Sierra had stripped the sproingy wires off a couple of telephone handsets. Kyle looped the cables around his waist and tied the other end to the handrail of the hover ladder. When fully extended, the safety rope would stretch out to a little more than twenty feet.

It should work.

"Be careful up there," said Akimi.

"Yes," said Sierra, who wasn't reading her book anymore. Apparently, watching a real live person risk his real live life by doing something really, really scary was one thing more exciting than reading.

Kyle locked his feet into the hover ladder's ski boot brackets. "Here we go."

Serious adrenaline raced through his body as he tapped the call number for *Huckleberry Finn* into the hover ladder's book locator keypad.

"When you open the window," said Akimi, "just shout, 'I found the way out!' and we win."

"Right," said Kyle. "All three of us."

"Huh?"

"Hey, Sierra came up with the safety rope idea. She's on our team now, too."

"Fine. Whatever. Just don't break your neck."

"Not part of the plan."

Kyle pressed the enter button on the control panel. The platform floated up off the ground and drifted slightly to the right.

"Be careful!" said Akimi. "Watch it!"

"I'm not doing anything," said Kyle. "This thingama-jiggy is doing all the work. I'm just along for the ride."

Kyle gripped the handles as the platform rose higher and higher. He sailed past books by Tolstoy and Thackeray. Tilting back his head, he looked up at the semi-transparent statues projected into the curved niches next to the arched windows.

They were a weird mix. A thoughtful African American man in a three-piece suit and a bow tie. A guy with long curly hair, old-fashioned clothes, and a looking glass. A long-haired dude in a scruffy shirt hiding behind cutouts of the letters "P" and "B." A bald guy with a beard.

Since the statues were really holographic projections, they had chisel-type labels floating in front of their pedestals identifying who the famous people were. The ones closest to Kyle were George Orwell, Lewis Carroll, Dr. Seuss, and Maya Angelou.

As he continued to climb, Kyle could hear the soft whir of the electromagnets invisibly lifting him toward the ceiling.

And then he heard something much louder.

"What a ridiculous idea!"

Charles Chiltington. He was standing on the second-floor balcony at the far side of the rotunda.

"You know, Keeley, I thought about doing the same thing. But then I noticed something you obviously overlooked: There's a wire mesh security screen on the other side of those windows."

The levitating platform stuttered to a stop.

"Enjoy staring at the ceiling, Keeley. I'm off to win yet another game!"

Kyle ignored Chiltington and grabbed hold of the ledge beneath Dr. Seuss's berth. He tried to haul himself up but his feet wouldn't budge.

They were locked in place by those ski boot clamps.

And this close to the skylights, Kyle could see that Chiltington was right—there was a security screen on the other side of the windows.

Kyle checked his wristwatch. It was one p.m. He and

his teammates had wasted an hour on the lame window idea. He sighed heavily and stared up at the quivering Seuss projection in the bowed niche above his head.

The Cat in the Hat's mouth started to move.

" 'Think left and think right and think low and think high.' "

Kyle recognized the voice.

It was Mr. Lemoncello.

" 'Oh, the thinks you can think up if only you try!' "

In other words, Kyle was back to square one. He needed to think up a whole new escape plan.

The ladder began a slow and steady descent to the floor—even though Kyle hadn't pushed a button.

"Don't listen to smarmypants Charles," Akimi coached as Kyle coasted toward the floor. "It was worth a shot."

"I agree," said Sierra.

A bloodcurdling scream came ringing up the staircase from the basement.

"That's Haley!" said Akimi. "I saw her go downstairs."

"That's where the Stacks are," added Sierra.

"Come on," said Kyle. "She could be in serious trouble."

"You should never help your competition, Keeley," scoffed Charles as he casually strolled down a spiral staircase. "Unless, of course, you *always* play to lose!"

Losers.

That's what Charles Chiltington thought about senti-mental saps like Kyle Keeley. A damsel in distress starts screaming and he forgets all about winning the game to go rescue her?

What a pathetic loser.

Unless, of course, Haley Daley was screaming because she had already found the alternate exit.

That made Charles laugh.

Impossible.

Although quite pretty, Haley Daley, the princess of the seventh grade, was a total airhead. There was no way a dumb girl like her could've outsmarted Charles Chiltington.

It was time to play his hunch.

Twice already, the head librarian, Dr. Zinchenko, had said, "The library staff is here to help you find whatever it is you are looking for." She said it once when they were just about to enter the library, again when she was reading the laundry list of rules.

Well, what Charles was looking for was a way out of the building that wasn't the front door and wouldn't set off any alarms.

That was why he kept coming back to the lobby with the gurgling fountain. Why he kept studying the display case labeled "Staff Picks: Our Most Memorable Reads."

"The staff is here to help," he muttered. "These are staff picks. Ipso facto, this has to be some sort of enormous clue."

Inside the sealed bookcase, Charles saw twelve book covers.

One for each of the twelve twelve-year-old players? he wondered.

The display items weren't actual books. They were cover art mounted on book-sized foam core. Three covers were lined up on each of the case's four shelves. Since they weren't actual books with spines, none of the covers included their call numbers.

Charles focused on the three books lined up on the bottom row.

Hoosier Hospitality was on the left. *In the Pocket: Johnny Unitas and Me* was in the middle. *The Dinner Party* was on the right.

Charles decided to concentrate on the Johnny Unitas

title. He moved into the rotunda and did a quick card catalog search on one of the desktop computers. When he typed *"In the Pocket,"* a matching cover image popped up.

But still no call number.

In the spot where the identifier should have been, there were instead a censor's thick black box and the words "I.D. Temporarily Removed from System."

Scrolling further down the screen, Charles came across a rather unusual annotation: "You didn't really think we'd make it that easy, did you?"

Charles grinned.

The computer was telling him he was on the right track.

He glanced up from the desk. The Children's Room was directly in front of him. The book about Johnny Unitas, with its cartoony cover depicting a football player wearing a number nineteen jersey and dropping back to launch a pass, was most likely a children's book.

Of course, it was also a sports biography.

So would it be shelved with sports books, biographies, or children's books?

Charles went back to the computerized card catalog. He read the book's description: "Billy wants to be a great quarterback like his hero, Johnny Unitas, but his coach is worried he'll get hurt."

It sounded like fiction. A made-up story. It had to be in the Children's Room.

As Charles crossed the slick marble floor, something else struck him.

This was like Hüsker Dü?, a memory game he had played when he was in kindergarten. He was on a hunt to find a hidden match for the football book cover he had just memorized. This was, in short, another memory game—that was why the Staff Picks display had been subtitled "Our Most *Memorable* Reads."

"Clever, Lemoncello," he mumbled. "Very clever indeed."

Charles entered the children's department. It didn't take him very long to find the book, because *In the Pocket* was propped up on a miniature stand on top of a shelf.

"Found it!" Charles proclaimed. Then, savoring the moment, he picked up the book and read the title out loud: *"In the Pocket: Johnny Unitas and Me."*

All of a sudden, a row of animatronic geese tucked into a corner of the room started honking and singing.

"They call him Mr. Touchdown, yes, they call him Mr. T."

The squawking birds startled Charles so much he dropped the book.

When he did, a four-by-four card fluttered out from behind its cover.

Charles bent down to pick it up.

Printed on the card was a black-and-white silhouette. A quarterback, wearing a number nineteen jersey (just like Johnny Unitas), was arching back his arm to throw a pass.

Charles grinned.

He was definitely on the right track.

He tucked the silhouette card into his pocket and hurried back to the lobby to memorize more book covers.

21

"Ouch! I'm stuck! Help!"

Haley Daley's cries sailed up the staircase as Kyle led the charge down the steps into the Stacks.

"So, what exactly are the Stacks?" asked Akimi, three steps behind Kyle.

"It's where the library stores its collection of research material," said Sierra, who was two stairs behind Akimi.

The three of them reached the basement. It was filled with tidy rows of floor-to-ceiling shelving units.

"Help!"

Haley sounded like she was on the far side of the room, behind the walls of metal storage racks crowded with boxes, books, and bins.

"What is all this stuff?" said Kyle, looking for a passageway, trying to figure out how to get to wherever Haley was.

"Mostly rare books and documents you can't check out," said Sierra. "But if you fill out a call slip, you can use this material up in the reading room."

With a whir and whoosh of its electric motor, a shiny robot the color of the storm troopers in *Star Wars* scooted across an intersection between bookshelves. It moved on tank treads and had what looked like a shopping cart attached to its front.

"Let's follow that robot!" said Kyle. "It might know the fastest way to reach Haley."

The trio dashed up a narrow pathway to where they saw the robot extending its quadruple-jointed mechanical arm to pluck a flat metal box out of a slide-in compartment. The box had been stored in a section of shelving with a flashing LCD that read "Magazines & Periodicals. 1930s."

"Somebody upstairs wants an old magazine?" said Akimi.

"They're probably researching the Gold Leaf Bank building," said Sierra. "I think it was built in the 1930s."

"Help!" screamed Haley. "I'm stuck."

"Hang on!" shouted Kyle. "We're coming."

"Well, hurry up already!"

"This way," said Kyle.

They scampered up another aisle, turned right, and saw Haley, her hand jammed through a horizontal slot near the top of the basement wall. To reach it, she'd had to stand on an elevated treadmill maybe thirty feet long. Since the thing was rolling, Haley was jogging in place so she wouldn't fall on her face. The high-tech conveyor belt was actually a series of rollers. Ten robot carts—staggered so no two were directly across from each other—were lined up on either side.

"I think it's an automatic book sorter," said Sierra. "That laser beam near Haley's ankles probably scans a book's tag and tells the conveyor belt which of the ten sorting trays to shove it into."

"You guys?" screamed Haley. "Hurry up and rescue me!"

Kyle stepped back. Tried to assess the situation.

"What is that slot you're hanging on to?"

"The bottom of the stupid book drop," said Haley, trotting on the treadmill. "I saw it on the floor plan. People can walk up to it on the sidewalk and return their books. I figured it had to lead down here."

"Smart move," said Kyle. "You could crawl through the slot and escape."

"*If* you were the size of a book," Akimi said sarcastically.

"I never got that far," said Haley. "The minute I stepped onto this belt thing, it started moving."

Kyle nodded. "Probably a weight-activated switch."

"A book falls in," said Akimi. "The sorter starts up."

"Clever," said Kyle. "Plus, it gives our game its first booby trap."

"Well, the game is no fun if you're the booby stuck in the trap!" said Haley.

Kyle turned to Sierra. "We need to stop the belt so Haley can yank her hand out of that slot without falling on her butt or cracking open her skull. Have you ever read a book where the hero outwits an escalator or a rolling checkout belt in the grocery store or something?"

"No," said Sierra. "Not really."

"How about one where the hero just flips an emergency shutoff switch?" asked Akimi. "Because that's what I'd do if, you know, I found one."

Akimi was standing next to a wall-mounted switch box. She flicked it down. The conveyor belt slowed to a stop.

"Ta-da! Another chapter for my amazingly awesome autobiography—if I ever write one."

Haley yanked her hand out of the book return slot. It sort of popped when it finally sprang free. She collapsed to her knees on the frozen treadmill.

"My hand feels flatter than a pancake," she moaned.

"Are you hurt?" asked Kyle. "Maybe we should tell the security guys that . . ."

"What? That I have a boo-boo and need to go home? Forget it, Kyle Keeley. You're not going to beat me that easily."

"I'm not trying to—"

Haley showed him the palm of her hand. "Save it, Keeley." She crawled off the conveyor belt. "One way or another, I'm going to win this game. I just hope starring in Mr. Lemoncello's commercials earns me some decent money."

She hobbled around the bookshelves toward the staircase up to the reading room.

When she was gone, Akimi raised her hand. "Question?"

"Yeah?" said Kyle.

"How come the guys inside the control room didn't flip a switch to shut down the book sorter when they saw Haley doing her cardio cha-cha-cha on it?"

Kyle shrugged. "Maybe they weren't watching."

"Actually," said Sierra, pointing to a square tile on the floor near the book sorter, "I think they were."

Kyle looked down. The tile was glowing like one of the tablet computer screens upstairs in the rotunda. Kyle read the words zipping across the illuminated square.

" 'Congratulations,' " he read out loud. " 'For helping Haley and being a sport, you've earned much more than a good report.' "

The tile popped open.

Inside a small compartment was a rolled-up tube of paper with a yellow card clipped to its end.

"Huh," said Akimi. "I guess somebody *was* watching."

Kyle pulled the yellow card off the paper tube. It smelled like lemons.

"What's it say?" asked Sierra.

Kyle flipped the card over so Sierra and Akimi could see what was printed on it:

SUPER-DOOPER BONUS CLUE.

22

"Oh, man, that was so dumb!"

Haley could not believe how idiotic she had been.

"Trying to crawl out of a book return slot? Chya. Like that was going to work."

She was giving herself a good talking-to as she trudged up the steps to the first floor.

When she entered the rotunda, she saw Charles Chiltington slipping out into the lobby again.

Chiltington was a snake. Worse. A garden slug. Maybe a leech. Something oily and slimy that left a greasy trail and liked to mooch off other people's ideas. That was why Chiltington had tailed the twin library nerds, Peckleman and Fernandez, upstairs during last night's dessert hunt. Haley was smart enough to know that Chiltington was hoping to steal the book geeks' ideas.

Actually, Haley was a lot smarter than anybody (except

her teachers and whoever scored her IQ tests) knew. With certain people, mainly grown-ups and silly boys, pretending to be a ditzy princess made getting what she wanted a whole lot easier.

And what she wanted right now was money. Lots of money. Her dad had been out of work for nearly a year. They'd run through all their rainy-day savings. They'd had to borrow from relatives and in-laws.

If Haley could win this competition and become Mr. Lemoncello's spokesmodel, her family's money woes would be over and they wouldn't have to sell their home. And once other people saw her on TV for Lemoncello games, they'd want her for their commercials, too. And movies. Maybe her own sitcom. Something on the Disney Channel.

But for all that to happen, Haley needed a winning idea—and fast. Something better than "crawl through a slot that's barely wide enough for your wrist." Maybe she should flush herself down the toilet and escape through the sewers like Charles did in that video game.

She headed over to the Book Nook Café so she could sit down and think.

She stepped into the room and checked out the snack table. There were trays of cookies, strawberries, bananas, and brownies. Sitting down to nibble on a macaroon, she studied the row of cookbooks displayed on the bookshelves lining the wall.

One in particular caught her eye: *Cupcakes, Cookies & Pie, Oh, My!*

Because the cover looked extremely familiar: two googly-eyed sheep made out of chocolate-frosted cakes with gobs of mini marshmallows for fleece. Haley had seen the cover before.

In the lobby!

It was in that glass case of memorable reads selected by the library staff.

She went over to the shelf and picked up the book. When she opened the cover, she discovered two cards.

One was a four-by-four piece of white cardboard with the black silhouette of a sheep on it.

The second card was yellow and about the same size as a Community Chest card in Monopoly. Haley sniffed the card. It smelled like lemons.

She grinned. "For *Lemon*cello!"

On one side of the yellow card was printed:

SUPER-DOOPER BONUS CLUE

On the other was the clue:

YOUR MARVELOUS MEMORY HAS EARNED YOU EVEN MORE MEMORIES. PROCEED TO THE LEMONCELLO-ABILIA ROOM.

LOOK FOR ITEM #12.

Haley slid both cards into the back pocket of her jeans,

pulled out her library floor plan, and found the Lemoncello-abilia Room. It was up on the third floor.

Making certain nobody (i.e., Charles Chiltington) was following her, Haley quietly dashed up a spiral staircase to the second floor. Checking for Chiltington one more time, she tiptoed up to the third floor, where she found the room labeled "Lemoncello-abilia: Mini-Museum of Personally Interesting and Somewhat Quirky Junk."

Haley opened the door and stepped inside.

The front room was like a storage warehouse. Cardboard boxes were stacked on top of wooden crates sitting on plastic bins stuffed with papers. All the boxes, bins, and crates were numbered. She saw one labeled "#576."

"Guess Mr. Lemoncello never throws anything away," Haley remarked as she scanned the heaps, looking for the #12 mentioned on her bonus card.

Weaving her way through the stacks and columns, Haley finally found her Super-Dooper Bonus. Item #12 was an old boot box from an Alexandriaville shoe store Haley had never heard of. Someone had taped a label on the lid: "Paraphernalia, Accoutrements, and Doodads from Mr. Lemoncello's 12th Year."

Haley lifted the lid. The box was filled with all sorts of confusing knickknacks: hand-whittled prototypes for game pieces; a star-spangled, red-white-and-blue "H-H-H Humphrey" button; a battered clasp envelope sealed up with tons of tape.

Someone had scribbled "First and Worst Idea Ever" on the front of the envelope with a Magic Marker.

There were also a felt pennant from Disneyland and a rubber-banded stack of cartoony cards for something called Wacky Packages. (The card on top was Weakies, Breakfast of Chumps.)

Haley knew this memory box had to be an important clue.

Why? She had absolutely no idea.

Kyle flipped over his lemon-scented Super-Dooper Bonus card and read what was written on the other side.

YOU WILL FIND THE ULTIMATE VERSION OF THIS BOARD GAME ON THE SECOND-FLOOR BALCONY CIRCLING THE ROTUNDA.

"Huh?" said Akimi. "What's that mean?"

"I don't know. Let's roll out the paper and see."

Akimi and Sierra helped Kyle anchor the edges of the scroll on the tiled floor.

"Okay," said Kyle. "It looks like the early sketch for a board game. See the circle in the center of the other circle? That's probably where you place the spinner. You move your pieces around the ten rooms. . . ."

He stopped.

"Wait a second."

"What?" said Akimi.

"Do you recognize the game?" asked Sierra.

"Yep," said Kyle. "I played it this week with my brother Curtis. It's Mr. Lemoncello's Bewilderingly Baffling Bibliomania. It takes place in a make-believe *library*."

"What about finding the 'ultimate version' up on the second-floor balcony?" asked Sierra.

Kyle grinned. "You'll see."

Coming up from the basement, Kyle saw Andrew Peckleman in the middle of the Rotunda Reading Room, opening a long metal box sitting on top of the center desk.

The holographic image of Mrs. Tobin was there, smiling patiently, as Peckleman pulled some kind of magazine out of the box. Miguel was also near the librarian's desk, apparently waiting his turn for a consultation.

"That's the box we saw the robot pluck off the shelf," whispered Akimi.

Kyle nodded. He motioned for the others to follow him and slipped around the circumference of the rotunda. Akimi and Sierra slunk after him.

In the shadows on the far side of the room, they saw Haley Daley heading for the staircase they'd just come up: steps that would take her back to the basement.

Kyle wondered if she'd found something else to crawl through. If so, he hoped it was bigger than a mailbox.

"Is this the *real* magazine?" he heard Peckleman shout at the hologram.

"Yes, ANDREW. This concludes your Librarian Consultation. Next? How may I help you, MIGUEL?"

"Not so fast," snapped Andrew. "I'm not done."

"Um, your consultation just concluded," said Miguel.

"Says who?"

"The librarian."

"MIGUEL?" said the hologram of Mrs. Tobin. "What is *your* question?"

"Sorry, bro. I told you."

"She's just like Mrs. Yunghans at school," snapped Peckleman. "All the librarians like you better than me!"

"Yo. Ease up."

"You'll see, Mrs. Tobin! You'll all see. I'm gonna beat Miguel Fernandez, big-time! And when I win, I'm gonna tell Mr. Lemoncello to fire you!"

"She's a hologram," said Miguel with a laugh. "You can't fire somebody who doesn't actually exist."

"Then I'll tell Lemoncello to pull her plug." Peckleman grabbed his magazine and stormed out of the rotunda into the lobby.

"I guess Andrew's planning on doing something with the front door," Kyle whispered to Akimi.

"Well, that's totally dumb. They already told us the way out isn't the way we came in."

"Maybe Andrew doesn't think Dr. Zinchenko was telling us the truth," suggested Sierra.

116

"Come on," said Kyle, leading his team toward the closest staircase up to the second floor. Glancing over his shoulder, he watched Miguel place a slip of paper on the table in front of the semi-translucent librarian.

"This item has been temporarily removed from the Stacks, MIGUEL," said Mrs. Tobin. "You will find it in a display case next to the original Winkle and Grimble scale model. Let me give you that location."

There was a grinding sound, like when movie tickets shoot up through the slot at the box office. Miguel snatched the small square of paper that popped up from the librarian's desk and spun around.

He froze the instant he saw Kyle, Akimi, and Sierra sneaking around the room behind him.

24

"Hey," said Miguel, hiding the tiny square of paper behind his back. "Yo."

"Yo," said Kyle. "Whazzup?"

"Nothin'. Just, you know, workin' the puzzle."

"Yeah. Us too."

"Okay. Later."

"Later."

Both boys thumped their fists on their chests like baseball players do. Miguel turned and ran for a staircase winding up to the second floor.

"Come on, you guys," said Kyle as he took off running for a different set of steps.

When Kyle, Akimi, and Sierra made it up to the balcony, they watched Miguel run up to the third floor. As soon as he disappeared into a room up there, Kyle unrolled the game sketch.

"Look at the drawing, then look down at the floor," said Kyle.

"They're the same!" said Sierra.

"Exactly. A circular room with a round desk at the center of that circle."

"Awesome," said Akimi. "And there are ten doors ringed around the balcony up here on the second floor, just like on the game board."

Kyle tapped the rendering of the spinner in the right-hand corner of the game plans. "See how the spinner is divided into ten different-colored sections numbered zero to nine?"

"It looks like the Wonder Dome," said Akimi, "when it's not doing its kaleidoscope thing or running a video that makes you think the building is hang gliding across Alaska, which totally made me airsick."

"Well, in the game, you have to go into all ten Dewey decimal book rooms and answer a trivia question about a book. If you answer correctly, you slip a book into your bookshelf and move on to another part of the library. When you have ten books, one from each room, it's basically a race to see who can exit the library first."

"Okay," said Akimi, sounding pumped. "This is good. This is major."

"Except one thing's missing," said Kyle.

"What?" asked Sierra.

"Mr. Lemoncello always works a clever back-door shortcut into his games. For instance, in Family Frenzy . . ."

"You can use the coal chute to slide into the millionaire's mansion at the end," said Akimi.

"Exactly. And in that castle game, Charles snuck out through the sewers. Anyway, when my brother Curtis beat me at Bibliomania . . ."

"You lost?" Akimi acted surprised.

"It happens. Occasionally. But only because Curtis used this shortcut." Kyle tapped a black square on the game diagram. "It took him straight out to the street. He beat me by one spin of the spinner."

"I don't see any black squares in the floor of our rotunda," said Akimi.

"Maybe," said Sierra, "for this new game, Mr. Lemoncello put the secret square someplace besides the main room."

Kyle nodded. "And maybe to win this *new* game we need to play the *old* one."

"You're a genius!" said Akimi.

"No. My brother Curtis is the genius. I just like to play games. So, do libraries even have board games?"

"Sure," said Sierra. "I think. I mean, the library in my dad's town has them."

"Which department?" asked Akimi, pulling out her floor plan.

"Young adult."

Akimi tapped her map. "Third floor. Stairs over there."

"Let's go!" said Kyle.

But before they could take off, they heard Mr. Lemoncello's voice echoing in the rotunda.

"Are you ready for your Extreme Challenge, Bridgette?"

Kyle and his teammates peered over the ledge of the balcony. Bridgette Wadge was alone in front of the librarian's desk, staring up at the ceiling.

"Yes, sir," she said.

"Are you sure?" Mr. Lemoncello's voice boomed out of hidden speakers. "You still have twenty-two hours to find the exit."

"I want to go for it now, sir. Get a jump on everybody else."

"Very well. Dr. Zinchenko? Reset the statues."

The ten holographic statues in their recessed nooks flickered off, leaving black and empty spaces.

"This Extreme Challenge is based on the classic Game of Authors card game," said Mr. Lemoncello. "Here are the authors in your deck."

Magically, new holographic statues appeared as Mr. Lemoncello rattled off the authors' names. "Charles Dickens, Raymond Chandler, Edgar Allan Poe, Agatha Christie, Patricia Highsmith, Mario Puzo, Frederick Forsyth, John Le Carré, Dashiell Hammett, and Fyodor Dostoyevsky."

"He wrote *Crime and Punishment,*" said Bridgette excitedly.

"Indeed he did."

"In fact," said Bridgette, "all those authors wrote crime novels."

"Correct again. However, that's the easy part. Dr. Z?

How do we make this authors game ridiculously difficult enough to qualify as an Extreme Challenge?"

"Simple," the librarian's voice echoed under the dome. "You will have two minutes, Bridgette, to name four books written by each of our authors."

Kyle gulped. "That's impossible," he whispered.

"Not really," said Sierra. She was about to start rattling off titles when Mr. Lemoncello said, "Go!" The sound of a ticking clock reverberated around the room.

"Um, okay," said Bridgette down on the main floor. "Agatha Christie. *Murder on the Orient Express, Ten Little Indians, Death on the Nile, The Mousetrap.*"

Somewhere, a bell dinged, and the British lady in the sensible shoes disappeared.

"Poe. *The Murders in the Rue Morgue, The Masque of the Red Death, The Purloined Letter, The Cask of Amontillado.*"

Another ding. Another statue vanished.

Bridgette kept going.

"Man," whispered Kyle, "what grade is she in? College?"

"Seventh," said Akimi, "just like us."

Bridgette Wadge kept tearing through the authors. The bell kept dinging.

But the clock kept ticking, too.

"Ten seconds," said Mr. Lemoncello.

Bridgette had saved the worst for last.

"Fyodor Dostoyevsky. *Crime and Punishment.* Um,

Crime and Punishment . . . The one about the brothers . . . *The Brothers* . . .”

And then she stalled.

She'd run out of gas.

A buzzer sounded.

“I'm sorry, Bridgette,” said Dr. Zinchenko. “But, as we advised you, the Extreme Challenges are extremely difficult. You will be going home with lovely parting gifts. Kindly hand your library card to Clarence and thank you for playing Escape from Mr. Lemoncello's Library.”

“That settles it,” muttered Kyle. “I am *never, ever* asking for one of those Extreme Challenge dealios.”

“Me neither,” said Akimi.

“I might,” said Sierra. “Maybe.”

And then she showed Kyle and Akimi the rumpled sheet of paper where she had written down *five* book titles for all ten authors.

Akimi grabbed the door handle to the Young Adult Room. "It's locked."

"Here," said Sierra. "Use my library card."

"Huh," said Akimi. "Your books on the back are different, too."

"I think they all are. I got *The Egypt Game* and *The Westing Game*."

"Two books about games?" said Kyle. "Sweet."

Akimi slipped Sierra's card into a reader slot above the doorknob. The door clicked. Kyle pushed it open.

The walls of the Young Adult Room were painted purple and yellow. There were swirly zebra-print rugs on the floor and a lumpy cluster of beanbag chairs. A couple of sofas were designed to look like Scrabble trays, with letter-square pillows.

Akimi nudged Kyle in the ribs. "Check it out."

In the far corner stood a carnival ticket booth with a mechanical dummy seated inside. A "Fun & Games" banner hung off the booth's striped roof. The dummy inside the glass booth?

He looked like Mr. Lemoncello.

He wasn't wearing a turban, but the Mr. Lemoncello mannequin reminded Kyle of the Zoltar Speaks fortune-teller booths he'd seen in video game arcades.

"That's not really him, is it?" said Akimi, who was right behind Kyle.

"No. It's a mechanical doll."

The frozen automaton was dressed in a black top hat and a bright red ringmaster jacket. Since the booth had the "Fun & Games" banner, Kyle figured you might have to talk to the dummy to get a game.

"Um, hello," he said. "We'd like to play a board game."

Bells rang, whistles whistled, and chaser lights blinked. The mechanical Mr. Lemoncello jostled to life.

"If you want a game, just say its name." The life-size puppet's blocky jaw flapped open and shut—almost in sync with the words.

"Do you have Mr. Lemoncello's Bewilderingly Baffling Bibliomania?"

"Did Joey Pigza lose control? Was Ella enchanted?"

"Huh?"

"Just say yes," suggested Sierra.

"Yes," said Kyle.

"Well, great Gilly Hopkins," said the Lemoncello dummy, "here you go!"

Kyle heard some mechanical noises and some whirring. Then, with a clunk, a wide slot popped open in the front of the booth and a game box slid out.

"Enjoy!" said the dummy. "And remember, it's not whether you win or lose, it's how you play the game. So be sure to read the instructions—so you'll know how to *play the game*."

Kyle took the box to a table.

"Okay," he said, raising the lid, "let's set it up and—"

There was a beep and the door opened. . . .

"Where is he?"

Andrew Peckleman barged into the room waving his antique magazine—something called *Popular Science Monthly*.

"Who're you looking for?" said Kyle.

"Mr. Lemoncello. I heard him. Is he in here?"

Kyle pointed toward the frozen Lemoncello doll sitting in the carnie booth. "It's a dummy."

Peckleman whipped his head around from side to side. "Is there a camera in here?"

"Right over the door."

Peckleman spun around to face it. Kyle, Akimi, and Sierra formed a human shield to hide their Bibliomania box.

"I want to use a second lifeline!" Peckleman shouted at the camera. "I want to talk to an expert!"

126

"Very well," said a calm voice Kyle immediately recognized as belonging to Dr. Zinchenko. "With whom do you wish to speak?"

"The guy who wrote this stupid magazine article about cracking open bank vaults in the 1930s!"

"I'm afraid we cannot arrange that for you, Andrew."

"Why not? The guy's a moron. He didn't tell me anything about how to open the front door, which is what my Google search said this magazine would do!"

"We told you the way out isn't the way in."

"That was just a red herring! A trick, to throw us off course."

"No, Andrew. It was not. What is the title of the article?"

" 'Newest Bank Vaults Defy the Cracksman.' "

"Ah. Well, that should have been a hint. Apparently, the reporter concluded that thieves could *not* break open the vault doors. When doing Internet research, it is important to—"

"Let me talk to the stupid idiot!"

"I am sorry. That magazine was published in 1936. The reporter is dead."

"Well, then, I want to talk to Mr. Lemoncello!"

"Excuse me?"

"I want to talk to Mr. Lemoncello!"

"This is highly irregular. . . ."

"And so's this game. You people have it rigged so

Miguel Fernandez will win. I know you do! That's why Mr. Lemoncello is afraid to talk to me."

Kyle heard the carnival booth dummy clatter back to life.

"Hello, Andrew. How may I help you?"

This Lemoncello didn't sound prerecorded. Apparently, the real deal was using the dummy to do his talking.

"Your library stinks!" shouted Peckleman.

"Oh, dear. Have you boys been playing that castle sewer game again?"

"No! But this stupid article should've given me the stupid answer but the stupid writer didn't write what he should've written."

"I see. And can you rephrase that in the form of a question?"

"How many can I ask you?"

"Just one. And then we're done."

"Okay. You're the expert on this stupid new library game. So where's your favorite contestant? Where's Miguel?"

"Is that your final question?"

"Yes!"

"Assuming our video monitors are correct, Mr. Fernandez is on the other side of the third floor, doing research in the Art and Artifacts Room."

"Thanks!"

Andrew bolted out the door.

The Lemoncello puppet bucked and drooped into its "off" mode.

Kyle sprang up from the table. "Come on," he said to Akimi and Sierra.

Akimi sighed. "*Now* where are we going?"

"To make sure Peckleman doesn't do something stupid that gets Miguel kicked out of the game."

"And why would we do that?"

"Because Miguel's our friend."

Akimi glanced at her floor plan. "The Art and Artifacts Room is on the other side of the circle."

"Sierra—stay here and guard the game box. Come on, Akimi."

Kyle and Akimi looped around the third-floor balcony to the other side. Kyle glanced at his watch. It was almost three p.m. They really needed to start focusing on The Game and not all this other monkey junk.

As they neared the Art & Artifacts Room, there was a shout, and the door flew open. Andrew Peckleman came running out.

Behind him were a woman with the head and tail of a lioness, and a Pharaoh in a cobra headpiece.

The Pharaoh stopped. "May onions grow in your earwax!" And a series of holographic hieroglyphics danced across the air.

Andrew Peckleman raced to a staircase, grabbed both handrails, and hurried down to the second floor. The Egyptians vanished.

Kyle and Akimi entered the Art & Artifacts Room and found Miguel seated at a desk with what looked like blueprints.

"You okay?" asked Kyle.

"Yeah, man. I'm fine. Thanks."

"Those guys chasing Andrew. Where'd they come from?"

"Holograms from the giant Lego Sphinx and Pyramid exhibit."

"So why'd they turn on Andrew?" asked Akimi.

"I don't know. One minute he's yelling at me. The next, the Pharaoh and Sekhmet are yelling at him."

"Sek-who?" said Kyle.

"Sekhmet," said Akimi. "The Egyptian lion goddess and warrior. Haven't you read *The Red Pyramid* by Rick Riordan?"

"It's on my list," said Kyle. Or it would be. He definitely needed to start a reading list soon so he could catch up with everybody else.

"I bet the security guards in the control room fired up the Egyptian holograms when they saw Andrew going berserk in here," said Akimi.

"Good," said Miguel. "A library is supposed to be a place for peaceful contemplation."

That was when Sierra Russell rushed into the room.

"You guys! Right after you left! The Mr. Lemoncello dummy spit out a bonus card!"

26

"Very clever," said Charles, pulling another silhouette card out of a book.

This cover had been easy to find. It was the third book on the top shelf of the Staff Picks display. The image on the front was a bright yellow yield sign. The title? *Universal Road Signs* by "renowned trafficologist" Abigail Rose Painter. Charles had found the matching book in the 300s room on the second floor. The 300s were all about social sciences, including things like commerce, communications, and—ta-da!—transportation.

The image also fit nicely with the pictogram he had found in the 700s room in a book called *The Umpire Strikes Back*. That baseball book was the first cover on the *second* shelf in the display case and had given Charles a card with the classic pose of an umpire calling an out.

Reading the images from left to right, then down—just like you'd read a book—Charles knew he was on the right track. The traffic sign book gave him "walk" and the umpire book gave him "out."

Put the two picture words together and he had "walk out."

Clearly, if he could find all twelve silhouettes, the Staff Picks display would tell him how to "walk out" of the library (although he had absolutely no idea what the first image he had found, the quarterback tossing a pass, had to do with escaping the library—not yet, anyway).

"Three down, nine to go," said Charles, winking up at the closest security camera. "And, Mr. Lemoncello, if you're watching, may I just say that you are an extremely brilliant man?"

Charles had never sucked up to a video camera before. He figured it was worth a shot. Maybe Mr. Lemoncello would send him a bonus clue or something.

Instead, when Charles stepped out of the 300s room, somebody sent him Andrew Peckleman. The goggle-eyed library geek was sputtering mad as he rushed down the steps and stomped around the second-floor balcony.

"Stupid library. Stupid Lemoncello. Stupid sphinx and Sekhmet."

"Why so glum, Andrew?" Charles called out.

"Because this game stinks. Mr. Lemoncello just sent a bunch of holograms hurling hieroglyphics after me. He could put somebody's eye out with those things."

"Really? With a hologram?"

"Hey, they're made with lasers, aren't they?"

"Indeed. Say, speaking of hieroglyphics, where might I find a book about picture languages?"

"Ha! Why should I help you?"

"Because Kyle Keeley is working with Akimi Hughes *and* Sierra Russell. I imagine it is only a matter of time before your friend Miguel Fernandez joins their team, too."

"Miguel isn't my friend! Besides, I'm better at navigating my way through a library than he'll ever be."

"I know. That's why I want you on my team."

"Really?"

Charles smiled. Kids like Andrew Peckleman were so easy to manipulate.

"Oh, yes. Work with me and I guarantee you the

133

world will know that *you* should be the head library aide at Alexandriaville Middle School."

"The four hundreds!" blurted Peckleman.

"Pardon?"

"That's where you'll find books on hieroglyphics and all kinds of languages. If you want secret codes, those are in the six hundreds room. The six-fifties, to be exact."

Charles shot out his hand. "Welcome to Team Charles, Andrew."

The new teammates stepped into the 400s room. For some reason, it was pitch dark and smelled like pine trees.

"*Bienvenida! Bienvenue! Witamy! Kuwakaribisha!* Welcome!" boomed a voice from the ceiling speakers. "This is the four hundreds room, home of foreign languages. Here, CHARLES and ANDREW, you can learn all about your American heritage."

A bank of spotlights thumped on.

Charles and Andrew were face-to-blank-face with a row of four featureless mannequins. An overhead projector beamed a movie onto dummy number two, turning it into a perky woman who looked like a flight attendant.

"Hello, and welcome to *your* American heritage. I'm Debbie. Let's begin your voyage!"

"That's okay," said Charles. "We're rather busy."

"Let's begin your voyage," the mannequin repeated.

Charles sighed. Obviously, there was no way to turn

this silly display off. He might as well speed things along by telling the dummy what it wanted to hear.

"Fine. But can we go with the abridged version? We're in a bit of a rush."

"Yeah," added Andrew, "we have to escape before noon tomorrow."

The woman, whose body remained frozen while a movie made her face and costume spring to life, reminded Charles of the graveyard statues from the Haunted Mansion ride at Disney World.

"While we research your family trees," she said, "please enjoy this short and informative film."

"Is this part of the game?" Andrew whispered to Charles.

"Possibly. Pay attention for any bonus clues."

"Okay. What do they look like?"

"Who can ever say?"

A screen behind the life-size dummies leapt to life with all sorts of scratchy images of people huddled together on the deck of a boat near the Statue of Liberty.

"For decades," narrated the ceiling voice, "public libraries have proudly served America's newest citizens— the immigrants who flock to these shores yearning for the freedom to build their own American dreams."

Charles really wasn't interested in this kind of stuff. His ancestors were all *Americans;* the only language they spoke was English.

"Yes, the library is where many new arrivals journey

first. To learn their new homeland's language. To keep in touch with the world they left behind. To search for the gainful employment that will make them productive residents of their newly adopted home!"

The movie dissolved into blackness.

"Thank you for your kind attention," chirped the cheerful Debbie. "We have completed your American family tree. Let's meet your first American ancestors!"

Two mannequins sprang to illuminated life, both of them dressed in traditional Thanksgiving pilgrim costumes.

"I know who they are already," said Charles. "That's John Chiltington and his wife, Elinor. They came to Plymouth Colony on the *Mayflower*. Can we move on to Andrew's family? Please?"

"Of course," said Debbie.

The mannequins quickly went through Andrew Peckleman's ancestry. Apparently, the family name had originally been Pickleman, because they made pickles. After a prolonged parade of pickle people, the dummies took on the guise of Andrew's most famous ancestor, a guy in horn-rimmed glasses and a tweed sports coat named Peter Paul Peckleman.

"I appeared on the TV game show *Concentration* in 1968," he announced, "and won a roomful of furniture and wood paneling for my rumpus room."

Charles smiled. He knew the TV game show *Concentration* was very similar to Mr. Lemoncello's Phenomenal

Picture Word Puzzler, one of the games he had picked up at the toy store. Peter Paul Peckleman's claim to fame was further confirmation that piecing together the picture puzzle would show Charles how to escape from the library.

He'd been right.

The dummies had just given him a bonus clue.

27

Excited by the sudden appearance of a second bonus card, Sierra read it out loud:

"'Two plus two can equal more than four. Put two and two together and you'll be closer than before.'"

Akimi raised her hand.

"Yes?" said Sierra.

"You do realize that Miguel here isn't on our team?"

"Oh. Right. Sorry."

Miguel turned to Kyle. "You guys are a team?"

"Yep. You want to join?"

"Maybe. Not sure. Check back with me later, man."

"No problem," said Kyle.

He fist-thumped his chest. Miguel fist-thumped his. They were flashing each other peace signs when Sierra said, "I think this means we should all play together as a team. Remember what it says on the fountain down in the lobby: 'Knowledge not shared remains unknown.' "

"Maybe," said Miguel. "Like I said—let me get back to you guys. I'm workin' on a few angles of my own. Flying solo."

"Sure. No problem." Kyle was about to do the whole fist-chest-bump-peace-sign thing again when he had a brainstorm. "Miguel? Quick question. What's on your library card?"

Miguel shrugged. "My name and the number one."

"Anything else? Like on the back?"

"Nothing really. Couple of books."

"Two?"

"Yeah."

"What're their titles?"

Miguel bit his lip. "Don't want to say."

"Because you think they might be clues?"

"Not saying what I might or might not be thinking, bro."

Kyle nodded.

"There are two different books on the back of every-body's library cards," said Akimi, thinking out loud. " 'Put two and two together and you'll be closer than before.' The book titles *are* some sort of clue. My books are *One*—"

"Um, Akimi?" Kyle shook his head. Nodded toward Miguel.

"Right. Sorry. My bad."

"Oh-kay, Miguel," said Kyle. "If and when you decide to team up with us, you can show us the two books on the back of your card; we'll all show you ours. We'll also split the prize four ways. Deal?"

"Deal."

"Come on, guys." Kyle gestured toward the exit.

"Where are we going?" asked Sierra.

Kyle dropped his voice. "The Electronic Learning Center."

"You want to play video games?" said Akimi. "Now? Seriously, Kyle, we may need to rethink your status as team captain."

"I don't want to play video games. I want to check out the discard pile."

"Huh?"

"The cards the players who went home early dumped into that goldfish bowl!"

"I'm comin' with you guys," said Miguel. "I've been thinking about those extra cards, too."

"Fine," said Kyle. "Whatever."

When they entered the game room, they saw Clarence, his arms folded across his chest genie-style. He was standing guard in front of the discard pile.

"May I help you?" he asked.

"Um, yeah," said Kyle. "We want to check out the cards in the bowl."

"Sorry," said Clarence. "You can't have them."

"But," said Mr. Lemoncello, his face suddenly appearing on every video screen in the room, "you can win them!"

Dressed in a polka-dotted bow tie and snazzy jacket like a game show host, Mr. Lemoncello had one arm resting on a slender Plexiglas podium. Behind him, Dr. Zinchenko—all decked out in a sparkly red minidress—looked like the models that point at prizes on TV.

"Are the four of you ready to play Let's Do a Deal?" When Mr. Lemoncello said that, he pushed a big red button in his podium. A prerecorded studio audience whistled, cheered, and applauded.

"Um, what's Let's Do a Deal?" asked Kyle.

"My first game to ever be turned into a TV show. Brought to you by lemon Pledge!"

Dr. Zinchenko started singing: *"Lemon Pledge, very pretty. Put the shine down, lemon good . . ."*

"Thank you, Dr. Z!" said Mr. Lemoncello, bopping the button to make the audience cheer again. "Now then, kids, here's the deal: Solve one simple picture puzzle and you four win the five library cards in the bowl."

"And if we lose?"

"Simple. Each of you loses his or her library card and adds it to the discard bowl for our next lucky contestants to try and win."

He banged the red button again. The audience cheered exactly the same way they cheered before.

Kyle turned to the others. "What do you say, guys?"

141

"Let's go for it," said Akimi.

Sierra nodded.

"Miguel?"

"I'm in, bro."

"You're joining our team?"

"Absolutely." They knocked knuckles to seal the deal.

Mr. Lemoncello must've whacked his button again, because the canned studio audience started cheering.

Kyle wondered what the sound effects would be if he and his friends lost their library cards playing Let's Do a Deal.

Probably groans.

And weeping. Lots and lots of weeping.

28

"Now then," said Mr. Lemoncello, "are you ready to play Risking Everything for Five Little Library Cards?"

Kyle swallowed hard. Then he nodded.

"All right, you Maniac Magees, here is your picture puzzle. The category is Famous Quotes. You have sixty seconds to solve this rebus."

"Wait a second," said Akimi. "What's a rebus?"

"You figure out the words in a phrase by looking at pictures and symbols," said Kyle.

"For instance," added Miguel, "the letters 'R' and 'E' plus a picture of a school bus would equal 'rebus.'"

"Oh. Okay," said Akimi. "If you guys say so."

"Are you ready to play?" asked Mr. Lemoncello.

Kyle looked at his teammates, who nodded.

"Yes, sir."

"Then on your mark . . . get set . . . go, dog, go!"

Mr. Lemoncello's image disappeared. Ticktock clock music started playing. The video screens all projected the same picture:

"We're officially dead," said Akimi.

"Fifty-five seconds," said Mr. Lemoncello.

"Okay, we break it up four ways," said Kyle. "The first and third rows are similar, I'll do them."

"I'll do the last one," said Akimi.

"I'll take the second row," said Miguel.

"I'm four," said Sierra.

"Fifty seconds," said Mr. Lemoncello.

Everyone went to work.

"Mine is some guy hitting himself in the thumb but with a 'gr' and an 'o'?" muttered Akimi. "Then the male symbol where the 'le' equals 'rx'? 'Marx'? Does that make sense? Hello? Kyle? Is my second half 'Marx'?"

Kyle didn't answer. He was too busy deciphering his own clue lines. " 'Outlet,' change the 'let' to 'side,' " he mumbled. " 'Golf' minus the 'g' and the 'l.' The letter 'A.' "

"Forty seconds."

" 'Dog.' " He dropped to the third line. He just needed the first word. " 'Bowling *pins*' without the 'p' but add an 'ide.' "

"Thirty seconds."

Kyle glanced at Miguel. He was moving his lips, mouthing out his part of the quote. Sierra, too.

"You guys ready?" Kyle whispered.

"Hang on," said Miguel.

"Twenty seconds."

"Okay. Go."

Kyle read the first line: " 'Outside of a dog . . .' "

145

Miguel picked up the thread: "'. . . a book is man's best friend.'"

Kyle continued. "'Inside of a dog . . .'"

Sierra took over. "'. . . it's too dark to read.'"

Akimi brought them home: "'Groucho Marx!'"

"Is that your final answer?" asked Mr. Lemoncello.

"Yes," said Kyle, and then he repeated the entire quote: "'Outside of a dog, a book is man's best friend. Inside of a dog, it's too dark to read.'—Groucho Marx."

Bells rang. Chaser lights flashed. The audience went wild. Akimi and Sierra actually squealed and hugged each other.

"You are correct!" shouted Mr. Lemoncello. "There's no dead end in Norvelt, not today! Take those five library cards, Team Kyle! You won them fair and square!"

Charles and Andrew heard a commotion on the third floor. Bells ringing. An audience whooping it up. Girls squealing.

"Come on," said Charles.

They raced up the stairs and peeked into the Electronic Learning Center. Kyle Keeley and his teammates were all hugging each other and slapping high fives. On every video screen in the game room, Charles could see a pictogram puzzle.

"What's going on in there?" whispered Andrew.

"They might be gaining on us," Charles whispered back. "We need to pick up our pace. Quick—where would I find a book called *Hoosier Hospitality* written by Eve Healy Aresty?"

"The nine hundreds room."

"Let's go."

Charles and Andrew scurried back to the second floor and the 900s room.

Where they found Haley Daley holding *Hoosier Hospitality* by Eve Healy Aresty.

"Oh, hello, you guys," she said, slamming the book shut.

Charles moved toward her. Slowly.

"Find anything interesting in that book, Haley?"

"Not really." She giggled. "Just a bunch of dumb junk about Indiana."

Charles knew she was hiding something.

"I wonder, Haley, if you and I might share a quiet word?" He turned to Andrew. "In private."

"Does that mean I'm supposed to leave?"

"Yes, Andrew. It's for the good of the team. Trust me."

"Okay. But I'll be right outside that door if you decide to double-cross me or something."

"Thank you, Andrew. This will only take a quick minute."

Peckleman left the room.

Smiling, Charles moved even closer to Haley. So close he could smell her bubble gum. Or shampoo. Maybe both.

"Let's step over here," he said, taking Haley by the elbow. "I found another fascinating book that I think you'll just love." He guided her to a spot behind a bookcase where their conversation couldn't be observed by the security camera blinking up in the ceiling.

Haley went with Charles.

If he had been looking for the same book she'd just found, that meant he was playing the library escape game along a similar path. Charles Chiltington might have clues Haley could use. Clues she needed.

"Rumor has it," Charles whispered, "that your parents wrote your library essay for you."

Inside, Haley was grinning. Obviously, Charles would try to bully her into joining his team. Fine. She'd pretend to be frightened.

"What?" she whispered back, pretending to be terrified. "That's a lie. My dad just helped me with some of the spelling."

"Aha! So you admit it. All the spelling in your essay wasn't your own?"

Okay. This was going to take more acting skill than usual. Having someone check your spelling wasn't against anybody's rules for anything.

She widened her eyes. Made her lips quiver. "What do you want, Charles?"

"For you to join my team."

"Why should I do that?"

"Two reasons. One, if you're on my side, your flagrant plagiarism remains our dirty little secret. Two, I know what to do with that silhouette card you just found in the *Hoosier Hospitality* book."

"You do?"

"Oh, yes. If we share our clues, the pictures will create a phrase telling us how to find the alternate exit."

Haley smiled. For real. This was working out perfectly. She'd get all their clues, and even if they all won together, Mr. Lemoncello would definitely make her the real star of his TV commercials. She had "zazz." Charles and Andrew did not.

"Okay," she said. "Deal. I'm on your team."

Then she handed Charles the clue she had found in the *Hoosier* book:

"Of course!" said Charles. "After all, Indiana is the Hoosier State."

29

"Oh, man," said Kyle, leading his team around the balcony, back to the Young Adult Room. "Nine library cards. This is fantastic!"

They gathered around a table.

"Okay, guys. Time for everybody to put their cards on the table. Literally."

The teammates set down their cards. Kyle spread out the five from the discard bowl. Akimi pulled out a pad and wrote all the information on one master list:

BOOKS/AUTHORS ON THE BACKS OF
LIBRARY CARDS

#1 Miguel Fernandez
Incident at Hawk's Hill by Allan W. Eckert/
No, David! by David Shannon

#2 Akimi Hughes
One Fish Two Fish Red Fish Blue Fish
by Dr. Seuss/Nine Stories by J. D. Salinger

#3 UNKNOWN

#4 Bridgette Wadge
Tales of a Fourth Grade Nothing
by Judy Blume/Harry Potter and the
Sorcerer's Stone by J. K. Rowling

#5 Sierra Russell
The Egypt Game by Zilpha Keatley Snyder/
The Westing Game by Ellen Raskin

#6 Yasmeen Smith-Snyder
Around the World in Eighty Days
by Jules Verne/The Yak Who Yelled Yuck
by Carol Pugliano-Martin

#7 Sean Keegan
Olivia by Ian Falconer/Unreal! by Paul Jennings

#8 UNKNOWN

#9 Rose Vermette
All-of-a-Kind Family by Sydney Taylor/
Scat by Carl Hiaasen

#10 Kayla Corson
<u>Anna to the Infinite Power</u>
by Mildred Ames/Where the Sidewalk
Ends by Shel Silverstein

#11 UNKNOWN

#12 Kyle Keeley
I Love You, Stinky Face by Lisa McCourt/
The Napping House by Audrey Wood

"Wow," said Sierra. "That's a lot of good books. But what do all those authors and titles mean?"

"It means we need Charles's, Andrew's, and Haley's cards," said Kyle.

"Really?" said Akimi. "Because if you ask me, we already have way too much information."

"Well," said Kyle, "maybe later we'll find a clue that'll tell us how to read *this* clue."

"And how are we going to do that?" asked Miguel.

"Have you ever played this?" Kyle pointed to the Bibliomania box.

"Nope. Always wanted to."

"We were just about to get up a game."

"Does this have anything to do with finding our way out of the library?"

"We sure hope so," said Akimi.

"Awesome."

"By the way," Kyle said to Miguel, "what'd you find in the Art and Artifacts Room?"

"Yeah," said Akimi. "All those papers you kept trying to hide from us."

Miguel grinned. "The original blueprints for the Gold Leaf Bank building."

"Clever," said Kyle. "That way you could look for old exits that might still exist behind new walls."

"Exactly."

"Find any extra exits?" asked Akimi.

"Nope. No hidden windows, either."

"Yeah, what's up with that? How come they built this place with so few windows?"

"To discourage bank robbers, I guess," said Kyle.

"Yep," said Miguel. "The only way in was through the front door. The fire exits could only be opened from the inside, like at a movie theater. The vault itself was all the way down in the basement."

"Mr. Lemoncello kept all that security," said Kyle, "and added his own."

"So it would seem."

"Well, hopefully Bibliomania will lead us to some kind of alternate exit."

"And fast," said Akimi. "Don't forget, we're not the only ones playing this game. One of those other guys is probably halfway out the door already."

"Okay," said Kyle, "game play is pretty simple. You spin the spinner and advance your piece the number of spaces the needle points to. You move around the library and go into each of the ten Dewey decimal rooms, where you can pick up a book by answering a clue card. If you guess wrong, you get a new clue card in the same room on your next turn. The first person to fill the ten slots in their 'bookshelf' and spin their way out of the library wins."

"It's sort of like Trivial Pursuit," said Sierra. "And the questions aren't all that hard because they're mostly multiple-choice."

"Let's hear one!" said Miguel eagerly.

The cards were separated into ten multicolored mini-stacks, one for each room. Kyle grabbed a green card.

"Okay, this is for the eight hundreds room. Literature. 'Deathly ill and pursued by the Ringwraiths, Frodo Baggins was carried safely across the River Bruinen on the gleaming white elf-horse of Glorfindel named: A) Asphodel, B) Asfaloth, C) Almarian, D) Anglachel.'"

Akimi shook her head like she was having a brain freeze. "Wha-huh?"

"I think the answer might be 'A,' " said Miguel.

"They're all 'A's,' " said Kyle. "Asphodel, Asfaloth, Al—"

"It's 'B) Asfaloth,' " said Sierra. "It's from J. R. R. Tolkien's *Lord of the Rings*."

Kyle flipped the card over and read the answer. " 'You are correct. You get a copy of *Lord of the Rings* to put in your bookshelf.' "

"So, Kyle," said Akimi, "how exactly is knowing the name of an elf-horse going to help us get out of the library?"

"Maybe it's like a secret code," suggested Miguel. "And the ten book titles will form a sentence telling us how to get out."

"Possibly," said Kyle. "But I see one problem."

"What's that?"

"It's too random. Mr. Lemoncello would have no idea which ten cards we might pick."

"Well," said Sierra, "maybe there are only *ten* questions. One for each room."

Akimi grabbed the card stacks, fanned them out. "Nope. They're all different."

"Hang on," said Kyle.

He was remembering something about another game: Mr. Lemoncello's Indoor-Outdoor Scavenger Hunt.

How his mother had been able to write to the company and request a fresh set of cards.

He turned to the video camera mounted in a corner. "I'd like my Librarian Consultation, please."

"What's up, Kyle?" asked Miguel.

"I'm playing a hunch."

The holographic Mrs. Tobin appeared behind the young adult librarian's desk.

"How may I help you, KYLE?"

"My friends and I want to play Bibliomania but we were wondering: Is there a new set of cards?"

"Yes, KYLE. There is."

And a fresh deck of cards popped up through a slot in the desk.

30

"We'll just play one bookshelf," said Kyle.

"Because we're a team now, right, bro?" said Miguel.

"Right. Plus, we don't have all day."

"Well," said Akimi, "technically we do. In fact, we have the rest of today and tomorrow till noon."

"We've got like nineteen hours left," said Miguel.

"But Charles and the others," said Sierra. "They could beat us."

"Right," said Kyle. "After all, he *is* a Chiltington. And according to Sir Charles, they never lose. Miguel, you're the newest member of the team. You spin first."

Miguel rubbed his hands together. Limbered up his fingers. Practiced flicking his index finger off his thumb. Made sure he had a good snap and follow-through.

"Would you hurry up and spin before my brain explodes?" pleaded Akimi.

"No problem." Miguel flicked the plastic pointer. It whirled around the cardboard square decorated with a sunburst of ten colorful triangles.

"Boo-yah! The triple zeros. General Knowledge."

"Um, that's not so great," said Kyle.

"How come?"

"You get to move zero spaces."

"Oh. Bummer."

Akimi shot up her hand.

"Yes?" said Kyle.

"Do we really have to spin and count spaces and all that junk? We have a deadline. Clocks everywhere are ticking against us."

"Maybe we can just pull a pink card," suggested Sierra.

"It's really not how you play the game," said Kyle.

"Um, we're not really playing this game, Kyle," said Akimi. "We're playing the other one. The Big Game. The one with the ginormous prize."

"I have to agree with Akimi," said Miguel.

"Fine," said Kyle. "It's against the rules, but pull a pink card."

"You sure, bro?"

"Just pull a pink!"

Miguel quickly sorted the new deck into ten stacks of different colors. He pulled the pink on the top of its pile.

"Hmmm. These are different from the regular cards."

He turned it over and showed it to the group.

$0 + 27 + 0.4 = ????$

"Easy-peasy," said Akimi. "The answer is twenty-seven-point-four, because the zero doesn't change the sum."

"Not in math," said Miguel. "But this isn't math. This is the Dewey decimal system and there's always three numbers to the left of the decimal point."

"We need to find a book with the call number 027.4," added Sierra.

"Fine," said Akimi. "But I guarantee you it isn't a math book!"

The team made their way around the balcony circling the Dewey decimal doors.

"Here we go," said Miguel. He slid his library card into a reader on a door labeled "000s."

"Okay," said Miguel, "in here we're gonna find General Knowledge. Almanacs, encyclopedias, bibliographies, books about library science . . ."

"It's a science?" said Akimi. "Where do they keep the chemicals?"

"In the library paste," joked Sierra, who was loosening up. She hadn't read one page of a book in hours.

"Found it," said Miguel, reaching up to pull a book off a shelf. "027.4. Man, it's old. Look how yellow the pages are."

"So what's the antique's title?" asked Akimi.

"*Get to Know Your Local Library* by Amy Alessio and Erin Downey."

Miguel held the book so everybody could see the cover. It was illustrated with a cartoony-looking detective in a checkered hat who was holding up a magnifying glass to examine books on a shelf.

"Looks like a library guide for kids," said Miguel, opening the cover to read one of the inside pages. "First publication was way back in 1952." He flipped through a few pages. "It explains the Dewey decimal system. Contains a glossary of library terms. A brief history of libraries . . ."

He reached the back of the book.

"Awesome."

"What?" asked Kyle as he and the others moved closer to see what Miguel had found.

"It's an old-fashioned book slip. From the Alexandria-ville Public Library."

"The one they tore down?"

"Yep. And this card, tucked into a sleeve glued to the back cover, comes from the olden days when they used to stamp the date the book was due on a grid and you had to fill in your name under 'issued to.'"

"And?"

"Look who checked this book out on 26 May '64!"

Kyle and the others looked.

"Luigi Lemoncello!"

* * *

Down on the first floor, Charles used his library card to open the door to Community Meeting Room A.

"Who is to have access to this room?" cooed a soothing voice from the ceiling.

"Me and my teammates," said Charles. "Andrew Peckleman and Haley Daley."

"Thank you. Please have ANDREW PECKLEMAN and HALEY DALEY swipe their cards through the reader now."

Both of them did.

"Thank you. Entrance to Community Meeting Room A will be limited to those approved by the host, CHARLES CHILTINGTON. Have a good meeting."

Charles and his team entered the sleek, ultramodern, white-on-white conference room. There were twelve comfy chairs set up around a glass-topped table and a cabinet filled with top-of-the-line audiovisual equipment.

"You can write on the walls," said Andrew. "They're like the Smart Boards at school."

"Excellent," said Charles, clasping his hands behind his back and pacing around the room. "Now, when we find all twelve pictograms and lay them out according to their position in the Staff Picks display case, they will create a rebus for a phrase that, I am quite certain, will tell us exactly how to exit this library without triggering any alarms. Therefore, it is time for all of us to lay our cards on the table."

Haley nodded. And pulled two more silhouettes out of the back pocket of her jeans.

"I found one of these in a cookbook," she said. "The other was in juvenile fiction. *Nancy Drew: The Mystery at Lilac Inn*."

"There are blank note cards in this drawer," announced Andrew. "We should use them as placeholders for the books we still need to find."

They laid out a three-by-four grid of cards on the tabletop:

"What does it mean?" said Andrew.

"Simple," said Charles. "It means we need to find those other six books!"

31

"So, does anybody have a clue as to why we were supposed to find this book?" asked Kyle.

He and his teammates were back in the Young Adult Room staring at the cover of *Get to Know Your Local Library.*

"Too early to tell," said Miguel. "Let's keep playing. This book will probably make more sense once we go into the other rooms and pick up more clues."

"Whose turn is it?" asked Akimi.

"Yours," said Kyle. "Flick the spinner."

Akimi finger-kicked the plastic pointer.

"Purple!" she yelled when the arrow slid to a stop. "The eight hundreds."

"That means you move eight spaces," mumbled Kyle.

"Except today." Akimi reached for the card on top of

the purple stack. When she saw what was written on it, she frowned.

"What's the clue?" asked Kyle.

"Something about Literature, Rhetoric, or Criticism?" asked Miguel.

"Nope," said Akimi. "It's a wild card. With a riddle."

"Read it!" said Sierra.

" 'I rhyme with dart and crackerjacks. Visit me and find a rhyme for Andy.' "

"Peckleman?" said Kyle. "How'd he get his name on a game card?"

"Bro," said Miguel, "nobody calls Andrew Peckleman 'Andy.' Of course, it could mean Andrew Jackson. The seventh president of the United States."

"Or Andy Panda," said Akimi.

"Or Andrew Carnegie," said Sierra. "He was a generous supporter of libraries."

"Okay," said Kyle. "Let's concentrate on the first part of the riddle. What rhymes with 'dart and crackerjacks'?"

"Smart and heart attacks?" suggested Miguel.

"Art and bric-a-bracs?" said Sierra.

"Art and *Artifacts*!" said Akimi, nailing it.

They hurried over to the Art & Artifacts Room.

"Everybody—check out the display cases," said Kyle. "See if anything rhymes with the word 'Andy.' "

"Well, this model of the old bank building is certainly 'grandy,'" said Miguel. "And the Pharaoh's pyramid and sphinx would be *sandy* if they weren't made out of Legos."

"True," said Kyle, sounding unconvinced about both.

"Check it out, you guys," cried Akimi, who was studying a row of Styrofoam heads sporting hats. "This plaid fedora from 1968 was worn by a guy named Leopold Loblolly."

"So?" said Kyle.

"According to this plaque, Loblolly was 'one of the notorious *Dandy* Bandits.' 'Dandy' rhymes with 'Andy.'"

"That it does," said Miguel. "However, 'Loblolly' does not."

"Neither does 'Leopold,'" added Kyle.

"'Candy' rhymes with 'Andy'!" said Sierra. She was staring at the objects in a display case under a banner reading "Welcome to the Wonderful World of Willy Wonka."

"Awesome!" said Miguel, hurrying over to admire the collection of Everlasting Gobstoppers, Glumptious Globgobblers, Laffy Taffy, and Pixy Stix displayed under glass in a sea of purple velvet.

"Mr. Lemoncello is a lot like Willy Wonka," said Kyle.

"You mean crazy?" said Akimi.

"I prefer the term 'eccentric.'"

"And Dr. Zinchenko is his Oompa-Loompa," said Sierra.

Everybody started giggling.

"Nah," Akimi joked, "she's too tall."

164

"And not nearly orange enough," added Miguel.

"The Willy Wonka book was written by Roald Dahl," said Sierra, who, Kyle figured, could name twelve other books the guy wrote, too. "In it, Mr. Wonka takes Charlie and Grandpa Joe home in a flying glass elevator that crashes through the roof of his chocolate factory."

Everybody thought about that for a second.

"So now we have to find a glass elevator?" said Akimi. "Because there isn't one on the floor plan."

"But Mr. Lemoncello is just wild enough to build one," said Kyle. "And if he did, he probably wouldn't put it on the floor plan."

"No way," said Miguel. "Everybody would want to ride on it."

"I know I would," said Sierra.

"So we're seriously searching for a secret glass elevator?" said Akimi.

"Maybe," said Kyle. "Maybe not. This is just another piece of a gigantic jigsaw puzzle. We won't see the whole picture until we collect all the pieces."

"Or someone shows us the box lid," cracked Akimi.

"Look, it's only six p.m.," said Kyle. "And we're collecting a ton of good information."

"You mean a ton of *random* information," said Akimi.

"Well," said Miguel, "once we have more clues, we can use Sherlock Holmes's famous 'deductive reasoning' method to make logical connections between all the random junk."

"Works for me," said Kyle. "But if we're going to play Sherlock Holmes, we need to go spin that spinner and dig up more clues."

"The game's afoot," said Sierra.

"Huh?" Kyle and Akimi said it together.

"Sorry. It's just something Sherlock says to Watson whenever he gets excited."

Sherlock Holmes. Kyle had just found another bunch of books to add to his reading list.

32

"Okay, Sierra," said Kyle, "your turn."

Sierra flicked the spinner. The pointy tip ended up in the yellow 200s zone, so she went ahead and pulled a yellow card.

"It's definitely for the two hundreds section," she said, showing her clue to Miguel before revealing it to Kyle and Akimi.

"Weird," said Miguel.

"What?" said Akimi before Kyle could.

"Well, the two hundreds are where they keep books on world religions."

"But there are *two* numbers on this card," said Sierra.

"Maybe this time we need to find *two* books?" suggested Kyle.

"I don't know," said Sierra, studying her card. "'220.5203' is obviously a call number."

"Obviously," said Akimi.

"But this other number isn't in the proper format. 'Two-twenty-fifteen.'"

"February twentieth, 2015!" said Akimi. "Quick—what happened on that date?"

"Um, nobody knows," said Kyle. "Because *it hasn't happened yet*."

"Oh. Right. Okay—how about February twentieth, *1915*?"

"That was the opening day of the Panama-Pacific International Exposition in San Francisco," said Sierra.

Jaws dropped.

"Sorry. I'm a big world's fair fan."

Everybody else just nodded.

Finally, Miguel spoke up. "Look, let's just go down to the two hundreds room and find 220.5203. We can figure out the second chunk later."

The team once again trooped down to the second floor and worked their way around the circular balcony.

"You guys?" said Sierra, looking across the atrium at the statues. "Remember how they switched all the hologram authors when Bridgette Wadge did her Extreme Challenge?"

"Yep," said Kyle. "She was doing good till she got to the Russian dude."

"What Russian dude?" asked Miguel, who hadn't witnessed Bridgette's elimination.

"Guy who wrote five or six books Sierra could tell you about."

"But look," said Sierra. "Now all the author statues are the same ones they were last night."

"So," said Kyle thoughtfully, "if they can switch 'em around . . ."

"These must be clues for our game!" blurted Akimi. She pulled out a pen and her notepad. "I'll write down their names."

"Start with the guy under the triple zeros wedge of the Wonder Dome," suggested Kyle.

"Right."

Akimi read the labeled pedestals and jotted down all the authors' names:

Thomas Wolfe, Booker T. Washington, Stephen Sondheim, George Orwell, Lewis Carroll, Dr. Seuss, Maya Angelou, Shel Silverstein, Pseudonymous Bosch, Todd Strasser.

"So," said Akimi when she'd finished writing, "do you think this game could get any more complicated?"

"Maybe," said Kyle. "It's possible that Mr. Lemoncello left a couple different paths to the same solution."

"Well, personally, I can only take one path at a time," said Akimi. "So let's go find two-twenty-point-whatever."

* * *

"Should be in the next row of bookcases," said Miguel. "Here we go. 220.5203. The King James Bible."

"*Ach der lieber!* An excellent choice," said a man with a thick German accent.

The four teammates spun around.

And were face to face with a semi-transparent guy in medieval garb with a fur-trimmed cap and a beard that looked like two raccoon tails sewn together under his nose and chin.

"I am Johannes Gensfleisch zur Laden zum Gutenberg," said the holographic image, who had ink stains all over his fingertips.

"You created the Gutenberg Bibles on your printing press!" gushed Sierra.

"Ja, ja, ja. Big bestseller. You need help with der Bible, I am at your service." He bowed.

"Oh-kay," said Akimi, turning to Miguel. "Take it away, Miguel."

"Herr Gutenberg, sir, we're looking for two-twenty-fifteen."

"*Das ist einfach.*"

"Huh?"

"That is easy. TWO, TWENTY, FIFTEEN is EXODUS, chapter TWENTY, verse FIFTEEN."

"Of course!" said Miguel. "Exodus is the second book of the Bible. Twenty and fifteen are the chapter and verse." He flipped through some pages. "Here we go. Exodus, chapter twenty, verse fifteen. It's one of the Ten Commandments: 'Thou shalt not steal.' "

33

"Let's put the two new cards on the table," said Charles.

He and his so-called teammates, Andrew and Haley (Charles planned on dumping them both right before he made his glorious solo exit from the library), had scoured the library together for hours looking for more book cover matches.

Peckleman wasn't nearly as good with the Dewey decimal system as he had claimed to be. And Charles needed someone to do that sort of thing for him. His father always hired tutors or research assistants for him whenever Charles had to do a major paper or report.

Finally, around six in, coincidentally, the 600s room, they scored twice, finding *Tea for You and Me* (641.3372) and *Why Wait to Lose Weight?* (613.2522).

Now their picture puzzle had only four blanks remaining:

"Okay," said Andrew, "I think it's pretty clear. 'Woolly BLANK walk up the skinny BLANK BLANK house Indian and nineteen BLANK.' "

Charles nodded and said, "Interesting," even though he knew Peckleman was way off.

"Uh, hello?" said Haley. "That doesn't make any sense."

"Sure it does," said Andrew.

"Uh, no it doesn't."

In his head, Charles had decoded the clues so far as

"Ewe (a female sheep) BLANK walk out the (t+h+e) way (weigh) BLANK BLANK Inn in passed (past) BLANK."

But out loud, he said, "I think we just need to tweak Andrew's translation a little."

"Fine. Go ahead. I don't care." Andrew slumped down in his seat to sulk.

"How about 'She BLANK walks out the skinny BLANK BLANK house five hundred and past BLANK."

"Where'd you get 'she'?" asked Haley.

"From 'sheep.' The card you gave us."

"Actually, I think the sheep is supposed to represent 'you.' Because a ewe is a female sheep."

"Fascinating," said Charles. "I didn't figure that out."

What he did figure out was that Haley Daley was much smarter than he had assumed. She could be a serious threat. And no way was Charles sharing his prize with anybody, especially her.

"And how did you get 'five hundred' from Indiana?" she asked.

"Simple. Indianapolis, the capital of Indiana, is home to a race known as the Indy 500."

"Okay. So how about 'You BLANK walk out the skinny BLANK BLANK in—because the Nancy Drew book was about an inn—five hundred pass, or *past,* BLANK."

Now Peckleman piped up. "That makes more sense than what you said, Charles."

"Indeed," said Charles, sounding magnanimous.

173

"Perhaps the clues are telling us to locate a secret skinny passageway five hundred paces past some landmark here in the library."

Andrew was excited. "This is like the pirate map from *Treasure Island*!"

"Or," said Haley, "maybe these clues are telling us we need to go out and find the four books we haven't found yet. We should split up. I'll go back to the four hundreds room."

"We've already been there," said Andrew.

"Well, you guys might've missed something."

"Good idea," said Charles. He figured if Haley Daley wasted time retracing steps he and Andrew had already taken, she would find nothing new and become less of a threat. "Let's meet back here at, say, seven."

"Fine."

Haley left the meeting room.

Charles went to the door and closed it.

"You know what we really need?" he said to Andrew.

"Chocolate milk and maybe some cookies?"

Charles shook his head. "No, Andrew. We need whatever clues Kyle Keeley and his team have found. Especially if they have our missing cards."

34

Veering left the instant she reached the second floor, Haley made her way toward the 400s room.

She figured that Charles and Andrew had probably missed something important in the foreign languages room because they'd spent too much time talking to "these awesome mannequins" that told them all about their "American heritage."

As she rounded the bend, Haley saw Kyle Keeley and his crew tumble out of the 200s room.

It looked like Miguel was carrying a Bible.

But a Bible wasn't one of the books on display in the Staff Picks case.

We're following separate paths to the same goal, Haley thought. *And somewhere, those two paths are going to collide.*

Haley slid her card key down the reader slot in the 400s door. The lock clicked and she pushed the door open.

The room was dimly lit.

"*Bienvenida! Bienvenue! Witamy! Kuwakaribisha!* Welcome!" boomed a voice from the ceiling speakers.

"Sorry," said Haley, blindly feeling her way forward and bumping into something hard and lumpy.

"This is the four hundreds room, home of foreign languages. Here, HALEY, you can learn all about your American heritage."

A bank of spotlights thumped on.

Haley was basically hugging a department store mannequin.

An overhead projector beamed a movie onto the dummy to her left, turning it into a perky woman who looked like Haley would probably look a couple of years after she graduated from college.

"Hello, HALEY. Welcome to *your* American heritage. Let's begin your voyage!"

"That's okay, I don't have time right now. I'm Haley Daley. My ancestors were Irish, okay? So can we skip the history lesson and . . ."

Suddenly, the two mannequins at the far end of the row turned into sepia-toned versions of her great-great-great-grandmother and great-great-great-grandfather. Haley knew it was them because her dad had a bunch of old photos hanging in their family room. The two dummies looked exactly like Patrick and Oona Daley did in their wedding portrait.

"No man ever wore a scarf as warm as his daughter's arm around his neck," said Patrick in his thick Irish brogue. "Yer da is proud of you, Haley."

"Thanks. But I really need to win this competition."

"Watch out for sneaky rascals," said Oona. "Them that would steal the sugar out of your punch."

Haley had to smile. It sounded like her ancestor had met Charles Chiltington.

"And always remember, Haley," said her great-great-great-grandfather, "every woman's mind is her kingdom. Rule it wisely, lassie."

"I'm trying!"

"This library can help," said her great-great-great-grandmother with a wink.

And when she did, a secret panel in the wall slid open.

"What's going on?" said Haley.

"You're our third visitor!" boomed the jolly announcer in the ceiling.

"So?"

"According to *The American Heritage Dictionary of Idioms*—available in our reference department, by the way—'the third time is a charm'! Therefore, as our third visitor, you have won this charming bonus."

Two bonuses in one day?

She was right! Mr. Lemoncello definitely wanted Haley Daley to win this game, because clearly he knew she'd be the perfect, best-looking spokesmodel for his holiday commercials.

"Don't worry, sir!" Haley said to the nearest TV camera. "I won't let you down."

She hurried through the open wall panel and into the 300s room on the other side.

Ta-da!

The first thing she saw was one of the books they'd been searching for all day long: *True Crime Ohio: The Buckeye State's Most Notorious Brigands, Burglars, and Bandits* by Clare Taylor-Winters.

She quickly opened the cover and found the hidden four-by-four card. It took her two seconds to decipher the clue:

"Bandits."

Haley remembered another bit of Irish wisdom, something her dad said all the time: "Never bolt your door with a boiled carrot!"

She decided to keep this new clue secret and secure. She wouldn't share it with Charles or Andrew.

Haley took off her left sneaker, folded the card in half, and slid the clue into her shoe for safekeeping. When her sneak was laced up tight again, she took the *True Crime Ohio* book off its display stand and tucked it into the bookshelf, making sure it was in the proper position: right between 364.1091 and 364.1093. That way, she'd know where to find it if, for whatever reason, she needed the book again.

Haley looked up at the nearest camera and flashed it her brightest toothpaste-commercial smile.

"Goooo, Le-moncell-ooooo! That's a cheer I just made up. We can use it in one of the commercials—after I win!"

35

"Entrance to Community Meeting Room B will only be granted to KYLE KEELEY, SIERRA RUSSELL, AKIMI HUGHES, and MIGUEL FERNANDEZ," said the soothing female voice in the ceiling after the four teammates had swiped their cards through the meeting room door's reader slot.

"This makes sense," said Akimi. "We needed a place to organize all this material, put it on the walls, and draw a chart like the FBI always does on TV when they're tailing the mob."

"Stole the meeting room idea from me, eh, Keeley?"

Charles Chiltington was standing in the doorway to Meeting Room A on the far side of the rotunda.

"No," said Kyle. "We just needed someplace to throw our victory party after we win."

"Not going to happen," Charles said smugly. "Must

I remind you? I'm a Chiltington. We never lose." And he disappeared back into Meeting Room A.

After Charles was gone, Kyle led his team into Meeting Room B.

Miguel posted the bank blueprints he had found up on the walls while Sierra set up the Bibliomania game board on the conference table.

"I'm glad this room won't let anybody else in," said Kyle.

"And by 'anybody' you mean Charles Chiltington, right?" said Akimi.

"Totally."

Akimi grabbed a marker and wrote a neat outline on the dry-erase walls:

CLUES SO FAR

DEFINITE CLUES

1) From the 000s room:
Get to Know Your Local Library book

2) From the Art & Artifacts Room:
Willy Wonka candy (rhymes with "Andy").
Find glass elevator?

3) From the 200s room:
Bible verse—"Thou shalt not steal."

PROBABLY CLUES

BOOKS/AUTHORS ON THE BACKS OF LIBRARY CARDS

#1 Miguel Fernandez
Incident at Hawk's Hill by Allan W. Eckert/
No, David! by David Shannon

#2 Akimi Hughes
One Fish Two Fish Red Fish Blue Fish
by Dr. Seuss/Nine Stories by J. D. Salinger

#3 UNKNOWN

#4 Bridgette Wadge
Tales of a Fourth Grade Nothing
by Judy Blume/Harry Potter and the
Sorcerer's Stone by J. K. Rowling

#5 Sierra Russell
The Egypt Game by Zilpha Keatley Snyder/
The Westing Game by Ellen Raskin

#6 Yasmeen Smith-Snyder
Around the World in Eighty Days
by Jules Verne/The Yak Who Yelled Yuck
by Carol Pugliano-Martin

#7 Sean Keegan
Olivia by Ian Falconer/Unreal! by Paul Jennings

#8 UNKNOWN

#9 Rose Vermette
All-of-a-Kind Family by Sydney Taylor/
Scat by Carl Hiaasen

#10 Kayla Corson
Anna to the Infinite Power
by Mildred Ames/Where the Sidewalk
Ends by Shel Silverstein

#11 UNKNOWN

#12 Kyle Keeley
I Love You, Stinky Face by Lisa McCourt/
The Napping House by Audrey Wood

MAYBE CLUES???

Statues ringed around the dome:

Thomas Wolfe, Booker T. Washington, Stephen
Sondheim, George Orwell, Lewis Carroll,
Dr. Seuss, Maya Angelou, Shel Silverstein,
Pseudonymous Bosch, Todd Strasser

"Wow," said Akimi, stepping back to study the walls. "What an incredible mess."

"Yeah," said Kyle. "Okay, guys—there are eight more book rooms to explore and who knows how many more wild cards. Whose turn is it?"

"Yours," said Sierra.

Kyle flicked the spinner. "Green. The five hundreds. Science."

He pulled the first green card from the deck.

" 'Four and twenty were once in a pie. 598.367 might tell you why.' "

"Blackbirds?" said Miguel.

"I guess."

"Well," sighed Akimi, "let's go check out *another* book. There's still like an inch or two left on our whiteboard."

The 500s room was like a miniature museum of natural history.

In addition to towering walls of books, there was a whole planetarium of stars and constellations projected on the ceiling. Models of planets whirled in their orbits. Sparkle-tailed comets shot around the corners of bookshelves.

Kyle and his teammates made their way back to the 590s—Zoology.

Shelving units were arranged in a square around an open area, maybe twenty feet by twenty feet wide. When the team entered the empty space, the lights dimmed and a guy with long wavy hair who looked like an artistic Daniel Boone faded into view. He was wearing some kind of bear-fur coat and toting a musket.

"*Bonjour,*" said the hologram.

"It's John James Audubon," said Sierra. "The famous ornithologist."

"He gives people braces?" said Kyle.

"No," Sierra said with a laugh. "He studied and painted birds."

A blackbird with a yellow beak flew into the open area and roosted on a tree branch. The bird and the tree were both holograms, too.

"This beautiful blackbird from Alexandriaville, Ohio," said the semi-transparent Audubon image, "can mimic in song the sounds it has heard."

And the bird started wailing.

"Wow," said Akimi. "That sounds exactly like a police siren!"

"Yo," said Miguel. "Freaky."

"To learn more," said Audubon, "be sure to read *Bird Songs, Warbles, and Whistles* written by Dr. Diana Victoria Garcia, with classic illustrations by *moi.*"

With that, Audubon sat down on a campstool. An easel appeared, the blackbird struck a pose, and the outdoorsy artist started painting the bird's portrait, while humming "Blackbird" by the Beatles.

"Okay," said Kyle. "This is the strangest clue yet."

"Well, here's the book at least," said Sierra, who had found 598.367 on the shelf.

"So what do a blackbird's wails and warbles have to do with finding our way out of the library?" said Akimi.

Just then, they heard a very different sound.

Behind one of the bookcases, something growled, then roared.

"Did you guys hear that?" said Sierra.

"Yeah," said Akimi. "I don't think it's a robin red-breast."

A very rare white Bengal tiger, with icy-blue eyeballs, crept out from behind a wall of bookshelves and stalked into the open area where Audubon sat painting his bird portrait.

"Uh, is that another hologram?" asked Miguel.

ROAR!

No one stuck around to find out.

36

Down on the first floor, Charles and Andrew were working their way around the semicircle of three-story-tall floor-to-dome bookcases filled with fiction.

It was nearly eight p.m.

"We need to find that blasted book," said Charles, craning his neck to study the shelves.

"I'm getting kind of hungry," mumbled Andrew.

"You had a snack this afternoon," snapped Charles.

"Well, now it's time for dinner."

"No. We need to find *Anne of Green Gables* first."

The classic by Lucy Maud Montgomery was the middle book on the top shelf in the Staff Picks display case. So far, Charles, Haley, and Andrew had not been able to find it anywhere in the library.

"Unfortunately," said Andrew, "they've temporarily erased the book's call number from the database."

"So we wouldn't know what to punch into the hover ladder's control panel," grumbled Charles.

"Actually," said Andrew, "they might've shelved it in the Children's Room. Or maybe the eight hundreds, with Literature. Could be in the four hundreds, too, because it was originally written in Canadian, which is, technically, a foreign language."

"So you have said, Andrew. Repeatedly. But we've already searched those other locations. Several times. It has to be here with the other fiction titles. You just need to fly up and find it."

"Well," said Andrew, "I'm kind of afraid of heights."

"Fine. Whatever. I'll go up and grab it. But you have to give me some kind of call number to enter into the hover ladder."

"Lucy Maud Montgomery wrote other Anne books. There's *Anne of Avonlea*. . . ."

Charles dashed over to the nearest library table and swiped his fingers across the glass face of its built-in computer pad.

"Here we go. *Anne of Avonlea* by Lucy Maud Montgomery. F-MON."

"Yes," said Andrew. "Fiction books are usually put on the shelf in alphabetical order by the author's last name. Nonfiction titles are classified according to the Dewey decimal system."

"How long have you known this?"

Andrew's nose twitched. "Since second grade."

"So all we ever needed was 'F-MON'? We could've found this book hours ago?"

Andrew gulped.

"You are such a disappointment." Shaking his head, Charles huffed over to one of the hover ladders. He quickly jabbed "F," "M," "O," and "N" into the keypad. The boot clamps locked into place around his ankles. "You owe me for wasting all this time, Andrew. You owe me big-time. If you let me down once more, I swear I will tell everybody you're a big blubbering baby. I'll Twitter it *and* post it on Facebook."

"Don't worry. I'll make you glad you picked me for your team, Charles! I promise."

The hover ladder lifted off the floor and gently glided up to the M section of the fiction wall. Shuttling sideways, it carried Charles over to a shelf displaying all the Anne books.

He grabbed a copy of *Anne of Green Gables*.

As soon as he did, the ladder started its slow descent to the floor.

"What'd you find?" asked Andrew when Charles landed.

"The clue we needed."

He showed Andrew the card that had been tucked inside the front cover.

"Okay," said Andrew. "It's 'C plus hat'! So the word is 'chat,' which, by the way, could also be *'chat,'* the French word for cat!"

"Well done, Andrew," said Charles, even though he knew the clue was really "C plus Anne," equaling "can," thereby making the puzzle "You *can* walk out the way BLANK BLANK inn in past BLANK."

The way what did what? he wondered. *And what does "inn in" mean?*

Charles desperately needed to find the three missing pictograms.

Suddenly, Mr. Lemoncello's voice boomed out of speakers ringing the rotunda.

"Hey, Charles! Hey, Andrew! Let's Do a Deal!"

Game show music blared. A canned crowd cheered.

Charles turned around and saw shafts of colored light illuminating three envelopes perched on top of the librarian's round desk. Clarence the security guard marched into the reading room and, folding his arms over his chest, took up a position near the three envelopes.

"We have a green envelope, a blue envelope, and a red envelope," said Mr. Lemoncello. "In two of those three envelopes are copies of two of the three pictogram clues you still need. In one, there is a Clunker Card. If you pick an envelope with a clue, you get to keep it—and you get to keep going. But once you pick the Clunker Card, you're done . . . and you must suffer the consequences."

Andrew raised his hand.

"Yes, Andrew?"

"What are the consequences?"

"Something bad," said Mr. Lemoncello. "In fact, something wicked this way will probably come. Do you want to do a deal?"

"Yes!" said Charles.

The canned audience cheered.

"All right, then! Charles, you roll first."

"Pardon?"

"Swipe your fingers across the nearest desktop computer panel. The dice tumbler app is up and running!"

Again, the prerecorded audience cheered. They sounded like they loved watching dice tumble more than anything in the world.

Charles slid his fingers across a glass pane. The animated dice rolled.

"Oooh!" cried Mr. Lemoncello. "Double sixes. That gives you a twelve."

"Is that good, sir?"

"Maybe. Maybe not. Okay, Andrew—your turn!"

Peckleman tapped the glass. The dice flipped over.

"Another set of doubles!" said Mr. Lemoncello.

"Yeah," muttered Charles. "Two ones. Snake eyes."

"Is that bad?" asked Andrew.

"Maybe," said Mr. Lemoncello. "Maybe not. Okay, guys—which envelope would you like to open?"

Charles thought about it while ticktock music played.

They were given this chance to play Let's Do a Deal

after they located the *Anne of Green Gables* clue. Coincidence? He didn't think so.

"We'll take the green envelope, sir."

Clarence presented the green envelope to Charles.

"Open it!" said Andrew. "Open it."

Charles undid the clasp. Pulled out a card.

A loud *ZONK!* rocked the room.

The card was black. With blocky white type.

"Uh-oh," mumbled Andrew. "What's it say on that card?"

" 'Sorry, kids, you're out of luck,' " read Charles. " 'So out of doors you're all now stuck.' "

Clarence picked up the blue and red envelopes and marched back toward the entrance hall.

"What's that mean?" said Andrew.

"Well," said Mr. Lemoncello, "Charles rolled a twelve and you rolled a two. What's twelve plus two?"

"Fourteen," said Charles eagerly, the way he always did in math when he wanted to remind the teacher that he was the smartest kid in the class.

"Oooh," said Mr. Lemoncello. "This is not good. In fact, I'd say it's stinkerrific."

"Stinkerrific?" said Andrew. "Is that even a word?"

"It is now," said Mr. Lemoncello. "J.J.? Tell them what they've lost."

An authoritative female voice boomed out of the ceiling speakers:

"Warning: Due to a Clunker Card, all ten Dewey decimal doors will lock in ten minutes, at exactly eight o'clock. If you are in one of those rooms, kindly leave immediately. The ten doors on the second floor will remain locked for fourteen hours."

Andrew panicked. "What? Fourteen hours?"

"I told you twelve plus two was bad," quipped Mr. Lemoncello. "Of course, it could've been good. If you had picked one of the other envelopes, you would've received a clue and a free fourteen-month subscription to *Library Journal*."

Charles did some quick math. "Sir? Does this mean we'll be locked out of the ten Dewey decimal rooms until ten o'clock tomorrow morning?"

"Bingo!" said Mr. Lemoncello. "It sure does!"

"This stinks," whined Andrew. "We need those stupid rooms to solve your stupid puzzle! Clunker Cards stink. This game stinks. Fourteen-hour penalties stink."

Charles did his best to block out Andrew's rant.

He needed to think.

And then it hit him: *Kyle Keeley's team had to be working on some other solution to the bigger puzzle of how to escape from the library.* Otherwise, Charles and his team would not have been able to find the nine clues they'd already picked up. Surely, if Keeley's team had been playing the same memory match game, they would've found at least one of the pictograms before Charles, Andrew, or Haley did.

They must be working a completely different angle.

Charles was certain that if he could use this downtime

to learn what Keeley and his team had in their meeting room, and combined it with his picture puzzle, he would emerge from the library victorious.

"Do not despair, Andrew," Charles said confidently. "We are still going to win."

"How?"

Charles leaned in and cupped a hand around his mouth so no security cameras could read his lips.

"Remember," he whispered, "you need to pay me back for wasting a ton of time in finding *Anne of Green Gables*."

"What? You're the one who picked the stupid green envelope with the stupid Clunker Card!"

Charles narrowed his eyes and chilled his hushed voice. "So?"

"Um, nothing," said Andrew nervously. "Just thought I'd, you know, point it out."

Charles turned his eyes into blue ice.

"So," whispered Andrew, swallowing hard, "what exactly do you want me to do?"

"Find a way to sneak into Community Meeting Room *B*."

Andrew wheezed in panic. "That's impossible."

"Don't worry. I have an idea."

"What is it?"

"Two words: Sierra Russell."

37

"Ever wonder if this could reek any worse?" said Akimi. "Because it couldn't."

"Yo, none of us pulled a Clunker Card," groused Miguel. "That means somebody on Charles's team did it."

"Akimi and Miguel are right, Kyle," said Sierra. "This really isn't fair."

"I know," was all Kyle could say. "But it's like in Mr. Lemoncello's Family Frenzy, where one player pulls the Orthodontist card and *everybody* has to move back seven spaces to buy their kids braces."

Kyle and his teammates were back in Community Meeting Room B. They'd been staring at the clue board, wondering what a wailing blackbird had to do with Willy Wonka and the Ten Commandments—not to mention that long list of books and all the statues—when the voice in the ceiling made its announcement about the Dewey decimal doors being locked for fourteen hours.

"Well, Mr. Lemoncello better have a *good* reason," said Akimi.

"Oh, I do," said Mr. Lemoncello.

His face appeared on one of the meeting room walls, which was really a giant plasma-screen video monitor.

"Team Kyle is not being penalized for Team Charles's blunder," he said. "Far from it. In fact, you are being rewarded."

Akimi arched her eyebrows in disbelief. "Really? How?"

"The other team's penalty gives you a wrinkle in time."

"A wrinkle in time?" said Kyle. "Is that a clue?"

"No. It's a book. And sometimes, Kyle, a book is just a book. But thanks to the Clunker Card, you have the gift of wrinkled time to seek clues *outside* the ten Dewey decimal rooms. Speaking of *Time*, a magazine available in our periodicals section, it's dinnertime!"

"So the game is basically suspended until ten o'clock tomorrow?" said Kyle.

"Well, Kyle, that's up to you. You can use this time as a bonus, to think, read, and explore. Or you can run upstairs and play video games all night long. The choice is yours."

"We want to win *this* game," said Kyle. His teammates nodded in agreement.

"Wondermous!" said Mr. Lemoncello. "Keep working the puzzle but try to avoid Mrs. Basil E. Frankweiler's files.

They're all mixed up. And before you turn in this evening, you might want to spend some time curled up with a good book."

"Um, they just said the book rooms are locked," said Akimi.

"The nice lady in the ceiling was only talking about the ten Dewey decimal rooms. There is plenty of first-class fiction in the Rotunda Reading Room. Dr. Zinchenko has even selected seven books specifically for our seven remaining contestants. After dinner, you'll find those books on her desk."

When he said that, Mr. Lemoncello started winking.

"I think you'll find the books to be very *enlightening*. Inspirational, even."

And then he winked some more.

"And now, I must return to my side of the mountain. See you in the morning, children! I have great expectations for you all!"

Mr. Lemoncello's image disappeared from the wall.

"Okay," said Akimi, "from the way Mr. Lemoncello was just winking, either somebody kicked a bucket of sand in his face or our recommended reading list is another clue."

On the other side of the rotunda, Charles huddled with Andrew in Meeting Room A.

"I don't trust Haley," he said.

"Why not?"

Charles placed his hand on Andrew's shoulder. "Well, my friend, I'm not sure if I should tell you this, but Haley told me she didn't think you were 'handsome enough' to appear in Mr. Lemoncello's holiday commercials with us when we win."

"Because of my glasses?"

Charles bit his lip. Nodded. "Of course, I totally disagree."

"I see," said Andrew, his ears burning bright red. "Then she doesn't get to see what we found in that *Anne of Green Gables* book."

"Very well, Andrew. If that's how you want to play it."

"You bet I do."

"Fine. Let's go see what's for dinner. I'm starving."

When Charles and Andrew entered the café, the Keeley team was already inside, filling their trays.

"Hey, way to go, Charles!" joked Miguel Fernandez. "You guys pulled a Clunker Card?"

"Indeed we did. However, not even that bit of bad luck can derail our juggernaut!"

"Huh?" said Akimi.

"He means we're still gonna win!" said Andrew.

Charles and Andrew crossed to the far side of the room to join Haley, who was sitting in a corner.

"You guys find any clues this afternoon?" she asked.

"Sadly, no," said Charles.

"All we found was that door-locking penalty," said Andrew, who could lie almost as well as Charles.

"How about you, Haley?" Charles asked. "Find anything interesting?"

"Nope. Nada." Then she yawned and finished her dinner. "I think I'll head upstairs and sack out."

"Really? It's only eight-forty-eight."

"I know. But I'm totally pooped." She yawned again. "Plus, I want to be up bright and early, before the Dewey decimal doors reopen. We have more clues to find. See you guys tomorrow. Unless we have more team business to discuss?"

"No. Nothing."

She walked out of the café.

38

"Very interesting," said Akimi, looking through the café's glass walls and into the Rotunda Reading Room.

"What?" said Miguel.

"I think Clarence just dropped off our books."

Kyle pushed back from the table. He could see the shadowy figure of the bulky security guard slinking away from the round desk at the center of the rotunda. He left behind a stack of books.

"Come on," he said. "Let's go see what sort of 'inspirational' reading Dr. Zinchenko has selected for us."

"What about those guys?" said Miguel, gesturing toward the table where Charles and Andrew were finishing their desserts.

Kyle was torn.

On one hand, he didn't want to give away the bonus his team had received thanks to the other team's penalty.

On the other hand, he didn't want people saying he and his friends won because Mr. Lemoncello had tossed them an extra clue.

He came up with a compromise.

"Hey, Charles? Andrew? We're all going to go grab some books to read to kill time till tomorrow morning. You two might want to do the same thing."

"No thanks." Charles stood up. "We pretty much have this thing figured out. In fact, I think Mr. Lemoncello steered us toward the Clunker Card so we wouldn't win too easily. I mean, how would it look if we escaped from his library in less than twenty-four hours?"

"Bad," said Andrew. "Real bad."

"Indeed," said Charles. "In fact, I suspect nobody would buy Lemoncello games anymore if we showed them how consistently easy they are to win. Anyway, we're going upstairs so I can give Andrew a tour of my private suite. Would any of you care to join us?"

"No thanks," said Akimi.

"Suit yourself. Oh, by the way, Mr. Lemoncello has a real video game console upstairs."

Kyle felt his mouth going dry.

"It's top-of-the-line equipment. And it plays real games. Not just educational stuff. Care to join us, Keeley?"

"Um . . ."

"We're going to play Squirrel Squad Six. The new edition. According to the game box, it won't be released to the general public until early December."

Kyle felt sweat beading on his forehead. His palms were moist. His fingers were twitching, itching to thumb-toggle a joystick.

But finally, after the inside of his mouth had turned to sandpaper, he said, "No thanks, Charles. We're just gonna, you know, read."

After Charles and Andrew headed up to the third floor to play what was probably the most awesome version ever of Mr. Lemoncello's most awesome video game ever (if Charles Chiltington was actually telling the truth), Kyle and his teammates hurried out to see what books were waiting for them on the librarian's table.

They found seven different versions of the same book: *The Complete Sherlock Holmes.* One was a leather-bound limited edition; another was a tattered paperback; three were hardcovers with different illustrations on their fronts; one was a bigger kind of paperback with lots of scholarly essays; and the seventh was an e-reader with only the one title loaded onto it.

"I think Mr. Lemoncello wants us to start a book club," said Sierra.

"What do you mean?" asked Kyle.

"You know—we all read the same book and then get together later to discuss it and share our opinions."

"It's fun," said Miguel. "We have a book group at school."

"Are you in it?" asked Sierra.

"Yeah. Maybe you'd like to join us sometime?"

"I would. Thank you, Miguel."

Akimi cleared her throat. "Now what?" she said to Kyle.

Kyle shrugged. "Like I told Charles. We read."

Everybody grabbed a copy of the Sherlock Holmes book.

Nobody went for the e-reader.

Upstairs on the third floor, Haley tiptoed around the Lemoncello-abilia Room.

When she had visited the mini-museum earlier, she hadn't really looked around. Now she hoped to find another book from the "memorable reads" display, a Little Golden Book called *Baby's Mother Goose: Pat-a-Cake,* which could've been something Mr. Lemoncello read (or had read to him) when he was a very young boy.

Haley made her way past the orderly stacks of boxes through a doorway and into what looked like a re-creation of Mr. Lemoncello's childhood bedroom—a cramped space crammed with two bunk beds that he had shared with his three brothers. Next to one of the lower bunks was a bookcase made out of plastic milk crates.

There it was, filed away with maybe three dozen other skinny, hardboard-covered picture books.

Haley pried open the cover.

Out plopped a four-by-four art card:

 + **ED**

She quickly folded it in half and stuffed it inside her sneaker with her "BANDITS" clue.

Because now she was pretty certain that "bandits" had, at one time or another, "crawled in" to this building back when it was a bank.

The silhouette of Indiana didn't represent the Indianapolis 500 like Charles had insisted.

It stood for "IN," the official post office abbreviation for the Hoosier State.

First thing in the morning, when the doors reopened, she needed to search through the Dewey decimal rooms to find a clue that would tell her exactly how and where the bandits had crawled in.

A tunnel? An air vent? A secret passageway on the first, second, or third floor between the old bank and the office building behind it?

There was only one thing Haley was certain of: They hadn't crawled in through a book return slot.

39

Everyone in the reading room was quietly lost in the adventures of Sherlock Holmes.

Kyle had just finished a pretty cool story called "A Scandal in Bohemia," about a king who was going to get married to a royal heiress with maybe six names. But the king was being blackmailed by an old girlfriend, an opera singer from New Jersey named Irene Adler.

Something Sherlock Holmes said to Dr. Watson early in the story really stuck with Kyle: "You see, but you do not observe."

Kyle figured that was why Mr. Lemoncello wanted them all to take a break from chasing clues and read these classic mysteries. Not to find new clues but to become better puzzle solvers. Had they been seeing things without really observing them? Probably.

Reading the story was also kind of fun. Kyle could

totally see Holmes's apartment at 221b Baker Street and the snooty king and the horse-drawn carriages on the foggy London streets and the disguises Holmes wore and the smoke bomb Dr. Watson tossed through a window and everybody on the street screaming, "Fire!"

It was like he was watching a 3-D IMAX movie in his head. Kyle couldn't wait to start the second story in the book, "The Adventure of the Red-Headed League."

"How's it going?" whispered Akimi.

"This book is pretty cool. This Sir Arthur Conan Doyle guy knows how to keep his readers hooked."

"His characters leap off the pages," said Sierra.

"Yeah," said Miguel. "I dig the 'consulting detective.'"

"Huh?" said Kyle.

"That's what Holmes calls himself sometimes."

"Oh. I've only read one story so far and . . ."

Suddenly, something seemed odd to Kyle.

"Hey—how come Conan Doyle isn't one of those statues up there?"

"What do you mean?" said Akimi.

"He's a famous author, right? How come they're projecting a statue of a modern writer like Pseudonymous Bosch but not the author who created a classic like Sherlock Holmes?"

"Good question, bro," said Miguel.

"I need to *consult* with my brother Curtis."

"How come?"

"Curtis has read more books than anyone I know,

except maybe Sierra. He scored an 808 on his SAT Subject Test in Literature."

"Uh, Kyle?" said Akimi. "I think the top score for any SAT test is 800."

"Yep. Then Curtis took it. They had to raise it."

"So maybe he can help us figure out what's up with all the statues," said Miguel.

"Exactly. Why these ten? Why not ten other writers?"

"Why not the same ten Bridgette Wadge had for her Extreme Challenge?" added Sierra.

Kyle looked around the room.

"Mrs. Tobin? Hello? Mrs. Tobin?"

The hazy holographic image of the 1960s librarian flickered into view.

"How may I help you, KYLE?"

"I'd like to talk to an expert."

"And whom do you wish to speak to?"

"Mr. Curtis Keeley."

"Your brother?"

"And an SAT-certified expert on the subject of literature and authors and other literary-type junk."

Suddenly, the hologram vanished and Dr. Zinchenko's voice came over the ceiling speakers.

"This is a rather irregular request, Mr. Keeley."

"Hey," said Akimi, "this whole game is rather irregular, don't ya think?"

"We just need some more data," said Kyle. "Because,

like Sherlock says to Dr. Watson, 'it is a capital mistake to theorize before one has data.' "

"I take it you're enjoying your book?" said the librarian.

Kyle gave the closest security camera a big thumbs-up. "Boo-yeah. Can't wait to see what's up with that league of redheaded gentlemen."

"Ah, yes," said Dr. Zinchenko. "A fascinating story. I recently reread it myself. Very well, Kyle. We will contact your brother to determine if he does indeed qualify as a literary expert. It may take a while."

"No rush," said Kyle. "I've got a good book."

Kyle was busy helping Holmes figure out that the Red-Headed League was just a clever ploy pulled by some robbers to get a red-haired pawnbroker to leave his shop long enough for them to dig a tunnel from his basement to the bank next door when the librarian's voice jolted him out of London and brought him home to Ohio.

"My apologies for the interruption."

Akimi, Miguel, and Sierra closed their books, too. It was eleven-fifteen. Everyone had sleepy, dreamy looks in their eyes because they'd been kind of drifting off in their comfy reading chairs.

"What's up?" said Kyle.

"We have arranged for your expert consultation with Mr. Curtis Keeley."

"Awesome! How do we do it?"

"You and your expert may have a five-minute video chat on my computer terminal, which is located behind the main desk."

Kyle hurried over to the round desk in the center of the room. His three teammates hurried right behind him.

"Your consultation begins . . . now."

And there was Curtis. Sitting at his computer in his bedroom.

"Hey, Curtis!"

"Hi, Kyle. How's it going in there?"

"Great."

Kyle's oldest brother, Mike, popped into the doorway behind Curtis.

"Ky-le, Ky-le," Mike chanted. "Whoo-hoo!"

Kyle had never had his own cheerleader before.

"We need you to give us one hundred and ten percent in there, li'l brother!" Mike squinted at the screen over Curtis's shoulder. "Who are those other guys?"

"My teammates, Miguel, Sierra, and you know Akimi."

"You guys are a team? Smart move. Even I can't win football games without help from ten other guys."

"Um, Mike?" said Kyle. "Curtis and I only have five minutes to chat."

"Cool. I'm outta here. Win, baby, win!"

Mike backpedaled out of the bedroom, making double fist pumps the whole way.

"You have four minutes remaining," advised Dr. Zinchenko.

"Okay, Curtis, here's my question. What do these authors have in common?"

Kyle rattled off the list of the statues in order.

And Curtis stared blankly into his computer cam.

For a real long time.

Then he shook his head. "I'm sorry, Kyle. I have no earthly idea."

"Really?" Kyle was astonished. "You've got nothing?"

"Well," said Curtis, "the only connection I can see is Thomas Wolfe wrote *Look Homeward, Angel* and Lewis Carroll wrote *Through the Looking-Glass*. Both titles have the word 'look' in them. But the two books are otherwise completely different. The two authors as well."

Kyle and his whole team stood in stunned silence.

Until Sierra started jumping up and down.

"Of course!" she shouted.

"Your time is up," announced Dr. Zinchenko.

"Um, okay," Kyle said to the computer screen. "Thanks, Curtis. That was, uh, really helpful."

"It was!" said Sierra, daintily clapping her hands together like a very polite seal. The computer screen faded to black.

"What's up?" asked Miguel.

"I think I know how to crack the statue code."

"There's a code?" said Akimi. "Who knew?"

"It'll take time," said Sierra. "And I need a computer."

"Oh-kay," said Kyle, who was sort of shocked to see Sierra so completely jazzed. "We'll be in our meeting room, putting together a list of new Dewey decimal numbers from the Bibliomania cards so we're ready to hit the ground running when the doors reopen at ten tomorrow morning."

While Sierra settled in at a desktop computer pad, the rest of the team returned to the Bibliomania board game.

"We should just start flipping over cards and putting together a list of call numbers," Kyle suggested.

"Sounds like a plan," said Akimi.

She plucked a purple card out of the pile.

Lose a Turn was all that was printed on the other side.

"Try a different color," urged Miguel.

Akimi flipped up a blue card.

Take an Extra Turn was printed on it. So Akimi flipped over all the other blue cards while Miguel flipped over all the purples.

The purple cards all said **Lose a Turn**. The blue ones all said **Take an Extra Turn**.

Kyle had been checking out the red and maroon piles.

"The reds all say 'Pick a Yellow Card,'" he reported. "The maroons say 'Grab a Green.'"

"The grays do the same thing," said Miguel. "Only they say 'Pick a Pink.' The tan cards say 'Go Grab an Orange.'"

"So that leaves the colors we've already played." Kyle flipped over a yellow card. "'In the square root of 48,629.20271209 . . .'"

"What the . . . ?" said Akimi.

"Hang on," said Miguel. "There's a calculator app in this desktop computer."

Kyle read the rest of the card: ". . . 'find half of 4-40-30.'"

"Well, that's 2-20-15, again," said Sierra.

"And the square root of forty-eight thousand what-ever is 220.5203," said Miguel. "The King James Bible we already found."

Akimi flipped through the rest of the yellow cards. "Same with these. They all send us into the Religion section to find that Bible verse."

"Ditto with the greens," reported Miguel. "All clues leading to *Bird Songs, Warbles, and Whistles*."

"And the pinks all lead back to 027.4," said Kyle. "I guess they really wanted to make sure we found *Get to Know Your Local Library*."

"Which leaves the wild cards," said Akimi. She examined the orange deck. "Find a rhyme for 'cart and paperbacks,' 'smart and zodiacs,' 'tart and potato sacks.'"

"The Art and Artifacts Room," said Miguel with a sigh.

"Where," Akimi continued, "we need to find a rhyme for 'Randy,' 'Sandy,' or 'Brandi.'"

"The Willy Wonka candy," said Miguel.

"So," said Kyle, "I'm guessing the Bibliomania game was only supposed to help us find the four clues we've already found."

"But we need to know more numbers," said Miguel. "Because a library should be a know-place for know-bodies."

When Miguel made his pun, Kyle and Akimi both groaned.

But then Kyle thought of something: "This is why Mr. Lemoncello called our time-out a bonus. He knew we'd need a ton of time to find a new source of numbers."

Just then Sierra burst into the meeting room.

"You guys! I found a whole bunch of new numbers!"

"What?" said Kyle, Akimi, and Miguel. "Where?"

"Up on the ceiling!"

41

"You need to look up at the Wonder Dome," said Sierra.

"Huh?" said Kyle.

Sierra and her whole team were standing together outside the door to Community Meeting Room B. She hadn't been this happy or excited in a long time.

"Um, Sierra?" said Akimi. "Why exactly are you suggesting we all give ourselves a crick in the neck by staring at the ceiling?"

"Okay. This is a game some of us play online called What's the Connection? I put up a list of authors and you have to figure out how they're linked by the titles of their books."

"Whoa," said Akimi, sort of sarcastically. "Sounds like fun."

"It is. But believe me, it's not easy."

"What'd you figure out?" asked Miguel.

"Well, like Curtis said, Thomas Wolfe wrote *Look Homeward, Angel* and Lewis Carroll wrote *Through the Looking-Glass*. That got me thinking. And running computer searches. Stephen Sondheim wrote a book called *Look, I Made a Hat*. Maya Angelou wrote *Even the Stars Look Lonesome,* and Pseudonymous Bosch wrote *This Isn't What It Looks Like*."

"They all have 'look' in the title," said Kyle.

"What about the other five authors?" asked Akimi. "Did they write 'look' books, too?"

"No, they're up there for a different word."

"Huh?"

"Booker T. Washington wrote *Up from Slavery* and Shel Silverstein wrote *Falling Up*."

"And Dr. Seuss?" said Kyle.

"*Great Day for Up*. George Orwell did *Coming Up for Air,* and Todd Strasser has a book called *If I Grow Up*."

"So the ten statues give us two words," said Miguel.

"Yep. 'Look' and 'up.' So I did. I looked up. At the Wonder Dome. There! Did you see it? That string of numbers that just drifted across the two hundreds screen under the Star of David?"

"220.5203," said Miguel.

Akimi knuckle-punched Kyle in the arm. "This is just like that bonus code thingie you showed me on the school bus!"

"Of course," said Kyle. "This is a Lemoncello game.

He always hides secret codes in screwy places. Way to go, Sierra!"

"Thanks," said Sierra, realizing how much more fun it was to play this kind of game with real friends instead of virtual ones on the Internet.

"But we already found that same two hundreds number playing Bibliomania," said Miguel.

"True," said Kyle. "Check out the sections for numbers the cards wouldn't give us."

Everybody craned their necks and focused on the graphics swimming across the ten panels overhead.

"Here comes another one!" said Sierra. "In the six hundreds. Right underneath the floating stethoscope."

"Got it!" said Kyle. "624.193."

"Whoo-hoo!" said Akimi.

"Sierra, you're my new hero," said Kyle. "You saved the day."

Sierra blushed. "Thanks."

"The spinner," said Akimi.

"Huh?" said Miguel.

"That was another clue. The Bibliomania game was pointing us to the ceiling, too. Because in Dewey decimal mode, the Wonder Dome looks like a giant 3-D version of the board game's spinner."

"Awesome, Sierra," said Miguel. "Absolutely awesome."

* * *

Sierra and her teammates stared up at the ceiling for over an hour. At 12:30, they finally lay down on the floor so they wouldn't cramp their neck muscles.

Because every fifteen minutes, the animated ceiling looped through call numbers for every Dewey decimal room in the library.

Except one.

And then the sequence repeated itself.

"How come there's no three hundreds number?" said Miguel.

"Probably because that's the one book we really, really, *really* need," said Kyle.

"That Lemoncello," said Akimi. "What a comedian."

Peering over the railing on the third-floor balcony at close to two a.m., Andrew Peckleman saw Sierra Russell sitting all alone in the Rotunda Reading Room.

Andrew had spent the night on the third floor losing video games to Charles.

And being reminded about how much he needed to break into Community Meeting Room B to "borrow" any clues Kyle Keeley's team had gathered, to pay Charles back for wasting so much of "the team's time" on the *Anne of Green Gables* clue due to his "foolish fear" of heights.

Andrew had promised Charles he'd do whatever it took.

"If anyone on Team Keeley is going to help us break into their headquarters," Charles had said, "it will be the shy girl who is constantly reading. Have you noticed what Sierra Russell uses for a bookmark?"

"No," Andrew had honestly answered.

"Her library card, which of course doubles as a key card for Meeting Room B. Find a way to borrow it."

"Isn't that illegal?"

"Of course not. This is a library. People borrow books, don't they?"

"Well, yeah . . ."

"Did I mention that I have three thousand Facebook friends? Two thousand Twitter followers? Each and every one of them will hear what a weenie and wimp you are if you don't do this thing to guarantee that our team wins."

So Andrew made his way down to the first floor.

Sierra, as usual, was reading a book.

As he moved closer, Andrew saw a flash of white.

Charles was right. Sierra was using her shiny white library card to mark her place in the book's pages.

He made his way to the cluster of overstuffed reading chairs.

"Good book?"

His voice startled her.

"Oh. Hello. Yes."

"Mind if I join you?" He slid into a crinkly leather seat opposite Sierra. "So, um, what're you reading?"

"*Charlie and the Great Glass Elevator* by Roald Dahl."

"Oh, yeah. I've heard about that book. Where's the rest of your team?"

"They went to bed. Want to get up bright and early. Before the doors on the second floor open again."

"Yeah. Haley and Charles conked out, too. Guess it's just us bookworms, huh?"

"Well, it is kind of late," said Sierra. "I'm going to go upstairs and . . ."

"May I take a look?"

"Hmmm?"

"At your book. I've never actually read it. I just tell people I have."

"Oh. Sure." Sierra handed it to him.

"Thank you."

Andrew flipped through the pages until he found the spot where Sierra had tucked in her library card. "Wouldn't it be cool if this library had a flying elevator like in that Willy Wonka movie? Especially if you could use it to crash through the roof like Charlie and Wonka did. That'd be a pretty cool way to escape from the library, huh?"

"Yeah. I guess."

That was when Andrew made the switch. He slipped his library card into Sierra's book and palmed hers.

Charles would be so proud of him!

"So," he said, closing the book, "did you ever read *The Elevator Family*?"

"No. I don't think so."

"It's all about this family that lives in the elevator of a San Francisco hotel. And let's just say, the book has its ups and its downs!"

Andrew laughed hysterically, because it was one of the

funniest jokes he knew. Sierra sort of chuckled. He handed back her book.

Overhead, the Wonder Dome dissolved out of its Dewey decimal mode and, with a swirl of colors, became a bright green bedroom with a pair of red-framed windows looking out on a blue night sky with a full moon and a blanket of twinkling stars. In the great green room, there was a telephone, and a red balloon, and a picture of a cow jumping over the moon.

The ceiling had become the bunny's bedroom from *Goodnight Moon*.

A quiet old lady bunny in a frumpy blue dress hopped into the Rotunda Reading Room. Two tiny cats followed her.

"Great," said Andrew. "Another stupid hologram."

"I think she's cute," said Sierra.

"Hush," said the bunny. "Goodnight clocks and goodnight socks. Goodnight, Sierra."

"Goodnight, Bunny." Sierra took her book and headed upstairs.

"Goodnight, Andrew," said the bunny.

"Right."

He pocketed the purloined library card. He couldn't do anything with it right away. Not while the holographic bunny's handlers were watching on the spy cameras.

But first thing in the morning . . .

"Goodnight old bunny saying hush," he called out.

And then, under his breath, he muttered, "In the morning, our competition we're gonna crush."

222

Up bright and early the next morning, Kyle made his way across the Rotunda Reading Room.

It was eight-fifteen. The Dewey decimal doors would open in one hour and forty-five minutes. The game would be over in less than four hours.

Kyle was totally pumped.

Sierra Russell, on the other hand, was sitting in a comfy chair reading a book.

"Hey," said Kyle.

"Hi," said Sierra, stifling a small yawn.

"Did you stay up all night reading?"

"No. I went upstairs around two. But there was a new stack of books on the librarian's desk when I came down."

"Oh, really? What'd you find?"

"Five copies of this."

She showed Kyle her book. It was *The Eleventh Hour: A Curious Mystery*.

"It's a rhyming picture book about Horace the Elephant's eleventh birthday party and the search to find out who ran off with all the food. There are hidden messages and cryptic codes all over the pages."

"Why's it called *The Eleventh Hour*?"

"The birthday feast was supposed to take place at eleven a.m. But since somebody stole all the food . . ."

Kyle laughed. "Eleven a.m."

"What?"

"The eleventh hour! The last possible moment." Kyle nudged his head up at the Wonder Dome. "How much do you want to bet that at eleven o'clock, on the dot, the clue we need most of all will pop up in the three hundreds section?"

Sierra smiled. "So this new book is a clue about our clue?"

"That's my guess. Did you eat breakfast?"

"Not yet."

"Well, what are you waiting for?" said Miguel as he strode into the room. "Today's the big day. We're gonna need our energy for the final sprint."

"He's right," said Akimi, climbing down the spiral staircase. "The doors open in less than two hours. Then we only have two more hours to figure everything out."

"But," said Kyle to his other teammates, "Sierra just figured out when we'll get the big three hundreds clue."

He gestured toward the picture book. "At the last possible minute."

"What?" said Akimi. "Eleven-fifty-nine?"

"Close. Eleven o'clock."

"Awesome," said Miguel. "It must be a very good clue."

Kyle and his team went into the café, where they found Haley Daley seated at a table, eating half a grapefruit and staring blankly through the glass walls into the rotunda.

"Hey, Haley," said Kyle. "How's it going?"

"Not bad. You?"

"Good. Win or lose, we're having a blast."

"We're the fun bunch," said Akimi.

"You guys really get along, huh?"

"Oh, yes," said Sierra. "I haven't had this much fun since I was six."

"Seriously?"

"What's the matter, Haley?" said Akimi. "Life not so good on Team Charles?"

"It's okay, I guess. I mean, we've pulled together some good clues and all. . . ."

"Well," said Miguel, "if you ever want to switch sides, we're always looking for new members."

"Can I do that? Just switch sides? Even though I know everything about what Team Charles did all day yesterday?"

"I think so," said Kyle. "I mean, there was nothing in the rules about teams."

"Huh," said Haley. "And Andrew's teamed up with you guys, too?"

"No," said Kyle.

Haley nodded toward the wall of windows behind Kyle. "Then why'd he just swipe his library card and go into your meeting room?"

44

Zipping across the slick marble floor, Kyle and his team, trailed by Haley, practically slid into Community Meeting Room B.

Where Andrew Peckleman stood with a notepad jotting down everything that was written on the whiteboard walls.

"Hey!" shouted Akimi. "That's cheating!"

Andrew spun around.

His eyes were the size of tennis balls behind his goggle glasses.

"Uh, uh, uh," he sputtered. "You guys left the door open!"

"No we did not," said Kyle extremely calmly, especially considering how much he wanted to throttle Peckleman. "It locks automatically; I checked."

"And I double-checked the door before we went to bed," said Miguel.

Kyle was surprised to hear it. "You did?"

"You bet, bro. It's what teammates do."

They knocked knuckles.

"Well, you don't have anything but a stupid list of stupid books and stupid authors and a stupid Bible verse. . . ."

"A verse which," boomed Mr. Lemoncello, whose face had just appeared on the video-screen wall, "you would do well to memorize, Mr. Peckleman. 'Thou shalt not steal.' "

Mr. Lemoncello was dressed in a curled white wig and a long black robe. He looked like a judge in England. He slammed down a rubber gavel on his desk. It made a noise like a whoopee cushion.

"Will everyone kindly join me in the Rotunda Reading Room? At once."

Everybody shuffled out of the meeting room and into the rotunda. They were shocked to see that Mr. Lemoncello himself was seated behind the librarian's desk at the center of the circular room. This was no hologram. This was the real deal.

Charles, all smiles, made a grand entrance, slowly descending one of the spiral staircases.

"Good morning, everybody," he called out cheerfully. "What's all the excitement? Did I miss something?"

"Just your man Andrew trying to cheat," said Miguel.

"What? Oh, good morning, Mr. Lemoncello. I didn't expect to find you here, inside the library. Isn't today your birthday, sir?"

"Yes, Charles. And there's no place I'd rather be on my

big day than inside a library, surrounded by books. Unless, of course, I could be on a bridge to Terabithia."

"Well, sir, I must say, you're certainly looking fit and trim. Have you been working out?"

"No, Charles, today I will be working *in*."

"I beg your pardon?"

"Today I will be working here, inside the library, supervising the final hours of this competition."

"Oh, I don't think it will take *hours,* sir," said Charles. "Not to brag, but I suspect some of us will be going home very soon."

"You are correct. For instance, Mr. Peckleman. He will be leaving right now."

"What?" whined Peckleman. "Why?"

"Because you cheated. You tried to steal the other team's hard-earned information."

Peckleman's eyes darted back and forth. "It wasn't my fault. It was Charles's idea." He whipped up his arm and waggled his finger. "Charles told me to do it. He *made* me do it!"

"Mr. Peckleman, please approach the bench, which, in this instance, is actually a desk. Let me see the library card you used to gain access to Community Meeting Room B."

Somewhat reluctantly, Andrew handed it over.

"Is your name Sierra Russell?"

"No, sir," Andrew said to his shoes.

"He stole my card?" said Sierra. She opened her latest book and pulled out the library card bookmark.

"Whose card do you have, Sierra?" asked Charles.

"Andrew Peckleman's."

"Aha," said Charles. "He pulled the old switcheroo, eh?"

"Because you told me to!" said Peckleman.

"Really?" Charles said, sniggering. "How dare you make such a scandalous accusation? Do you have any proof?"

"I don't need any stupid proof. You bullied me into stealing Sierra's card!"

Mr. Lemoncello banged his gavel again. "And thus ends the story of Andrew and the terrible, horrible, no good, very bad day. Mrs. Bunny?"

A hologram of the old lady bunny from *Goodnight Moon* hopped on top of the librarian's desk.

"Goodnight, Andrew," said the bunny. "Your time with us is all through."

Clarence and Clement, the security guards, appeared and escorted Peckleman out of the building.

"Sir?" said Sierra. "Would you like Andrew's library card for the discard pile?"

"No, thank you. That card is now property of Team Kyle."

Haley Daley raised her hand.

"Yes, Haley?"

Kyle saw her shoot a withering glance at Charles.

"How may I help you, dear?" asked Mr. Lemoncello.

"Well, sir, if it's okay with you, I'd like to switch sides. I want to join Kyle Keeley's team."

45

"Zap!" said Mr. Lemoncello, waving his arms like a magician. *"Zip!* You're now on Kyle Keeley's team!"

"Haley?" said Charles. "How can you desert me?"

"The same way you just deserted Andrew."

"Um, do we get *her* library card, too?" asked Kyle.

"Indeed you do. Plus any and all information she chooses to share with you. And so, Charles, I ask you: Would *you* like to quit your team and join Kyle's?"

"Excuse me?"

"You know, all for one and one for all?"

"Sir, with all due respect, that may have worked for those three musketeers in a trumped-up work of fiction, but I'm sorry, that is not how things work in the real world. Out here, it's every man for himself. What good is a prize if everyone wins it?"

"I see. But Haley knows all the clues you've collected."

"True, sir. But I doubt she realizes what any of them mean."

Kyle could see Mr. Lemoncello's nose twitch when Charles said that. And it wasn't a happy-bunny kind of twitch, either.

"It was a joke, sir." Charles must've seen the nose twitch, too.

"Oh. I see. Like the one about the boy named Charles. Hilarious. Remind me to tell it to you sometime. Anyway, be that as it may, I insist that you be given a few extra clues to compensate for the fact that all your teammates are either being kicked out of the game or abandoning your ship." Mr. Lemoncello reached under the desk and pulled out a white envelope. "This, Charles, is for your eyes only."

Charles stepped forward and took the envelope.

"Thank you, sir. That is very generous."

"I know. You may also ask me one question. But please, don't waste your question asking me, 'Where is the alternate exit?' because I do not know."

"You don't know?" Kyle said it before Charles could.

"Haven't a clue. This entire game was designed by my head librarian, Dr. Yanina Zinchenko, as my birthday present."

"But," said Akimi, "you could just ask Dr. Zinchenko how to get out, right?"

"Akimi Hughes? Are you one of those people who read the last chapter of a book first to see how it ends?"

232

"No, but . . ."

"Good. It's much more fun when the ending is a surprise. Dr. Zinchenko is the only one who knows how and where to exit this building without setting off all sorts of fire alarms. Any clues I personally delivered during the course of this game were completely scripted for me by Dr. Z."

"Okay," said Charles, "here's my question. . . ."

Mr. Lemoncello raised a hand. "Before you ask it, be advised: Your opponents will also hear my answer."

"Fine. Why is the book on the bedside table in your private suite *From the Mixed-Up Files of Mrs. Basil E. Frankweiler* by E. L. Konigsburg?"

"Because when I was your age, Mrs. Tobin, my local librarian, gave it to me."

Miguel raised his hand.

"Yes, Miguel?"

"Can we have one bonus question, too?" he asked politely.

"No," said Mr. Lemoncello. "However, I will give you one bonus answer, which Charles, of course, will also hear. Your bonus answer is 'lodgepole, loblolly, and Rocky Mountain white.'"

"What are three different kinds of pine trees?" said Charles, just to show off—and to let Kyle's team know their bonus answer didn't give them any kind of advantage.

"I am told that is correct," said Mr. Lemoncello, touching his ear.

He reached under the desk again and this time pulled up a three-foot-tall hourglass, a giant version of the red plastic timers that came as standard equipment in a lot of his games.

He turned it over.

"It's the jumbo, three-hour size," he said as the sand started trickling down. "Because it is now nine o'clock and you have only three more hours to find your way out of the library. Good luck. And may the best team—or, in Charles's case, the best solo effort—win!"

46

"Let's see what kind of *real* bonus clues Mr. Lemoncello is serving up today," Charles said to his empty conference room.

He really didn't mind flying solo. It meant he wouldn't have to share his prize when he won it.

Winner won all.

Losers lost all.

That was just the way the world rolled.

And Charles knew he would win.

After all, he was a Chiltington. They never lost.

Even if he had wasted his question about the *Mixed-Up Files* book. Turned out that Mr. Lemoncello was just a sentimental sap like Kyle Keeley. The book was there because his beloved librarian gave it to the old fool when he was the same age as all the library lock-in contestants. Boo-hoo. Big whoop.

And what was all that nonsense about pine trees?
Preposterous.

Unclasping the sealed envelope, Charles found two silhouette cards. Each of them was numbered, in case Charles couldn't figure out which books they would've been hidden in.

#8

Babied? Charles wondered. *No. Crawled!*
He examined the second free card.

#12

Three dinners? Three couples? A restaurant?
This one was difficult.

Charles decided to put the two new pieces into the puzzle, to see if their meanings would become clearer:

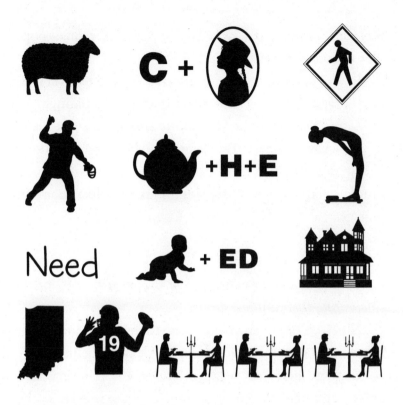

Charles was missing only one clue, but he had everything else.

"You can walk out the way BLANK crawled in in passed restaurant."

No. That didn't make sense.

In fact, all he was really certain about were the first two lines: "You can walk out the way."

The way what? Past the restaurant? The Book Nook Café? And what about the image of the football player?

It came from the Johnny Unitas book. Maybe Johnny Unitas, who had played football back when Mr. Lemoncello was Charles's age, had owned a restaurant? Perhaps a popular national chain?

If so, there might've been one in Alexandriaville. Maybe right here in the old Gold Leaf Bank building.

Could the last bit be "In Johnny Unitas's Restaurant"?

Or what if Andrew Peckleman had been right all along and it was the NINETEEN that was the clue from the football player card? That would make the final line "In nineteen . . ." WHAT? *Diners? Couples?*

No.

Anniversaries!

The three couples in the bonus clue were obviously celebrating their anniversaries!

Nineteen anniversaries? Was today the nineteenth anniversary of some major event in Alexandriaville?

Charles shook his head. He knew the phrase would make sense only *after* he had completed the third line, the only one that still had a blank in it: "BLANK, CRAWLED, INN."

What if the missing image is an eyeball? Then the third line could be "I crawled *in*."

Hang on, Charles thought. The one book in the Staff Picks display case nobody had found yet was *True Crime Ohio: The Buckeye State's Most Notorious Brigands, Burglars, and Bandits* by Clare Taylor-Winters. The last image was going to be a criminal of some sort.

That one, single missing book might tell Charles who had crawled into the bank and, more importantly, *where* they had crawled in. Was this the nineteenth anniversary of a famous bank robbery?

Charles realized he needed help.

It was time to use his Ask an Expert.

That made him laugh.

Because Charles knew the top library expert in all of America, maybe the world. Someone much more important than Dr. Yanina Zinchenko.

Kyle Keeley and the rest of that bunch didn't stand a chance.

Eager to find out all he could in the final minutes before the Dewey decimal doors reopened on the second floor, Kyle listened as Haley Daley detailed everything she had learned on Team Charles.

Meanwhile, Akimi added Andrew's and Haley's library cards to the list on the whiteboards in Community Meeting Room B.

"We were piecing together a picture puzzle," said Haley. "It was like a memory match game, or that old TV show *Concentration.*"

"We played one of those, too," said Miguel. "A rebus."

"Right. So far, I'm pretty sure it says something like 'You walk out the way bandits crawled in.'"

"'Thou shalt not steal,'" said Kyle, tapping the Bible verse they had found in the 200s room. "That points to bandits, too."

"And the blackbird," said Sierra. "It wailed like a police siren."

"Chasing bandits!"

"Hang on," said Miguel. "What about Willy Wonka? Were there criminals in the chocolate factory?"

"No," said Sierra.

"And what about all this?" said Akimi, pointing at the list of library cards. "I added the new cards but it still doesn't make much sense."

BOOKS/AUTHORS ON THE BACKS OF LIBRARY CARDS

#1 Miguel Fernandez
Incident at Hawk's Hill by Allan W. Eckert/
No, David! by David Shannon

#2 Akimi Hughes
One Fish Two Fish Red Fish Blue Fish
by Dr. Seuss/Nine Stories by J. D. Salinger

#3 Andrew Peckleman
Six Days of the Condor by James Grady/
Eight Cousins by Louisa May Alcott

#4 Bridgette Wadge
Tales of a Fourth Grade Nothing
by Judy Blume/

Harry Potter and the
Sorcerer's Stone by J. K. Rowling

#5 Sierra Russell
The Egypt Game by Zilpha Keatley Snyder/
The Westing Game by Ellen Raskin

#6 Yasmeen Smith-Snyder
Around the World in Eighty Days
by Jules Verne/The Yak Who Yelled Yuck
by Carol Pugliano-Martin

#7 Sean Keegan
Olivia by Ian Falconer/Unreal! by Paul Jennings

#8 Haley Daley
Turtle in Paradise by Jennifer L. Holm/
A Wrinkle in Time by Madeleine L'Engle

#9 Rose Vermette
All-of-a-Kind Family by Sydney Taylor/
Scat by Carl Hiaasen

#10 Kayla Corson
Anna to the Infinite Power
by Mildred Ames/Where the Sidewalk
Ends by Shel Silverstein

#12 Kyle Keeley
I Love You, Stinky Face by Lisa McCourt/
The Napping House by Audrey Wood

"Wow," said Haley. "What a mess."

"Tell me about it," said Akimi.

"I don't think it's another author-title game," said Sierra, "like up on the Wonder Dome."

"Huh?" said Haley.

"Long story," said Miguel. "We'll save it for later."

"What we need," said Kyle, "is some kind of clue to show us how to unscramble this list. Remember what Dr. Zinchenko said when the game started: 'Your library cards are the keys to everything you will need.' This clue is the big one, guys. We need to crack it."

That's when Mr. Lemoncello popped his head in the door.

"Hello, hope I'm not interrupting. We have twenty minutes till the doors open upstairs. Anybody up for an Extreme Challenge?"

48

"In case you forgot," said Mr. Lemoncello, "Extreme Challenges are extremely challenging and sometimes extremely dangerous."

"Is Charles doing one?" asked Akimi.

"He might. I'm going to ask him if he'd like to next."

Mr. Lemoncello had changed out of his judge's costume into some kind of cat burglar outfit—black pants, ribbed black turtleneck, and sporty black beret.

"Is that costume a clue?" asked Haley. "Because it goes with the whole bandit theme."

"Don't know. But Dr. Zinchenko told me to wear it for the big finale. Is there going to be a finale?"

"Maybe with Charles," mumbled Kyle. "We're sort of stuck."

"At least till eleven," added Sierra. "That's when the most important clue will appear on the ceiling."

"Really?" said Mr. Lemoncello. "That Dr. Zinchenko. The woman knows how to build suspense."

"So let's do the Extreme Challenge," said Haley. "What do we have to lose?"

"Um, the whole game," said Akimi.

"Not for all of us," said Kyle. "I'll do the challenge. After all, I'm the team captain."

"You are?" said Haley.

"We had an election," said Akimi. "Yesterday."

"Oh. Cool."

"But, Kyle," said Miguel, "if you blow the Extreme Challenge, you lose, bro."

"Not if my team wins."

"No," said Mr. Lemoncello. "If you lose, Kyle, you *lose*. You will not be allowed to share in the big prize."

"Fine."

"I'm going with you," said Haley.

"No, you're not," said Mr. Lemoncello.

"I have to. Look, we both know I'd be a *fabulous* spokesmodel for your games and stuff, but I can't just glom on to everything Kyle and his team have already dug up. I have to earn my place on this team."

"Sorry, Haley. Extreme Challenges are, and always will be, solo efforts."

"But . . ."

Mr. Lemoncello held up his hand. "No buts. Kyle must face this challenge alone. However . . ."

"Yes?"

"The rest of you can watch his progress on the video screens and cheer him on over the intercom system. You are a cheerleader, aren't you, Haley?"

"Yep," said Kyle. "But she's never cheered for me."

"Well, I will this time. I promise."

"Excellent," said Mr. Lemoncello. "By the way, Kyle, there is no backing out once you commit to the challenge."

"Fine," said Kyle. "Let's do it."

"Go, Kyle, gooooo!" shouted Haley.

Akimi flinched. "Um, a warning next time . . . please?"

"Sorry."

Mr. Lemoncello touched his ear again. "Here is your Extreme Challenge. Dr. Zinchenko tells me:

" 'The answer you seek . . .' "

He paused to listen.

" ' . . . the key to this code . . .
is a memory box . . .
that holds the mother lode.' "

"What?"

Mr. Lemoncello shrugged. "Sorry. I don't write 'em. I only recite 'em. Wait. There's more:

" 'Forget the Industrial Revolution;
my first idea is your certain solution.' "

The room was silent.

Mr. Lemoncello touched his ear once more and continued, " 'And now, it's time for the addendum.' "

"Huh?"

"A last-minute addition:

" *'The box had been here*
but now it is there.
Poor Kyle. Your fate
is up in the air.' "

Mr. Lemoncello stood there grinning. For several seconds.

"Is that it?" said Kyle.

"Yes. Find what you're looking for before the second-floor doors open, and it is yours. Fail, and you, Kyle, will be eliminated from the game, and your team, due to that series of unfortunate events, will be forced to struggle on without you. Good luck. You have fifteen minutes."

And Mr. Lemoncello left the room.

"Dude," said Miguel, shaking his head. "You are so dead."

"Wait a second," said Haley. "I think I know how to find what Mr. Lemoncello was talking about!"

"You do?" said Kyle.

"I better. I'm the one who moved it from 'here' to 'there'!"

"Now then, Charles," said Mr. Lemoncello, "would you like to utilize any of your remaining lifelines? Perhaps an Extreme Challenge? An Ask an Expert?"

"Yes, sir," said Charles. "And may I just say, it's kind of you to come in here and ask me that question."

"Well, it's cloudy with a chance of meatballs and I had nothing better to do."

"Pardon?"

"Nothing. Just a brief flight of fancy, my mind sailing off past the phantom tollbooth. So, which lifeline would you like to use?"

"My Ask an Expert, sir."

"Fine. See Mrs. Tobin at the main desk. I must go to my office to monitor Kyle's Extreme Challenge."

"What's he doing?"

"Trying to beat you. Tootles!"

Mr. Lemoncello raised his beret by its stem, turned on his heel, and headed for one of the bookcases on the far side of the rotunda.

Charles watched him tilt back the head on a bust and press a red button in the middle of what would have been the man's neck. A door-sized section of the bookcase swung open. Mr. Lemoncello stepped into the darkness. The bookcase swung shut.

Charles hurried to the librarian's desk at the center of the Rotunda Reading Room.

"Mrs. Tobin?" He clapped his hands. "Mrs. Tobin? Chop-chop. I'm in a bit of a rush. The doors upstairs will be open in thirteen minutes. Mrs. Tobin?"

The holographic librarian finally appeared.

"Good morning, CHARLES. How may I help you?"

"I need to use my Ask an Expert."

"Very well. Whom do you wish to consult with?"

"Someone who knows his way around a library."

"If that is all you require, CHARLES, perhaps I can be of assistance."

"I need to talk to my uncle Jimmy."

"Your uncle Jimmy? Could you please be more specific?"

"Yes. Of course. James F. Willoughby the third."

"*The* James F. Willoughby the third?"

"Yes, ma'am."

"The *head librarian* of the *Library of Congress* in *Washington, D.C.,* is your uncle?"

"That's right. If my mother's brother, Uncle Jimmy, the top librarian in all of America, can't help me find the one book I'm looking for, nobody can!"

50

"The memory box is down in the Stacks," Haley told Kyle.

So he raced down to the basement. The very long, very wide cellar was just as he remembered it: filled with tidy rows of floor-to-ceiling shelving units.

Kyle looked up at the closest security camera.

"Where to next?"

"I hid it way over on the far side," said Haley through the ceiling speakers. "On a shelf near that horrible book-sorting machine."

Kyle hurried up the center aisle.

Suddenly, a heavy metal bookcase thundered in from the right, sliding like it was on roller skates.

"Watch it!" shouted Haley.

The bookcase skidded to a screeching halt, blocking Kyle's path forward.

"Go left," suggested Miguel.

The whole team was watching and cheering him on.

Kyle went left.

And another steel shelving unit shuffled in from the side.

"Jump back!" shouted Akimi.

The shelf slammed to a stop two inches in front of Kyle's feet.

"Kyle? You okay?"

"Yeah."

"This is like the hedge maze in the Triwizard Tournament," said Sierra.

"Huh?"

"Harry Potter. Book four. *Goblet of Fire*."

"Right. Need to read that one, too."

Kyle, of course, realized he'd just discovered the most "extreme" part of his Extreme Challenge. Each one of the sliding floor-to-ceiling bookcases was loaded down with heavy cardboard cartons, books, or metal storage bins. They probably weighed several tons each. If Kyle was in the wrong place when a shelving unit came shooting in from the side, he'd be flattened like a pancake under a steamroller.

"Warning," announced the official-sounding lady in the ceiling. "You have twelve minutes to complete this challenge."

He had to keep going. Like Mr. Lemoncello said, there was no turning back now. Unless, of course, he wanted to go home a loser.

Ha! Never!

Kyle jogged up an alleyway between two walls of bookshelves.

"Left turn!" Haley shouted. "Now!"

The wall on Kyle's right swung open, revealing six swiveling sections, each pivoting panel maybe twenty feet long, all skittering sideways and gliding backward to create new walls and reconfigured pathways.

"You've only got like ten more yards to go," coached Haley.

Kyle weaved his way around the randomly shuffling shelves.

But as soon as he was on any kind of straightaway, the walls started to rearrange themselves again.

Finally, Kyle scooted down a corridor so tight he had to turn sideways to squeeze through. The walls stuttered to a stop.

And the voice made another announcement. "Warning. You have eight minutes to complete this challenge."

"I'm trapped!" Kyle shouted. "There's no exit."

None of his teammates said anything for a real long time.

Finally, Sierra's voice rang out from the overhead speakers.

"Put your hand on the right wall," she said.

"What? Why?"

"When I was little, I played a lot of maze games. If the walls are connected, all you have to do is keep one hand in contact with one wall at all times and eventually you'll reach the exit or return to the entrance."

"Do it," coached Akimi.

"It'll work, bro," added Miguel.

So Kyle kept his right hand firmly planted on the right wall of shelves and started inching his way forward.

"Go, Kyle!" cheered Haley. "Hug that wall! Hug that wall!"

The passageway widened. Kyle kept his hand glued to the right wall and went around corners, through switchbacks, until finally, he stepped into an opening near the book return conveyor belt.

"You made it!" shouted Haley. "Whoo-hoo!"

All the shelves streamed back into their orderly church pew positions.

"Good," said Kyle. "Getting out should be easier than getting in. Where's the box, Haley?"

"I put it on the shelf."

"Which one?"

"That one."

"Warning," announced the calm female voice in the ceiling again. "You have THREE MINUTES to complete this challenge."

Kyle stared up at a nearby camera. "Um, Haley? What exactly am I looking for?"

"A cardboard box. In a drawer."

"Okay. There are like a billion of those. . . ."

"I flagged it with a piece of pink tissue."

Kyle raced to a shelf.

"TWO MINUTES," announced the calm lady.

"This one?" said Kyle.

"Yes! Look in the steel drawer."

"I thought you said it was cardboard. . . ."

"It is. Open the lid. Not that lid. The other one."

"This one?"

"No! The one under it!"

"ONE MINUTE."

"Hurry, Kyle!"

"I'm hurrying."

"Flip it open."

Kyle did as he was told. He flipped up the lid on a steel drawer and found a battered boot box.

Every member of Kyle's team shouted the same thing: "Grab it!"

"And run!" added Akimi.

Kyle did.

He tucked the boot box under his arm and ran like he had never run before.

He sprinted across the basement floor. He raced up the steps, two at a time.

When he hit the rotunda, his heart was pounding against his ribs.

"THIRTY SECONDS."

He speed-skated across the marble floor. It was so slippery he lost his balance.

He fell forward.

Dropped the box.

It flew out of his hands, hit the slick floor, and slid like a hockey puck across the threshold into Community Meeting Room B.

A buzzer sounded.

"Time is up," announced the calm voice.

"Yo," shouted Miguel, "you made it, bro!"

And Kyle started breathing again.

51

Having made his request, all Charles could do was wait.

"Apparently," said Mr. Lemoncello when he came back into the rotunda, "your uncle Jimmy is a very, *very* busy man. Reminds me of a spider I once knew. But it is a Sunday morning. We will attempt to track him down at home."

"Thank you, sir. I told Uncle Jimmy to stand by. That I might need him this weekend."

"And now—*WHOOSH!* He's as elusive as the wind in the willows. You'll have to discuss this with him the next time your family gets together for Thanksgiving dinner. Now, if you will excuse me, it is currently nine-fifty-eight a.m. Almost time to reopen the Dewey decimal chambers."

Mr. Lemoncello opened a filing cabinet and pulled out a megaphone.

"Is there some room you should be ready to run to? Isn't there some clue or book you need to go find?"

"Just one," said Charles. "And I need my uncle Jimmy to tell me which one it is. Will you keep looking for him? Please."

"Of course." Mr. Lemoncello pointed to a smudge on Charles's shirt. "If you like, I will also have Al Capone do your shirts."

All Charles could do was nod, smile, and wonder when Al Capone had opened a laundry.

52

"Everyone, please pay very close attention," cried Mr. Lemoncello through a squealing, screeching megaphone. "The Dewey decimal doors are now open and, unlike Tuck, this game will not be everlasting. Therefore, it is time to race upstairs like the rats of NIMH!"

Kyle and his teammates heard Mr. Lemoncello's announcement but stayed inside Community Meeting Room B so they could examine the dusty old boot box.

"It's from when Mr. Lemoncello was our age," said Haley. "Here. I'm pretty sure this is what we need." She handed Kyle a large manila envelope sealed up with tons of tape. "First and Worst Idea Ever" had been scribbled on the front.

"Awesome," said Kyle as he started undoing the tape. "The clue said his first idea might be our best solution."

Inside the envelope were a stack of cards, a bunch of rubber stamps, an ink pad, and a sheet of three-ring-binder paper filled with a fifth grader's sloppy hand-writing.

Kyle read out loud what the young Luigi Lemoncello had written: "'Presenting First Letters: the Amazingly Incredible Secret Code Game.'"

Haley held up some of the cards. Each one showed a cartoony drawing and a single letter: Apple = A, Bee = B, Carrot = C, and so on.

Kyle continued reading: "'Want to send your friend a secret message to meet you after school? Just use your super-secret rubber stamps.'"

Miguel examined a couple of the wood-handled stamps. "The stamps match the cards."

"So how exactly do you use this junk to tell your friends to meet you after school?" asked Akimi.

"This is so bad," said Kyle. "'Moon, Elephant, Elephant, Tiger. Moon, Elephant. Apple, Flamingo . . .'"

Akimi held up her hand. "Okay. Stop. I get it."

"Maybe it was for little kids," said Sierra.

"Definitely," said Kyle. "Because anybody over the age of six could crack this code in like ten seconds."

And then he froze.

"This is it!"

He went to the wall with the list of library cards. "What would happen if we played First Letters with these book titles?"

BOOKS/AUTHORS ON THE BACKS OF LIBRARY CARDS

#1 Miguel Fernandez
Incident at Hawk's Hill by Allan W. Eckert/
No, David! by David Shannon

#2 Akimi Hughes
One Fish Two Fish Red Fish Blue Fish
by Dr. Seuss/Nine Stories by J. D. Salinger

#3 Andrew Peckleman
Six Days of the Condor by James Grady/
Eight Cousins by Louisa May Alcott

#4 Bridgette Wadge
Tales of a Fourth Grade Nothing
by Judy Blume/Harry Potter and the
Sorcerer's Stone by J. K. Rowling

#5 Sierra Russell
The Egypt Game by Zilpha Keatley Snyder/
The Westing Game by Ellen Raskin

#6 Yasmeen Smith-Snyder
Around the World in Eighty Days
by Jules Verne/The Yak Who Yelled Yuck
by Carol Pugliano-Martin

#7 Sean Keegan
Olivia by Ian Falconer/Unreal! by Paul Jennings

#8 Haley Daley
Turtle in Paradise by Jennifer L. Holm/
A Wrinkle in Time by Madeleine L'Engle

#9 Rose Vermette
All-of-a-Kind Family by Sydney Taylor/
Scat by Carl Hiaasen

#10 Kayla Corson
Anna to the Infinite Power
by Mildred Ames/Where the Sidewalk
Ends by Shel Silverstein

#11 UNKNOWN/CHARLES CHILTINGTON

#12 Kyle Keeley
I Love You, Stinky Face by Lisa McCourt/
The Napping House by Audrey Wood

"Okay," said Miguel, moving to a clean space on the wall. "Here are the first letters of all the titles."

I N O N S E T H T T A T O U T A A S A W ? ? I T

"It still makes no sense," said Akimi.

"Wait a second," said Sierra. "If the title starts with an article, drop that word, and use the letter from the second word."

"Got it," said Miguel.

I N O N S E T H E W A Y O U T W A S A W ? ? I N

"Okay," said Akimi. "It's making some sense."
She went to the board and broke Miguel's string of letters into words.

I /N O N /S E T /H E /W A Y/ O U T/ W A S /A /W ? ?/ I N

"Hang on," said Kyle. "It could be . . ."

I N/ O N /S E/ T H E /W A Y/ O U T/ W A S /A /W ? ?/ I N

"What's 'In on se'?" said Akimi.
"Wait! Look!" said Miguel. "The books on the second and third library cards actually start with *numbers*!"
Kyle grabbed a marker:

I N/ 1 9 6 8/ T H E /W A Y/ O U T/ W A S /A /W ? ?/ I N

"Hang on," said Haley. "You know all those questions in the trivia contest Friday? I did so badly, I Googled a bunch of them later that night. They were all from 1968."
"You guys?" said Sierra. "I did some research, too.

Mr. Lemoncello was born in 1956. That means he turned twelve in 1968."

"Oh-kay," said Akimi. "Is this something besides a fun fact to know and tell?"

"You bet it is," said Kyle. "Nineteen sixty-eight is key. And we don't need Charles's library card to finish this phrase." He went to the whiteboard.

IN 1968, THE WAY OUT WAS A WAY IN.

"So what happened in 1968?" said Haley.

"Was that when *Charlie and the Chocolate Factory* came out?" asked Miguel.

"No," said Sierra. "Nineteen sixty-four."

"So what's up with the candy clue from the Art and Artifacts Room?"

"We messed up," said Akimi. "We need to go back and find a new rhyme for 'Andy'!"

"Really?" said Haley. "I thought he got kicked out for cheating."

"Another long story," said Miguel.

"For later," said Kyle. "Right now, we need to be on the third floor!"

53

Back in the Art & Artifacts Room, Kyle felt confident they were pretty close to figuring out, well, whatever it was they were supposed to figure out.

How it would help them escape from the library was still anybody's guess.

"It's ten-forty-four," said Akimi. "The last clue should pop up on the Wonder Dome in sixteen minutes."

"Okay, you guys," said Kyle. "Spread out. We need a new rhyme for 'Andy.'"

"This model of the bank building came in *handy*," added Miguel.

"The Dandy Bandits!" shouted Akimi, once again studying the display of hats.

"Yes!" said Haley, pulling off her shoe so she could show everybody her clue card.

+ ITS

"Bandits! I found this in the three hundreds room."

"That's the room clue we're waiting for," said Kyle.

"Because the Dewey decimal number for True Crime books always starts with the number three," said Miguel. "When we find that book, it'll tell us how and where the 'bandits crawled in in 1968.'"

"Listen to this, you guys," said Akimi. She read a placard in the display case: "'This plaid fedora from *1968* was worn by bank robber Leopold Loblolly, one of the notorious *Dandy* Bandits.'"

"Loblolly!" Miguel shouted.

"The smell-a-vision clue," said Kyle. "That's why everything kept smelling like pine trees."

"Loblolly was one of the pine trees in the answer Mr. Lemoncello gave you guys!" said Haley.

"Whoop-whoop-whoop," said Mr. Lemoncello as, banana shoes squeaking, he stepped into the room. "Well done, Miss Daley . . . and Miss Hughes."

"See?" said Akimi. "I was right the first time we came in here. I said 'dandy' and everybody else said, 'Noooo, *candy*. Willy Wonka . . .'"

"Yes, it's all coming back to me," said Mr. Lemoncello.

"Nineteen sixty-eight. I was pondering an idea for a game at the old public library."

"And," said Kyle, "you were so totally focused, you didn't hear the police sirens screaming past the library as they raced to the Gold Leaf Bank. . . ."

"The blackbird was from Alexandriaville," said Sierra. "The police siren wail was from that day."

Miguel finished that thought: "When the Dandy Bandits tried to crawl into the bank!"

"My goodness," said Mr. Lemoncello. "How could you kids know all that?"

"From the game clues," said Kyle, "and from the story Dr. Zinchenko told us on Friday night when somebody asked her why a library building needed a bank vault door."

"She was already feeding us clues!" said Akimi.

"The time is now ELEVEN a.m.," announced the ceiling lady. "This game will end in ONE hour."

"Come on," said Kyle, heading for the door. "It's the eleventh hour. We need to go check out the Wonder Dome again."

They raced to the balcony.

"There it is!" said Sierra.

"364 point 1092!" shouted Miguel.

"Whoo-hoo!" cried Akimi. "We're gonna win!"

54

On the first floor, Charles was at long last video chatting with his uncle, James Willoughby III, the librarian of Congress, who had finally shown up for the Ask an Expert call.

"Sorry for the delay, Charles."

"That's okay, Uncle Jimmy," Charles said, straining to smile and not scream.

"The time is now ELEVEN a.m.," announced the annoyingly placid lady in the ceiling. "This game will end in ONE hour."

Charles had to hustle.

"Sir, I know you're a very important, very busy man, so I just have one quick question: If I were a book on true crimes in the state of Ohio, where would you shelve me?"

"Library of Congress classification?"

"No, sir. Dewey decimal."

"Ah. Easy. 364 point 1. What comes after the one will depend, of course, on how many books a library . . ."

Charles didn't stick around to hear the rest of his uncle's answer.

He took off running for the closest spiral staircase up to the second floor. As he ascended the steps, two at a time, he saw Kyle Keeley and his entire entourage running down a staircase from the third floor.

Charles reached the second-floor balcony first.

He darted around the bend, past the door to the 500s room, the 400s.

Keeley and his crew were coming from the opposite direction, but Charles reached the door to the 300s room before them.

He swiped his library card, yanked on the handle, and dashed into the room.

He scanned the shelves and headed to his right.

He heard Keeley enter the room.

Glancing over his shoulder, Charles saw Keeley go left.

Charles dashed up an aisle between bookcases. He read the number at the end of each row of shelves.

310.

320.

330.

One of those robots with the book baskets came rumbling across his path, but Charles was able to dodge it.

340.

350.

Keeley's footsteps pounded up the passageway on the other side of the shelving units to his left.

In the middle of the 300s room, they entered an open space with a judge's bench and witness box.

Charles was getting closer to the True Crime section.

But so was Kyle.

Charles saw Keeley read something off his palm.

He had the whole call number!

It was time to change tactics.

Charles hung back and let Keeley take the lead.

Kyle rushed toward a bookcase.

Charles sprinted after him.

"Got it!" Kyle shouted as he reached for a book on the shelf.

But before he could completely pull it out, Charles grabbed hold of the book, too.

They both yanked it off the shelf.

Kyle had the spine; Charles had hold of the top.

They tugged it back and forth.

While they wrestled with the book, Keeley's teammates caught up to them.

"Careful, Kyle," cried Sierra Russell. "Don't hurt the book."

Charles grinned. Keeley, the sentimental sap, was listening to the silly, bookish girl and easing up on his grip.

Giving Charles his chance.

He body-checked Keeley. Slammed into him with his

shoulder. Sent him flying, the book tumbling. Charles snatched it off the floor.

He had the book. He quickly flipped through the table of contents. Saw chapter 11 was about a robbery at the Gold Leaf Bank in Alexandriaville.

He knew he'd won the game.

Charles used his free hand to slap an "L" on his forehead.

"Loser," he sneered at Keeley.

A tiger roared, a whistle blew, and Mr. Lemoncello entered the room, accompanied by Clarence, Clement, and what looked like a rare Bengal tiger.

"Mr. Chiltington?"

Charles smiled. He knew Mr. Lemoncello was about to congratulate him for defying the odds and winning the game. He had single-handedly defeated Kyle Keeley's entire team! "Yes, sir, Mr. Lemoncello?"

"Do you remember Dr. Zinchenko's number one rule?"

"You bet, sir. No food or drink except in the Book Nook Café."

"No," said Mr. Lemoncello, touching the tip of his nose and making a buzzer noise. "Dr. Z? Tell him what he should've said."

Dr. Zinchenko's voice purred out of the ceiling speakers. "Be gentle. With each other and, most especially, the library's books and exhibits."

"I know," said Charles. "That's why I had to stop Kyle

Keeley. He was ready to rip the cover off this poor book. Heck, sir, everybody at school knows that Kyle Keeley is a maniac. He'll do anything to win a game."

Mr. Lemoncello turned to Keeley.

"Is that true, Kyle? Would you actually destroy property if it stood between you and your prize?"

"W-well, sir . . ."

Keeley was stammering. The fool didn't know how to lie.

Charles quickly opened the book to chapter 11 and slipped in his library card to bookmark the location.

"You should ask Keeley about the window he broke, sir."

Mr. Lemoncello turned to face Charles again.

"The window?"

"Yes, sir. The whole school heard about it. See, Kyle Keeley and his two brothers were playing some sort of wild scavenger hunt game and . . ."

Mr. Lemoncello pointed at the book. "That's clever. You use your library card as a bookmark?"

"Yes, sir, I sure do," said Charles, turning on the charm. "Of course, I can't take full credit for such a clever idea. On Friday night, I saw Sierra Russell doing it and . . ."

"You told Andrew Peckleman to 'borrow' her card."

Charles blinked. Several times. "I beg your pardon?"

"You broke Dr. Zinchenko's number one rule. You

were not gentle with your teammate Andrew. In fact, you bullied him into stealing Miss Russell's library card, which you knew she always used as a bookmark."

"No, sir. I did not."

"Yes, Charles. You did." Mr. Lemoncello touched his right ear. "In fact, Dr. Zinchenko has spent the past few hours combing through security tapes, and guess what she just found?"

Charles heard his own voice ringing out of the ceiling speakers:

"Have you noticed what Sierra Russell uses for a bookmark?"

"No."

"That was Andrew," said Mr. Lemoncello. "This is you again."

"Her library card, which, of course, doubles as a key card for Meeting Room B. Find a way to borrow it."

"You told Andrew to steal Sierra's library card."

"How could you record that?" said Charles. "I was whispering!"

"And *I* have very good microphones. You're done, Charles. Dr. Zinchenko? Tell our departing guest what he has just won."

"Absolutely nothing," said the voice of the Russian librarian. "But please, Mr. L, tell Charles the correct answer to the final pictogram."

"Ah, yes!" Mr. Lemoncello reached into his back

pocket, pulled out a four-by-four card, and showed it to Charles.

Charles stood there fuming.

"Anyone care to help Charles out?"

"Hmmm," said Kyle. "Is it 'six eat'?"

"You are very close," said Mr. Lemoncello.

There was a pause and then Haley laughed. "Did it come after the football player?"

"Yeah," said Charles. "So?"

"Andrew was right all along," said Haley. "The football player clue wasn't 'past,' it was 'nineteen.'"

Mr. Lemoncello shifted into his game show voice. "So, Haley Daley, would you care to solve the puzzle?"

"Sure: 'You can walk out the way bandits crawled in in nineteen six ate.'"

"I don't get it," said Charles.

"Nineteen, six-ate," said Akimi. "You know: 1968."

"Ah, yes," said Mr. Lemoncello. "The year *From the Mixed-Up Files of Mrs. Basil E. Frankweiler* won the Newbery Medal for excellence in children's literature. Another clue you completely missed, Charles."

"Wow," said Miguel. "And I thought Chiltingtons never lose."

"There's a first time for everything," said Mr. Lemoncello. "Clarence? Clement? Kindly escort young Mr. Chiltington from the building."

"Buh-bye," said Akimi. "There goes this game's biggest loser."

55

"Open it!" Akimi said to Kyle. "We only have like forty minutes to figure out how Loblolly and the Dandy Bandits crawled into the bank back in 1968!"

Kyle flipped through *True Crime Ohio* to the place where Charles had slipped in his bookmark.

"Well?" said Miguel.

" 'Chapter Eleven. The Dandy Bandits Burrow into a Bank Vault.' "

"Even though thou should not steal," said Akimi.

"And I'll bet they crawled in, right?" said Haley.

" 'The clever thieves,' " Kyle read from the book, " 'took up residence in an abandoned dress factory next door to the Gold Leaf Bank and spent weeks tunneling from its basement into the bank vault.' "

"Which," said Miguel, "according to those old

blueprints I found, was down where the book-sorting machine is now."

"That explains the first clue," said Kyle. "The book title was *Get to Know Your Local Library*. Dr. Zinchenko meant we needed to get to know *this* library. This also explains why she wanted us to read those Sherlock Holmes stories."

" 'The Adventure of the Red-Headed League,' " said Sierra. "The story about robbers tunneling into a bank from the building next door."

Kyle nodded. "Dr. Zinchenko told me *she* had just reread it. I'll bet that's where she got the idea for this whole game."

"Hey, Charles should've stuck with crawling through sewers like he did in that video game," joked Miguel. "He might've found the Dandy Bandits' tunnel before we did."

"Come on, you guys," said Haley. "We need to be back in the basement."

"I'm coming with you," said Mr. Lemoncello. "I just have to see how this story ends!"

Clutching the *True Crime* book against his chest, Kyle led the way down to the Stacks.

"Why are you bringing that book?" asked Akimi.

"We'll put it on that conveyor belt thing," Kyle explained. "Whatever basket the scanner sends it to, I'm guessing that's where we'll find our 'black square.' "

"Our shortcut out of the library!"

"Exactly."

As the team trooped down the steps to the basement, Mr. Lemoncello turned to Kyle and said, "So, Mr. Keeley, did you have fun this weekend?"

"Yeah."

"Good. Congratulations, Miss Hughes, it seems *you* have already won."

Akimi sort of blushed.

"What do you mean?" asked Kyle.

"In her essay, your extremely good friend wrote, and I quote: 'I want to see the new library so I can tell my friend Kyle Keeley how cool it is.'"

"You wrote your essay about me?"

"Maybe," mumbled Akimi.

"Wow," said Kyle. "No one's ever done that before."

"Well, no one's ever going to do it again if you blow our chance at winning this thing. So can we please stop yakking and find our way out of here?"

"Works for me."

"Warning," said the calm voice in the ceiling speakers. "This game will terminate in THIRTY minutes."

Everybody moved a little faster.

Fortunately, when the group reached the basement, the floor-to-ceiling bookshelves didn't start sliding into another maze formation.

"The automatic book sorter is straight up this path, near the far wall," said Kyle.

They made it to the conveyor belt.

"From what I remember from the old blueprints," said Miguel, "the vault was right here, in the same spot as this machine."

"Okay, you guys," said Kyle. "Whatever robo-basket this book ends up in is probably sitting right on top of the entrance to the tunnel."

"Here goes everything." Kyle placed *True Crime Ohio* into the array of crisscrossing beams.

Nothing happened.

"What's going on?" cried Miguel. "Why isn't it working?"

"Maybe this book isn't heavy enough." Kyle pushed down on the cover of the book a bit.

Still nothing.

They stared, dumbfounded, at the book sitting on the immobile belt.

"It wouldn't *stop* moving yesterday," muttered Haley.

"That's it!" cried Akimi. She hurried to the wall and flipped the emergency shutoff switch back to the "on" position.

Several red laser scanners sprang to life under the book drop slot.

The belt started moving. Slowly.

The single book worked its way down the line like a

candy bar on a wrapping machine. When it reached the third robo-basket from the end, a set of rollers popped up and shunted the book off to the side into the waiting wire basket.

The conveyor belt stopped rolling. The robo-cart rolled away.

Nothing else happened.

"That's it?"

"Warning," said the calm voice. "This game will terminate in TWENTY minutes."

"It didn't work," said Haley.

"We're toast," added Akimi.

"Wait," said Kyle, pointing to a square tile on the floor where the robo-basket had been. It was glowing, like one of the touch-screen computers in the desks upstairs. "It says 'Howdy. Dü you like fun games? Get Reddy.'"

"Excellent!" Akimi giggled. Then she and Kyle cracked up, remembering the box tops from their first puzzle in the Board Room on Saturday morning.

"Now it says we're going to get an anagram," said Kyle.

"My favorite kind of cookies," said Mr. Lemoncello.

"Okay, everybody," said Kyle. "Gather round. Get ready."

Kyle, Akimi, Sierra, Miguel, and Haley knelt on the floor in a circle around the square. Mr. Lemoncello hovered behind them.

"Here we go," said Kyle as game instructions scrolled across the screen.

GIVE ME SIXTEEN WORDS MADE FROM
THESE SIXTEEN LETTERS
IN SIXTY SECONDS OR LESS.

A sixty-second clock popped up at the bottom of the screen. And then a four-by-four Boggle jumble of letters:

L U I G
I L L E
M O N C
E L L O

"Luigi L. Lemoncello," mumbled Kyle.

The sixty-second clock started ticking down.

Sierra shouted out, "Lemon!" and a *ding* sounded from the speaker above. The five teammates started shouting out words:

"Cello!"

"Eon!"

"Elm!"

"Lion!"

"Mole!"

"Leg!"

"Oil!"

"Thirty seconds left," said Mr. Lemoncello.

"One!"

"Cell!"

"Cone!"

"Lone!"

"Glen!"

"Lime!"

"Eh, mole."

"We already said that."

"Melon."

"That's fifteen," said the voice in the ceiling.

"Um . . ."

"Ten seconds left."

"Anybody?"

"Five."

"Four."

"Colonel!" shouted Haley.

The computer screen flashed "Congratulations!" and "Winners!"

Somewhere, a game show audience cheered, fireworks rockets whistled through the air, and several geese honked out a "Hooray!"

"Please stand back," said the soothing voice in the ceiling.

Kyle and his teammates did as they were told.

"Warning," the voice continued. "This game will terminate in FIFTEEN minutes."

"We still need to get out, you guys!" said Akimi. "Hurry, floor. Do something!"

The eight tiles surrounding the glowing tablet also started to glow. First yellow, then orange, then purple.

"Our secret square," said Akimi.

There was a series of clicks, and the tiles began folding up on themselves and retracting into the floor, opening up like an origami trapdoor.

"Look," said Haley, "there's steps."

Mr. Lemoncello peered down into the hole at the well-lit staircase and tunnel. "My, my. Dr. Zinchenko has certainly cleaned things up since Mr. Loblolly was here."

"Of course she did," said Haley. "So we 'can walk out the way bandits crawled in in nineteen six-ate.' "

"Hurry, everybody!" said Mr. Lemoncello. "I don't want to be late to my own birthday party."

56

Kyle led the way up the tunnel and brought his team (plus Mr. Lemoncello) into an empty basement filled with mannequins and cardboard boxes.

"This must be the cellar of one of the clothing shops in Old Town," said Kyle.

"The Fitting Factory," said Haley, reading a tag on a shipping crate. "It's one of my faves."

"And," said Sierra, "back in 1968, it was the real dress factory that Leopold Loblolly and the Dandy Bandits used."

"There's some steps over here," said Miguel, climbing a wooden staircase. "And a door." He jiggled the knob. "Oh, man—it's locked."

Kyle looked up at the dingy casement windows, about ten feet above the cellar floor.

He couldn't help grinning.

It reminded him of another game he'd won once. This time, he'd just have to reverse things a little.

"Help me drag over a couple cartons," Kyle said to Miguel. "We can stack them on top of each other underneath this window."

After they built a step unit out of boxes, Kyle climbed up and examined the window latch.

"Great," he said.

"Don't tell me," said Akimi. "Another game?"

"Yep. There's a combination lock—the kind with four wheels of random letters."

"Warning," said the voice.

"What?" said Akimi. "Dr. Zinchenko put loudspeakers in this basement, too?"

"This game will terminate in FOUR minutes."

"Yo, open the lock, Kyle!" said Miguel.

"Hang on. It's some kind of word game."

"Is there a clue?" asked Haley.

"Of course." Kyle read the tiny slip of paper taped to the glass. " 'Once you learn how to do this, you will be forever free.' "

Everyone started laughing.

This last puzzle was ridiculously easy.

"Ready, children?" said Mr. Lemoncello. "All together now!"

And they all shouted it at the same time: "READ!"

Kyle thumbed the wheels to spell R-E-A-D. The lock clicked. The window opened.

And this time, he didn't need to shatter any glass to win the game.

Kyle and Mr. Lemoncello stood on top of the highest box and helped the others up and out of the basement.

When Haley crawled through the window frame, someone in the crowd that had gathered around the library for the game's big finale saw her and started screaming.

"Look! It's Haley Daley! She's the first one out. She won! With just two minutes to go!"

"Nuh-uh!" Kyle heard Haley shout in her perky cheer-leader voice. "I'm just one member of a super-amazing team. We're all winners. Whoo-hoo!"

When Akimi climbed through the window, the crowd chanted her name.

"How do you people know my name?" Kyle heard her say. "Dad? Did you tell them?"

Sierra Russell was set to crawl out next.

"Mr. Lemoncello?"

"Yes, Sierra?"

"What time does the library open tomorrow?"

"For you, Sierra, nine a.m.!"

Smiling, she stepped into their hands and climbed out the window.

Kyle felt bad when Sierra stood up on the sidewalk. Who was out there to cheer for her?

But then he heard Haley shout, "Hey, you guys. You gotta meet our amazing new friend, Sierra Russell! She's so smart, she could tell you who wrote the phone book!"

The crowd went crazy. "Sierra! Sierra! Sierra!"

"Okay," said Kyle, "you're next, Miguel."

"And, Miguel," said Mr. Lemoncello, "if your summer schedule permits it, I'd love for you to head up my team of Lemoncello Library Aides."

"Thank you, sir. It'd be an honor."

"And please invite Mr. Peckleman to join you."

"But Andrew thinks this library is stupid."

"All the more reason for him to spend time getting to know us a little better. Now, off you go!"

They gave Miguel a boost up and out the window.

The chanting outside grew even louder.

"Miguel! Miguel! Miguel!"

"You guys?" Miguel shouted. "This library is like a good book. You just gotta check it out!"

The crowd laughed. Kyle groaned.

"You're next, Mr. Keeley," said Mr. Lemoncello.

"Okay. Can I ask one last question?"

"Certainly. And I hope it won't be the last."

"Are you really going to put all of us in your television commercials?"

"Oh, yes. You'll be quite famous."

"Cool."

287

"Indeed. Who knew spending time in your local library could be such a rewarding experience?"

Kyle smiled. "You did, Mr. Lemoncello."

"And now you do, too."

Kyle put his foot in Mr. Lemoncello's hands and grabbed hold of the window frame.

"See you at the birthday party, sir!"

"Oh, yes. And you know what, Kyle?"

"What?"

"There might be balloons!"

AUTHOR'S NOTE

Is the game really over?

Maybe not.

There is one more puzzle in the book that wasn't in the story. (Although a clue about how to find it was!)

If you figure out the solution, let me know. Send an email to author@ChrisGrabenstein.com.

THANK YOU . . .

To R. Schuyler Hooke, my longtime editor at Random House, for his incredible patience, faith, and input on this project.

To designer Nicole de las Heras and artist Gilbert Ford, who made the book look so darn good.

To my wife, J. J. Myers, who is a terrific first editor.

To Ms. Macrina, librarian, and all the folks at P.S. 10 in Brooklyn, whose library gave me the initial inspiration for this story.

To Darrell Robertson, Gail Tobin, Amy Alessio, Erin Downey, Yanna Zinchenko, Scot Smith, and all the other librarians and media specialists I have met in my travels as an author, at public libraries and in schools. When I see how you inspire the love of reading on a daily basis, I realize you are much more amazing and incredible than Mr. Lemoncello.

CHRIS GRABENSTEIN

is the coauthor (with James Patterson) of the number one *New York Times* bestseller *I Funny*. He is also an award-winning author of books for children and adults, playwright, screenwriter, and former advertising executive and improvisational comedian. Chris was a writer for Jim Henson's Muppets and is a past president of the New York chapter of the Mystery Writers of America. He also cowrote the screenplay for the CBS TV movie *The Christmas Gift,* starring John Denver. He lives in New York City with his wife, three cats, and a rescue dog named Fred, who starred in *Chitty Chitty Bang Bang* on Broadway.

You can visit Chris (plus Fred and the cats) at ChrisGrabenstein.com. He also loves hearing from readers, so send your email to author@ChrisGrabenstein.com.

So Say the Fallen

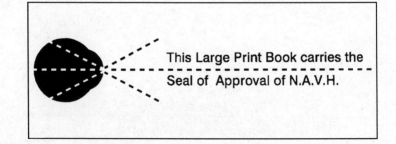

This Large Print Book carries the
Seal of Approval of N.A.V.H.

So Say the Fallen

Stuart Neville

THORNDIKE PRESS
A part of Gale, Cengage Learning

GALE
CENGAGE Learning·

Farmington Hills, Mich • San Francisco • New York • Waterville, Maine
Meriden, Conn • Mason, Ohio • Chicago

GALE
CENGAGE Learning®

LIBRARY OF CONGRESS CATALOGING-IN-PUBLICATION DATA

Names: Neville, Stuart, 1972– author.
Title: So say the fallen / by Stuart Neville.
Description: Large print edition. | Waterville, Maine : Thorndike Press, 2017. |
    Series: Thorndike Press large print Bill's bookshelf
Identifiers: LCCN 2016046290| ISBN 9781410497314 (hardcover) | ISBN 1410497313
    (hardcover)
Subjects: LCSH: Women detectives—Ireland—Fiction. |
    Murder—Investigation—Fiction. | Widows—Fiction. | Large type books. | GSAFD:
    Mystery fiction. | Suspense fiction.
Classification: LCC PR6114.E943 S67 2017 | DDC 823/.92—dc23
LC record available at https://lccn.loc.gov/2016046290

Published in 2017 by arrangement with Soho Press, Inc.

Printed in Mexico
1 2 3 4 5 6 7 21 20 19 18 17

For Jo, who has given me so much.

"I can't just live for the other world. I need to live in this one now. So say the fallen. So they've said since time began."

— Dennis Lehane, *The Drop*

1

Detective Chief Inspector Serena Flanagan
focused on the box of tissues that sat on the
coffee table between her and Dr. Brady. A
leaf of soft paper bursting up and out, ready
for her tears. Just like when she'd been
diagnosed with cancer. A box like this one
had sat close to hand on the desk. She
didn't need one then, and she didn't need
one now.

Dr. Brady had no interest in abnormal
cells, growths, tumours. Flanagan's mind
was his concern. He sat cross-legged in the
chair on the other side of the table, chewing
the end of a biro. It clicked and scratched
against his teeth, a persistent noise that trig-
gered memories of exam halls and waiting
rooms, and made Flanagan dig at her palms
with her nails.

The counsellor pursed his lips and inhaled
through his nose in a way that Flanagan
found even more irritating than the click-

scratch of the pen. Irritating because she knew it preceded another question that she had no desire to answer.

"Do you feel you owe anything to Colin Tandy's family?" he asked.

"No," Flanagan said. "Nothing."

"You're quite emphatic about that."

"He made his choice," she said. "He set out to kill me that morning. He failed. So I killed him."

Dr. Brady paused, his gaze fixed on hers, a small smile on his lips that might have appeared kindly to anyone but Flanagan.

"But you didn't kill him," he said. "You killed the other one, the gunman. Colin Tandy rode away on the motorbike. You had nothing to do with him winding up under a bus."

Flanagan saw herself outside the small terraced house on the outskirts of Lisburn where she'd taken a statement from an assault victim. She remembered the street, the graffiti painted white on red brick. She saw the bike, the two men, the semiautomatic pistol aimed at her, felt the Glock 17's grip in her hand. Something hot splitting the air close to her ear. Then the pillion passenger's helmet cracked open, the jammed pistol useless in his hand. She felt the empty cartridge, sent spinning from the chamber of the Glock, bounce off her cheek. In her mind she heard the brass hit the pavement, a sound like a Christmas bauble falling from the tree, but she knew she couldn't possibly have heard it over the noise of the traffic and the screaming.

She saw the passenger — Peter Hanratty, she later learned — lean back on the motorcycle's pillion seat. Then she put one in his chest. This time the cartridge spun into her hair before falling away, falling like the passenger — except he didn't. His torso hung over the motorcycle's back wheel, his arms suspended at his sides, feet caught on the rests.

Flanagan moved her aim to the rider, saw the fear in his eyes as she aligned the forward and rear sights of her pistol.

Not armed.

The thought pushed through the terrible stillness of her mind. She couldn't shoot him. He wasn't armed. But still she kept pressure on the trigger; a fraction more and the next round would discharge, sending the bullet through the visor of his helmet to pierce him somewhere between his left eye and the bridge of his nose.

They stayed there, both of them, frozen for a second that felt like a day. He knew he was going to die. She knew she was going

11

to kill him.

But she couldn't. He wasn't armed.

Flanagan eased her finger from the trigger, released the pressure. He saw the movement of her knuckle, and the bike launched away, spilling the dead passenger to the ground.

She wouldn't find out until later that bike and rider wound up under a bus only two streets away.

Tandy didn't die. Not then. He lived on, if it could be called living, for another five years before what remained of him slipped away. Detective Superintendent Purdy had told her in the canteen at Lisburn station during lunch a few weeks ago. Perhaps he could have chosen a better time and place, but how was he to know? Flanagan herself wouldn't have dreamed the news would tear her in two.

She broke down there in the canteen, in front of everybody — constables, sergeants, inspectors, detectives, cooks, cleaners. They all saw her collapse, levelled by a desperate grief for a man that deserved none from her.

Six sessions she'd had, now. At the end of the first, as Dr. Brady glanced once again at the clock on the wall behind Flanagan, he told her what she'd already figured out for herself: every possible emotion she had about that morning more than five years ago had been wrapped up, tied down, stowed away while Tandy lived the non-life he had condemned himself to. Only when his body followed his brain into death did the memory rupture and every distorted feeling spill out where she could no longer deny it. Guilt at the men's deaths, fear at almost meeting her own, elation at surviving, sorrow for their families. These things had grown there in the dark, swelling and bloating like the rogue cells in her breast, until the whole of it flooded her at once, drowning her, more emotion than she could hold within.

Flanagan didn't remember much about the incident now, the initial breakdown, only how frightened DSI Purdy had looked, the shock on his face. Looking back now, weeks later, it seemed as if she had watched herself from across the room, seeing some other woman splinter into jagged pieces. And if she could, she would have told that woman to pull herself together, not to make a spectacle of herself.

A week of leave and three months of counselling had been prescribed. As if that would fix everything, as if this smug doctor could plaster over the fissures in Flanagan's mind by simply talking about the incident.

She and Alistair used the unexpected break to book a last-minute holiday in Portstewart on the north coast. An apartment near the old golf course, overlooking the sea. It was a good week. Days spent at the Strand, the long sandy beach at the other end of the town, even if the weather didn't justify it. They ate at the new restaurant between the dunes, a converted National Trust building, little more than a shack on the beach. Glorious breakfasts and lunches devoured before returning to the sand and the water.

Almost a week of peace, as near to happiness as they'd come in the last year.

One night, as sea spray whispered on the bedroom window, they talked about the proposed counselling. "What harm could it do?" Alistair asked.

More than you can imagine, Flanagan had thought. But she said, "All right, I'll give it a go."

And Alistair had put his arms around her and they had made love for the first time in months. He had no nightmares that night, had barely any during the week by the sea. But after, when they returned to their house outside Moira, the terrors came back. There had been little intimacy between Flanagan

14

and her husband since.

"Time," Dr. Brady said, smiling that fake smile of his.

Flanagan looked over her shoulder and saw that the session was done. She quietly thanked God and left the room with the most cursory farewell she could get away with.

2

Roberta Garrick walked him along the hall to the rear sitting room of her beautiful house. The room that had been converted to a hospital ward. Reverend Peter McKay followed her, feeling as if she dragged him by a piece of string. Conflicting desires battled within him: the desire for her body, the fear of the room beyond, the need to run. But he walked on regardless, as much by Roberta's volition as by his own.

Mrs. Garrick. After all that had happened, he had only recently stopped thinking of her by that name. Even when he had bitten her neck at the force of his climax, her thighs tight around his waist, she had still been Mrs. Garrick to him. She was Roberta now, and the intimacy of using her first name frightened him.

She stopped at the door, snug in its frame, and took the handle in her palm. For the hundredth time, McKay noted the length of her fingers, the smooth near-perfection of her skin, the nails just long enough to scratch. She turned the handle and pushed the door.

Her husband, still Mr. Garrick to him in spite of all the hours McKay had spent at this bedside, lay where he'd left him last night. But dead now. Even from the doorway, from the other side of the room, it was obvious a corpse lay there. McKay imagined if he touched Mr. Garrick's forearm the skin would be cold against his fingertips. Like a side of meat.

Bile lurched up into McKay's throat at the thought, and he swallowed it. Now was not the time to be squeamish. He had been a rector for two decades, presided over more funerals than he could remember, seen hundreds of cadavers lying in a waxy illusion of sleep. This was no different.

Keep hold of yourself, he thought. Whatever happens, keep hold of yourself.

Roberta took slow, measured steps from the threshold to her husband's side. McKay followed, keeping back from the bedside. What had once been a spacious sitting room was now cramped, with a wardrobe and a chest of drawers, a bedside table, a television on the wall and, facing that, the electric care bed.

17

A care bed. Not a hospital bed. Mr. Garrick had been quite clear about the distinction, though McKay could see little difference between this and the beds that populated every hospital ward he'd ever visited. Cost thousands, Mr. Garrick had said. It lay positioned so that he could see through the patio doors, out onto the beautifully tended garden and the trees beyond. Now the curtains were drawn, and the sun would never shine on Henry Garrick again.

McKay put a hand on Roberta's firm, still shoulder and felt the warmth of her through the fabric of her light dressing gown. Warm skin, not cold, like her husband's would surely be. McKay swallowed bile once more. He squeezed gently, but if she felt the tightening of his fingers she did not let it show.

Her husband lay like a man in sound sleep, his mouth open, his eyes closed. A snore should have rattled out of him.

What devastation, McKay thought. How Mr. Garrick had lived this long was mystery enough. A little less than six months ago he had been driving his favourite car, an early seventies Aston Martin V8 Vantage, through the country lanes that surrounded the village. The investigators had estimated his

18

speed at the time of the accident as approximately fifty-five miles per hour. Charging around the bend, he had managed to swerve past all but one of the cluster of cyclists he had come upon. One of them, a young father of two, had died within moments of being struck, his helmet doing him little good against the force of the impact with the Aston's bonnet.

Mr. Garrick had not been so lucky. As the car swerved then spun, it swept through a hedgerow before barrel-rolling across a ditch and into a tree. The car's front end buckled, forcing the engine back into the cabin, taking Mr. Garrick's legs.

The fire had started soon after. The cyclists who had such a narrow escape did all they could, one of them suffering severe burns as he dragged what remained of Mr. Garrick from the wreck. Another was a nurse, well experienced in trauma surgery. They kept him alive, whether or not it was a merciful act.

Regardless, now he lay dead, drool crusting on his scarred chin. Pale pink yogurt clinging to the wispy strands of his moustache. The same yogurt his nightly sachet of morphine granules was mixed with. Ten empty sachets lay scattered on the table over his bed, behind the row of framed photo-

19

graphs. One of Mr. Garrick's parents, long gone, one of him and Roberta on their wedding day, another of his wife, tanned and glowing, smiling up from a beach towel. Then finally a small oval picture of Erin, the child they had lost before her second birthday.

Reverend Peter McKay had presided over that funeral too. One of the hardest he'd ever done. Grief so raw it had charged the air in the church, made it thick and heavy. McKay had heard every sob trapped inside the walls, felt each one as if it had been torn from his own chest.

Roberta reached out to the picture of the smiling child, touched her fingertips to the face. McKay moved his hand from her shoulder, down her arm, until his fingers circled her slender wrist.

"It's maybe best you don't touch anything," he said. "For when the police come."

Then Roberta's legs buckled and she collapsed to her knees beside the bed. She reached for her husband's still hand, buried her face in the blanket, close to where his legs should have been. McKay watched as her shoulders juddered, listened as her keening was smothered by the bedclothes. The display of grief quietly horrified him, even though his rational mind knew hers was a natural and inevitable reaction. But his irrational mind, that wild part of him, clamoured, asking, what about me? What about me? What about us?

McKay kept his silence for a time before touching her shoulder once more and saying, "I'll make the phone calls."

He left her to her wailing and exited into the hall.

Such a grand place. Mr. Garrick had built it for his new wife when they first married seven years ago. Six bedrooms, half of them with bathrooms, three receptions, a large garage that held Mr. Garrick's modest collection of classic cars. An acre of sweeping lawns and flower beds. Enough money to pay for a gardener and cleaner to look after it all.

They should have had a long and happy life together. But that was not God's will, Mr. Garrick had once said after he and Reverend McKay had prayed together.

God had no part in it, McKay had almost said. But he held his tongue.

McKay seldom thought of God any more, unless he was writing a sermon or taking a service. Reverend Peter McKay had ceased to believe in God some months ago. Everything since had been play-acting, as much out of pity for the parishioners as a desire

21

to keep his job.

No God. No sin. No heaven. No hell.

Reverend Peter McKay knew these things as certainly as he knew his own name.

He went to the telephone on the hall table, picked up the handset, and dialled.

3

Flanagan stood at the kitchen sink, a mug of coffee in one hand, looking out over the garden. Rain dotted the window, a lacklustre shower that had darkened the sky as she watched. Behind her, Alistair sat at the table with Ruth and Eli, telling them to eat their breakfast, they'd be late. Flanagan had showered and dressed an hour ago; she had her holster attached to her belt, the Glock 17 snug inside, hidden beneath her jacket, her bag packed and ready for the day. Still half an hour before she needed to go.

Mornings had been like this for months now. She rising early, still tired, her night's sleep fractured by Alistair's gasping and clutching. A year had passed since the Devine brothers had invaded their home, since one of them had plunged a blade into her husband's flank. A year since she had pressed wadded-up bedding against the wound, begging him not to die.

He blamed her. She brought this upon their family. He hadn't said so after that first night in the hospital, but she was certain he still believed it. Once, he had asked her to think about getting out of the force. Or at least leaving the front line, taking an admin role. Her reaction had been angry enough that he had never asked again.

Last night had been bad. Flanagan had lain silent, pretending to sleep as Alistair wept in the darkness. Choked, frightened sobs. Eventually, he had got up and left the room. She had heard the faint babble of the television from downstairs. At some point she had fallen asleep, only to be disturbed by the bed rocking as he got back in. He lay with his back to her. She rolled over and brought her body to his, her chest against his shoulders. He stiffened as she reached over and her hand sought his.

"You don't have to," he said, his voice shocking her in the quiet.

"Have to what?" she asked.

"Pretend," he said. "With the children, maybe. But not with me."

"I don't . . ."

Words hung beyond the reach of her tongue. Anger rose in her, but the root of his bitterness remained so veiled that she could form no argument against it. Instead, she rolled over and crept to her cold edge of the bed. She did not sleep again, rose with the sun, and set about preparing for another weary day.

So now she stood apart from them, as she did more often every day. Her husband and children at the table, she at the window, no longer even trying to make conversation with her family. An intruder in her own home, just as those boys had been.

Alistair's voice cracked her isolation. She turned her head and said, "What?"

"Your phone," he said, a tired sigh carrying the words.

Her mobile vibrated on the table, the screen lighting up.

She crossed from the sink and lifted it. Detective Superintendent Purdy, the display said.

Purdy had only a fortnight left on the job, retirement bearing down on him like a tidal wave. He had confided in Flanagan that although it had seemed like a good idea a year ago when he'd first started making plans, the reality of it, the long smear of years ahead, now terrified him.

Flanagan thumbed the touchscreen. "Yes?"

"Ah, good," Purdy said. "I wanted to catch you before you left for the station.

25

There's been a sudden death in Morganstown. The sergeant at the scene reckons suicide, so —"

"So you thought of me," Flanagan said. "Thanks a million."

Flanagan hated suicides. In most cases, the minimum of investigation was needed, but the family would be devastated. Few grieve harder than the loved ones of someone who has taken their own life. They'd be coming at her with questions she could never answer.

"You're closer to Morganstown than you are to Lisburn," Purdy said, "so you can go straight there."

"I'll leave now," she said.

"Take your time. From what the sergeant said, it looks pretty straightforward. You remember that road accident about six months ago? The car dealer?"

Yes, Flanagan remembered. The owner of Garrick Motors, a large used car dealership that occupied a sprawling site on the far side of Morganstown. He had been badly burned, lost both of his legs, if Flanagan recalled correctly. A popular churchgoing couple, good Christians both. Close friends with one of the local unionist politicians. The community had rallied around them. After all, Mr. Garrick had contributed much to the area over the years.

"The wife found him this morning," Purdy continued. "She phoned the minister at her church first. He went to the house, then he called it in. The FMO's on scene already."

Flanagan knew the steps by heart. When a sudden death was reported, a sergeant had to attend to make an initial assessment. Was it natural? Had the deceased been ill? Was it suspicious? If the latter, including a suicide, the scene would be locked down, the Forensic Medical Officer summoned, and an Investigating Officer appointed.

Today, it was Flanagan's turn.

"What's the address?" she asked, pulling the notebook from her bag. She held the phone between her ear and shoulder as she uncapped the pen and scribbled it down.

Alistair looked up at her from his plate of buttered toast. Ruth and Eli kicked each other under the table, giggling.

"I can be there in ten minutes." Flanagan stuffed the notebook back into her bag, then hoisted the bag over her shoulder. "I'll call DS Murray on the way."

She was halfway to Morganstown, trees whipping past her Volkswagen Golf, when she realised she hadn't said goodbye to her husband or children.

■ ■ ■ ■

A uniformed constable opened the door to
Flanagan. A beautiful house, inside and out,
at the end of a sweeping drive. Not long
built, by the look of it, and finished with
enough taste to prevent its grandeur stray-
ing into vulgarity.

"Ma'am," the constable said when Flanagan showed her warrant card. "In the back."

He looked pale. Flanagan wondered if it
was his first sudden death. At least the next
of kin had found the body, and the constable
had been spared delivering the death notice.
Flanagan remembered the first time she'd
been given that duty, calling at the home of
a middle-aged couple whose son had lost
control of his new car. Everyone has to do
it some time, the senior officer had said,
might as well get it out of the way. Even
thinking about it now soured Flanagan's
stomach, and she had done dozens more
since then.

She stepped into the hall, past the young
officer. "Where's the sergeant?" she asked.

Wooden floors. A staircase with polished
banisters rose up to a gallery on the first
floor, cutting the hallway in two. Art on the
walls, mostly originals, a few prints. Framed

28

scripture verses. A large bible ostentatiously open on the hall table.

Serious money, here, Flanagan thought. So much money there was no need for another penny, but still you couldn't help but make more. And yet it didn't save Mr. Garrick in the end.

"In the living room," the constable said, "with the deceased's wife."

Flanagan looked to her right, through open double doors into a large living room. A stone fireplace built to look centuries old. No television in this room, but a top end hi-fi separates system was stacked in a cabinet, high quality speakers at either end of the far wall. A suite of luxurious couches and armchairs at the centre, all arranged to face each other. The widow, Mrs. Garrick, red-eyed and slack-faced sitting with a man whom Flanagan assumed to be the clergyman, even though he wore no collar. Her hands were clasped in his. The other uniformed officer sat opposite them: a female sergeant she recognised but whose name Flanagan could not recall.

She got up from the couch, and said, "Ma'am." She carried a clipboard, held it out to Flanagan.

"Are you my Log Officer?" Flanagan asked, keeping her voice respectfully low.

"Yes, ma'am."

"Have you done this before, Sergeant
. . . ?"

"Carson," the sergeant said. "A few times.
I know the drill."

"Good," Flanagan said, taking the offered
pen. She saw Dr. Phelan Barr's signature
already scrawled on the 38/15 form. She
signed beneath and handed the pen back.
"DS Murray's on the way. When he arrives,
send him back, and I'll come and speak with
Mrs. Garrick. Then I want you on the door
to the room, understood?"

"Yes, ma'am."

"Is there a clear path from the door to the
body?"

"Yes, ma'am."

"Okay, make sure anyone you let in knows
to stick to that."

Flanagan looked over Sergeant Carson's
shoulder to see Mrs. Garrick and the rector
watching from their place on the opposite
couch. Flanagan nodded to them each in
turn. "I'll be with you in a few minutes,"
she said.

She walked along the hallway to the right
of the staircase. On the other side, she saw
the dining room with its twelve-seater table,
and the kitchen, all white gloss and black
granite. And here what had once been

another reception room but now was a makeshift care unit.

The Forensic Medical Officer, Dr. Barr, stood over the corpse, writing on a notepad. Flanagan looked from him to the bed and the scarred ruin of a man beneath the sheets. She let a little air out of her lungs as she always did at the sight of a body. A tic she had borrowed from DSI Purdy.

Barr heard and turned to her. A small man in his late fifties who always managed to look dishevelled no matter how smartly he dressed. He was known to have a drink problem, had lost his marriage over it, yet Flanagan had never so much as caught a whiff of it on him, he kept it so well hidden.

"Ah, DCI Flanagan," Barr said. "Never a pleasure."

"Likewise," Flanagan said.

A small joke they always shared over a body. Neither of them enjoyed the company of the dead, but it was when they most frequently met. Flanagan took a step inside the room, smelled the hospital smell, and the death.

"Well?" she asked.

"I'll call it suicide," Barr said, "unless something remarkable turns up. I expect the post-mortem to confirm an overdose of morphine granules." He waved his pen at

31

the wheeled overbed table that had been pushed aside, presumably to give Barr access to the body. "I count ten sachets of granules. One mixed in with a carton of yogurt would be enough to give him a good night's sleep. I expect he dumped the lot in and chewed them up. He just swallowed and went to sleep. Simple as that."

Flanagan saw the pot on the table, and the spoon in Mr. Garrick's hand. And the framed photographs lined up on the table. She couldn't see them from here, but she assumed they were of loved ones, living and dead. Hadn't she heard something about the couple losing a child? A wisp of a memory, a conversation overheard in the supermarket in Moira, did you hear about the Garricks? The wee girl drowned when they were on holiday, isn't it terrible?

Tragedy clustered around some families. Most lived their lives untouched by the kind of sorrow that plagued a few. One child lost, then another years later. Or illness of one kind or another taking a mother while her children were tiny, then a sibling, an uncle, or a cousin. Some families drew such misfortune to them like the pull of gravity.

Flanagan went to ask a question, but something stopped the words on her tongue. She looked again at the table pushed close

32

to the patio door, one end pressed into the drawn curtain.

"What?" Barr asked, shaking her loose from her thoughts.

"Nothing," she said. "Any note?"

"No," Barr said, "but I don't think we need to wonder too hard about his motivation."

Flanagan could not begin to imagine what the last six months had been like for this man, or for his wife. What kind of life could this be? Then she scolded herself. She knew plenty of police officers left mutilated by bombs who had fought back, fought hard, and made new lives for themselves. Painful lives, maybe, but meaningful nonetheless.

From the doorway, a voice said, "Ma'am."

Detective Sergeant Craig Murray, still nervous around her despite being her right-hand man for almost nine months. He had worked out well so far. Conscientious, reliable, smart enough to know when to shut his mouth. She'd keep him as long as she could. Good assistants were hard to come by; her last, DS Ballantine, hadn't worked out, even as capable as the young woman had been. The trust between them had broken down — it couldn't have done otherwise — and without trust, the relationship would not work. Ballantine would be all right. Flanagan wouldn't be surprised if she made Detective Inspector within the next few years.

"What do you need me to do?" Murray asked.

"Stay here," Flanagan said. "Help Dr. Barr with anything he needs. I'll be speaking with Mrs. Garrick."

She left them, walked along the hall to the double doors leading into the living room. Flanagan paused there and watched.

Mrs. Garrick and the rector, hands still clasped together, staring at some far-off memory. Each looked as battered as the other, as if the rector grieved as hard as the widow. The policewoman noticed Flanagan, stood, and said, "Ma'am."

Flanagan entered the room and said, "Thank you, Sergeant Carson, I can take it from here. You know what to do."

Carson left them, and Flanagan walked to the centre of the room, stood in front of the minister and the widow. "Mrs. Garrick," she said, "I'm very sorry for your loss. I'm Detective Chief Inspector Serena Flanagan. Can we have a quick chat?"

The minister stood, releasing Mrs. Garrick's hand, and reached for Flanagan's. A small and slender man, narrow-shouldered, salt-and-pepper hair, a neatness about him

34

that bordered on prissy. As they shook, he said, "I'm Peter McKay, the rector at St. Mark's. Do you have to do this now, or could it wait for another time?"

"It's usually best to have an initial conversation as soon as possible," Flanagan said. "Mrs. Garrick isn't obliged to talk to me, of course, but the sooner we get it out of the way, the better."

McKay looked down at Mrs. Garrick, who remained seated, worrying a tissue between her fingers. She still wore her silk dressing gown over her nightdress, red hair spilling across her shoulders. A good-looking woman, mid thirties. If not beautiful, then at least the kind to make men look twice. The kind teenage boys whispered to each other about, tinder for their adolescent fires.

"It's all right," Mrs. Garrick said, her voice firm despite the tears. "Let's get it out of the way."

"Thank you," Flanagan said, sitting on the couch opposite. "I'll be as quick as I can."

McKay took his place once more beside Mrs. Garrick, slipped his fingers between hers. He squeezed, Flanagan noticed, but Mrs. Garrick did not return the gesture. Flanagan took her notepad and pen from her bag, readied them.

"Mrs. Garrick," she said, "can you please tell me, as simply as you can, what happened last night and this morning."

Mrs. Garrick took a breath, held it as she closed her eyes, then exhaled. Her eyelids fluttered, releasing another tear from each. She wiped at her cheeks, sniffed, and then spoke.

"Everything was normal," she said. "Or as normal as it can be, I suppose. I made dinner for us both, cottage pie, easy for Harry to eat with a spoon, you see. I ate with him, with the tray on my lap. We do that every evening. Then Harry always has his yogurt for dessert. That's what he mixes the morphine granules with."

"You didn't do that for him?" Flanagan asked.

"No. I did at first, but Harry insisted on doing it for himself a few days after he came home from the hospital. He hates being waited on. He wants to do as much for himself as he can, whether he's fit to or not." Mrs. Garrick's eyes went distant for a moment. "He wanted to, I should say. Everything's past tense now. It'll take a while to get used to that, like when —"

She froze there, mouth open, words that would never leave her tongue. Flanagan remembered the photograph of the child

36

and kept her silence.

After a while, Mrs. Garrick blinked, inhaled, and continued.

"We kept the box of little morphine packets by the bed, where he could reach them. One sachet to get him through the night. The doctor told us he's not to chew the granules. They're supposed to be swallowed whole so they dissolve in his stomach as he sleeps. Best way to take them is to mix a packet with yogurt and just eat it with a spoon. So he ate his dinner as normal, then I helped him do his toilet. Then the doorbell rang, and it was Reverend Peter."

The rector spoke up. "I sometimes call by to see Mr. Garrick. Just to chat, see how he's doing. We pray together."

"I gave Peter the yogurt to take to Harry," Mrs. Garrick said.

"He didn't eat it, though. He said he'd keep it for later."

Mrs. Garrick turned to McKay. "You were with him for, what, half an hour?"

"Something like that."

"You didn't look in on him after Reverend McKay had left?" Flanagan asked.

"Reverend Peter," McKay said. "Or Reverend Mr. McKay. But not . . ."

The rector's voice faded as his gaze dropped, his cheeks reddening.

Mrs. Garrick cleared her throat and said, "Just to kiss him goodnight. The yogurt was still there, and I told him to eat it up and get some sleep. I didn't go in after that. Some nights I do, some I don't. Depends how tired I am. I just cleared up, did the dishes, and went to bed myself."

"And this morning?"

"I woke up before five, before the alarm went off. I usually wake Harry around six-thirty, and I like to have an hour or so to myself. When it's quiet."

"I know the feeling," Flanagan said, offering Mrs. Garrick a hint of a smile.

"Anyway, this morning, I don't know why, but I decided to look in on him earlier than usual. Funny, that, isn't it? This morning of all mornings. I went to his door and I knew straight away something was wrong. He always snores when he's on the morphine. You can hear him on the other side of the house."

Mrs. Garrick's eyes brightened. "Maybe that's why I went in to him, do you think? Maybe I wasn't conscious of it, but I didn't hear him snoring when I came downstairs, so that's why I went to his room. Is that why?"

She looked to Flanagan for an answer, as if being right would make everything better.

"Possibly," Flanagan said, giving another kind smile.

This time, Mrs. Garrick returned the gesture, but only for a moment before the smile fell away. "So I opened the door," she said, "and I just knew. He hadn't turned his light off, the one by the bed. He was just lying there, all quiet and still, and I knew he was dead. My first thought was his heart, it'd just given up. Then I saw he'd moved the pictures from the bedside table, put them in front of him, and I wondered why he did that. And then I saw the spoon, and the box of sachets beside him on the bedclothes. So I knew then what he'd done."

"But you didn't call an ambulance or the police," Flanagan said.

"No," Mrs. Garrick said, now squeezing McKay's fingers between hers. "Maybe I should have, but I suppose I wasn't thinking straight. Peter's been with us since the accident, every step of the way — before that, even. He's always been such a rock for us. Him and the Lord Jesus. So Peter was the first person I thought of."

The rector spoke up. "I came over as soon as Mrs. Garrick called. And when I saw Mr. Garrick, I called the emergency services."

"Then we came in here and prayed," Mrs. Garrick said.

Flanagan pictured them both, kneeling, eyes closed, mouths moving, talking to nothing but air. Stop it, she told herself. They need their belief now. Don't belittle it.

"How about Mr. Garrick's mood in recent days?" she asked. "Had you noticed any change?"

"No," Mrs. Garrick said. "His mood was up and down, it has been — had been — since the accident. Good days and bad days, like you'd expect. But he always had God with him. He always clung to that. Didn't he, Peter?"

McKay nodded. "Harry always said God must have let him live for a reason. He wouldn't leave him to suffer like that if there wasn't a purpose behind it."

"And what did you say?" Flanagan asked. The question rang more curtly than she'd intended and the clergyman flinched a little, before his expression hardened.

"I agreed," he said. "I could never say otherwise. It's what I believe."

"Of course," Flanagan said. "But what changed?"

McKay's shoulders slumped. "Who knows? Sometimes faith isn't enough, I suppose, no matter how much I'd like it to be. Sometimes faith lets us down."

Flanagan saw something in his eyes in the

40

moment before he looked away. An image flashed in her mind: a man falling. The image lingered long after her questions were done.

4

When it came to matters of faith, Reverend Peter McKay had lied so long and so often that he sometimes couldn't tell the difference himself. And no matter what he believed, or rather didn't, Mr. Garrick had survived this long purely on the certainty that there was some greater reason for his agonised existence. McKay would never have told him otherwise.

This policewoman terrified him.

He wore his mask with such practised skill, he didn't think she could see through it, but still, the fear swamped him like cold water. She can't see, he told himself. She is blind to my sin.

If she knew what he had done, if she knew where his hands had been, what wicked sweetness he had tasted, her questions would not be so cordial. Her tone would not be so sympathetic.

"I think that's all for now," she said. What

42

did she say her name was? Flanagan, wasn't it? Yes, Flanagan. "I will have more questions for you both once the coroner's report is done. And I'll need to get formal statements, but there's no immediate rush."

She leaned forward, spoke softy.

"Mrs. Garrick, there are things we need to do here. For your husband. Things you might not want to see. Things you might not want to hear. Is there somewhere you can go, maybe? Just for the next few hours?"

"My house," McKay said. Perhaps too quick, too eager. As he watched Flanagan's face for a sign that she'd noticed, Roberta twitched her fingertips against his palm.

A warning. Careful. She'll know.

She'll know the things we did together.

But Flanagan's expression did not change from one of warm sympathy.

"That sounds like a good idea," she said. "And I'll know where to reach you if I need to. If that's all right with you, Mrs. Garrick?"

Roberta hesitated, then nodded, and said, "Of course."

"Good," Flanagan said. "Perhaps you want to go to him. We can give you a few minutes alone, if you like. I'd just ask you not to touch anything."

"Yes," Roberta said. "Please."

She stood, and Flanagan and McKay did the same.

Flanagan took Roberta's hands in hers, saying, "And once again, I'm truly sorry for your loss."

McKay went to follow Roberta, but she turned, put a hand to his forearm, telling him, no, just me. Alone. He watched her leave, a feeling he could not identify biting at the edge of his consciousness.

"St. Mark's, you said?"

Startled, he turned back to Flanagan. "Yes," he said. "Morganstown. At the end of the main street."

"I know it," she said, scribbling on her pad. "I think I've been to a couple of funerals there. You probably conducted the ceremonies."

"Probably," he said, walking away, towards the doorway. He stopped there, one hand against the frame. He watched the medical officer leave the rear room, stand respectfully outside it with his hands folded in front of him, next to the sergeant with her clipboard. Beyond them, Roberta, standing over her dead husband.

Don't weep, McKay thought. Don't weep. At least give me that.

But she wept, and for a moment so fleet-

44

ing he couldn't be sure it had ever been at all, he hated her.

5

The photographer had finished his work long ago. Now the coroner-appointed undertakers wheeled the trolley into the room, the black body bag upon it open and ready to receive Mr. Garrick. The empty morphine sachets, the yogurt pot, the spoon, had all been bagged up and taken away.

The undertakers rolled back the bedclothes, exposing what remained of the lower portion of Mr. Garrick's body. One of the undertakers, a young man showing his inexperience, hissed through his teeth. A buttoned pyjama top covered Mr. Garrick's torso, an adult nappy enclosed his groin. And the stumps of his legs beneath. Still wrapped in bandage and gauze, still stained brown and yellow with serous fluid. He rested on a layer of medical absorption pads, the kind Flanagan remembered from having her children, one of the indignities of childbirth no one mentions in polite conversation.

"Can't blame him, really, can you?"

The same undertaker who'd hissed a moment before. Flanagan looked up at him, but did not reply. He couldn't hold her gaze, though she hadn't meant it as a challenge. But what he'd said . . .

Can't blame him.

Blame him for what?

The older man said, "I apologise for my colleague."

The younger man's face flushed red as he whispered an apology of his own.

They counted off, then hoisted the corpse onto the trolley. They folded the body bag around Mr. Garrick and zipped it closed, an ugly sound in this quiet room, then wheeled the trolley out to the hall. Dr. Barr entered as they left.

"You still here?" Flanagan asked.

"I was going to ask you the same thing," he said, walking to the patio doors. "Are you going to close the scene now?"

"I suppose so," she said. "Everything useful has been packed up. DS Murray's gathering up any other medication in the house. I don't think there's anything more to do here, do you?"

Barr shook his head and pulled aside the curtain, showing the room in natural light

47

for the first time since Flanagan had arrived. Flanagan moved the table back towards the bed, gave him room. As she did so, one of the framed photographs toppled forwards, almost fell to the floor, but Flanagan caught it. She put it back in its place, a picture of a child, in the row of loved ones who'd kept watch over Mr. Garrick's last peaceful breaths.

Except they hadn't.

A strange thought. Flanagan tried to connect it to whatever had started to tug at her mind shortly after Mrs. Garrick and the minister had left. Like an itch she couldn't reach.

Barr said something, but Flanagan didn't hear.

The photographs.

She studied them, one after the other. The itch deepened.

Barr spoke again. "I said, he'd have had a nice view from here."

Flanagan turned her head, followed his gaze. A well-kept garden, an expanse of healthy green lawn, an assortment of shrubs, a few rock and water features, all bordered by a small wood, leaves beginning to brown, late afternoon sunshine spearing through the branches.

"A nice view," Flanagan said, returning

her attention to the photos. "But not much of a life."

Dr. Barr buried his hands in his pockets. "It would have got better, though. He still had a lot of healing to do. A lot of pain to suffer. I spoke to his doctor earlier. Mr. Garrick had lost too much muscle tissue for it to be wrapped over the bone, so healing was slower than below-the-knee amputations. That and a couple of infections had made it an even harder road for him. But given time, he'd have got there. He could've been mobile again. He wasn't going to be locked in here forever."

"Then why did he do it?"

"With a journey that tough, that painful, maybe he couldn't see the end of it."

Flanagan hesitated, then asked: "Are you definitely citing suicide?"

Dr. Barr turned to her, his eyebrows drawing together. "I haven't seen anything here that suggests otherwise. Have you?"

"No," Flanagan said. "Not really. Just . . ."

"Just what?"

She indicated the photographs, put words to what had bothered her. "We've both attended suicides before. We've both seen something like this. The pictures of family. When people take that step, they often want to see their loved ones."

49

"Yes," Dr. Barr said. "And?"

"He couldn't see them," Flanagan said. "They were facing away from him. I didn't realise when I first came in, the way the table was sitting by the patio doors. But when I moved it back . . ."

Dr. Barr looked down at the table, from one framed photograph to the next, a frown on his lips. "Maybe he wanted them close, but he couldn't stand to see them. Or let them see what he was about to do. Who knows? When a person is about to take their own life, rationality doesn't come into it. Anyway, it's in the coroner's hands now. Hope not to see you again too soon."

"Likewise," Flanagan said as Dr. Barr exited.

Alone, now.

She stared at the table and the photographs for a few seconds longer before blinking and shaking her head, chasing the notion away. Another question she could never answer, one of a long list that spanned her career. This was a suicide, and no photograph would change it into something else.

Flanagan turned in a circle, surveying the place where Henry Garrick had spent the last miserable months of his existence. The bible on the nightstand to one side of the

50

bed, the selection of motoring magazines on the other. Above the bed, another framed verse of scripture, like those in the hall. Flanagan whispered the words.

Isaiah 41:10: Fear thou not; for I am with thee: be not dismayed; for I am thy God: I will strengthen thee; yea, I will help thee; yea, I will uphold thee with the right hand of my righteousness.

She stared at the verse, suddenly aware of the currents of air around her, warm and cool. The sound of other people in the house. Birdsong outside.

"Ma'am."

She stifled a gasp as she spun on her heel to see DS Murray in the doorway, a plastic bag full of medicines and pills hanging from his hand, Sergeant Carson behind him.

"Shit," she said, catching her breath.

"Sorry, ma'am," Murray said. "Is there anything more you need us to do? We're all kind of twiddling our thumbs here."

Flanagan walked to the doorway. "Close the scene, Sergeant Carson."

Carson scribbled on the scene log as she bit her lower lip in concentration, then handed the clipboard to Flanagan. With her signature, Flanagan authorised the closure.

"You did good work today," she said to Carson.

A faint bloom flushed on Carson's cheeks. "Thank you, ma'am."

As the sergeant walked away, Flanagan spoke to Murray. "I'll lock up here. Send the uniforms on their way, and you head back to Lisburn. Make a start on the paperwork. The FMO's going to report suicide, to be confirmed by the coroner. You know what to do."

"Yes, ma'am," Murray said. "Keys are on the hall table. Two sets, so I'm not sure Mrs. Garrick took hers with her."

"All right, I'll see to it. Get going."

Flanagan listened to their muted voices and the scuffing of their boots as they left, the front door closing, two engines igniting, tyres on driveway. Then silence, even the birds outside seeming to have hushed.

This rarely happened, that she was left alone at the scene. Normally, she would come and go from the site of a murder, the body lying *in situ* for as long as it took to explore every inch of its surroundings. But not today. This is simply a house of the bereaved, Flanagan thought, as if Henry Garrick had died of some illness on a hospital ward.

What, then, do we do for the dead?

It had been years since she or Alistair had lost a family member. Before the children, in fact, when Alistair's father had died. She remembered his going around their home, closing blinds, shutting out the light. She had wanted to open them again, saying no one would see their isolated house. But Alistair had insisted. It's what you do, he'd said. A mark of respect.

So now Flanagan went back to the patio doors and pulled across the curtain that Dr. Barr had opened. Then she walked from room to room, doing the same, the darkness deepening as each window was blotted out. She noted the objects, the artwork, the furniture, the ornaments, the electronics. Wealth she would never know in her lifetime. If the Garricks weren't millionaires, they must have been close.

Flanagan walked through the kitchen, again pulling down blinds, so the granite worktops changed from glistening sheets of black to dark pools. Through to the utility room, top of the range washing machine and tumble dryer amid more cupboards and a sink. A door leading to the rear of the property; she checked it was locked. Another door, open, a small bathroom. A third door, a key in the lock. She tried the handle, then turned the key, snick-click.

The door opened outward. A step down into a large dim garage. Flanagan felt around the door frame for a light switch, found it, and fluorescent tubes flickered into life.

Glistening metal from one side of the garage to the other. Space for five cars, but only four were lined up here. For a moment Flanagan wondered where the fifth could be. She hadn't seen anything other than the modest cars of the visitors when she pulled up, but then she remembered: the car Mr. Garrick had been driving when he crashed.

She looked at the rest, marvelling at the money invested in these machines. She recognised a Porsche 911 by its profile, and a vintage MG, and a Mercedes convertible, the long boxy kind she remembered seeing on television as a child. Closest of all, a Mini Cooper, no more than a year or two old. The far wall was lined with racks of alloy wheels and tyres, and a large red tool chest. All of it appeared too clean to have seen much use. The cleanliness of the cars, however, suggested Mrs. Garrick had continued to enjoy them, even if her husband could not.

Flanagan turned off the lights and locked the door behind her, leaving the key where she'd found it. Back through the kitchen, out to the hall and its wide central staircase. She climbed up to the gallery landing above. From up here, the hall looked all the more impressive. Facing the top of the stairs, a set of double doors. The master bedroom, Flanagan assumed. For no reason she could grasp, she went to the other rooms first, all blandly decorated spaces for guests, all neutral colours and beech veneers. Once all of them were darkened, Flanagan returned to the master bedroom and opened the double doors.

This room was not like the others. Her eyes were drawn first to the cherrywood four-poster bed and its silk canopy. Flanagan guessed it cost more than her car. Everywhere else, furniture that at least appeared to be antique. She stepped inside, felt the depth of the carpet underfoot. A scent of perfume hung in the air. On the dressing table beneath the window, a selection of bottles, Chanel, Dior, Yves Saint Laurent, and more that she guessed were too expensive to be familiar to her.

Flanagan looked to the other side of the room, and the two doors at either end of it. One stood ajar, showing the bathroom beyond. She guessed where the other led to, and opening it proved her right: a dressing room. A light flickered on automatically and she saw rows of dresses in cellophane shrouds, drawers of jewellery, racks of shoes. She lifted one of the dresses down from its rail, checked the label. Not only could Flanagan never afford such a thing, she'd also never fit into it. Not now, anyway.

Something turned inside her, a hard, ugly thing. An emotion she felt so rarely that it took a few moments to recognise it.

Envy.

I covet these things. I covet this life.

No you don't, Flanagan thought, as she felt a ridiculous blush heat her cheeks. She returned the dress to its rail, backed out of the dressing room, and closed the door. Why had she even entered? She had no business in there. What had begun as a courtesy to the dead man and his widow had turned into a sordid exploration. A familiar sense of intrusion crept into her, the same as she felt when she searched any victim's home, a house full of secrets revealed to a stranger. Except this time, she was indeed an intruder.

Time to go, she thought. She went to turn towards the window and its open blind, but something caught her attention on the wall. What? She let her eyes defocus and refocus until they found what had snagged her: a picture hook on the wall, centred over a tall chest of drawers. The dusty shadow of a frame that had once hung there.

Flanagan's gaze moved to the chest's top drawer, and the single brass knob at its front.

I have no reason to look in there, she thought.

"I have no reason," she said aloud.

Even so, she reached for the knob and pulled. The drawer slid open with no resistance. She took one step closer so she could better see inside. Bundles of papers, brown envelopes, a scattering of hairbands and clips.

And a large framed photograph of the child, perhaps a year old, held in masculine arms. Bright-eyed, smiling, two small teeth in the lower gum. A wisp of hair on her head.

Dead and gone, Flanagan thought. And I envied this life.

She pushed the drawer closed, held her fingertips against the wood as she pictured her own children, at school now. The Garrick child would have been close to six, a year younger than Eli. They might have been in the same playground, chasing and teasing each other.

The chime of the doorbell made her cry out.

6

Roberta hadn't spoken on the short drive to McKay's house. Her gaze had remained fixed ahead, her face cut from flint. When they arrived at St. Mark's and the adjoining rectory, she waited in the passenger seat for him to open the door. He had offered her his hand to help her out, but she ignored it, climbed out by herself. She walked to the door of the house where he had lived alone for a decade and stopped there, not looking back as he approached.

The house had been built at the same time as the church, a century and a half ago, from the sandstone quarried near Armagh. Like all rectories, it was large, with four bedrooms and three receptions. Had he and Maggie ever had children, then they might have made good use of the space. But there were no children, Maggie was ten years in her grave, and McKay couldn't remember the last time some of those rooms had been opened. Cold and damp, draughts slipped through every closed window and door. He sometimes imagined himself a ghost haunting the dark hallways.

The church grounds stood behind an iron fence at the south-western end of Morganstown's main street, the last buildings before the countryside. The Morgan family had paid for the building of the church in order to serve the community that earned its living in its linen mill. The mill had died with the linen industry, but the rows of redbrick two-bedroom houses remained, as did Morgan Demesne, the mansion seated in acres of woodland at the other end of the village, now owned by the National Trust.

These days, the village was mostly populated by young professionals who took advantage of easy access to the motorway that served Belfast, but few of them ever saw the inside of McKay's church. His congregation was drawn from the older generations who had stubbornly refused to be bought out of their homes, and the dozens of farms that sprawled across the surrounding countryside.

Main Street — in truth, Morganstown's only real street — stretched to just a few hundred yards, a filling station with a small shop at the north-eastern end. Clusters of modern houses, built during the property boom, branched away from Main Street, SUVs and executive sedans parked on their driveways. Apart from a handful of band parades every summer, it was as uneventful a place as could be imagined. Sometimes McKay enjoyed the peace here; sometimes the quiet made him want to scream.

He unlocked the door and stood aside to let Roberta enter. Still she did not speak, not even to thank him. He followed her into the hallway, watched as she paused at the bottom of the stairs, looked up, then back at him. Then she walked into his living room. He remained in the hall, looking at the stairs. No, not at them, but at the memory of them. That Sunday four months ago.

She had smiled at him from the second to last pew as all others around her bowed their heads in prayer. He had stood in the pulpit, his stare fixed on her as he recited the words, just shapes in his mouth, no meaning to them whatsoever.

Roberta sat there, glowing like an ember among the sad, grey, slack faces. Farmers, most of them, scrubbed-up for their weekly duty. Broad-backed wives, thick-fingered children. Boys who could drive tractors before the age of seven; girls who longed for the monthly socials and the chance to spin around in the arms of some pimply lad.

He'd been dreading this service, just as he dreaded every one. He felt certain they would see the sin on his face, know what he'd done. And they would point and hiss, and call him hypocrite, how dare he preach to them after he'd taken her into his bed, after his weakness had betrayed them all.

He watched as Roberta stood, sly and silent as a cat, and made her way to the door. She gave him a glance over her shoulder, her eyes meeting his, and he could not help but stumble over the prayer. The door closed silently, and a few seconds later, as he found his place again, he felt the cold wash of displaced air.

After the service, after he had shaken hands with the departing congregation, after he had listened and laughed and consoled and thanked, he let himself into his cold and lonely house. With a fluttering in his stomach, and a heavy heat beneath that, he went straight to the living room, knowing she waited for him.

But she did not.

"Not here," he said to himself. A mix of relief and disappointment flooded him. He let the air out of his lungs, feeling himself deflate.

McKay backed out of the room, intending to go upstairs to change. It wasn't until he put his right foot on the bottom step that he saw the pair of shoes there, two steps above. Two steps higher, her coat. Halfway up, her blouse, slung over the banister.

He swallowed and began to climb.

At the top of this flight, at the turn, her skirt. Then tights, underwear, leading to his bedroom, the door open for him like an eager mouth.

Roberta lay in his bed, the duvet pulled up to her chest, the flame of her hair lying across her bare shoulders. He knew he should tell her to get out, tell her this had gone far enough, tell her this madness had to end.

But she threw aside the duvet, offered herself to him, and he pulled the white collar from his black shirt and claimed the madness for his own.

Now, two hours after McKay had driven her away from her home and her dead husband, Roberta stood at the centre of his small living room, glowering where she had once glimmered. He had left her there earlier while he went to the kitchen, where he had remained until now, unable to face the question he needed to ask. He waited in the doorway to the living room, afraid to cross his own threshold. He cleared his throat. She turned her head to him, her eyes still red and brimming.

"What now?" he asked.

She stared at him, as if she expected him to answer his own question.

He cleared his throat again and said, "Maybe we should talk."

"About what?" she asked.

McKay opened his mouth and found no words there. He opened his arms, showed her his palms, tried to speak once more, but fear closed his lips.

Say it now, he thought. Say it now or say it never.

"About us."

Roberta held his gaze for a moment, then looked away. She said, "I'd like to be alone for a while. If you don't mind."

He wanted to protest, but tightened his jaw to trap the words in his throat. He brought his hands together, balled them into one fist, felt his nails dig at his palm. Somehow, he wrestled a smile onto his lips that at least felt kindly, even if it might have looked more like a grimace. Not that she could see it anyway. She stared at the fireplace, her arms folded across her breasts.

"All right," he said. "Of course. I'll be upstairs if you need me."

McKay closed the door behind him and climbed the stairs. No trail of clothes to follow now. No sweet insanity waiting for him in his bedroom. Only the cold loneliness that had slept with him for the last ten years. He sat on the edge of his bed, trying not to remember the scent of her there, how, every time she left, he had smelled her on the pillows and the sheets, how he had brought them to his face and breathed deep.

He covered his eyes with his hands, rested his elbows on his knees.

Now he recognised the feeling that had crept in on him as he had watched Roberta go to her husband's corpse: the sensation of the thing he desired slipping through his fingers.

"Dear God," he whispered. "Please don't take this from me. Not now. Please don't."

Then he remembered he didn't believe, hadn't believed in months, and he despaired.

7

Flanagan went to the bedroom threshold, saw the front door open and a slender middle-aged woman enter. She carried a large tote bag strapped over her shoulder.

"Hello?" the woman called as she closed the door behind her. Unbidden, she walked towards the rear of the hall, out of Flanagan's view. Flanagan descended the stairs.

"Hello? Mr. Garrick, where . . . what's . . ."

Flanagan saw the woman standing in the doorway to the dead man's room, her bag hanging from her hand. She wore a nurse's tunic and trousers, and the kind of plain black shoes favoured by someone who spends the day on their feet.

"Please don't go in there," Flanagan said.

The woman gasped and spun around. "Jesus!" She put her free hand to her heart. "You scared the life out of me. What's going on? Where's Mr. Garrick? Who are you?"

Flanagan took her wallet from her jacket pocket and showed the woman her warrant card as she approached. "I'm Detective Chief Inspector Serena Flanagan. Mr. Garrick is dead."

The woman dropped her bag. "What? No. How?"

"We believe suicide. I was just locking up when you came in. And you are?"

"Thelma Stinson. I'm a nurse. I come out every other day to change Mr. Garrick's dressings and help bath him. I'm used to just letting myself in if the door's not locked. I wondered why all the blinds were drawn. I can't believe it. He was doing so well. Why would he go and do that? God love him."

She reached down for her bag, looked back into the room.

"I suppose there's no point in me hanging around, then."

"I suppose not," Flanagan said.

The nurse nodded a farewell as she passed on her way to the door.

"Actually," Flanagan called after her, "maybe we could have a quick chat, if you've time for a few questions."

"Love, I've got the next two hours free. But do you mind if I step outside for a smoke? Just to settle my nerves."

Flanagan followed Thelma out to the front step where the nurse's Škoda Fabia sat parked next to her own Volkswagen. Thelma took a ten-pack of Lambert & Butler from her bag, folded back the lid, and removed a cigarette and a disposable lighter. She offered the pack, but Flanagan declined.

Once she'd sparked up, Thelma said, "Ask away."

"How long have you been coming here?"

Thelma exhaled a long blue plume that was swiped away by the breeze. "Ever since he came home from the hospital. That was, what, four months ago, give or take a week?"

"How was Mr. Garrick's mood in that time?" Flanagan asked.

"Better than you'd think," Thelma said. "I mean, he had his ups and downs, of course. He did better than I ever could if that happened to me. But then, I've no religion."

"You think his faith helped him?"

Another plume of smoke. "Oh, yes. He always said to me, if that's what God intended for him, then there had to be a reason for it. What was it he said? There's not a leaf falls from a tree without God's say-so. I don't know, if God did that to me, I'd tell him to go fuck himself."

The nurse turned to Flanagan, open-mouthed, her hand extended in apology.

"Oh, I didn't think, you're not religious, are you?"

Flanagan smiled and shook her head. "No, not really."

"Thank God for that, I wouldn't want to offend you. My sister's all into that, but I could never be bothered with it." She winked at Flanagan. "I'm always too hungover on a Sunday morning for church, anyway."

"How was Mrs. Garrick coping?" Flanagan asked.

The smile left Thelma's mouth. "God love her, I think she took it worse than he did. I mean, she's what, thirty-four, thirty-five, something like that? And now she's got to care for him like he's a baby for the rest of his days. He didn't have much of a life after the accident, but Jesus, it was no laugh for her either. No matter how much you love someone, it's hard to face cleaning up after them day in and day out. And when I say cleaning up, I mean *cleaning up.* Like, down there."

Thelma waved her fingers at her own crotch while her face creased, and Flanagan knew exactly what she meant. She imagined the rituals the Garricks had to go through morning and night, the shame and resentment that would surely take root and grow between them. True love can only stretch so far.

"And nothing changed recently?" Flanagan asked. "No mood swings? Any arguments between Mr. and Mrs. Garrick?"

"Not that I noticed."

"All right. Thank you, you've been a help."

Thelma stubbed the cigarette out on the sole of her shoe, slipped the remains into the packet, and stowed it in her bag. "No worries, love. If you need anything else, you can get me through the local trust."

She went to her car and paused as she opened the door.

"It's an awful shame," she said. "He was a nice man. He'd every right to be bitter about things, but he wasn't. God love him. God love the both of them."

Flanagan closed the front door as the Škoda's engine hummed away. She went to the hall table and found the two sets of keys there, resting on the open pages of the huge bible. The paper silken and cool against her fingers. In the dimness of the hall, she saw the first page of the New Testament.

The Book of Matthew.

Chapter One. Verse One. The genealogy of Christ, who begat who, the names cascading down the page.

69

She pulled her gaze away from the words, grabbed the keys, and left.

8

McKay froze when he heard the knock on the door. He'd been standing over his kitchen sink, staring out of the window. He almost lost his grip on the handle of the mug, tea long cooled spilling over the rim, over his fingers and into the steel bowl.

Another knock, and he placed the mug on the draining board before going out to the hall. He saw the form through the rippled glass in the door. Was it Flanagan?

McKay advanced along the hall until he reached the door to the living room. He looked in and saw Roberta staring back at him.

"It's that policewoman," she said in a voice too angry to be a whisper. "I don't want to talk to her."

McKay nodded and went to the door. He paused for a breath before he opened it.

"Yes?" he said, shocking himself with the force of his own voice.

A flicker of concern on Flanagan's face before she said, "Reverend McKay."

"Reverend Peter," he said. "Or Reverend Mr. McKay."

"Oh, yes," she said. "You corrected me earlier on that. I'll try to remember."

He paused, swallowed, and said, "Sorry, I don't mean to be rude. It's been a long day."

"I can imagine," Flanagan said. "How's Mrs. Garrick holding up?"

"She's resting. She doesn't want to see anyone."

"I understand." She held out a set of keys. "I just came by to drop these off. Mrs. Garrick is free to go home any time she wishes. I'd only ask that she stays out of the room Mr. Garrick died in and doesn't allow anyone else to enter. Just in case we need to reopen the scene. If she doesn't object, I'll hold on to the other set, to save bothering her if we need access over the next day or two."

He took the keys from Flanagan's hand. "That's fine. I think she might stay here at least a couple of days."

"Okay. I'll need to come by tomorrow and ask some more questions. Routine stuff, so no need to worry. I'll call in advance."

"All right," McKay said. "Thank you."

He waited for her to leave his doorstep,

but she lingered.

"I'd invite you in, but Mrs. Garrick . . ."

"No, that's fine," she said. "I have to get on, anyway."

She turned towards the church on the far side of the grounds.

"It's a beautiful building," she said. "How old?"

"Mid nineteenth century," he said.

"How often do you have services?"

"The times are on the board at the gate."

"Oh," she said, offering him a polite smile. "Thank you."

Without another word, McKay watched her get into her car, start the engine, and pull out of the gate. She did not pause to look at the board. He closed the door and rested his forehead against the cool glass for a moment. Then he went back to the living room where Roberta waited.

"Well?" she said. "What did she want?"

"To give you these." He held the keys out to her. When she did not reach for them, he placed them on the coffee table. "She said you could go back home, but I said you'd maybe stay here for a couple of days."

"I'll go to a hotel," she said.

McKay took a step closer to her, knocked his shin on the edge of the coffee table, making the keys rattle. "No, please, stay here," he said.

"I can't," she said. "How would it look?"

"You don't have to sleep with me," he said.

"It's not a question of whose bed I'm in."

"Please," he said. "Stay here. With me."

Roberta closed her eyes for a moment, then said, "All right. But I need to get some things from home. You'll drive me."

It was an instruction, not a request. And he didn't mind one bit.

Fifteen minutes later, Roberta unlocked the front door of the house her husband had built for her and stepped inside. McKay followed, sensing that keeping a distance would be best. He closed the door behind him as she walked to the open room in which Mr. Garrick had died.

"You're not to go in there," he called. "That policewoman said no one's allowed in."

Roberta changed course as if he had said nothing, as if it was purely her own decision. She walked beneath the staircase and towards the kitchen door on the other side. She opened it and peered into the gloom.

"They closed the blinds," she said. "All of them. All over the house."

"Did they?" he said. "Out of respect, I suppose."

She turned and he saw the hardness in her features. "If they'd any respect they'd have left everything alone. I need to get my things."

He couldn't hold her gaze. Instead, he retreated to the front door and waited there with his back against the wood as she walked upstairs to the double doors of her bedroom. She opened them wide and switched on the light. He watched as she went to one side of the room, out of his view, and returned with a leather bag. Then she froze at the foot of the bed, staring at a place he could not see.

After a while, she said, "Someone's been in here."

Her voice resonated in the high-ceilinged hallway, its metallic edge cutting at his senses.

He swallowed and said, "I suppose they had to search the house."

If she heard, it did not show. She dropped the bag on the bed and walked towards whatever had caught her attention, disappearing from view once more. A minute later, she reappeared.

"That woman was in my drawer," she said, anger sharpening her words. "Where I keep my . . . private things."

McKay moved closer to the foot of the

stairs, daring himself to speak. "They have to look. I've seen suicides before, and they always look around the house. They always do."

She stepped out of the room, to the top of the stairs. "Not my fucking house."

He moved back to the door, felt the wood against his shoulders, as the last reverberations of her voice faded.

"No," she said, raising a finger as if admonishing a wilful child. "She doesn't go through my private things. I won't have it."

Some foolish part of him wanted to argue with her, to tell her nothing was private until it was all settled. But his rational mind closed his mouth.

"Go and wait in the car," she said. "I'll get my things, then I want away from this house."

Reverend Peter McKay did as he was told.

Flanagan missed dinner with her children, which was not a rare event, particularly in recent months. When she let herself into the house by the back door she found Alistair at the kitchen table, stacks of exercise books in front of him, marking homework.

"Everyone all right?" she asked as she looked in the fridge for a plate covered with foil.

"Fine," he said. Barely a grunt.

She set the plate on the worktop, removed the foil. Cottage pie.

Mr. Garrick's last meal. Flanagan's appetite deserted her.

"Actually, do you mind if I don't?"

Alistair looked up from a teenager's spidery handwriting. "Do what you like. Chuck it in the bin, whatever you want. I'm not bothered."

"I'm sorry, it's just . . ."

He scribbled a note on the exercise book

in front of him, not hearing anything she said. She scraped the cold food into the bin and put the plate in the dishwasher.

"How are the kids?" she asked.

"You could ask them yourself if you were ever around."

"That's not fair," Flanagan said, surprised more at her own anger than his words.

Alistair rubbed his eyes as he inhaled and exhaled. "Look, I've got a lot of work to do here. We can argue another time."

"All right," Flanagan said, and walked to the kitchen door and the hallway beyond. He called after her, but she pretended not to hear. She went to the stairs and climbed, feeling the smooth varnish on the old wooden banisters. Alistair had sanded and finished them himself, and he had been so proud.

It should have been a happy memory, but instead it made Flanagan mourn for the life they once had. In the quiet hours, when she couldn't sleep, she promised herself they would get back what they'd lost, maybe something even better. If only they could hold it together a little longer, find their way through this.

And what, exactly, was this? She didn't know. How could she fix anything if she didn't know what had been broken?

Reaching the landing, Flanagan found Eli's bedroom door slightly ajar, just as he liked it. But Ruth's was tight shut. When had she started closing her door at night? She was ten years old; Flanagan had been into adolescence before the need for privacy had outweighed her fear of the dark. Even then, she needed a light on in the room. She'd still have one now if Alistair would tolerate it.

She knocked on Ruth's door and listened. After a few seconds, she opened it a crack and peered inside. Ruth stared back from her bed, an open book in her hand.

Flanagan opened the door fully and said, "Late to be up reading, love."

"I was just finishing," Ruth said, folding down the corner of the page.

"Can I come in?" Flanagan asked, realising this was the first time she'd ever sought permission.

"Uh-huh," Ruth said, the expression on her face seeming to ask if she was in trouble.

Flanagan closed the door behind her and approached the bed. Ruth tucked her legs up to make room, and Flanagan sat down on the edge. She reached for her daughter's hand.

"When did you get so grown up?" she asked. "How did I miss it?"

"Because you're never here," Ruth said.

"Nonsense. I saw you this morning. And last night before bed."

"That's not much. It's not like you hang out with us or anything. It's always Dad takes us if we're going anywhere. You never do anything with us. You're never here, not even just to watch TV."

Flanagan tightened her hold on Ruth's hand. "I've been very busy with work, love, you know that. But I'll try to do better, I promise."

Ruth nodded her acceptance and looked down at her free hand.

After a few moments, Flanagan reached out and touched her cheek. "What, love? Tell me."

Ruth took a breath, her eyes brimming. "Are you and Dad going to split up?"

"No," Flanagan said, her voice harder than she'd intended, making Ruth flinch. "No, not at all. Why would you think that?"

"You and Dad haven't been talking to each other for ages, not properly. Not even to argue."

"Course we have," Flanagan said, the lie bitter in her mouth. "We were talking just now, downstairs, before I came up."

Ruth gave her a hard look that said she knew the truth.

"We were, honest."

"What about?" Ruth asked.

"You and Eli," Flanagan said without hesitation.

Ruth shrugged and looked down to her hands once more. "If you do split up, we'll be all right. I know lots of kids whose mums and dads aren't together, and they're all fine."

Flanagan was about to dismiss the idea when a question occurred to her. "Did your father say something?"

Ruth kept her gaze down. She was a terrible liar, always had been, so now she wasn't even going to try.

"What did he say?" Flanagan asked.

Ruth looked to the far corner, biting her lip.

"Tell me." The sharpness of the words startled them both.

"Just that, sometimes, if a mum and dad aren't happy together, it's better for everybody if they split up."

Flanagan felt that anger surface again, the same as she'd felt a few minutes ago in the kitchen. She pushed it away, saved it for later.

"Well," she said, "sometimes that's true. But me and your dad are happy together. We're just having a bit of a rough patch,

81

like all mums and dads do. We'll get over it and things will be better."

"When?" Ruth asked in the earnest way only children can.

Flanagan smiled and said, "Soon. I promise. I promise. Now, it's time to go to sleep."

Ruth lay down, and Flanagan set the book aside. She leaned over and gave her daughter a kiss.

"Light off?"

Ruth nodded against her pillow, and Flanagan did as she was told. She stood and went to the door.

As she stepped through the door, Ruth called, "Leave it open. Just a little."

Flanagan did so. Then she went to her own bedroom, lay on the bedclothes, and cried in the dark.

She dreamed of Mr. Garrick, dead in his back room, except it was a room in Flanagan's home and she wondered why and how he had come to be here. And dead Mr. Garrick pointed to the photographs in their frames, all lined up on the table, facing away from him, facing Flanagan.

Turn them around, dead Mr. Garrick said, turn them around, I want to see.

Flanagan reached for the picture of his wife, but he said, no, my baby, I want to see my baby.

She woke the moment her fingertips touched the frame, confused, at first weightless, then heavy on the bed, her body sinking into the mattress. She wanted to go downstairs to the back room, let poor dead Mr. Garrick see his baby's photograph, but reality untangled itself from her dream and she knew Mr. Garrick lay in a mortuary miles away.

Flanagan moved her arms, felt the clinging of fabric, and realised she had fallen asleep fully dressed. She turned her head on the pillow, saw Alistair staring up at the ceiling.

"You awake?" she asked, even though she knew the answer.

"No, I'm spark out," he said.

She rolled onto her side, facing him, and inched closer. "Do you want to talk?"

"I want to sleep."

She reached for the hand that lay by his side. He did not pull away. "Seeing as neither of us is doing that, do you want to try the first option?"

"Go on, then," he said.

She told him what Ruth had said, that their daughter seemed to believe their marriage was over, as if the terrible thing had already been done.

"Is that how you see it?" Flanagan asked. "Are we done?"

She listened to him breathing for a time before he said, "I don't know."

"We can't give up just like that. All these years thrown away. We can't."

"No?" he said. "You seem to be giving it a bloody good try."

"Me? What . . ." She stopped, told herself to not get defensive, it wouldn't help. "I know I've not been around as much as you'd like, but you know how work is these days."

"It doesn't make much difference if you're here or there, though, does it? Even when you're here, it's obvious you wish you weren't."

"That's not true, and it's not fair," Flanagan said, defensive now whether she liked it or not.

"Really? It's like you're a lodger here, for Christ's sake."

"Because you've frozen me out. Ever since you were hurt, you've kept me at arm's length."

"Oh, so it's my fault."

"I didn't say that. But I know you blame me for what happened, and maybe you're right to, but I can't change it no matter how much I wish I could."

84

"Yes," he said, spitting the word into the darkness. "You're right. I blame you. It was your fault I got stabbed. It's your fault those boys came into our home. It's your fault I still have nightmares about it. And the one thing I asked of you to try and make it better, you won't do it."

"What?"

"You know."

And she did know, much as the idea horrified her. "Quit my job," she said.

He remained silent until she had no choice but to speak.

"I won't do that. If that makes me selfish, then so be it, I'm selfish. But I do good work, I help people, or at least I try. Sometimes I wonder what I do it for, sometimes all I get is grief for my trouble, but I try. And I'm going to keep trying."

Alistair's hand slipped away from hers. "Then there's nothing more to talk about, is there?"

He pushed back the duvet and got out of bed.

"Alistair, wait," she said as he pulled on his dressing gown and slippers. "Wait, darling, please."

He closed the door softly as he left, and Flanagan placed her hand on the warm place where he had been. She did not know

85

how long passed before she slept again, but she dreamed once more of dead Mr. Garrick and the photographs, turn them, please turn them, I want to see . . .

10

As dawn crept in through the cracks in the shutters, Reverend Peter McKay lay quite still beside Roberta and watched her sleep. He had offered her his bed while he took the small spare room, and she had not hesitated in accepting. At some point in the night he had woken with a start, disorientated in the single bed in the room across the landing. Once his senses had aligned, an idea occurred to him, simple and clear: get up and go to her.

Why not?

They had slept together before on several occasions. Not through the night, of course, but many times, as the sweat cooled on their tangled limbs, they had each drifted into soft warm nothing. Why should they not sleep together now?

Decided, he got out of bed, and left the spare room. Wearing his T-shirt and boxers, he crossed the landing to the door of his own bedroom. He thought about knocking, but dismissed the idea almost as soon as it had appeared. Instead, he reached for the handle and opened the door.

Quiet like a church mouse.

The image almost made him giggle, and he brought a hand to his lips as he closed the door behind him. He crossed the room, mindful of creaking floorboards, and stood over her for a while. So peaceful there, her hair pooled on the pillow, her cheek resting on the palm of one hand. He eased back the covers and lowered himself into the bed.

As he drew up the bedclothes, she lifted her head from the pillow, her eyes barely open, her mind clearly far away.

"But you can't walk," she said.

He realised she was still tangled in a dream about her dead husband, no wall between the real and the unreal.

"It's all right," he whispered. "Go back to sleep."

She lowered her head to the pillow and closed her eyes. He leaned over and placed a kiss, so soft it wouldn't have woken a baby, on her forehead. At that moment, as he looked up from her, he noticed the framed photograph of Maggie, turned to face the wall. Even though he could not see her face, he couldn't bear to look.

He had slept little in the hours since, stirring every few minutes, roused by the heat of Roberta's body just inches from his own. Now she lay on her back, one arm curled around her head so that he could see the stubble there where he had kissed her so many times. He watched her eyes move behind the lids, listened to her breathing, took in her heated scent.

She had promised.

With his hands clasped in hers, she had sworn on her dead child's soul that they would be together. One day, they would be together. He did not believe in the soul, but he accepted her oath nonetheless, because he wanted her more than anything in the world. He needed her more than he needed his own conscience.

And now, surely, Roberta was his. Wasn't she?

And if she wasn't?

McKay's mouth dried, his stomach turned. Cold on his forehead as sweat seeped from his skin.

No, it was unthinkable. To even consider the possibility would strip away the last of him, unman him as brutally as the Aston's engine had unmanned her husband. So he would not consider the idea. He forced himself, instead, to resume his study of her.

He had lost Maggie a decade ago. Eight years they had together before that. Happy years. From here, it seemed like some soppy television romance, all hazy sunlight and meadow picnics. There had been some sadness — their inability to conceive a child being the darkest stain on the memory — but even so, those eight years retained a golden glow in his mind.

Then one morning, at breakfast, Maggie complained of a headache. As she sat at the kitchen table, head in her hands, a mug of tea going cold in front of her, McKay searched the cupboards for ibuprofen or paracetamol. Eventually, he decided to give up and walk the few hundred yards to the filling station at the other end of the village's main street.

"Don't be too long," she said. "It really hurts."

Five minutes there, five minutes to buy what she needed, five minutes back.

Fifteen minutes, that was all.

He found her on the kitchen floor, the chair toppled over, her face slack, her hands clawed in front of her chest. He wept as he called the ambulance, wept as he kneeled over her, prayed with all his heart.

She died on the way to the hospital. The paramedics restarted her heart twice before they could get her hooked up to the machines. In the early hours of the following morning, the doctor told McKay she was long gone. They could keep her heart beating, keep her lungs inflating and deflating. But Maggie McKay, who blushed when he touched her, who cried at Audrey Hepburn movies, who was kind and sweet to the very root of her being, everything that she was had ceased to exist. Now she was a vessel of organs and blood and bones and skin and nothing more. When they switched the machines off, he crawled onto the bed beside Maggie and held her as the life wheezed and rattled out of her.

Anything you need, Mr. Garrick had said, anything at all, just ask.

Mr. Garrick's first wife had left him just the year before, had run off with one of the salesmen at the car dealership. But Mr. Garrick had his faith to keep him strong, and the fellowship of his church. And so did McKay. The congregation gathered around him in his time of need, and he was grateful. And most of all, McKay had prayer, and the knowledge that his wife's passing had been God's doing. There had to be a reason.

Not a leaf falls against His will. Hadn't he always said that?

Nonsense. All a lie. His wife's passing had

been caused by a random malfunction of her brain; God had nothing to do with it.

There is no God, McKay knew. No God, only us and our sordid desires to drive us through our days until we're too old or too sick to desire anything. And then we are meat in a box, or ash in an urn, nothing more.

McKay could recall the exact moment he had ceased to believe. It had not been a process, a gradual degradation of his faith. It had been a sudden and total realisation that it was all a lie. The moment had been when she first brought her mouth to his, four months ago. For days and weeks she had been coming to him so that they could pray together, to help her through the terrible time after her husband's accident.

And they had grown close, talking together long after their praying was done, and as they talked, he noticed her in ways he hadn't before. The curve of her upper lip, the long and slender fingers, the toned form of her thigh as she crossed one leg over the other.

Then one morning, before he knew what was happening, his hands were lost in her red hair, and he felt her warm breath on his neck.

And his mind screamed, *sinner, sinner, sinner!*

But there is no sin. Is there? There is no sin because there is no God.

And then her mouth found his, her tongue quick and nimble and eager, and he knew beyond all certainty. Later that day, when it was done, he turned Maggie's picture to the wall.

The path from there to here had been the only one. There had been no other way but this. No other destination than his bed, the morning sunlight burning in her hair. He reached out, touched the glowing red strands, traced them back to the heat of her scalp.

She gasped, eyes opened wide, her gaze flitting around the room until she found him, inches away, staring back at her.

No recognition there, only confusion. Then realisation, and her expression turned from fear to anger.

"Get out," she said.

He reached for her again, his fingertips seeking the soft skin of her cheek.

She slapped his hand away. "Get out."

"But —"

"Get out!"

A shout now, her voice cracking.

"But we've —"

She struck him, her palm against his cheek, glancing off his nose.

"Get out!"

He brought his hands up as she swiped at him again. Then she pushed, first with her hands against his chest until he teetered at the edge of the bed, then she curled her legs up, and planted her feet against his stomach and pushed again.

McKay landed on the floor, shoulders first, the back of his head cracking on the floorboards. His legs followed, bringing the tangled duvet with them.

Up on her knees now, naked, pointing to the door. "Get the fuck out!"

He scrambled to his feet, fell, got up again. "Get out!"

McKay didn't look back as he crossed the room, opened the door, exited, closed it behind him. He stood on the landing, shaking, shame creeping in on him, a sickly wave of it.

He went to the spare room and slipped inside, silent, and climbed back into the small bed. Pulled the duvet up over his head, blacking out everything.

It took an hour for the shaking to pass.

11

At eight A.M., the pathologist's assistant opened the door to the Royal Victoria Hospital's mortuary and allowed DCI Flanagan and DS Murray to enter. Flanagan had spent several minutes assuring Murray that he could leave at any point if he really needed to. Sooner or later, he would have to attend a post-mortem in her stead, and he might as well break his duck with this one. With no trauma involved, no bullet fragments to seek, no stab wounds to count, this would be about as clean as an autopsy gets.

The assistant led them to the post-mortem table. The body bag lay on a trolley beside it, Mr. Garrick's remains within. Dr. Miriam McCreesh, the forensic pathologist, waited for them. A tall woman, the kind whose girlhood awkwardness turned to grace as an adult, she had an efficiency about her movements and her words. She wore surgical gloves, and a cap that strangely matched the green of her eyes.

"Morning," she said.

Flanagan and Murray returned the greeting.

McCreesh consulted the clipboard on the wheeled table at her left hand.

"Dr. Barr's initial assessment is death by suicide," she said. "Do you concur?"

Flanagan hesitated, then said, "I'm undecided."

McCreesh looked up from the notes. "I see." She returned her attention to the clipboard. "Going by the liver temperature taken at the scene, the rigor, and the lividity, I'm estimating time of death between eleven P.M. and midnight on Sunday the 4th of October. Dr. Barr observed no sign of recent trauma, as well as the presence of ten empty morphine granule sachets. There was an empty yogurt pot, and the spoon with which the yogurt was eaten. I understand the deceased was in the habit of using the yogurt as a means of administering his nightly dose of morphine, correct?"

"That's my understanding," Flanagan said.

"All right," McCreesh said. "Shall we begin?"

■ ■ ■ ■

Murray endured the early stages of the ritual. Flanagan watched him from the corner of her eye. He showed no signs of defeat as the body was taken from the bag, transferred to the post-mortem table using a ceiling-mounted hoist, and then photographed. Nor when the pyjama top was removed, or even the dressings on the stumps of Mr. Garrick's legs. Only when the adult nappy was removed, and the damage to the dead man's lower abdomen was revealed, did Murray flinch.

In truth, so did Flanagan.

They watched as McCreesh took samples — hair, skin, matter from beneath the fingernails. Murray cleared his throat as she swabbed what remained of Mr. Garrick's genitalia. Then she began the slow crawling external examination of the body, starting at the head, working down the left side, then up the right. Occasionally, McCreesh paused to lift her magnifying glass and look closer at some hair or fibre, before nodding and putting it back.

Eventually, she said, "All right. I concur with Dr. Barr, no external sign of trauma."

She looked to her assistant, who immediately acted on the unspoken command, wheeling a trolley laden with tools to the table.

Flanagan leaned in close to Murray. "How are you holding up?"

"I'm okay, ma'am," he said. "So far."

McCreesh checked Dr. Barr's notes once more. "The FMO mentions that the morphine granules were to be swallowed whole, not chewed, so the dose would be released gradually in the stomach."

"That's right," Flanagan said.

McCreesh took a small penlight from her pocket and leaned over Mr. Garrick's still open mouth. She shone the light inside, peering into the back of the throat.

"Hm," she said and reached for a clear plastic tube containing a swab stick. She removed the stick, and inserted the swab into Mr. Garrick's mouth, moving it around his back teeth. When she was done, she examined the swab with her magnifying glass.

"I've got a mixture of a pink substance, the yogurt presumably, and crushed granules. I'd say that's the morphine he chewed to get it to release more quickly. Tests will confirm."

She returned the swab stick to its tube, sealed it, and handed it to her assistant, who wrote on the tube's side with a permanent marker. Then McCreesh turned to her trolley and selected a scalpel.

Murray nodded towards her. "Is she going to . . . ?"

"Yes, she is," Flanagan said.

Murray exhaled and said, "I'm okay. I'm okay."

His breathing deepened as the Y-shaped incision was made from the body's shoulders to its groin. He did not speak again until McCreesh began to saw away the ribs and clavicle to remove the breastplate, the grinding noise resonating between the tiled walls.

Murray leaned in and said, "Ma'am, may I be excused?"

"Can't you stick it out a little longer?" Flanagan asked. "The organ examination's where the real work gets done."

"Oh, Christ," Murray said, and rushed past her to the doors, where he slapped at the green button with his palm until they swung open.

McCreesh looked up from her work. "He didn't do too bad."

"No," Flanagan said. "Not too bad at all."

Two hours later, Flanagan sat at McCreesh's desk, opposite the pathologist. She had sent DS Murray back to Lisburn to chase up the searches made of the Garricks' MacBook and iPad, as well as the notes from the door-to-door inquiries carried out in Morganstown by the two detective constables under his command.

"I'm reporting death by suicide to the coroner," McCreesh said. Her blonde hair now flowed free of the cap she'd worn during the autopsy.

"All right," Flanagan said, nodding.

"You don't seem convinced," McCreesh said.

"I'm not disputing your assessment."

"But?"

"But there's something . . . details, really, just details."

McCreesh rested her elbows on the desk. "Go on," she said.

"I spoke with the nurse who came in to help Mrs. Garrick with her husband, change his dressings and so on. She thought he'd been doing well, or as well as could be hoped for. She said his mood was generally good, that he had his faith, that he was strong-willed."

"Is that so unusual?" McCreesh asked. "Haven't you ever seen a suicide that came out of the blue, that baffled everybody around the deceased?"

"Of course, but this seems . . . different."

"Different," McCreesh said. "You'll have to do better than 'different' to sway the coroner."

Flanagan swallowed, considered letting it go, then she said, "It's the photographs."

McCreesh sat back. "Photographs?"

"That's the one detail that doesn't sit right. He had photographs of loved ones arranged around him."

"Suicides often do."

"But they were facing away from him. If he wanted to see them as he died, they would have been facing him. Why put them there at all if he couldn't see them?"

McCreesh sighed. "I don't know. We probably never will. What I do know is I found what appear to be crushed morphine granules on his teeth and the rear of his tongue, which is consistent with him chewing them before swallowing. The stomach contained exactly what we expected to find there, the mass spectrometer tests on the liver and blood samples will confirm the lethal morphine levels. All of it adds up. This was a suicide. I can't see it any other way, and I'm going to advise the coroner accordingly. I expect him to sign the interim death certificate, Mrs. Garrick will put her husband to rest, and until the inquest, that will be that."

"Fair enough," Flanagan said. "But I can disregard your findings, and the coroner's report, if I so wish."

McCreesh bristled. "That's your prerogative. But you're just making grief for yourself."

A sudden smile burst on Flanagan's lips, in spite of everything, surprising her. "Oh, I'm good at that."

McCreesh returned the smile. "I know," she said. "Anyway, enough business. How've you been?"

"Okay," Flanagan said. "Still on the tamoxifen for the foreseeable future, still having the check-ups, still terrified I'm going to find another lump. You?"

McCreesh's eyes glistened. She blinked. A tear threatened to spill from the lower lid. "I found something. I have an appointment at the Cancer Centre first thing on Friday."

Flanagan reached across the desk, took McCreesh's hand in hers.

"It'll be a cyst," Flanagan said. "Just like the last time."

"That's what I keep telling myself," McCreesh said. "Over and over. But I can't drown that other voice out. You know what it's like."

"I know," Flanagan said, squeezing McCreesh's fingers tight.

"All I can think of is, how will I tell Eddie, what will I say to the kids? What if it's worse this time? What if it's not been caught soon enough? What if it's spread to the lymphatic system? What if, what if, what if?"

Now McCreesh squeezed back, sniffed hard, blinked again.

"But I won't be beaten now," she said. "Six years clear. I'm not fucking letting it get the better of me after six years clear."

"Good," Flanagan said.

They embraced, and Flanagan walked from the mortuary wing out to the car park. She paid at the kiosk and found her car. Before she inserted the key into the ignition, she closed her eyes and said a small prayer for Miriam McCreesh.

12

Reverend Peter McKay left Roberta Garrick alone in his draughty house and crossed the grounds to the church. The morning prayer service, a daily tradition few parishes maintained. But McKay opened the chapel two mornings a week for the handful of parishioners who still wanted to commune with God on a Tuesday or Thursday morning.

Mr. McHugh waited at the vestry door, a folder full of sheet music under his arm. A retired schoolmaster, he'd taught music and religious education at a grammar school in Armagh for forty years. Now he turned up at each service to play organ for the faithful.

"That was a bad doing, yesterday," Mr. McHugh said. "How's Mrs. Garrick?"

"She's coping," McKay said.

"Well, tell her Cora and I are thinking of her."

"I will, thank you."

Mr. McHugh touched McKay's sleeve. "We had the police at the door last night. Asking about it. A fella and a girl, I think they said they were constables. They were asking all sorts. Made me and Cora uncomfortable, if I'm honest."

"I suppose they have to do these things," McKay said.

"Well, I didn't like it," Mr. McHugh said. "It's not respectful. To us or the Garricks."

McKay gave no response. He opened the door and allowed Mr. McHugh into the vestry and through to the church beyond, before entering the code to disable the burglar alarm. Over the next half hour, while McKay donned his black cassock and white surplice, while he scribbled notes on loose sheets of paper he took from the old printer in the vestry, a scattering of people, more women than men, mostly elderly, sat in the pews. More of them than usual. Death brings out the God-fearing.

And there, near the front, Jim Allison, MLA. Forty-something, tanned and well-dressed, owner of a print business on the outskirts of Moira. He'd been an elected Member of the Legislative Assembly at Stormont since the re-establishment of the devolved Northern Ireland government in

2007. A man of influence who'd fought battles for many in the parish, from denied benefits claims to planning refusals, Allison had tackled bureaucrats in every government department on behalf of his constituents.

Although the MLA and his wife were regular attendees on Sundays, McKay struggled to remember a time when Allison had bothered with a weekday service, save for funerals or weddings. But he knew why Allison was here this morning. The parish had suffered a terrible tragedy and the local politician had come to show his solidarity with his people.

Such a cynical thought, but McKay had been given to cynical thinking over the past few months. Since his own faith had left him, he had questioned the belief of every other person who stepped inside his church. We're all just playing along, aren't we? Just going through the motions, doing what's expected of us.

And so McKay worked his way through the service, point-by-point as prescribed by the Book of Common Prayer: the gathering of God's people, the sentence of scripture, the opening hymn, the exhortation, the confession, the Lord's Prayer. Like an actor who'd performed the same lines every night for twenty years, he recited each segment with detached authority.

But today was different, wasn't it?

Today, they listened harder. This morning, every word he spoke carried the weight of Mr. Garrick's death. He had chosen the hymns and readings carefully to reflect the sombre mood the congregation expected from him. And this morning, he would go further. A sermon, a rarity in a weekday service. After the canticles and the psalms were done, he turned over two pages of scribbles that would carry him through the next ten minutes.

He heard the door open, felt a cool breeze, and looked up from his own barely legible scrawls. The policewoman, Flanagan. McKay's throat dried. She slipped into the second to last pew, exactly where Roberta Garrick had sat all those months ago. Her eyes met his, held his stare.

Start talking, he told himself.

Start talking now.

"My friends," he said, or at least he tried. The words came out as a crackling whisper. He cleared his throat, looked down at his notes, and tried again.

"My friends, this morning we come into the Lord's house carrying the great weight of tragedy. You all know the Garrick family, and you all know they have endured more heartbreak than any family should. First, with the loss of little Erin Garrick, not even two years old, in a terrible accident four years ago. Back then, Mr. and Mrs. Garrick sought the solace of their faith, their Lord God and His son, Jesus Christ. And they sought the support of the congregation of this church, they turned to their friends here, and with your help, and the Saviour's, they survived the loss of their only child."

McKay glanced up once more. Flanagan still watched him.

And why shouldn't she? Everyone else watched him too. That's what they're here for. Stay calm, he told himself. She can't see inside you. She can't read your thoughts. She doesn't know the terrible things you've done.

And still she watched him.

He coughed once more, and recommenced his sermon.

"Then six months ago, another accident almost took Mr. Garrick's life. He survived, but with the loss of his legs, and the cost of a lifetime of pain. And still, Mr. and Mrs. Garrick turned to the only ones who could help them through such a torturous time: their God and their church.

"Now, if Mr. Garrick had reacted to this

life-changing accident with anger, all of us would have understood. Wouldn't any one of us have been angry? We'd have had a right, wouldn't we? But Mr. Garrick was not angry. He and I talked and prayed together many times over the last few months, and not once did he speak a word of bitterness. What he did say was that if it was God's will that he should survive, there had to be a reason."

McKay looked once more to the back of the church. Now, at last, Flanagan did not stare at him. Instead, she looked up to the vaults of the ceiling, around at the commemorative plaques, the stained-glass windows, the military standards hanging at intervals along the side walls, the harvest displays of pumpkins, root vegetables, sheaves of wheat, all arranged around the church by Miss Trimble and the other elder ladies of the congregation. He guessed Flanagan seldom visited a church unless someone needed burying. He returned his attention to his notes.

"And this morning, we gather here knowing yet another tragedy has struck the Garrick family. All indications are that, on Sunday evening, Mr. Garrick took his own life. I want you all to know that he died peacefully, without pain. We'll never know what brought Mr. Garrick to this final decision, but we understand that six months of tremendous suffering have taken their toll. But I want to believe that when Mr. Garrick closed his eyes for the last time, he did so with his faith as strong as it had been four years ago when he lost his daughter, and six months ago when he came so close to death. Because without faith, what do we have left?"

McKay knew the answer to that question. Nothing. Without faith, we have nothing.

13

Then I have nothing, Flanagan thought.

She felt a piercing spike of self-pity, an emotion she detested above all others. Get out of me, she thought, I'll have no more of you.

Reverend McKay wrapped up his sermon and said, "Let us pray."

Flanagan kept her head upright while the rest of the congregation lowered theirs. And McKay too, his eyes open as he turned to the prayer desk, side on to the congregation.

"Dear Lord, we pray this morning for the soul of our departed friend, Henry Garrick. We pray that he is now at peace, that the depth of his faith in You brought him into Your eternal embrace, that his suffering is at an end, and that he is made whole again through Your grace and compassion.

"And Our Father, we also pray for Roberta Garrick, that she can find strength in us, her friends, and in You, that You can guide her through this difficult time. Lord, guide us in our efforts to provide comfort for the bereaved."

McKay looked up from the desk, turned his head. His eyes met Flanagan's.

She felt a hot flush of shame, like a child caught stealing. She dropped her gaze to her hands, bowed her head like the others.

As McKay recommenced the prayer, Flanagan wondered at the power of this place to make a middle-aged woman bow her head even if she didn't believe. The memories a church roused in her, the little girl she had once been, the ritual of putting on her best Sunday clothes, fidgeting beside her mother as a minister droned on, then the Bible classes led by plain women, and how the stories frightened her.

When had Flanagan last attended a service? A year ago, she thought, when her friend Penny Walker had been buried along with her husband. And Flanagan had prayed then, just as she prayed an hour ago for Miriam McCreesh.

Prayed to whom?

If Flanagan did not believe, then why did she pray so often? She rationalised it as a form of self-talk, an internal therapy session. Wasn't that it? Or were those Sunday

112

mornings spent in places like this so rooted in the bones of her that deep down she believed this nonsense, even if her higher mind disagreed?

McKay's voice dragged her back to herself, the words, "Our Father, who art in heaven."

With no conscious decision or effort, Flanagan recited the Lord's Prayer along with the rest, every word floating up from her memories of school assembly halls and windswept gravesides. As the syllables slipped from her tongue she weighed the meaning of each.

And she thought of her daughter, and the question she'd asked last night: was their marriage over? She had denied it, but truthfully, she didn't know. And she thought of the cold distance between her and her husband, his anger stoking hers. If it really happened, if they really split, she knew Alistair would fight for the children. And he might win. With a job like hers, with the hours she kept, she couldn't be sure the court would favour her. There was a real risk she would lose her children because of her job. A job that had once given her days meaning, now a daily mire of futility.

McKay had asked: without faith, what do we have left?

Without the job, Flanagan thought, what do I have left?

Her family should have been the answer. But even that seemed to be slipping beyond her reach.

The service over, the small congregation left their seats and drifted towards the exit. Flanagan felt the cool draught on the back of her neck as the door opened. McKay did not look at her as he joined his people in the late morning light. She heard snatches of hushed conversation between him and the parishioners.

Yes, a tragedy. She's bearing up. Keep her in our prayers.

The church empty now, Flanagan alone, her thoughts seeming to echo in the hollow space around her. She closed her eyes, leaned forward, her hands on the back of the empty pew in front of her, her forehead resting on them.

Oh God, what do I have left?

I am my job. I am my children. What am I without them?

Flanagan turned her mind away from the question, because she knew the answer was there, waiting to snare her and drag her further down. She opened her eyes, lifted her head, and saw Reverend Peter McKay standing over her, his hands in his pockets, his cassock and white gown draped over the back of another pew. Reflexively, her palm went to her cheek, wiped away a tear that wasn't there.

"Sorry," he said, "I didn't mean to interrupt your prayer. Please go on."

"I wasn't praying," Flanagan said, and immediately wondered why she would lie about such a thing in this of all places. "Not really. Just thinking."

"It's a good place to think," he said, his expression warmed by a soft smile. "And to pray. Sometimes they're the same thing. Anyway, I quite often come here to do both. At night especially, when it's quiet, when there's no traffic outside, just silence. We all need a peaceful place to hide in now and then."

Flanagan returned his smile, was about to speak, but he took a breath.

"Listen, I'd like to apologise if I was curt yesterday evening when you dropped the keys off. It'd been a stressful day."

"No need to apologise," Flanagan said. "I understand."

"So what can I do for you?"

Flanagan stared up at him for a moment before she recalled why she had come here. "Oh, sorry," she said, reaching for her bag beside her on the pew, and the pen and notebook within. "Just a few follow-up questions. All right to do it here?"

"Of course," McKay said, lowering himself into the pew in front. "Has the post-mortem been done?"

"This morning," Flanagan said. "I've just come from the Royal. Dr. McCreesh, the pathologist, is going to report suicide to the coroner, who'll probably issue an interim death certificate in the next day or two. Then the remains will be released to Mrs. Garrick."

"And the inquest?" McKay asked.

He clearly knew the procedures, Flanagan thought; this wasn't the first suicide in his parish, and it wouldn't be the last.

"At least the spring," Flanagan said. "Maybe the summer."

"It takes a long time to decide what everyone already knows," McKay said. When Flanagan didn't respond, he said, "You had questions for me."

She readied her pen. "About the Garricks. How long have you known them?"

"I've known Mr. Garrick as long as I've been here. That's, what, twenty years? His first wife was still around then."

"And when did they split?"

"About eleven or twelve years ago, I think."

"What were the circumstances?"

"It's no secret," McKay said. "She was having an affair with one of the salesmen at the dealership. It'd been going on for months, apparently. She lifted £50,000 from one savings account, £70,000 from another, and just disappeared one morning. She and the salesman flew to Greece and bought a villa. The money ran out, of course, and the former Mrs. Garrick had to take a job in some tourist bar. Last I heard, the salesman left her for some girl who was passing through on holiday."

"How did Mr. Garrick take it at the time?" Flanagan asked.

"He was devastated. But his friends in the church gathered to him, so did I, and we helped him through. That's what people outside don't tend to appreciate. That a church is not a building." He waved his hands at the empty air around him. "This is not a church. The stained glass, the altar, the pews, none of this makes a church. A church is a community, a group of human beings brought together by their faith, so close they become a family. And when one of our family is hurt, we help them."

He dropped his gaze, smiling, ran his fingertips through his salt-and-pepper hair. "Sorry, I didn't mean that to sound like a

117

recruitment drive. Anyway, you get the picture."

Flanagan smiled and nodded. "When did Mr. Garrick meet his second wife?"

"About seven, eight years ago," McKay said. "They met online. I suppose people do that nowadays."

"So I hear," Flanagan said.

"They'd been seeing each other a few months before he brought Mrs. Garrick — Roberta Bailey, she was then — before he brought her along one Sunday morning. Everyone was taken with her straight away. She had this glow about her. Like the sun in winter."

For a moment, McKay was lost in his memory of her. Flanagan measured the distance in his eyes, the years they peered through. Then his mind returned to the present and he focused on Flanagan.

"I married them a couple of months after that. I'd never seen Mr. Garrick so happy."

McKay's smile broadened to emphasise the point, but somehow it stopped at his lips, the rest of his features untouched.

"What about Mrs. Garrick's life before that?" Flanagan asked. "Who was Roberta Bailey?"

The smile left McKay's mouth, his face slackened. "I don't really know. I suppose I never thought to find out. She just seemed to fit right in here, became a part of the community straight away, joined the choir, everything. There never seemed to be anything outside of the church for her, other than her husband."

"What about the wedding?" Flanagan asked. "She would have had friends and family there."

McKay shook his head. "She and her parents . . . Listen, does this have to go any further?"

"You're not under caution," Flanagan said. "Nothing you say is admissible to the inquest or any other investigation."

He sat back, his brow creased. "Any other investigation?"

"If a further investigation of Mr. Garrick's death should be required."

"You said the pathologist was satisfied it was suicide, that he'd made his report."

"*She* has reported suicide to the coroner. But I am not bound by that report. If I'm not satisfied with the finding, I'm free to look at other possibilities."

"Surely there are no other possibilities," McKay said.

"There are always possibilities," Flanagan said. "I'm not disputing the pathologist's findings, I'm simply not closing any other doors for the time being. Anyway, as I was saying, nothing you say today is admissible in any court."

"All right," McKay said. "It's just I'm getting reports about your officers doorstepping people from this congregation, asking questions."

Flanagan opened her mouth to speak, but McKay held up a hand.

"I know, I know, it's routine, you have to do it. But this is a very close-knit community. Everyone talks. If anything I said to you wound up in a question to somebody else, it'd get back to Mrs. Garrick. She's been through enough. I don't want to see things get worse for her."

Flanagan looked him hard in the eye. "I promise you, this investigation will be handled with discretion. You have my word."

McKay gave a single nod. "All right. What I was going to say is, Mrs. Garrick had something of a troubled past. She and Mr. Garrick told me about it before they married. There were some issues with addiction, alcohol, drugs — nothing too heavy, you understand, but enough to have caused her some problems. Enough to estrange her from her parents. When she found God she left that life behind, including whatever friends and family she had then. So when she and Mr. Garrick were married, the bride's side of the church was filled by people from this congregation."

"They had a child," Flanagan said.

McKay's face darkened. "Yes. You know what happened to her?"

"That she drowned. I don't know the detail."

"Do you need to?"

Flanagan wished she could say no, she didn't need to hear about a child's death. Instead, she said, "Everything helps."

McKay's shoulders fell as he exhaled. "They were on a short holiday in Barcelona. Wee Erin wasn't quite two. They went to the beach, somewhere out of the city centre, I don't know it, I've never been. Anyway, I believe Mr. Garrick stayed on the sand while Mrs. Garrick took Erin out into the water, paddling at first and then carrying her in her arms. Apparently Mrs. Garrick was up to her waist, the water was calm, Erin was giggling, saying the water was cold. Mrs. Garrick didn't see the shelf under the water. It dropped a few feet, I was told. She lost her balance, and both she and the baby went under. In the confusion, the child slipped out of Mrs. Garrick's arms.

"Mr. Garrick didn't know anything was wrong until people started running past him to the water. Mrs. Garrick almost drowned trying to save Erin. They were able to revive her. But not the child."

"You seem to know a lot of detail," Flanagan said, "considering you weren't there."

"Mr. and Mrs. Garrick told me what happened many times," McKay said. "Many, many times. So, three years after I married them here, almost to the day, I conducted their little girl's funeral service. About the worst day of my career, to tell you the truth."

As he stared at some faraway place, Flanagan had an urge to touch him, offer comfort. She ignored it.

"How did it affect their relationship? Many marriages don't survive a loss like that."

McKay shrugged. "They had a difficult year or two, there's no denying it. But once again, they had their faith and their church to cling to." He turned to Flanagan. "There's nothing God can't help you survive, if you'll only open your heart to Him."

Had he aimed those words at her? Maybe, she thought.

"What about more recently, before Mr. Garrick's accident? Had there been any problems?"

"None at all," McKay said. "At least none

that I know of. Erin's death was hard to get past, of course, but they both threw themselves into church life. And community work. Mr. Garrick put a lot into the local community. He'd done well in life and he felt he owed something back."

"And then the accident," Flanagan said.

"And then the accident," McKay echoed. "As if they hadn't been through enough."

"Some might ask why a benevolent God would do such a thing to a good Christian family. Why would He heap tragedy upon tragedy like that?"

"Believe me, Mr. Garrick and I had that conversation many times over."

"And did you come up with an answer?"

Reverend McKay touched his fingertip to his lips while he thought for a moment, then his gaze met hers. "May I take a wild guess at something, Inspector Flanagan?"

Flanagan nodded. "Go on."

"Doing what you do for a living, I assume you have much faith invested in the science of your work. In the crime scene, all that CSI sort of thing you see on the television. I'm sure it's not terribly accurate, that TV stuff, but I know there's a science to it. Forensics. Fingerprints, DNA, blood spatter, tests, measurements, readings, numbers, results. Correct?"

"Correct," Flanagan said.

"And even presented with all that science, that evidence, all those hard facts, all these tangible things that you can see and touch, do you always get the answers you need?"

"No," Flanagan said. "Far from it."

"Well then," McKay said, "if your faith in science can't answer all of your questions, why expect my faith in God to answer all of mine?"

Flanagan exited the church, tucking her notebook and pen away. She had found the small car park full when she arrived, and had left her Volkswagen out on the road, its inside wheels mounted on a grass verge.

She was halfway to the gate when a voice called, "Inspector Flanagan, isn't it?"

Flanagan stopped and turned. Jim Allison, MLA, leaning against his Range Rover. She walked back towards him.

"Yes," she said. "We've met before, Mr. Allison."

"At the Policing Board meetings," Allison said.

He extended his hand, and Flanagan shook it. She had sat across a table from him on more than one occasion as he questioned her and other senior officers about their work. The Policing Board was largely a bureaucratic exercise, a sop to those in the community who distrusted the police, but Allison always seemed to take his civic duty more seriously than the other public representatives who had been appointed to the board.

"I would say it's good to see you again, but not under these circumstances. I take it you're investigating Mr. Garrick's case."

"That's right," Flanagan said. She resisted the urge to wipe her fingers on her trousers.

"Glad to see it's in capable hands," Allison said. "I hope you're making progress."

Flanagan told him she was, and once more explained the pathologist's report to the coroner, and the inquest ahead.

"Good," he said. "Listen, here's the thing. I know a suicide requires almost as much digging as a murder case, and I know you have a job to do, and I trust you'll do it thoroughly and diligently. But I'll also ask that you conduct it sensitively. Mrs. Garrick is a close personal friend of mine, just as her husband was, and I don't want her to suffer any more distress than she has already."

"Of course," Flanagan said, offering only enough deference to satisfy his ego. "I always try to tread as gently as I can when I go about my work. This case will be no different. Have a good day."

She went to leave, but his fingers closed on her upper arm. She turned back to him, stared down at his hand until he got the message and lifted it away.

"Try won't be good enough this time, Inspector Flanagan. I'll be keeping a close eye on things, and if I suspect Mrs. Garrick has been caused any more distress than is absolutely necessary I won't hesitate to go to the Assistant Chief Constable."

Flanagan took a step closer. "Like I said, I will conduct this investigation with the utmost sensitivity, as I always do, but let me stress, it is my investigation. One other point, Mr. Allison."

He put his hands in his pockets and leaned back on his car.

She stepped closer still, inches between them, her eyes hard on his. He blinked, but did not look away.

"Do I have your full attention, Mr. Allison? Then listen well." Closer now, so close he couldn't hold her gaze any longer.

"Don't ever touch me again," she said.

14

McKay slipped out through the vestry, closed the door behind him, locked it. He crossed the grounds to his house, opened the door. Inside, alone, he called out, "Roberta?"

Not in the living room, he could see from here. Perhaps the bedroom. He hesitated to go up there after what had happened this morning, but he had no choice, he had to talk to her. He took the stairs two at a time, found the bedroom empty.

Where had she gone?

Then he knew.

McKay descended the stairs and let himself out. He crossed back to the church, skirted around to the rear, and the small graveyard on the other side. Only the wealthiest families could afford a burial here. The Garricks were one such family, three generations buried in their plot.

Roberta sat on the low marble wall that

surrounded the plot, one hand resting in the gravel, smooth white stones between her long fingers. Two headstones at the top of the grave, one for Mr. Garrick's grandparents and parents, the inscription updated over a span of thirty years.

The other headstone bore the name Erin Susan Garrick, the dates only twenty-two months apart: our cherished daughter, taken into the Lord's arms where we will see her again.

McKay slowed his step as he approached, his shoes crunching the loose stones on the concrete path. She heard him, clearly, but did not lift her head to acknowledge his presence. He stopped beside her, considered lowering himself down to sit next to her, decided against it.

"Are you all right?" he asked.

She sighed and said, "What do you think?"

"I was worried when I didn't find you in the house."

She kept her eyes on the grave. "Do I need permission to go out?"

"That policewoman was here."

Now she looked up. "Flanagan? What did she want?"

"Follow-up questions."

Roberta got to her feet. "What did she ask?"

"About you and Mr. Garrick," McKay said. "About how long I've known you, about the accident, about Erin."

Roberta flinched at her daughter's name.

McKay swallowed and said, "She suspects."

"No she doesn't," Roberta said too quickly, shaking her head. "Why would she? What did she say?"

"Nothing specific. But the questions, they seemed to be leading somewhere."

She reached for him, grabbed a fistful of sweater. "Leading where? Tell me exactly what she said."

He searched his memory, seeking words and intents. His mind scrambled through the fragments, trying to piece them together.

"I . . . I don't remember, not exactly."

"Think!" She pushed and pulled him. "What did she say?"

McKay staggered to one side, shuffled his feet for balance. Fear threatened to blot out his higher mind entirely.

"I don't know, I don't remember, I can't think, I can't . . ."

Roberta let go of his sweater and said, "All right, calm down."

"What'll we do?" he asked, his throat tightening, his voice rising. "What'll we do? It's not just her, it's the other police, they're going around the village, asking questions."

She placed her palm, still cool from the gravel, on his cheek. "Shut up and calm down."

"What if she —"

"Shut. Up." Her fingers moved from his cheek to the side of his neck, warmer now, the heat cutting through the clamour in his mind. "Calm down. Are you calm?"

She spoke as if he were a child, and in truth, wasn't he? Held here in her palm, he was an infant, blind and helpless, mewling for her succour. And she gave it to him. She reached her arms up and around his neck, drew her body close to his, her nose and mouth seeking the hollow between his jaw and his shoulder. He had no choice but to wrap his arms around her waist, lose himself in her embrace.

"Be strong," she said, her voice low, her breath rippling across his skin. "Remember everything we talked about. Everything we're going to have together."

"Together," he said. "You promised. To-gether."

"I know," she said, releasing herself from his arms, bringing her hands to his face. "And I keep my promises."

15

Flanagan knocked on the door of DSI Purdy's office and opened it without waiting for permission. She leaned in and saw him at his desk, the telephone handset pressed to his ear. He raised his hand and beckoned her to enter.

"I understand that," he said into the mouthpiece.

Flanagan took the seat opposite him.

"I do," he said. "I do understand."

She watched as he closed his eyes in exasperation.

"I don't know, but what I can tell you is that DCI Flanagan is one of the best police officers I have ever had the good fortune to work with."

Flanagan's skin prickled. She pointed to the door, eyebrows raised, silently asking if Purdy wanted her to leave. Purdy shook his head and pointed to the chair she already sat in.

"That's as may be, but this is DCI Flanagan's case, and she will conduct it as she sees fit with no interference from me. If that's not good enough for you, then feel free to complain to the ACC next time you have a round of golf with him. Have a good day."

He slammed the handset into its cradle and said, "Fucking prick."

"Allison?" Flanagan asked, even though she knew the answer.

"Yep," Purdy said, leaning back in his chair. He took off his glasses, tossed them onto the desk, and rubbed his eyes. "Was I a little abrupt with him?"

"A little," Flanagan said.

"Good. If he thinks being on the Policing Board means he can start telling me my job, he's got another thing coming. He tries that shit again, I'll bury my boot up his hole."

Flanagan smiled, partly at the image, partly at the knowledge that Purdy had stood his ground for her. He was a good man. She had spent much of her career working under his command, and although those years weren't without friction — they had both made mistakes they regretted — he had been as good a mentor as she could have wished for. She would miss him when he retired.

Not long now. Boxes were stacked against one wall of the office, his personal items packed in one pile, paperwork filling the rest. A man's career wrapped up and ready to be taken away.

"So, what's the deal with this suicide?" Purdy asked. "Are you near ready to close it up?"

Flanagan took a breath and said, "No, I'm not."

"Explain," he said as he reached for his glasses.

"It's probably a suicide," Flanagan said. "Everything's pointing that way. More than likely, once we've got the coroner's report, I'll close the investigation and leave it to the inquest."

Purdy tapped the leg of his spectacles against his teeth. "But?"

"But I'm not sure. Not a hundred per cent."

"Care to elaborate?"

"Something doesn't feel right." Purdy went to speak, but Flanagan raised her hand. "No, let me finish. I know I need more than a feeling to go on, you don't need to tell me that, but there are details that don't add up."

"Such as?"

"The photographs."

133

Flanagan explained the arrangement of the photo frames around the corpse, how they faced away, how Mr. Garrick couldn't see his loved ones as he slipped into the dark. She told him of the conversation she'd had with the nurse, how she'd said Mr. Garrick had been in good spirits right up to the end.

"That's pretty flimsy," Purdy said. He rested his chin in his hand and blew air out through his lips. "Do you need a calculator?"

"Sir?"

"Well, you're adding two and two and coming up with Christ knows what."

"We won't have the coroner's report for a day or two yet, Murray's still working on the laptop and iPad, the DCs are still doorstepping in the village, and the body won't be released until the end of the week. I've got a few days to dig a little deeper."

"All right," Purdy said. "But go easy. Remember, there's a bereaved woman at the centre of this. Don't cause her any more hardship than you absolutely have to. Understood?"

"Understood," Flanagan said.

An email from DS Murray awaited Flanagan when she returned to her office. A preliminary examination of the laptop found in Mr. Garrick's room showed searches over several weeks for lethal doses of morphine. The cookies stored on the machine showed that whoever made the searches had been logged into Mr. Garrick's Google account. There was more information to be gleaned from the computer, but these searches had been what they were primarily looking for. Everything that built towards a suicide, anything that showed intent or planning.

"It's a suicide," Flanagan said aloud to herself. "Admit it's a suicide and let it go."

Problems, Reverend Peter McKay had said. Addiction.

Even so, she logged into her computer and opened the interface for the ViSOR database. She entered the names B-A-I-L-E-Y and R-O-B-E-R-T-A, narrowed the region to Northern Ireland. One result. Flanagan clicked on the name, and the record appeared.

A different woman entirely, this one forty-seven years old, a haggard face, a history of minor assaults and public order offences. Now living in a hostel in Newry.

Flanagan closed the ViSOR interface and opened the DVA database. This time, she entered Roberta Garrick, along with the address of the grand house.

Roberta Bailey had applied for a provisional driving licence twelve years ago, aged twenty-three, and her full licence six months later. Seven years ago, the surname was changed to Garrick, and the address updated. A few months after that, a speeding offence, and three points. Then another, and another.

Those cars, Flanagan thought.

No more points after that. Mrs. Garrick's heavy foot could have earned her a driving ban, but she had apparently learned to slow down. The points had expired by the time the licence was renewed two years ago.

"Who are you?" Flanagan asked the screen.

Next, a straight Google search, combinations of the name and social media sites.

'Roberta + Garrick + Twitter'

No Twitter account under that name. She didn't seem the type, anyway.

'Roberta + Garrick + Facebook'

Half a dozen matches, three of them in America, one in New Zealand, one in England, and here, at last, Mrs. Garrick smiling from the screen. An informal portrait for her profile picture, a glowing white-toothed smile. A little over a hundred friends. A handful of likes, including her church and her husband's car dealership.

Flanagan scrolled down through the sparse timeline. Nothing but occasional Bible quotes, and photographs she'd been tagged in, the choir here, the floral society there, and precious little else. Had she no life outside her marriage and the church?

She clicked the link to look closer at the likes list. Almost nothing. No music, no films, no books, only a few local businesses and religious groups.

"Just for show," Flanagan said aloud. Roberta Garrick had a Facebook account because that's what people do, not because she wanted one for herself. As artificial as keeping the good towels for guests.

"You're a work of fiction," Flanagan said.

A nonsensical idea. She scolded herself for allowing the very thought to form in her head. Not everyone wants to use social media, or even knows how. Flanagan had never bothered with any of those websites. Why did she expect Mrs. Garrick to have any real presence on them?

Roberta Garrick has done nothing wrong, Flanagan thought.

Then why does she bother me so?

Flanagan decided then that she needed to speak with Roberta Garrick today.

16

McKay woke alone, the sheets cool beside him. Roberta had left some time ago.

He had dreamed of Maggie, as he often did. A year ago, he would have woken with the lingering memory of her, despairing that the dream had not been real, that she was not back here with him, returned from whatever strange journey she had taken. Now, he felt relief that she had not come back from the dead to condemn him for what he'd done, that she would never see who he had become.

He reached for the framed photograph on the bedside table, turned it back from the wall. Maggie smiling, pretty as she'd ever been. So pretty he couldn't stand to look at her for another second. He turned her to face the wall once more.

McKay checked his watch. Two hours he'd been asleep. He swung his legs out of the bed and reached for his clothes. A few minutes later he descended the stairs, slowly, quietly, feeling like a thief come to rob his own house.

He found her at the kitchen table, typing on his old Dell laptop. It took a few moments for her to notice him watching from the doorway. Her eyes flashed in fear or anger for an instant, he couldn't be sure which, before she gave him the faintest of smiles. A few more clicks and keystrokes, then she closed the computer, placed her hands on top of it.

"What are you doing?" McKay asked.

"Nothing," Roberta said. "Just reading emails."

"Be careful. They can check that sort of thing these days. See what you've been saying, what you've been looking at."

"I know," she said. "It's nothing for you to worry about."

He was about to ask her if she wanted something to eat when the doorbell rang, startling them both. McKay looked back over his shoulder towards the front door. He exhaled when he saw the now familiar shape.

"Is it Flanagan?" Roberta asked.

"Yes," he said.

"Tell her to go," she said. "I'm too distraught to talk."

"What if she insists?"

"She can't force me to talk to her unless she arrests me. Tell her she can't see me."

McKay looked from the door to Roberta and back again. The doorbell rang once more. "It might look bad. Maybe you should —"

"Just fucking tell her," Roberta said, her words cutting the air between them.

McKay nodded. He was halfway along the hall when he realised he was barefoot, only half dressed. Too late to turn back. She could see him through the frosted glass.

He reached for the chain lock and slid it into place before he opened the door as far as the chain would allow.

"Inspector Flanagan," he said.

"Reverend," she said. She looked at the chain. "No need for that, is there?"

He stared back at her through the gap, his mouth opening and closing, searching for a reason to disagree. When he could find none, he smiled and said, "Sorry, force of habit. I've been robbed twice by bogus callers." He slid the lock free, let the chain hang loose. Easing the door open a few inches more, he asked, "What can I do for you?"

"I'd like to speak with Mrs. Garrick," she said, looking past him into the hall.

He couldn't help but follow her gaze to

the closed kitchen door. He imagined Roberta on the other side, her ear pressed against the wood.

"No," he said, turning back to Flanagan. "Not today. She's really not fit for it."

"It won't take long," she said. "Fifteen, twenty minutes at most."

"No, she can't."

"I will need to speak to Mrs. Garrick at some time in the next day or so. If I could get it out of the way now, before the coroner issues the interim death certificate, it'd leave Mrs. Garrick to make the arrangements for the funeral."

"No, I'm sorry," he said, his voice firm enough to make his point. "So if there's nothing else I can do for you, I was just going to take a shower."

Flanagan's shoulders fell as she exhaled. "All right. But please tell Mrs. Garrick I'll need to speak with her by tomorrow at the latest. You have my number. I'd appreciate it if you called me as soon as Mrs. Garrick is ready to talk."

"I will," he said. He watched her walk back to her car, then closed the door.

Roberta waited in the kitchen, standing by the table. "Thank you," she said.

"You'll have to talk to her some time,"

McKay said. "You can't put her off much longer."

"I need a shower," she said, and walked past him out of the room.

McKay watched her climb the stairs, heard her enter the bathroom, then running water. Then he went to the table and opened the laptop. The web browser still showed the BBC news article he'd read last night. He clicked on the History tab. Only the last few pages he'd browsed. She'd used the private browser window, the computer recording no traces, no history, no cookies.

She'd been covering her tracks, hiding from him.

Hiding what?

That sick feeling again, deep in his stomach. Like the ground shifting beneath his feet.

I will suffer for this, he thought. I will suffer and I don't care.

17

Flanagan entered the darkened utility room, closed the back door behind her. She passed through the dim kitchen, then out into the hallway. The sound of her footsteps on the wooden floor reverberated in the grand space, rippling through the still air. She froze and listened for a few moments, trapped by the quiet of the house, as if it held its breath, waiting for her to speak.

Intruder, it would say. Get out. Leave us in peace.

But I need to know her better, Flanagan would reply, I need to know her secrets.

She had toured this house the day before, room to room, and saw nothing to shed light on Roberta Garrick. Only the same tasteful shows of wealth Flanagan had already seen and desired for herself.

The bedroom. If the truth lay anywhere in this house, it would be there. Flanagan climbed the stairs to the double doors, opened them, stepped through. Light in here. Someone had opened the blinds. Either Mrs. Garrick or the rector. A few items of clothing lay on the bed, considered for wearing and then discarded.

Flanagan's gaze went to the wall above the dresser, the space where the missing picture had been. She walked to the dresser and opened the top drawer. The same portrait of the child, hidden here among the papers and letters. Flanagan lifted a bundle of envelopes and leafed through them. Bank and credit card statements. A car insurance renewal notification. Passports in Mr. and Mrs. Garrick's names, both with several years left on them. Medical cards. Reissued birth certificates for both of them, a marriage certificate. And here, kept together, the birth and death certificates for the child, the latter issued in Spain.

"Can I help you?"

A cry escaped Flanagan's throat before she could stop it. She turned towards the voice.

Roberta Garrick stared at her from the threshold, her face blank.

"Mrs. Garrick," Flanagan said. She swallowed, searched for something to say. "How are you feeling?"

"What are you looking for?" Mrs. Garrick

asked, stepping into the room.

"Nothing specific," Flanagan said.

"It's hard to find something if you don't know what it is," Mrs. Garrick said. "I'll give you anything you need, but I'd consider it a courtesy if you'd ask before you go rummaging through my personal items."

Flanagan held Mrs. Garrick's stare. "I would have asked if I'd been able to speak with you. But Reverend McKay wouldn't allow it."

Mrs. Garrick put her hand to the drawer, began to push it closed.

"Why do you keep your daughter's photograph in there?" Flanagan asked.

Mrs. Garrick's hand paused, the drawer still half open. "Because sometimes it's too hard to look at her. Sometimes I can't bear it, other times I want to see her, then I take the picture out and hang it up." She pushed the drawer the rest of the way, sealing the framed photograph inside. "You wanted to talk with me. Let's get it out of the way."

They sat opposite each other in the living room, the blinds open, sunlight reflecting off the polished surfaces. Flanagan, pen in hand, set her notepad open on her lap.

"Reverend McKay tells me you met your husband online," Flanagan said.

Mrs. Garrick nodded. "That's right. Lots of people meet like that these days."

"True," Flanagan said. "And how long after that did you marry?"

"A bit less than a year."

"That was quick," Flanagan said.

"We knew we were right for each other," Mrs. Garrick said. "Why wait?"

"And you had your little girl within a year. Was she planned?"

"Not really. Harry was a bit older than me. He wasn't sure about having a baby at his age. But when I realised I was expecting, then we accepted the Lord's blessing."

"How did he take your child's death?"

Mrs. Garrick's features hardened, her lips thinned. "That's a ridiculous question," she said. "How do you think he took it?"

"Well, I'm told he coped well with the consequences of his car accident, under the circumstances. Was he able to deal with your child's death in the same way?"

"No. No, he wasn't. It almost destroyed him. It almost destroyed us both. We put a brave face on it, but we barely held our marriage together. It took a year to come back to anything resembling a normal life. Even then, it was still difficult. But the Lord got us through it eventually."

"And Reverend McKay helped."

"He's been very good to us. I don't think we could have coped without him."

"You and he are particularly close," Flanagan said.

Mrs. Garrick nodded. "He's a good friend."

An idea flitted across Flanagan's mind, a question. Too much? Too hard? She asked anyway. "More than that?"

Mrs. Garrick stared, her eyes burning. "How dare you?"

Yes, it had been too much, but Flanagan kept her face impassive, would not take it back. "It's just a question."

Mrs. Garrick stood. "We'll have to do this another time."

Flanagan remained seated. "Can't we just keep —"

"Another time," Mrs. Garrick repeated, a tremor in her voice now. "Please."

"Mrs. Garrick, if we can —"

"Isn't it enough?" she asked, her voice rising, breaking. Her hands shaking. "When is it enough? I have nothing left to give."

Now Flanagan stared. "I don't understand," she said.

Mrs. Garrick blinked, seemed to return from somewhere. "First my little girl," she said, her voice thinner, softer. "Now my husband. Just when I think God might let me breathe, let me live, He burns it all down again. I don't know if I can take any more."

Mrs. Garrick collapsed back onto the couch, her body limp. Tears spilled.

Flanagan sat frozen, caught between her instinct to comfort this bereaved woman and the need to follow her suspicion.

Mrs. Garrick shook her head as she spoke, her face contorting as she turned it up to the ceiling, her voice aimed beyond. "I can't, I can't take any more. If you want to kill me, then kill me. Don't make me suffer this, please, I've had enough. No more, please, no more."

Flanagan thought of the white coffin, the devastated car, the body she'd watched being taken apart that morning.

"Christ," she whispered. She set her pen and notebook aside, then crossed to the couch, beside Mrs. Garrick. She slipped her arm around the other woman's quivering shoulders, gathered her in.

Mrs. Garrick curled into Flanagan's lap, muttering, "No more, no more, no more . . ."

Back in her car, Flanagan called DS Murray's mobile.

"Are you at the station?" she asked.

"Yes, ma'am. Just got the last of the info

back from the computer searches."

"Anything to trouble us?"

"No, ma'am, not that I can see."

"All right," Flanagan said.

She closed her eyes, placed her free hand on the dashboard, concentrated on the sensation of the soft plastic on her skin, the coolness of it, allowed it to settle her mind.

"Ma'am?"

Flanagan opened her eyes again. "Gather up all the paperwork, all the reports, get everything in order for me to sign off on."

"You're going with suicide?"

"Yes," Flanagan said. "Yes I am."

18

McKay waited for her in the kitchen, a mug of tea long cold in front of him. It had occurred to him to prepare a meal, but he didn't know what she'd want to eat. What if he made something she didn't like? The idea of displeasing her caused a small terror in him.

Could that be right? If he loved Roberta, how could he be afraid of her? And yet he was. McKay banished the thought. To seek logic in the madness of recent days was the maddest idea of all.

Roberta had said she wouldn't be long, no more than an hour. It had been more than two going by the clock over the kitchen door, and he had been picking at a thread of worry for thirty minutes now. As the notion that she might not return, that she had fled, began to take form in his mind, the front door opened.

From the kitchen table, McKay watched

Roberta, the fading evening light silhouetting her on the threshold as his fear dissolved. She closed the door and approached the kitchen.

"Don't worry about the policewoman," she said.

"Why?" McKay asked, fear returning, colder and brighter than before. "What happened?"

"Never mind why," Roberta said. "We don't have to worry about her any more, that's all."

McKay studied her face, but it was unreadable. He wiped his fingers across his dry lips and said, "There was a call from the coroner's liaison. They've declared it suicide, pending the inquest, and they'll have the interim death certificate ready by tomorrow."

"What does that mean?" she asked.

"It means you can bury him."

Her shoulders fell. She placed a hand on the table to steady herself.

"Then it's all done," McKay said. "It's over."

She exhaled, a long, whispery expulsion of air. "Over," she said. She pulled out the chair opposite McKay and sat down, rested her palms on the table. Stared at some point miles beyond his shoulder.

"We can talk after the funeral."

Her gaze returned to him. "About what?" she asked.

He swallowed. "About us."

She blinked once and said, "I'll go back home first thing tomorrow morning."

"You don't have to."

"It'd be best."

He looked down at his hands. "All right."

Without speaking further, she stood and left the kitchen. When she reached the bottom of the stairs, he called after her.

"Can I bring you something to eat?"

She did not reply as she climbed the stairs, and the idea that he had lost her reared up again. And again, he told himself no, no she is mine now, always and forever.

To think otherwise might kill him. Might kill them both.

19

Alistair looked up from his plate as Flanagan let herself through the back door and into the kitchen. Ruth and Eli both glanced in her direction, but neither spoke. Bolognese sauce smeared Eli's chin. Ruth went back to spinning spaghetti onto her fork.

"Anything for me?" Flanagan asked.

Alistair nodded towards the stove. "There's a little left in the pot. I wasn't expecting you home."

Flanagan put her bag on the worktop, slung her jacket over the back of a chair. "Well, I wanted to make sure and eat with everyone tonight. I haven't done that enough lately."

Alistair shrugged and picked up his fork. "If you'd let me know, I would've made more."

She scooped the few spoonfuls of minced beef and pasta from the pot onto a plate. "This is plenty," she said, even though it wasn't. An empty jar of ready-made sauce sat by the cooker. She took a fork from the drawer and brought the plate to the table. She sat down opposite Alistair, with Ruth and Eli at either side.

The children stared at their food. Alistair stared at the wall.

Flanagan reached for the last piece of garlic bread, broke it in two, chewed a mouthful without tasting it. She swallowed and said, "So, any news?"

No one answered.

"Ruth, what about school? Anything happening?"

Ruth shrugged and said, "Same as usual."

Flanagan reached for Eli's hand and asked, "What about you, wee man?"

Eli looked down at Flanagan's hand, kept his gaze there until she released her hold on him. His hand retreated to his lap.

"All right," she said, forcing a laugh into her voice. "I'll just shut up, then, will I?"

Alistair's fork clanked on his plate. "You can't just waltz in here and expect us to act like everything's fine. You've barely spoken to your children in months, and you think they're going to be all over you just because you decided to show up tonight? You know I had to go and see Eli's teacher today?"

Flanagan shook her head.

"Mrs. Cuthbertson," Alistair said. "Do you even know that's who his teacher is? No? Well, I had to go and see her today and be told he's been picking on other kids."

She turned to her son. "Oh, Eli, why —"

"Save your breath, I've already talked to him about it. The point is, you have no idea what's going on with your own family. You think it's just another late night on the job, what does it matter? And every night I'm having to make excuses for you when they ask where you are. Now, I'm at the end of my bloody rope with this. You need to decide if you're part of this family or not."

Ruth pushed her plate away and left the table. Only when she'd gone did Flanagan notice the tiny pools where her tears had fallen.

"If you want to stay with us," Alistair continued, "then stay with us. But be *here* with us. Or else there's no point. Or else you might as well pack up and get out."

Now Eli stood and left. His fork rang as it hit the tiled floor.

"Well?" Alistair said. "Are you going to say anything?"

Flanagan brought her hands together to suppress the tremor of anger. "Of course I want to stay here. This is my home. Those are my children. But what are you? You've been pushing me away for a year now. Longer than that. Ever since I was first diagnosed, it's like I was tainted."

"That's not fair." Alistair sat back, his hands on the table. "I did everything I could for you while you were having the treatment."

"Everything except be my husband."

"What does that mean?"

"You know what it means."

Alistair's chair scraped on the tiles as he stood. He said nothing as he left.

Flanagan brought her hands to her face, rested her elbows on the table.

"Fuck," she said. "Fuck."

Flanagan woke in the night, stirred by her son's cry.

A few seconds of disorientation scrambled past before she remembered she had gone to sleep in the spare room, on the lower landing, next to the bathroom. Eli's cry had come from in there, echoing against the tiles. She threw back the duvet and went to the door, the creeping tendrils of a dream still snaking through her mind.

She found Eli crouched over a puddle on the floor, his soaked pyjama bottoms bundled beside it. He held a wad of toilet paper in his hand, mopped at the liquid with it.

He looked up as she entered, shame and fear on his round face.

"I couldn't hold on," he said, tears coming. "I tried really hard, but I couldn't."

Flanagan kneeled down next to him. "It's all right, love, don't worry about it. It's just an accident, that's all. We'll get it sorted."

She pulled more paper from the roll and mopped up the rest then tossed the pyjama bottoms in the laundry hamper. After washing her hands, she reached for the buttons on Eli's pyjama top.

"Let's pop you in the shower for a second."

Eli pulled away. "I want Dad to do it."

Flanagan reached again. "Dad's sleeping."

"No, I want Dad."

"He's sleeping. Come on, I can do it."

"I want Dad!" His voice rang in her ears.

Flanagan stood and said, "Okay." She left Eli there, climbed the short flight of stairs to the top floor and entered the bedroom she should have shared with her husband. She nudged him and said, "Eli needs you."

Alistair sat up in the bed, blinking in the light from the landing. "What?"

"Eli needs you," she said. "He's in the bathroom."

She returned to the spare room, closed the door, and got back into the cold bed.

The tears came then, and she covered her mouth and nose so no one would hear.

20

McKay set Roberta's bags on the hall floor.

"I can bring them upstairs for you if you want," he said.

Roberta followed his gaze up to the double doors of her bedroom. "No," she said. "They're fine here."

She turned and walked to the end of the hall and the closed door to her husband's death bed. She turned the handle, opened it. McKay saw the bed, the wheeled table, the photographs. The framed verse on the wall.

"Just two days ago," she said.

"It's done now," McKay said. "No going back."

"No," she said as she pulled the door closed. "No going back."

They stood at opposite ends of the hall for a time, he staring at her, she staring at the door.

"Look," he said eventually, "I'll leave you

in peace. I can come over this evening, if you like."

"Why?" she asked.

That cold feeling in his stomach again. He realised it was somehow worse that she hadn't understood why he offered than if she'd simply said no.

He cleared his throat. "Well, they're bringing him home tomorrow. With the wake and all the fuss, tonight might be the last chance we have to . . . to . . ."

He waved his hand towards her bedroom door, feeling heat creep up his neck and into his cheeks. Don't make me say it out loud, he thought.

She walked the length of the hall to him, the click-clack of her heels resonating through the house. "It's best we be discreet," she said before placing a dry kiss on his cheek.

"For now," he said. "You're probably right, let's keep things simple for now."

She nodded, smiled, took his elbow and turned him towards the door.

McKay saw DCI Flanagan's Volkswagen Golf as he pulled into the church grounds. He parked his Fiesta by the house and crossed to where she waited, the driver's door open. She looked up at him as he ap-

160

proached, but couldn't hold his gaze.

With terror in his heart, McKay asked, "What can I do for you, Inspector?"

She glanced up at him and away again, indicated the building that cast a shadow over them both. "I thought I might come to the morning service," she said.

"Oh," he said, unable to keep the surprise from his voice. "Sorry, only Tuesdays, Thursdays and Saturdays for matins."

"Matins?"

"Morning prayers."

"I see," she said. A tear rolled down her cheek. "It's just . . . I . . . I think I need to pray."

She took a seat at the end of the third row, gripped the rolled top of the pew in front of her. Her fingers flexed and relaxed, gripped again. Real strength there, but they were not masculine hands. McKay's eyes were always drawn to a woman's hands before any other part of her. The touch of cool soft skin, hard bones within. These were the sensations he recalled when he thought of the few women he had been with in his life.

"Am I supposed to kneel?" Flanagan asked.

He looked from her hands, along her arms, her shoulders, up to her face. How frightened she looked. And yet he suspected this was a woman who feared little in the world.

"You can kneel if you want," he said. "Or you can sit, or you can stand, or you can run laps around the church."

He gave her a smile, but the joke seemed lost on her.

"Sorry," he said. "What I'm trying to say is, God doesn't much care what you do when you pray. All He wants is for you to open your heart to Him."

"Okay," she said, returning his smile now, if only a flicker. She looked towards the altar, her eyes wet, reflecting the greens and reds of the stained-glass windows.

"Shall I leave you alone?" he asked, pointing his thumb back to the vestry.

She opened her mouth, her voice crackling in her throat before she found the words. "I don't know what to do. I don't know what to say. I don't believe in this."

"Then why are you here?" McKay asked.

Flanagan shook her head. "I don't know."

McKay hesitated a moment before sliding into the pew in front of her. He rested his arm on the back. Her hands lifted from the wood, hung in the cool air, then returned, knuckles showing white beneath the skin as she gripped.

"In my experience," he said, "whether you believe in prayer or not, just saying something out loud can make it smaller, take away the power it has over you."

"I've been having counselling sessions," she said. "Dr. Brady, once a fortnight, fifty minutes of me talking and him pretending to listen."

"Has it helped?"

"Not one fucking bit." She gave him a shamed glance, then dipped her head. "I'm sorry."

"Don't be," he said. "Swearing does the soul good. Keep it to yourself, but I've been known to let the odd f-word slip myself."

She smiled, held it on her lips a little longer this time before it slipped away. She took a breath before she spoke. "There was an incident a few months ago. I suppose it wasn't a full-blown breakdown, but it wasn't far off. A man died. I didn't kill him, it was entirely his own doing, but all the same I felt like I had. He and another man had tried to shoot me five years ago. The shooter was the pillion passenger on a motorcycle. His pistol jammed, and I shot him. One in the head, one in the chest. He died right there.

"The other, the one driving the bike, he took off. A couple of streets away, he ran a

163

red light right into the path of a bus. Took him five years to die. Like I said, it was his own stupid bloody fault, but when I found out he'd died, I fell to pieces. I know it doesn't make any sense. I've spent my career dealing with killers. I've seen the cost of what they do. And I'm one of them. Doesn't matter that I didn't choose to be."

McKay's mouth dried as she spoke. He put a hand over his lips and nodded.

She can't see inside me, he thought. She can't.

"Have you buried any murder victims?" Flanagan asked.

He managed a nod as he took his hand from his mouth. "Just one," he said, his voice a whisper.

"Then you know what it does to the people left behind. It blows families apart. Destroys marriages. Ruins children's lives."

Tell her.

The thought rang clear and bright in his mind.

Tell her and be done with it.

His hand went to his mouth once more, teeth hard on his palm. He nodded again.

Tell her or save yourself, he thought. One or the other. Do it now.

Flanagan stared at him. His skin burned where her gaze touched. She went to speak.

Do it now.

"But that's not why you're here," McKay said. No quiver in his voice. "Is it?"

She dropped her eyes, and he exhaled.

"Is it?" he asked again.

Flanagan's left hand shook as she lifted it from the pew back and wiped fresh tears from her cheeks. McKay waited, left room for her, knowing the confession would come before long.

Finally, she said, "I'm losing my family."

A sob from deep in her chest, and she looked away.

Fear leaving him, relief taking its place, McKay put a hand on her wrist and said, "Tell me."

21

Flanagan couldn't be sure what had brought her here this morning. She'd left the house before Alistair rose, before the children stirred, and had driven to Lisburn and the fortress-like station. Her office door locked, she sat at her desk, paperwork laid out across its surface. All of it meaningless to her, nothing but shapes and scrawls on pages.

Some time before nine, she messaged DSI Purdy, said she was going to follow up on the last details for the Garrick suicide. She went to her car and drove the small roads across country as far as Lurgan, then circled back east towards Moira, with the intention of going home for an hour. Just an hour to think, that was all.

But to get there, she had to pass through Morganstown, with its one main street, the church at one end, the filling station at the other. She made no conscious decision to hit the indicator, to slow, to pull the steering wheel to the right. And yet she found herself parked by the grey wall of the church, reaching for the key to kill the ignition.

She sat there for a time listening to her own breathing, hearing its strange dry resonance in the car, before it seemed the glass all around was only an inch from her skin. Then she opened the driver's door and felt the cool morning air wash in.

So quiet here. No traffic on the street. Nothing but the whisper of leaves on trees, silvery threads of birdsong between the branches.

She knew no one else was here, hers was the only car on the grounds, even McKay's was gone. Looking across the car park, she saw the old house and wondered if Mrs. Garrick was in there, grieving the desperate angry grief of those robbed by suicide. She remembered the widow's tears and felt a sting of guilt.

Why had she been so determined to find some dark stain on this woman? A woman who had borne more loss than most would in a lifetime. What had Flanagan seen in Mrs. Garrick that she wanted to believe her husband's death had been anything more than it appeared? Was it bitter envy for all

Mrs. Garrick had?

Flanagan would never have believed herself capable of such a base emotion, but there it was. She had been ready to torment Roberta Garrick further in her time of grief in pursuit of a truth that existed only in her own mind. Mrs. Garrick's husband had been physically devastated by a terrible accident, and months of agonising recovery had left him unable to face more. That was all, and Flanagan had to let it go.

But the photographs . . .

No, too thin. Too much of a reach. Still wanting Mrs. Garrick to be guilty of something just because she disliked her.

"Enough," she said aloud, startling herself.

Only when she looked around to see if anyone had heard did she notice Reverend Peter McKay walking towards her. Now he was sitting in the pew in front of her, his warm hand on her wrist, and she wanted to tell him every rotten thing that festered in her soul.

She told him about the Devine brothers, Ciaran and Thomas, how they came to her home a year ago with the intent to do her harm, and how instead Ciaran stabbed her husband in their bedroom while their children cowered downstairs. She told him how the case came to an end on a beach near

Newcastle, how everything that she'd done had helped no one, least of all the young man the brothers had murdered in a Belfast alleyway. Over the following twelve months, as she drifted from her husband and children's reach, she had wondered over and over what she had achieved in her career. Had it been worth the loss of her family?

"Then quit," McKay said.

She stared at him for a moment, disoriented at being pulled from her spoken thoughts. "What?"

"If your job's making you miserable, then quit," he said. "Simple, isn't it?"

Flanagan shook her head, fumbling for an answer. "No, it's . . . it's not . . ."

He smiled that kind smile of his, the one that warmed his eyes. "No, it's not that simple, is it? We have this in common, you know. Neither of us has a nine-to-five job we can leave behind at the end of the day. We don't work in some office, watching the clock, waiting for home time. You don't stop being a police officer when you go home any more than I stop being a priest. Not even when we go to sleep at night. Do you dream much?"

"Every night," Flanagan said. "About the ones I couldn't help. They stare at me. They point at me. They tell me I should have tried harder, asked one more question, turned over one more stone."

"Then you are your job, your job is you. Same for me."

"And I am my family. I need them, even if they don't need me."

His fingers tightened on her wrist, a small pressure. "Then the answer lies somewhere between the two. It's like two sides of an arch. One can't stand without the other."

"Then what do I do?" she asked, another sob catching in her throat.

"What you came here for," McKay said. "You pray."

As new, hot tears spilled from her eyes, McKay got to his feet.

"Now I'll leave you to it," he said. "Let yourself out when you're ready."

As he stepped away, Flanagan reached for his hand. He turned and looked down at her, and she suddenly realised how tired he appeared, darkness beneath his eyes, lines deepened by the light and shade of the church. She regretted the insinuation she'd made the day before when interviewing Mrs. Garrick, that there might be more to the minister's and the new widow's relationship. It had been unfair and uncalled for. She decided she would apologise to Mrs. Garrick, if she got the chance.

"Thank you," Flanagan said. "You're a good man."

Something flashed across his face, something quick and furtive, gone before she could fully see it.

"A good man," she said again.

He nodded, smiled, squeezed her hand, then left her alone with the God she did not believe in.

22

McKay closed the vestry door behind him, leaned his forehead against the wood.

Shakes erupted out from his core, to his hands, to his legs. His knees buckled and he collapsed into the door, then staggered across to the desk beneath the window.

A good man.

The words clawed at him.

"I am not," he whispered. "I am not."

A good man.

Maybe once. But not now.

I killed a man so I could have his wife.

Go back out. Go back out and tell her.

Tell her there is no God, that she is praying to air and stone and glass and nothing else.

Tell her this good man is a killer who deserves hellfire for his sins.

But McKay went nowhere. Instead, he remained at the desk, wishing he had a God to pray to.

23

Flanagan spent the next two days in prayer. An hour in the silence of the church before the stillness of the air seemed to press against her, squeezing her chest tight. Then in the car. Then in her office with the door locked. Then in the bed in the spare room, duvet pulled up to her mouth.

On the second night, she left the spare room, climbed the small flight of stairs to the master bedroom. She knocked lightly on the door. After a few moments, Alistair opened it.

"Can I sleep with you tonight?" she asked.

"It's your bed," he said. "You don't need to ask. And you don't need to knock."

She followed him to the bed, climbed in beside him, into his open arms. Warm and familiar and shocking. She rested her head on his chest.

"I'm sorry," she said.

A few seconds passed before he asked,

"What for?"

"For not being here for you and the kids. And for the distance I've put between us."

She felt his chest fall as he exhaled.

"I'm as responsible for that as you are," he said. "I've been thinking about it all day. I've been pushing you away since before what happened last year. I think I need to talk to somebody about it. Get some counselling."

She almost told him about the prayer that had brought her back to their bed, but felt suddenly shy. They did not believe in such things, she and her husband. And anyway, her prayers were between her and whatever listened.

"Maybe we should both talk to someone," she said. "As a couple, I mean."

"Maybe," he said.

"But listen." She moved her head so she could see the profile of his features in the darkness. "You have to understand, I need to do my job. It's what I'm good at. It's what I've worked for my whole adult life. You can't ask me to choose between my job and my family, because it's not really a choice. I need both. I'm not me without them. Both of them."

Quiet, the only sound their breathing in the dark.

Then Alistair spoke. "All right. But you have to leave your work outside. When you come into our home, all that other stuff, it stays outside."

"Says the man who spends his evenings marking homework," she said, smiling.

"I'm serious."

"I know. And I promise I'll try. And you have to promise not to push me away."

"I promise," he said.

They kissed and slept hard into the morning.

Flanagan arrived early at the church, but still she had to park a hundred yards down the road, wheels up on the kerb. She had known it would be a big funeral — Henry Garrick had been a well-liked man in the community — but even so, she was surprised. Before she got out of the car, she sent a text message to Miriam McCreesh, wishing her luck with the appointment at the Cancer Centre.

Before she pressed send, she checked her watch, realised the test might have already happened. She knew the routine: the probing, the scanning, the sting of the biopsy. The hours between being sent away and coming back for the results. A long and lonely day, even if you had someone to hold

175

your hand.

Flanagan walked towards the church, buttoning her black jacket. Groups of men and women, some younger, most older, moved in the same direction, and Flanagan found herself part of the tide. She listened as people exchanged greetings, their polite laughs, their remembrances of past encounters. A strange comfort in these voices, and she recalled funerals she'd attended in the past, the coming together of family and friends, aunts or uncles seldom seen, cousins she barely recognised.

The farewell to an elderly relative often had a muted joy about it. If their time was due, and the suffering and indignities of their withering years were at an end, then wasn't that a good thing? Sad, yes, but wasn't life itself?

But this kind of funeral was different. Mr. Garrick had not been taken by heart failure after days wired to machines in a hospital side ward. There had been no long and slow decline to be endured. True, Mr. Garrick had spent his last months in terrible pain, but even so, it was not his time. Flanagan had gone to enough suicide funerals to know there was no joy or gratitude to be found here.

Police cones at the gates to the grounds to

keep them clear for the hearse and the family cars. As Flanagan walked towards the church, she checked her watch. Quarter past eleven. The service was to start at noon. As she entered, an elderly gentleman handed her an order of service printed on folded A4 paper. He smiled and said good morning as he did so, and Flanagan couldn't help but return the smile.

Inside, she found a place in a pew two rows from the back. Soft organ music played, sending warm waves of sound through the church. It was already two thirds full. With the first two rows reserved for family, the place would be packed tight.

As she let her gaze wander the congregation, Flanagan noticed a middle-aged man, slender, well dressed. Mid fifties, or perhaps younger but prematurely grey. It was difficult to tell from this angle. He sat across the aisle, two rows forward. Flanagan watched as he bowed his head, rested his knees on the prayer stool, and clasped his hands together. She could just make out the movement of his jaw as he spoke to his God.

Right there in front of everyone. As if it was the most natural thing in the world.

And wasn't it?

It is a church, after all, Flanagan thought. If he can't do it here, where can he?

She looked around. No one paid him any attention. No one cared.

Flanagan put her hands on the back of the pew before her, brought them together, twined her fingers. Then she slid forward until her knees rested on the padded bench. She took one more look around, saw no one watching, then bowed and closed her eyes.

"Dear God," she whispered in a voice so low only the Creator could possibly hear. "Thank you for my blessings. Thank you for my children, for my husband, for keeping them well, and for keeping us together. Thank you. And please help Miriam with her test this morning. Please let it be good news."

She raised her head and said aloud, "Amen."

When she got back up onto the seat, she looked back towards the middle-aged man whose prayer had inspired her own. He sat turned in his pew, watching her. Flanagan froze as if caught in some misdeed. She saw now that the man was older, perhaps near sixty, and his eyes were tearful and hollow. He nodded to her, and she returned the gesture, realising his features were familiar. The man turned away, and Flanagan studied the back of him, digging for a memory, anything to reveal his identity.

She spent the next forty-five minutes wondering about him as the church filled. By the time the coffin arrived, shoulders pressed against hers at either side. The hum of chatter faded as the widowed Mrs. Garrick arrived, walked up the aisle to the reserved seats, arm-in-arm with another woman.

Then Flanagan heard Reverend McKay's voice behind her, coming from the vestibule. She turned her head, but she could not see him.

"We receive the body of our brother Henry Garrick with confidence in God, the giver of life, who raised the Lord Jesus from the dead."

When he finished the verse, the congregation said, "Amen." Flanagan said it too.

She watched as McKay led the group of six men along the aisle, the coffin resting on their shoulders. Two undertakers guided the coffin onto the waiting trolley at the front.

McKay went to the lectern and said, "We meet in the name of Christ who died and was raised by the glory of God the Father. Grace and mercy be with you all."

The congregation said, "And also with you."

Flanagan said it too, beats behind everyone else. As she said the words, McKay's

179

eyes met hers, and from the back of the church, even over this distance, she saw despair in them.

24

McKay recited the words with no aware-ness of their meaning. They were only shapes in his mouth, movements his tongue had made hundreds of times over the years.

He looked out to the people, his gaze find-ing Flanagan.

Save me, he thought.

She stared back, and she saw it on him, he was sure. He looked away, looked any-where but at her. Then he found Roberta in the front row, and she did not look at him.

She had barely looked at him the day before, during the wake. All the same people, the congregation of this church, milling around the house. Cups of tea, small sandwiches, biscuits, cakes, sausage rolls. The kitchen a production line of kindly women, the hall lined with folding chairs, borrowed by the vanload from the old school hall across the road from the church that served as a community centre, now bearing the weight of middle-aged men holding cups and saucers.

The chatter of voices and the clink of china, this was the sound of a wake to Reverend Peter McKay. The smell of tea and sweat.

Roberta had the coffin put in the back room where Mr. Garrick had spent his last weeks. McKay didn't want to see it, didn't want to look at the face of the man he'd killed. But such was his duty. When he arrived at the house in the early afternoon he lingered in the hall as long as he could, shaking hands, patting shoulders, refusing cups of tea.

Soon there was no more avoiding it. He walked to the room at the rear of the hall, paused in the doorway. A small cluster of men greeted him, and he stepped inside. They moved out of his way, allowed him space. As fear pushed up from his belly and into his throat, threatening to choke him, McKay approached the coffin. Varnished oak, gold-plated handles, glistening in the light from the window. McKay swallowed and looked inside.

Silk covered the body to the waist, disguising the missing legs, the gnarled hands powdered to hide the scarring. And the face, waxen and hollow, like a doll.

I'm sorry, he wanted to say. I wish I could take it back. I shouldn't have done this terrible thing, and I'd give anything to take the poison from your mouth.

And every unspoken word was true. As he fought the urge to weep, McKay startled at the sound of a voice at his shoulder.

"Sure, you'd think he was sleeping, wouldn't you?"

He turned to see Mr. McHugh staring into the coffin.

"They can do wonderful things, these days, the undertakers. I remember when we buried Cora's mother it looked as if they'd made her up as a clown."

McKay knew he should have replied, perhaps enquired after Cora's health, was she getting out at all lately? Instead, he walked away, out of the room, and struggled through the kitchen full of trays and steam and gossip until he found the door to the utility room and the small bathroom off that.

Had he still believed in God, McKay would have thanked Him that the bathroom was unoccupied. He closed and locked the door, leaned against it. A small space, no more than six feet by four, the toilet at one end, a washbasin at the other, lit by a narrow frosted window.

For the first time in a decade, he felt the craving for a cigarette. That dry need at the back of his throat, in his lungs, waiting for tarry blue smoke. He had never smoked more than ten a day, even as a young man, but still the desire was great.

Later.

Later, he would go to a shop in some other town and buy a packet of cigarettes and smoke them until he hacked up grey phlegm, until he was dizzy and nauseous. But now he had to pull himself together. Get through the next forty-eight hours. That was all.

Last night she had given him hope.

Roberta still hadn't wanted him to come over — discreet, she'd said — but her voice had been warm and kind. Loving, even. Enough to let him think there might be an after, a beyond. If he survived, there could be a future for him and Roberta, as tainted as it might be.

His thin surface of calm restored, McKay left the bathroom, back out through the kitchen, into the hall, avoiding every hand that reached out for him, every seeking face that wanted to snare him in banal conversation. He kept his focus on the door to the good sitting room, where he knew Roberta would be, the queen on her throne holding dominion over her subjects.

She did not look up as he entered the room. A cup of tea on a saucer held on her lap. Black skirt, white blouse, minimal make-up. A beautiful young widow mourning her husband. McKay crossed the room, swerving between the feet and knees of those seated here, towards the one narrow space on the couch, opposite her.

"Excuse me," he said to Miss Trimble, the aged spinster who always insisted on giving him a critique of his sermons. She moved sideways, leaving him just enough cushion to squeeze onto.

Now the widow saw him.

"Reverend Peter," she said.

"Mrs. Garrick," he said. "How are you holding up?"

A gentle smile. She tilted her head. "Not too bad." She shared the smile with the people all around. "Everyone's been very kind."

With that, she turned away from him. A clear instruction. Don't talk to her.

And he wanted to slap the cup and saucer from her hand, grab her shoulders, shake her. And tell her what? He loved her? He hated her?

He said nothing. Sat with his hands on his knees, exchanged greetings with the good people as they came and went, while magnificent fury burned inside him.

"We have come here today to remember our dear friend Henry Garrick," McKay said, his voice carrying over the congregation. The echo of the loudspeakers sent his words back to him, a booming muddle of vowels and dull consonants. "To give thanks for his life, to leave him in the keeping of God his creator, redeemer and judge, to commit his body to be buried, and to comfort one another in our grief, in the hope that is ours through the death and resurrection of Jesus Christ."

Words upon words upon words. He worked through each stage of the ceremony, the prayers, the hymns, the psalm, the calls and responses, the standing and sitting. All the time he avoided the policewoman's gaze, and Roberta avoided his.

He read from the First Epistle of John, asking the congregation to reflect on the fleeting nature of life on this earth, because one's gaze should be beyond. He almost choked on his hypocrisy as he came to verse fifteen.

"Love not the world, neither the things that are in the world. If any man love the world, the love of the Father is not in him.

For all that is in the world, the lust of the flesh, and the lust of the eyes, and the pride of life, is not of the Father, but is of the world. And the world passeth away, and the lust thereof: but he that doeth the will of God abideth forever."

He watched Roberta as he read the words lust and flesh, but she did not react.

Then he moved to the pulpit for the sermon, the usual recounting of the deceased's life and loves, their hobbies, their foibles, their losses, their victories. Roberta smiled and nodded when appropriate. When McKay spoke of the drowned child, she bowed her head, pulled a tissue from her sleeve and dabbed at her cheeks while Miss Trimble put a comforting hand on her shoulder.

Now a final glance up at him, so quick, so sly. Barely enough for him to see the dryness of her eyes as he said her dead daughter's name once more.

He stared down into the open grave, the fine wood of the coffin marred by the handfuls of earth that had broken on its surface. The Lord's Prayer murmured around him, and for an insane moment he wondered who had prompted the gathered people to recite it before he realised he spoke it

187

himself. He faltered over the final lines, but the voices around him carried him to the finish.

"Lord," he said, "you will show us the path of life: in your presence is fullness of joy, and from your right hand flow delights for evermore."

A moment of stillness, only the breeze rustling through the trees, then the crowd began to disperse. McKay shook hands with a few as they passed on their way to Roberta to give their final condolences.

He backed away, worked towards the periphery. The day was far from over; tea and sandwiches were to be served in the community centre, please join us, all welcome. At least two more hours of small talk and handshakes, two more hours of swallowing the scream that had been coiled in his throat since the coffin entered the church.

But a moment, please, a moment of quiet. He made for the church, imagining the silence of the vestry. He could take his time removing his cassock and surplice, hanging them up, putting on his jacket. The half-full packet of Marlboros was hidden in the safe, along with a packet of mints. No one would miss him for fifteen minutes, surely? He nodded and smiled to the stragglers on the path back to the church, ignored any attempt to slow him, to talk to him.

"Reverend McKay."

A woman's voice, behind him.

"Reverend McKay?"

He knew whose. He kept his head down, quickened his step. She was quicker.

DCI Flanagan touched his arm. "Reverend McKay."

He turned, feigned surprise, hoped she wouldn't see the fear on him. "Ah, sorry, Inspector, I was in a world of my own. And it's Reverend Peter."

"Reverend Peter," she echoed. "Sorry to keep you back. I just wanted to thank you for the other day. For taking the time to talk with me. It helped, it really did."

McKay felt the fear slip away almost entirely, replaced by something else. What was it? He couldn't be sure; his emotions had become a confused jumble in recent days, and he struggled to tell one from another.

He wetted his lips and asked, "And did the prayer do any good?"

"Yes," she said, a smile blooming on her mouth. "I'm still not sure who or what I was praying to, maybe I was just talking to myself, but it helped me see things more clearly. My husband and I had a good talk

189

last night. Things are looking better."

"Good, I'm glad," he said, meaning it.

In that moment, he saw something in Flanagan that alarmed and calmed him all at once: her decency. In all the filth he had allowed himself to wallow in for the last few months he had lost sight of that most human of qualities. And here, confronted by this woman's basic goodness, he felt awed by her. Once more he wanted to tell her everything, throw himself on her mercy.

It must have told on his features, because a crease appeared on her brow.

"Is everything all right?" she asked, putting her hand on his arm again.

"Fine, fine," he said, backing away. "It's been one long day after another, is all. Sorry, I need to get these robes off and get over to the hall. Will you be joining us? You're very welcome."

Even as he asked the question, he regretted it. A small burst of relief when she shook her head.

"I have to get to work," she said, moving towards the gates. "Thanks again."

She walked to the drift of people exiting the grounds. When he'd lost her among them, he went back to the church, into the cool and the quiet. He ignored Mr. McHugh who was packing away his sheet music at

190

the organ and headed straight for the vestry. The door closed and locked behind him, he pulled the surplice over his head, let it fall to the floor, unbuckled the belt at his waist, threw the cassock off. He got down on his knees, hit the four-digit combination on the safe, reached inside for the lighter and cigarettes, pinched one between his lips, sparked the thumbwheel, inhaled.

Oh, glorious heat, filling his chest, that crackling through his veins, into his skull.

He exhaled a long plume of smoke, felt a dizzy wave wash across his forehead, took another drag. Once the wave passed, he got to his feet and went to the small window protected by a wire grille. He opened the top pane, blew smoke through.

I've gotten away with it, he thought.

Such a certain and reasonable idea, he couldn't question it. Flanagan had moved on, more concerned with her own life now than his or Roberta's. The coroner had ruled it suicide. If he held his nerve just a little longer, if he could keep a wall around the crushing guilt that threatened to break him, if he could do that, he had gotten away with it.

A high whoop of a laugh escaped him, followed by a stream of tears.

He had gotten away with it.
They had gotten away with it.

25

Flanagan edged through the cluster of mourners at the gate, fighting against the flow towards the community centre. She wanted to turn right, head towards her car, but she was swept onto the road. She persevered through the dark suits and sharp-cornered handbags, excuse me, excuse me, thank you, excuse me, until she emerged into clear air. There, she joined the thin trickle of people who didn't want to partake of tea and sandwiches.

Her Volkswagen in sight, she kept her head down, walking along the roadway, avoiding the bottlenecks of people on the footpath.

From behind, "Excuse me!"

Another person trying to escape the crowd. She kept going.

"Excuse me! Hello?"

Footsteps jogging behind her. Flanagan turned, feeling suddenly defensive for no reason she could comprehend.

That man, from the church. The middle-aged man who knelt in prayer, the familiarity of whose features had nagged at her throughout the ceremony. He slowed his pace, fighting for breath.

"Can I help you?" she asked, trying to ignore her growing wariness.

"Are you the police officer who's handling Harry's case?" he asked between gulps of air.

"That's right," she said. "DCI Flanagan. What can I do for you?"

"My name's George Garrick," he said. "Harry's brother."

It made sense, then, the familiarity. The scarring had blurred the dead man's features, but enough remained for the likeness to his brother to be clear. For a moment, Flanagan felt she knew what Henry Garrick had looked like in life, tall and gently handsome. She wondered if he had spoken with the same country softness to the consonants as George Garrick. With the wondering came a sadness that he had gone and no one would hear his voice again.

She pushed the thought aside and said, "I see. I'm sorry for your loss."

He fussed at his well-worn suit jacket. "Thank you. I recognised you from the

194

news. I wanted to have a word, if you've time."

She looked towards her car, thought of the paperwork at the station that needed doing, then turned back to him. "Of course."

"It's about Harry," he said. He looked to the crowd filtering into the old school hall before speaking again. "And Roberta. I need to tell you something about her."

"Go ahead," Flanagan said.

She noticed the redness of his eyes, realised he had been weeping for his brother. The grief lingered beneath the surface, its vague form visible to her through his skin.

"That woman," George Garrick said. "She's evil."

"I stayed near the back," he said. "Out of the way. I daren't have let her see me there."

George Garrick sat in the passenger seat of her car, his knees pressed against the glovebox, his head nearly touching the roof lining. Some of the other cars had started to move away. He looked over his shoulder, put his elbow on the door, his forearm shielding his face from outside.

"Why not?" Flanagan asked.

"She would've made sure I got driven out. She wouldn't stand to have me about the place. I haven't been welcome around here for four years now."

"Why?" Flanagan asked.

"Roberta made sure of it. The lies she told about me. The things she accused me of."

The last words caught in his throat, and he brought his hand to his mouth, his eyes brimming. Flanagan did not prompt him, allowed him to find his own way.

"I never touched her," he said eventually, wiping at his veined cheeks. "I swear to my Lord God above, I never touched her. I swore to Harry, I swore to the rest of them, and I swear to you, I never laid one hand on that woman."

He wept now, tears running free to drip onto his shirt.

"And I have to tell you this. I've never said it to anyone, not once. But I have to say it now."

Flanagan reached across, put her hand on his forearm. "Go on," she said.

"Oh God," he said. He hissed through his teeth as if the pressure of his secrets might burst him at the seams. He looked skyward, then closed his eyes. "Oh God. Dear God forgive me, I think she killed her child."

Fat raindrops slapped against the car's windscreen. Flanagan's nerves jangled, electricity coursed across her skin.

"From the start," she said. "Tell me what happened."

He sat there for a while, his head gently shaking, a tiny movement, almost nothing at all. His breathing settled, the tears dried. He took a breath and began.

"I was so happy for Harry when he met her," he said. "He'd been struggling since his first wife cleared out. He put a brave face on it, he was always a proud man. Not in a sinful way, I mean, but he was the sort of fella wouldn't tell anyone his problems. But I knew he was struggling. He was lonely. He had all this money, and no one to share it with. All he had was his business, that and the church. If he'd been a drinker like me, he probably would've let that eat him up.

"Anyway, when Roberta came along I was delighted for him, the same as everyone else. You could see how happy he was. I knew he was going to marry her before he did. I was best man at his wedding. Second time I did that for him. I started to see less of him after the wedding, but I thought, sure, that's only natural. He's got a lovely wife now, why would he be bothered with his useless auld lump of a brother.

"She threw herself into the church, joined in all the activities, all the clubs. Really

197

made herself a part of the community. Everyone loved her. So did I. She just pulled people to her. Then she got pregnant and everyone was over the moon. You'd think the whole town and country was an uncle or an aunt to that child."

A smile broke on his face, wide and toothy. Flanagan couldn't help but reflect it. He blushed, dropped his gaze.

"Wee Erin. She was a beautiful wee girl. An awful good baby. They never had any trouble with her. She fed well, she slept well. She was talking away by the time they went to Barcelona. She couldn't make a whole pile of sense, but you could see the personality coming through, who she was going to grow into. Who she might have been.

"It was Reverend Peter phoned me to let me know. I remember it like it was five minutes ago. It was evening time, I was having a wee whiskey, watching the snooker on TV. The wife was washing up. I answered the phone and he told me, and I hung up and I went and put that bottle to my mouth and I never took another breath till it was gone.

"Oh God, the funeral. It was the worst I'd ever seen. The crying. People cry at funerals, course they do, but not like this. And me and Harry carried that wee white coffin and, oh God, I wanted to take Harry and pull all the pain out of him and take it for myself.

"And I remember, I stood by the graveside, that same grave she stood by today, and I looked across and I saw Roberta. And I knew it was an act. Everyone else was too worked up to see it, but I saw it, like she was wearing a mask.

"I started wondering then. I started drinking, too, more than I should have. Maybe if I'd laid off the drink for those few months, maybe I would've made more sense of it. But here's the thing. She was a swimmer. A good swimmer. Not everyone knew that, but I did. She used to go to Lisburn, and I saw her there, doing lengths. She cut through that water like she could win a medal. And somehow she goes out into the sea and loses her child? Nearly drowns herself?

"The more I thought about it, the more I couldn't make sense of it. And the way she'd looked at the funeral. Maybe I should've gone to Harry about it, or the police, or just kept my bloody mouth shut. But one Sunday after church, Harry and Roberta had me and the wife to theirs for lunch. I'd had a few wee nips from a quarter bottle in my pocket, the wife didn't approve, but I felt like I needed it. Anyway, usually Janet and

Roberta would've done the dishes, but I insisted Janet sit down and take it easy.

"So there's me and Roberta in the kitchen, loading up the dishwasher, sorting out the pans, and I says to her about wee Erin. I say, tell me again how it happened, and she sort of closed up, said she didn't want to go over it again. But I didn't let it go. I says to her, I don't understand it, as good a swimmer as her, and she couldn't help wee Erin. Even if she lost hold of her, how come she couldn't get her back? How come she nearly drowned herself?"

George went quiet, his eyes distant, the memory holding his mind there in the past. Flanagan wondered how many hours he'd lost to it over the years, locked there.

"How did she react?" Flanagan asked.

"She just stared at me for a minute," George said. "I remember the two of us standing there, her with a stack of plates in her hands, me with my hands in my pockets. And then I saw who she really was. Like she'd taken off this disguise she was wearing, and I could see what she really was underneath. And I knew then she killed her daughter. And she knew I knew. We stood still like that for I don't know how long, not saying anything, just knowing each other. I saw something inside her, something that's sick, that's not human. I see it every night when I try to sleep. I see it every time I think of my brother, and when I remember wee Erin. I think of the monster she showed me that day.

"She dropped the plates. There was this almighty crash, pieces going everywhere. And then she screamed, stop it, stop it, let go of me, and she ran for the door. Harry came in then, and she ran right past him and upstairs. I went and got Janet and said, let's go, and I got out of there.

"Harry called me that night. He said he didn't want to see me ever again, not at home, not in the street, and not at church. Before I know it, it's all around the town and country that I grabbed my brother's wife, tried to feel her up when she's still grieving for her child. And of course, the rumour got worse the further it spread. Janet started hearing all sorts of things on the street. She stuck by me for a month, but it got too much for her, all the talk and all the looks she got. She couldn't take it any longer, even though she knew it was nonsense. She moved back to Bushmills, where she's from."

He seemed diminished, shrunken into the seat, as if telling all this to Flanagan had bled something out of him. He shook his head and looked at her.

"That woman destroyed me. She might as well have put a gun to my head and pulled the trigger. It's years since I set foot on this street. And now my brother's dead. My brother, who was the strongest man I ever knew in my life, who thought suicide was the worst sin a person could commit. I tried, but I never got to see him after the accident. I know he was in bad shape, but if he had a thread of life to hang on to, he never would have given up. I know that. I know it in my heart. My brother did not kill himself."

Flanagan remained silent and still, her mind racing.

"Have you nothing to say?" he asked. "Tell me I'm mad, at least. Tell me something."

"The coroner has reported it as suicide," she said.

"I know that, but —"

"I was there when the pathologist did the post-mortem examination. Everything pointed towards suicide. Everything."

"You sound like you're trying to convince yourself more than me," he said.

Flanagan shook her head. "I don't know what else to say."

"Well, at least I told someone." He reached for the door handle. "I don't have to go to my grave carrying this thing around with me. I suppose what you do with it is up to you. But I had to tell you. You understand that, don't you?"

"I do," Flanagan said. She put her hand on his arm. "And again, I'm sorry for your loss, I really am."

He nodded and opened the passenger door, climbed out, ducked down to look in at her.

"Whatever happens," he said, "just remember what she really is."

He closed the door before Flanagan could reply, and she watched in her rear-view mirror as George Garrick slipped between the parked cars and out of her vision.

26

"You're looking terrible, Reverend Peter," Miss Trimble said.

McKay had tried to avoid her, had veered around a row of chairs, but she had ducked through a gap and headed him off.

"Have you not been sleeping?" she asked.

He looked past her, beyond the rows of people with their combination plates and saucers, cups of tea or coffee balanced on one side, mounds of sandwiches and sausage rolls on the other. At the long table at the top of the hall, by the curtained stage, Roberta sat, people leaning in from all sides to offer their kinship, like Christ at the Last Supper. One empty chair at the table where McKay should have sat. He had spent as much time as he could touring the room, shaking hands, smiling, saying thank you for the compliments on his sermon. Miss Trimble had not been the first to comment on his gaunt appearance.

Now, as people began to say farewell, the room emptying, he had no choice but to take his seat. First, he went to the long table laden with trays and cups and plates, two large urns at one end. He took a plate, lifted a few scraps of food, paying no mind to what he had chosen.

"Tea or coffee, Reverend?" Mr. Wellesley asked.

"Yes, please," McKay said, watching her across the hall.

"Which?"

"Oh," McKay said, turning back to Mr. Wellesley. "Tea, please."

Mr. Wellesley poured him a cup and set it on the outstretched plate. McKay thanked him and walked towards the stage, and the table before it. She glanced up as he approached, looked away again, leaning across to listen to whatever drivel Jim Allison spouted.

McKay sat down between them, forcing Allison to speak around him.

"I was just saying, it was a good service."

"Thank you," McKay said.

"I saw that policewoman talking to you outside the church," Allison said. "Has she been bothering you? I can deal with her if she has."

McKay shook his head. "No. She's been

205

nothing but courteous and professional. I think we'll not be hearing from her again until the inquest next year."

"Okay, good," Allison said. "I need to be off, but I'll see you on Sunday."

He stood and patted McKay's shoulder before crouching down and putting an arm around Roberta. "Take care, now, and let me know if you need anything. Anything at all."

McKay watched Allison's back as he left, saw him shake hands and smile his way through the thinning crowd.

"You don't like him, do you?"

He turned to Roberta, startled at the teasing in her voice. "It's not up to me to like or dislike my congregation. My job is to care for them, whoever they are."

"He's not that different from you," she said.

"He's nothing like me."

"You sure about that?"

He tried to read her face, even though he should have known by now that she was unreadable. Was she mocking him? Was it playfulness or spite? Or were they the same thing to her?

"You were right," he said.

"About what?"

"About DCI Flanagan," he said. "We

don't have to worry about her. She's not
—"

Roberta squeezed his arm, stopping the words in his mouth. She looked around the room, at those close by, those still at the table.

"I need the bathroom," she said. Then she lowered her voice. "Follow me in two minutes."

She left the table without waiting for a reply. McKay watched her walk to the entrance hall, avoiding encounters with sympathetic friends, moving through the people like a snake through grass. He checked his watch, counted the seconds. Someone at the table spoke his name. He pretended he didn't hear.

When two minutes had passed, exactly, to the second, he rose from his chair and made his way to the entrance hall. No one tried to talk to him, no one reached for his elbow. He rounded the corner to the two unisex toilets out of view of the hall. One stood open and empty, the other an inch ajar. He went to it, put his fingertips to the wood, pushed.

Roberta stood at the washbasin, examining her face in the mirror above. She turned to him as he closed the door, locking them both inside.

McKay opened his mouth to speak, but before a word could find his tongue, her hand lashed out, her palm hard across his cheek. He staggered back, tried to speak again, but she lunged at him, caught his throat between her fingers, pushed him against the door. The back of his head connected with the wood. Her fingers tightened, closing his windpipe. Black dots speckled his vision.

"Don't ever talk like that again in public," she said through bared teeth. "If someone heard, we'd both be finished. Watch your fucking mouth. Do you understand me?"

He tried to speak, but no air could pass through his throat.

She eased her grip and repeated, "Do you understand me?"

"Yes," he said, a thin croak between gulps of air. He put a hand on the wall to steady himself as his head seemed to drift away from his shoulders.

"Good," she said, stepping back. She wiped the back of her hand across her mouth, her eyes burning. Then she lunged forward again.

McKay said, "No," and brought his hands up, tried to keep her away. But she grabbed his wrists, pulled his arms aside.

Please don't, he would have said, but her

lips closed on his, her tongue soft and warm, her body in tight to him. Her hands went to his waist, his belt, the button, the fly. She took his lower lip between her teeth, and he felt a hot sting and tasted metal.

As chattering voices drifted in through the small bathroom window, Roberta dropped to her knees. She pulled fabric aside, baring him to her.

She grinned up at him, a red smear of his blood on her teeth.

27

Flanagan found DS Murray at his desk, engrossed in paperwork. She knocked on the wood to get his attention. He looked up, startled.

"Sorry, ma'am," he said, blinking as if he'd come out of a slumber.

"Get on the phone to Barcelona, get hold of whoever in the Mossos d'Esquadra dealt with the death of Erin Garrick four years ago."

"Who?"

"The Garricks' little girl," Flanagan said, her voice rising with her impatience. "She drowned at a beach there. I want to speak with whoever dealt with the case. Today, if possible. Organise a translator if one's needed."

She walked away, and he called after her.

"Ma'am, what's going on?"

"Just get it sorted," she said without looking back.

Flanagan went to her office, fired up her computer. A minute later she had the telephone number for the British Consulate in Barcelona. One minute more and she was on hold for the Third Secretary. She had to wait five more before an answer came.

"This is Julia Heston-Charles, how can I help?"

The accent was stiffly English, public school through and through.

"This is Detective Chief Inspector Serena Flanagan, Police Service of Northern Ireland, based in Lisburn. I need to discuss the case of a child, a British national, who drowned at the beach in Barcelona four years ago. Her name was Erin Garrick, her parents were Henry and Roberta Garrick."

A moment of hiss in the earpiece before Heston-Charles said, "Yes, I remember."

"You dealt with this?"

"Yes. It was just before I went on maternity leave. I was seven or eight months pregnant at the time. Not a pleasant case to deal with when you're about to have a child of your own."

"No, I suppose not," Flanagan said.

"What do you need to know?"

"Anything," Flanagan said, her pen ready. "Whatever you can remember about it."

"All right," Heston-Charles said. The line

went quiet as she gathered her memories. "If I recall correctly, the initial contact came from the police officer who dealt with the case. Can't think of his name, but he was an inspector. He called a few hours after the accident. In these situations, the Consulate needs to liaise with the police, the coroner, the local government, the undertakers, the airline for getting the body home, all on the family's behalf. It's quite an operation to oversee."

"Did you have much contact with the Garricks themselves?" Flanagan asked.

"Some. They were still at the hospital when I first met them. The mother was in the emergency ward herself, she almost drowned trying to save the little girl. The father was just wandering the corridors, he didn't know what to do with himself. I sat him down and talked him through the procedures. He was in a terrible state, understandably. Confused, angry, despairing. It was a difficult conversation."

"I can imagine," Flanagan said, remembering the many death notices she'd delivered, facing the denial and fury of the bereaved. "And what about the mother? How was Mrs. Garrick?"

"She was different," Heston-Charles said. "Whoever pumped the water out of her lungs cracked one of her ribs in the process, so she was in physical pain as well as emotional. The doctors had given her morphine, as much to sedate her as to kill the pain, I think. It all seemed to be washing over her, as if she was watching this happen to someone else. She was almost serene, I remember. Almost smiling, at times. I didn't deal with her much; it was mostly Mr. Garrick after that. He pulled himself together over those few days, got everything dealt with. I believe his brother flew over to help, too."

Flanagan took a breath before asking, "Were there ever any questions about what happened?"

A pause, then, "What do you mean?"

"The police, the coroner, did anyone dispute the Garricks' version of events?"

"Goodness, no. Can I ask, what's this about? That little girl drowned four years ago. Why are you digging into it now?"

"Sorry, I can't discuss that," Flanagan said. "It's nothing for you to be concerned about."

Heston-Charles's voice hardened. "But it concerns me enough that you need to interrupt my working day to question me about it."

"I do appreciate your time," Flanagan

said. "I'm sure you understand why I can't discuss what I'm dealing with here."

"I understand. Doesn't mean I have to like it. Now, is there anything else you need to know?"

Flanagan scanned her notes. "Not at the moment. You've been very helpful, thank you. Can I get back in touch if need be?"

"I suppose so. Good afternoon."

The line died, and Flanagan looked at the handset. "Fuck you too," she whispered before hanging up.

Her fingers hadn't left the telephone before it rang. She picked it up.

"DCI Flanagan," she said.

"What's going on?" DSI Purdy asked, not even bothering with a greeting.

Flanagan closed her eyes as she searched for something convincing. "Just following up on some details, sir," she said, knowing he wouldn't accept such a weak explanation.

"Some details," he echoed. "I was chasing young Murray for some paperwork and he tells me you have him tracking down someone in Spain for you. To do with the Garrick case, I'm told. Exactly what details can a cop in Barcelona clarify for you?"

Flanagan winced as she spoke. "I just had a few questions about the little girl's death."

"I fail to see the relevance," Purdy said.

She would have to tell him, there was no getting around it. "This morning, at the funeral, Henry Garrick's brother found me, said he had to talk to me."

"And?"

Flanagan told him all of it, every detail. When she'd finished, he said nothing for a while. When he did speak, he said, "All right, but tread carefully. I don't need that Allison prick annoying me because you stuck your nose where it didn't belong. Understood?"

"Understood, sir," Flanagan said. "Thank you."

Relieved, Flanagan hung up and turned back to her computer and its web browser. A few search phrases later, she had Roberta Garrick's Facebook profile open once more. A string of condolence messages had been posted by her friends, but otherwise nothing had changed. Including the irrational feeling that this woman did not really exist in the world. No schools listed, no former places of work. As if she'd sprung into life fully formed seven years ago.

Flanagan returned to Google and combined Roberta Garrick's name with that of every social network site she could think of, even those that had fallen from fashion

215

years ago, as well as every major shopping site in case she'd ever reviewed anything online.

Still nothing.

After an hour's fruitless searching, Flanagan realised she had forgotten to eat. She went to the canteen and ordered some toast and a coffee. She ate alone, the only other customers being a cluster of uniformed officers discussing a protest they were to attend in Belfast city centre to make sure it didn't get out of hand. Their relaxed manner suggested they didn't expect any trouble.

Just as she swallowed the last mouthful of toast, her mobile pinged to tell her a text message had arrived. Flanagan looked at the display. From Miriam: *You were right — it was a cyst. Thank God!* A smiley-face emoticon finished the message, and Flanagan felt a smile spread on her own face.

She went to reply, but the phone trilled and vibrated in her hand. DS Murray's desk number on the display.

"Yes?"

"Ma'am, I have an Inspector Guillermo Sala, retired, on the line for you."

Flanagan smiled at Murray's fumbling at a Spanish accent when he said the name. She got to her feet and walked towards the canteen exit. "Give me a minute, I'll take it in my office."

Once at her desk, she turned over to a fresh notebook page, lifted the telephone handset, and hit the blinking call waiting button. Murray had said the retired inspector's English was excellent, so no translator was needed.

When Murray had connected them, Flanagan said, "Inspector Sala?"

"Yes," he said. She could hear the grit of age in his voice.

"I'm Detective Chief Inspector Serena Flanagan, Police Service of Northern Ireland. I'd like to ask you about a case you dealt with four years ago."

"Yes, the sergeant, he told me this," Sala said. "About the baby girl."

"That's right," Flanagan said.

"It was very sad," he said. "I don't like to remember. What do you ask me?"

"If you can, please tell me what happened the day the child died."

He exhaled a sorrowful sigh, and Flanagan sensed the recollection pained him. "I come to the beach after. A *Sotsinpector,* he go first, then he call me. When I go, the mother, she is already gone to hospital. The father, he is there on the beach. He is crying, crying, crying, he says do something for her, the baby, but the paramedics say,

217

no, she is gone, we can do nothing. It was difficult. It is more time before I know what happened. The mother carries the baby out into the sea, but there is a drop, the water is deeper, and she lets go of the baby. She cannot get her back, and she goes under water also."

Flanagan noted it all down, the events matching what McKay had told her a few days before.

"The mother, she is hurt. A broken rib. They stay her in the hospital, and I call the British Consulate. I talk to the mother and the father the next day."

"What was your impression of them?" she asked.

"Ah, I don't know this meaning."

"What did you think of them?" Flanagan said. "Did you like them? Not like them?"

"Ah, *si*. Yes, first I like them. They are good people. The mother is, how do I say it, cold? No feeling. But, you know, a child dies, how do you act? The father is very sad, very angry, he cries all the time. I am sad for him."

"You said, at first you liked them. Did something change?"

Sala clicked his tongue as he thought. "I don't know I should tell. The father, Mr.

Garrick, he tells me say to no one. Is a secret."

"Inspector Sala," Flanagan said, "anything you can tell me will be helpful. I'd really appreciate it."

"Why do you call me?" he asked. "Four years ago, this is. Why call now? What happens there?"

"I'm investigating the apparent suicide of Mr. Garrick," Flanagan said.

"Ay, ay. This is bad news. Tell me, please, did they have more children?"

"No, they didn't."

"Is sad. Is very sad. He was a good man. A good father, I think."

"Inspector Sala, can you tell me what Mr. Garrick said to you?"

Silence as he considered it, before he said, "Okay. Mr. Garrick is dead, so I can tell. He was very sad in this time, you understand, very weak. So weak he tells me this thing."

"What did he tell you, Inspector Sala?"

"He tells me, she beat him. Not all the time, but some time, she beat him. And she calls him stupid, weak, a bad man. He cries when he tells me this in my office. He tells me he is afraid of her. Then he tell me not to say."

"And you agreed?"

"What can I do? They take the baby home, back to Ireland, they go together. I cannot arrest her for what he tells me. I tell him go home, go to police, ask they help you."

"Seems like he didn't," Flanagan said.

"You know, I think Mr. Garrick is big in his heart, how to say it . . . proud, yes?"

"Proud," Flanagan echoed, thinking of what George Garrick had told her about his brother.

"A proud man, is difficult to say a woman beat him. It makes him feel like he is not a man. Do you understand?"

"I do," Flanagan said. And pride was not an exclusively male trait. She had known women who refused to report abuse by their husbands simply because they couldn't bear the shame of it. It was easier to take the beatings than it was to admit they had been taken.

"One last question," she said. "Was there ever any doubt about what happened on the beach that day?"

Sala's voice thinned, as if the speaking of his answer diminished him. "I wondered," he said. "I wondered about the mother. I think, maybe, can she do this? Then I think, no, a mother cannot do this. And the coroner says an accident, I don't argue. But

220

sometimes at night, when I don't sleep. I lie in bed and I think, maybe? Maybe?"

A pause before he spoke again.

"Please, Inspector Flanagan, will you make a promise to me?"

"All right," she said.

"If you find out maybe is yes? If you find out she kill the baby? Please. Don't tell me. I don't want to know."

28

McKay stared at the ceiling, Roberta beside him on his bed.

They had emerged from the bathroom five minutes apart. No one had seen them, no one had noticed their absence in the time they were gone. When McKay had returned to the main hall, only a few stragglers remained; the ladies had already begun clearing the tables.

Ten minutes later, within earshot of Miss Trimble, Roberta had said she felt tired, unwell, could she please go over to Reverend McKay's house for a lie-down? Of course, he had said, and he escorted her through the hall, pausing for a few polite farewells, and across the road to the church grounds.

She had taken everything he could give her, taken it so voraciously it had frightened him. Now they both lay spent and exhausted, the blinds drawn, the room dim around them. They had lain for an hour, neither of them speaking. He had drifted in and out of a thin and whispery sleep, jerking awake as the images that played in his mind grew more scarred and bloody.

The drowsiness passed, and the urge to move took its place. Perhaps she sensed the change in him because she rolled onto her side to face him. He turned to look at her. Her eyes just inches from him, glittering in the points of light that pierced the blinds. She brought her hand up, rested her palm on his cheek.

"I've been thinking," she said.

"Yes?"

"Maybe we shouldn't see each other for a while."

She waited as if to let him argue, object, but his mouth was empty.

"Just for a few months," she continued. "Maybe six. Until the dust settles. Then we won't have to sneak around any more. We can be together, like we talked about."

He searched for something to say to her, a reason they shouldn't be apart, even if it was only for a few months. But he couldn't defend against her cold logic.

Her hand moved to his chest, her fingers spread wide.

"I'm going to go away for a couple of weeks," she said. "Maybe more. I need to get out of this village for a while. Miss Trimble and all that lot will be torturing me, bringing me cakes and cottage pies and lasagnes when all I really need is to be left alone."

At last he found a word to speak. "Where?"

"Somewhere warm," she said. "South of France, Montpellier's lovely, or the Canaries. Just so long as it's away from here."

"Away from me?"

The words escaped him before his right mind could intervene. He felt her body first stiffen against him, then go loose once more.

"Don't be silly," she said. "We've come this far together. It won't fall apart now. I just need some space. We need to think about the long term."

"It's just . . ."

He lacked the courage to finish the sentence.

She propped herself up on her elbow. "Just what?"

"I feel like you've been pushing me away since . . . you know . . . like I'm being closed out. Like you're putting distance between us."

"Nonsense," she said.

"And you've been . . . angry at me."

"It's been a stressful few days. You know that."

She seemed so calm, so reasonable, his fears seemed trivial when spoken aloud. But inside him they remained barbed and tangled. Try to explain, he thought. Make her see.

"If all this was for nothing," he said. "If I did what I did just for you to turn away from me, then I don't think I could survive that."

She kissed him and said, "I'm not turning away. Just being pragmatic. Now, I need a shower."

The bed rocked as she got up. He watched her naked back as she left the room and he told himself to believe her, not to let the doubt eat at him. Truly, he didn't know what he would do to himself if she left him now. He didn't know what he would do to her.

He imagined her throat squeezed between his hands.

No, he could not do that.

But hadn't he thought, all those weeks ago, that he'd never be able to kill a man?

In this very bed, another sunny afternoon sealed out of the room, when she said, "Kill him for me." Hadn't he said, "No, no I can't"? And she hadn't argued. Simply gone quiet, clinging to him as if he was all she needed in the world.

She had asked again two days later.

Like before, she had been talking about her husband's suffering. How the pain never left him except at night, when the morphine shut him down. The indignities of his existence. The urine and the excrement she had to clean away in their daily rituals. The ruin of him. How he would never be a husband to her again.

"But he'll get better," McKay had said. "It'll be hard, but things will improve. The pain, the healing, all that has to be got through to get to the other side. He'll be mobile again one day, even if it's just a wheelchair."

"Years," she said. "The doctors say it'll take years before he can even try to move. And they said there's a good chance he won't be able to use artificial limbs when there's so little left of his legs. And the suffering he'll have to go through to get there."

"But he's strong," McKay said. "He's been so positive when I've prayed with him."

She buried her face in the pillow. Her shoulders fell and rose again. "That's what everyone says." The pillow muted her voice, but the bitterness still cut through. "They come and visit for half an hour, they can't stand any more than that, and they come out of his room saying, oh, isn't he doing well? Isn't he cheerful, considering." She lifted her face, and he saw the tears as her voice cracked. "But when they're gone, when you're gone, I see what it's really like for him. He can barely stand breathing, it's so hard for him. He tells me when I wake him in the mornings, he's sorry he didn't slip away in the night. That's what he told me: he wants to just go to sleep one night and not wake up."

She covered her eyes and wept, tears dripping onto McKay's arm.

"Just imagine what it's like for him," she said between sobs. "Imagine living in constant pain. Imagine being unable to move, to care for yourself. Imagine staring at the same four walls all day, every day, for years and years. Imagine being a grown man and your wife having to clean up your shit and your piss like you're a baby."

He couldn't look at her. He couldn't get past the truth of it. "It'll get better," he said, knowing what he said meant nothing.

"When?" she asked. She spat the words at him. "When will it get better? Tell me. When will I be able to face a day that doesn't feel like hell to me and him both. For Christ's sake, we're kinder to dogs."

So the following day, Reverend Peter McKay went to Mr. and Mrs. Garrick's beautiful house outside the village. He sat down with Roberta on the luxurious couch in the living room and took her hands in his.

He asked, "How do I do it?"

The answer was simpler than he could have believed. Every night, Mr. Garrick ate a pot of yogurt — he preferred strawberry flavour — laced with the prescribed morphine granules the pharmacist delivered once every two weeks. One sachet per night, fourteen sachets per delivery. The granules were to be swallowed whole to allow them to disperse slowly in the stomach. The doctor had given dire warnings that they shouldn't be chewed lest too much of the drug be released at once: mixed with yogurt was the best way to consume the granules. And so had begun the nightly ritual of Mr. Garrick finishing his small evening meal — he didn't need a great deal of calories, but the nutritionist had insisted on an abundance of protein to promote healing — followed by a pot of yogurt spoonfed to him by his wife, or occasionally by a concerned friend. Like McKay.

They talked about it over the weeks that followed. It seemed an abstract idea, not something they would actually do. Like the way a couple might talk about leaving their jobs to buy a vineyard in France, or take a round-the-world trip. A fantasy to pass time in each other's arms, not a real act to be undertaken in earnest. But the plan grew flesh, details emerged, problems were revealed and resolved.

The granules would have to be crushed, but that was easy, just use a pestle and mortar, ditch them after. But surely they'd know he hadn't chewed them? Simply rub some of the yogurt and crushed granule mix onto his teeth with a cotton bud. But wouldn't the cotton bud leave traces of its fabric on the teeth? Then use a finger in a rubber glove.

But even though a course of action emerged clear and firm from their wonderings, McKay never truly believed it to be real. Even on Sunday night past, when he arrived at the Garricks' house, he didn't truly think he'd go through with it. Even when he saw the ceramic pestle and mortar on the kitchen worktop, the open box of morphine sachets beside it, along with a box of the surgical gloves she used when cleaning her husband.

"There," she said, pointing at them, as if he hadn't seen them as he entered the room.

She took a step back, showed him she would take no further part in it. It was up to him, and him alone.

He looked at her, and she saw the question on his face.

"Yes, tonight," she said. "Just like we talked about. It has to be tonight."

He stayed where he was. "Are you sure?" he asked.

"Yes," she said. "Go on."

McKay moved to the worktop. Slow steps, as if a noose waited for him there. He reached for a sachet.

"Gloves first," she said.

A latex glove protruded from the dispenser box. He plucked it, then the second that sprouted in its place. Tight. He struggled to put one on, then the other.

"Two pairs," she said. "To be safe."

He took another pair, pulled them on over the first. Talcum powder dusted the worktop.

"You'll need to wipe this down," he said.

She did not answer. He took the first sachet, tore along its top edge, and poured the milky white granules into the pestle.

"Ten, you reckon?"

"I think so," she said.

One after another, he tore them open, emptied their contents into the bowl until ten empty packets lay on the worktop and granules mounded in the pestle. He gripped the pestle in his right hand, the edge of the mortar in his left, and set to work. It didn't take long. The cracking and crunching of the larger pieces breaking down gave way to a sandy grinding that made him think of the beach in Cushendun where he had spent childhood summer Saturdays.

When the morphine had been reduced to a gritty powder, McKay lifted the bowl and showed it to Roberta.

"Good enough?" he asked.

"Good enough," she said.

She went to the fridge and fetched a large pot of strawberry yogurt, the expensive kind, the kind they advertised with beautiful actresses licking the spoons, purring words like creamy and decadent. Not the type he usually had, the type the supermarkets sold in packs of six, bound together at the rim to be snapped apart.

Roberta took a teaspoon from a drawer and joined McKay at the worktop. She set the pot down and peeled back the lid, put it aside. McKay held the pestle for her while she scooped spoonfuls of powdered morphine into the yogurt. She worked with a steady care and precision, not letting a single grain fall from the spoon, stirring oc-

231

casionally as she went.

When the last of the morphine had been scraped from the pestle, McKay set it down next to the yogurt pot. Roberta pulled a crumpled-up carrier bag from the cupboard beneath the sink, opened it wide while McKay put the pestle and mortar inside, along with the gloves. She tied the handles in a loose knot.

"Are you ready?" Roberta asked.

"I'm ready," he said.

She lifted the yogurt pot, the spoon standing inside it, and handed them to him. He followed her out of the kitchen, across the hall, to the closed door of Mr. Garrick's room. Roberta knocked once and opened it.

Mr. Garrick lay on the bed, its back raised, pillows propping him up. He seemed to be adrift somewhere inside himself, his eyes open but unfocused. A sharp breath and he came back, looked towards the door.

"Oh, what's this?" he said, the scarred mouth stretching into a smile.

"Reverend Peter dropped in to see you," Roberta said.

"Oh, that's nice," he said. "Good to see you, Peter. It's been a while."

Mr. Garrick had always called McKay by his first name, ever since he first took over the parish.

"Been busy," McKay said, following Roberta into the room. It was a lie. In truth, he had avoided seeing Mr. Garrick as much as possible since he'd taken the poor bastard's wife into his bed. "I brought you your pudding."

"Good man," Mr. Garrick said.

Cheery. Always cheery. When he had all the reasons in the world not to be.

Roberta gathered up the plate and cutlery from dinner, clearing space on the wheeled table that overhung the bed.

"Thanks, love," Mr. Garrick said.

As McKay went to the chair by the bed, Roberta carried the plate to the door, out into the hall, and started to close it behind her.

"Are you going?" McKay asked, a hard edge to his voice he hadn't intended. He cleared his throat. "I thought you might stay and chat with us."

She shook her head. "Sure, you boys chat away and I'll get the dishes done."

If not for the panic in his breast, he might have noted for the hundredth time how her accent took on her husband's soft country lilt when she was around him.

The door closed, and McKay stared at the wood until Mr. Garrick said, "Sit down, Peter, sit down."

McKay did so, holding out the yogurt pot.

"Oh, she's got me the fancy stuff this time. Set it on the table, there, I'll have it in a wee bit."

McKay put the pot on the table, then put his hands on his knees. His mind scrambled for something to say, anything, anything at all.

"For a man who came to chat, you're awful quiet tonight," Mr. Garrick said. "No crack with you?"

McKay swallowed and said, "No, nothing at all, just work at the minute. How've you been?"

"Oh, much the same, good days and bad days. More bad than good, if I'm honest. If it wasn't for Ro, I wouldn't be able to stick it."

Ro. His pet name for her. McKay could never call her that.

Mr. Garrick winked, the gesture creasing the pink scar tissue on his cheek. "Still no movement in your love life, then? No wee Dilsey-Janes chasing after you?"

McKay felt heat in his cheeks. "No," he said. "I've no time for that."

"Then make time." Mr. Garrick raised a clawed hand to him. "*Cherchez la femme,* as the man says. You should try online.

There's no shame in it these days. Sure, I did all right out of it, didn't I?"

"Yes, you did," McKay said. "You have that to be thankful for, at least."

"At least," Mr. Garrick echoed. "Speaking of thanks, maybe we should say a few words to Him upstairs, what do you think?"

"Would you like to?"

Mr. Garrick's eyes glistened. "Yes, I'd like to."

Even though there was nothing he wanted less at that moment, McKay said, "All right."

He leaned forward, bowed his head, put his hands on the edge of the bed, brought them together. He inhaled, ready to speak, but Mr. Garrick started first.

"Dear Lord," he said, "I just want to thank you for all my blessings. I've had some hard times, but You've blessed me with good friends. And I thank You for bringing Ro to me, and I pray that You give her the strength to care for me the way she has done so far."

McKay felt knuckles nudge his shoulder.

"And Dear God, I pray You put some sense into this man's head, and help him get up off his backside and find a decent woman, because he deserves one as much as he needs one. Amen."

In spite of himself, McKay smiled and

said, "Amen."

He looked up at the table, the yogurt pot, the spoon.

"Maybe you don't want that," he said, standing as he reached for it. "I'll put it into the bin for you."

Mr. Garrick hooked his clawed hand around the pot. "No, you're not taking that off me. That's the good stuff, and I'm not wasting it."

With his right hand he was able to grip the spoon between his thumb and index finger. He scooped yogurt into his mouth, worked it around his tongue, and swallowed. He opened and closed his mouth a few times.

McKay sat down again, watching.

"Texture's a bit funny," Mr. Garrick said. "Tastes good, though."

He took another spoonful, then another. With the next one, the spoon slipped in his grasp before it reached his lips, spilling yogurt down his chin. He tutted and shook his head.

"Here, let me," McKay said. He reached for a napkin from the table.

"These spoons are too small," Mr. Garrick said. "I can't keep hold of them like the big spoons."

"I'll help," McKay said.

He used the napkin to grip the spoon handle, scooped some yogurt out of the pot and into Mr. Garrick's mouth.

When he'd swallowed, Mr. Garrick gave a dry laugh. "Look at me, like a baby. Don't be making choo-choo noises, now."

He giggled, and his head rocked forward then back onto the pillow. "She's kicking in quick tonight, boy."

"Good," McKay said, scooping as much as he could into the spoon. "The sleep will do you good."

Into his mouth, there, don't spill.

"I remember feeding our wee Erin," Mr. Garrick said, his eyes focusing and defocusing, the pupils growing. "She was a great eater. You remember our wee Erin?"

Another spoonful.

"Of course I do," McKay said.

Mr. Garrick's head nodded forward but didn't fall back again. "She's getting big," he said. "She's near up to my . . . what?"

McKay put a finger beneath Mr. Garrick's chin, lifted it until the weight of the head carried it back. His eyes glassy now.

Don't go yet, McKay thought. If he passed out too soon he might not get enough morphine. He might wake and know what they'd tried to do. McKay clicked his fingers in front of Mr. Garrick's face until he blinked and said, "What?"

Another spoonful in, and Mr. Garrick swallowed by reflex. And another.

The eyelids fluttering.

"I . . . I . . . don . . . wan . . ."

Another, and another, then McKay scraped the bottom of the pot for the last drops. He tipped them into the open mouth. Mr. Garrick smacked his lips together then went very still. McKay stood there over the bed, the napkin-wrapped spoon suspended in one hand. He held his breath, felt the silence press in on him.

Then Mr. Garrick inhaled with a long, low, guttural snore and McKay let the air out of his lungs. He reached across and placed the spoon handle between the fingers of Mr. Garrick's right hand, feeling the dying man's breath upon his cheek. He shivered and stood up straight.

Simple as that.

And wasn't Roberta right? Wasn't it a mercy?

No, it wasn't. McKay was a murderer. The truth of it threatened to flood his mind, drive all reason from him. Be calm, he thought. You're not done yet.

Roberta had googled suicide, the methods and investigation. Often people place photographs around themselves, watch them as they die. McKay took another napkin from the bundle on the table. He moved each of the framed pictures from the bedside table and arranged them in front of Mr. Garrick. There, good.

He went to the door, opened it, out into the hall, across to the kitchen.

Where was Roberta? No time to think of that now.

He squeezed his hands into another two pairs of surgical gloves then gathered up the empty morphine sachets, bundled them in one hand, lifted the box with the other. Back in Mr. Garrick's room, he spread the sachets on the table, put the box on the bedclothes, just within Mr. Garrick's reach.

That done, he surveyed his work. Yes, everything was as they'd discussed and planned. All he had to do now was leave the room and close the door.

Then he noticed the utter silence. No snoring. Not even a whisper of a breath.

Some time between McKay's leaving this room and returning, Mr. Garrick had died.

A wave of panic swelled in him, and he began to shake as adrenalin surged through his body, telling him to run, run, get away, get out of here.

"Stop it," he said. "Stop it now."

Breathe. For Christ's sake, breathe.

He willed his lungs to obey, air in, air out, until the tremors subsided enough for him to be able to step back through the door and close it behind him.

Done.

God help him, he had done it.

Suddenly, all air left the hallway. McKay inhaled as deep as his lungs would allow, but there was no air. Breathed out, and in again. No air. He reached for his collar, pulled aside the white tabard, found the button at his throat, undid it. Inhaled again, but no good, there was no air. His vision narrowed, closed in.

McKay's legs gave way, and he tried to put his hands out to break his fall. The wooden floor slammed into his knees. His heart boomed behind his breastbone, and he felt that the next thunderous beat would burst it inside him.

An idea pierced through the chaos behind his eyes: Heart attack. I'm having a heart attack and I'm dying. One hand on the floor to stop him toppling over, the other clutched at his heaving chest, his lungs pulling at the air that wasn't in the hallway.

He didn't see Roberta approach, didn't hear her shoes on the floor, only realised she was by his side when her hands gathered him up to her.

"Panic attack," she said. "It's just a panic attack. Try to breathe. Come on. Breathe."

And he did. Somehow, slowly, sweet air returned to the world. Thin at first, but thickening so that he could take a gulp, then another, and another until the booming of his heart eased.

He didn't know how long passed as he kneeled on the floor, his head on her breast. Eventually she said, "It's over. It's done."

"Yes," he whispered as he pushed himself up to sit alongside her.

"I'll find him in the morning," she said. "Just like we talked about."

"Then you'll call me," he said between breaths.

"That's right. You should go now. I'll take care of everything else."

She helped him to his feet as he asked, "What about the pestle and mortar, the bag?"

"I'll take care of them." She pushed him towards the front door. "Now go."

A minute later, he steered his Ford Fiesta through the gates at the end of the driveway. Branches and hedgerows blurred as they passed through the glare of his headlights. Without thinking, he headed west, skirted Moira, and found his way onto the motorway, south, left it again.

Lurgan, the signs said. A service station. Houses, sixties boxes and newbuilds.

After a few turns, he came to a round-about. He circled it once, twice, three times, unable to choose which exit to take. Finally, he jerked the wheel at the next junction he saw, not caring where it might lead. He found himself on a straight stretch of road, railings on either side. Then he saw the wide stretch of water he crossed, reflecting the weak moonlight: the River Bann. He slowed the car, stopped at the centre of the bridge, the river rolling away either side of him. Darkness everywhere.

He climbed out of the car, put his hands on the metal railing, felt the cold of it seep through the flesh and into the bones. Trees hissed at him. He wondered for a moment what it would feel like, the fall, only a second or two, then the sudden cold of the water. Would his body fight to live? Or could he allow himself to sink, to drown down there in the black?

He saw the beam of the headlights illuminating the pale skin of his hands before he heard the engine. It'll pass, he thought. The driver will see me and think I'm odd standing here at night, but that's all.

The car did not pass. Its engine note dropped in pitch, stepping down as the driver moved through the gears. McKay heard the tyres rumble on the road, a faint high whine as the brakes gripped the wheels, then the engine died. He didn't have to turn his head to know the car had pulled in behind his own. But when he heard one door open, then another, he did turn his head and his heart froze.

Two police officers closed the doors of their patrol car. One, the driver, lit a torch and shone it at McKay. He squinted, brought his hand up to shield his eyes.

Did they know what he'd done? Had they tracked him here? Would they arrest him?

No, no, they can't know. Be calm.

"Everything all right, sir?" the policeman asked.

If he answered, would they hear the terror in his voice? He had no choice. He swallowed and said, "Fine."

The policeman paused as the torchlight found the white collar at McKay's throat. "Any reason why you're out here this time of night?"

McKay put his hands in his pockets to hide his trembling. "Oh . . . I, uh . . . well, I was just out for a drive, and I saw how pretty the moonlight on the river was, so I wanted to just stop and have a look. Take it all in, you know?"

"Just out for a drive," the policeman echoed. "Do that often, do you?"

"Occasionally," McKay said. "I have trouble sleeping sometimes, so I find a nice drive settles me a little bit."

The policeman turned his torch towards McKay's car, shone it through the windows, examined the empty seats. "I see," he said. "Will you do me a favour, though?"

"Yes?"

"Get on the move again. We've had a few hijackings in the area over the last couple of weeks, young lads taking cars and rallying them around the place then burning them out. I wouldn't want them getting a hold of you. These wee bastards wouldn't go easy on you just because you're a minister."

McKay nodded as the torch beam glared at him once more. "All right," he said. "I'll do that. Thanks for the warning."

He went to his car, opened the driver's door.

"Take care, now," the policeman called as he and his colleague returned to their vehicle.

"You too," McKay said as he lowered himself in. He watched the rear-view mirror as he closed the door and put on his seatbelt. Waved as the patrol car pulled out and passed him. When the other car was out of sight, he leaned his head against the steering wheel, kept it there until the shaking stopped.

29

Flanagan took the seat opposite DSI Purdy.

"Well?" he said.

"I want to question Roberta Garrick," Flanagan said.

"I thought you already did."

"Here," Flanagan said. "I want to bring her in, do it in an interview room, put the fear of God into her."

Purdy chewed the end of his spectacle arm for a few seconds before saying, "No, absolutely not. You can't hit her that hard with so little to go on."

She considered arguing, but knew this was not a fight worth having. "Do you have any objection to me questioning her at home?"

"What sort of tone?" he asked.

"Firm," Flanagan said. "I'll not let her know what I'm after specifically, but I want her to know I'm suspicious. If she's innocent, it'll probably go over her head. If she's guilty, it'll rattle her. Put her on the back foot. I'll learn a lot just from her re-action."

"Prearranged or drop-in?"

"Drop-in. Not tonight, of course, but to-morrow."

Purdy nodded and put his glasses back on. He leaned back and said, "You know, I've got mixed feelings about this. On the one hand, I've no desire for this to turn into a murder investigation, so I hope you're wrong. On the other, if you are wrong, if you've been pursuing a recently bereaved woman for no good reason, then you'll have gone down in my estimation."

"I understand that, sir," she said, feeling the weight of his gaze on her.

"This will be the last investigation of yours that I oversee before my retirement. What I said to Allison on the phone the other day, that was true, you're probably the best I've ever worked with. I don't want my last memory of you to be a monumental fuck-up."

She looked at her lap. "No, sir."

He leaned forward, his elbows on the table. "Look at me," he said.

She did so. "Sir?"

"I'll give you one chance, right now, to drop this. You let it go, and I'll forget everything you told me about the brother and the baby, all of that. You can put this case behind you and move on, no harm done."

"I can't do that," she said, keeping her eyes hard on his.

"All right. But know this: if you go chasing after a murder and the whole thing blows up in your face, there'll be sweet fuck all I can do for you."

"I know, sir."

"Okay. Have at it, then."

Flanagan made it home before dinner, in time to eat with her family. It seemed like the first time in forever. She called Alistair on the way, asked if he'd started cooking anything yet. He hadn't, and she offered to grab a Chinese takeaway. She picked up a bottle of wine and some beer while she was at it, and now all four of them sat around the table, sharing sweet and spicy food. Flanagan took a mouthful of cold Czech lager, savoured the sharp taste, the burn of the carbonation on her tongue, and felt a gladness in her heart.

Ruth and Eli talked about school, their friends, the film they were looking forward to at the cinema. Some new superhero nonsense with a character Flanagan had never heard of.

"We'll go tomorrow," Alistair said. "Let me see."

He thumbed his smartphone, clicked his tongue behind his teeth as he searched. "There," he said. "There's a morning showing in Lisburn — 2D, I'm not squinting at the screen for two hours in those stupid 3D glasses — and we can go and get burgers after. How does that sound?"

Ruth and Eli threw their hands up and cheered.

"Actually," Flanagan said.

Alistair's smile fell away. He stared across the table at her. "Actually, what?"

"I need to do something for work in the morning," she said.

"On a Saturday morning?"

"Yes." She felt the temperature drop around the table, the smiles gone. "But I'll probably be done by lunchtime. I can meet you guys in Lisburn, we can get something to eat, then go to an afternoon showing. Have a look, see what times there are."

He sighed and swiped his thumb up and down the phone's screen. "Well, yes, but the times aren't so good. We'd be hanging around for an hour and a half."

"Then we can go bowling for an hour," she said. "We haven't done that in ages. Or Sunday. What about Sunday?"

Alistair put his phone down. "Sure, we'll figure something out."

"Don't be like that," Flanagan said. "Let's just pick a time and go."

"Never mind," Alistair said. "I'll just take the kids to the film in the morning, and if you're done in time, you can meet us for lunch. Or you can leave it. Or whatever."

She felt anger build, but held it back. The children ate, quiet now, their disappointment tainting the air between them. Flanagan would not have another argument in front of them. She forced a smile and said, "All right, we'll play it by ear, then."

They didn't speak for the rest of the meal.

That night in bed, Alistair reached for her hand. "Sorry about earlier," he said.

"Me too."

He squeezed her hand and let go. Sleep soon took her, but she was woken in the dark hours by Alistair's gasping. She lay quiet and still as he woke from his nightmare, got up and went downstairs. Flanagan returned to her rest by the soft murmur of the television downstairs. Her last thought before her mind darkened was that she'd forgotten to reply to Miriam Mc-Creesh's text message. Never mind, she would do it in the morning.

But she didn't.

Flanagan drove the short distance to Morganstown in less than ten minutes, passing along its main street as the clock on the Volkswagen's dashboard showed eleven. Another few minutes took her out the other side and to the driveway of the Garrick house. She applied the handbrake and shut off the engine. The house seemed quieter now, more grey, less grand on this overcast morning.

As Flanagan got out of the car, she looked at the sitting room window. Roberta Garrick stood there, looking back, wearing a dressing gown, a mug held in both hands. By the time Flanagan got to the front door, Mrs. Garrick had already opened it.

"Good morning," she said, a polite smile on her mouth. "What can I do for you?"

Flanagan put one foot on the doorstep. "Just a few follow-up questions," she said. "Can I come inside?"

Mrs. Garrick's smile remained in place, but her eyes narrowed. "I thought everything was settled."

"Almost," Flanagan said. "I'll try not to take up too much of your time."

"I was hoping to have today to myself. It's

been a difficult week, and I'd like some peace."

Flanagan moved her other foot onto the doorstep, closer to Mrs. Garrick. "Like I said, it won't take too long."

Mrs. Garrick gave her a hard stare, then said, "All right."

She stepped back, allowed room for Flanagan to enter.

"Coffee smells good," Flanagan said, looking at the mug in Mrs. Garrick's hand.

With a rigid smile, Mrs. Garrick asked, "Would you like some?"

"Yes, please," Flanagan said. "Black." Without invitation, she walked towards the kitchen.

"Why don't you take a seat in the living room?" Mrs. Garrick asked.

"No, kitchen's fine," Flanagan said, not looking back. She proceeded to the tiled and shining room, placed her bag on the granite-topped island at the centre.

Mrs. Garrick followed her into the room and went to the coffee machine. She placed a mug beneath the spout, put a pod in the top, pressed a button. The machine gurgled.

"I've been meaning to get one of those machines," Flanagan said.

Mrs. Garrick turned to her. "Shall we get started?"

Flanagan ran her fingertips over the shining black granite. "You have a beautiful home."

"Thank you," Mrs. Garrick said. "Can we start?"

"Your husband had it built, is that right?"

"Yes, when we married. Please, can we start?"

Flanagan sat on a stool by the island and took her notebook and pen from her bag. She opened the book to a fresh page and asked, "How long ago? We have started, by the way."

Another hard stare. "It'd be seven years now."

"How did you two meet?"

"Online."

"So, he saw your profile and messaged you, or was it the other way around?"

"Actually, I messaged him."

"What did you say?"

"I don't think that's any of your business."

Flanagan gave her an apologetic smile. "I'm just trying to get the broader picture."

"I don't remember what I said in the message. Something short, I think, that I liked his profile, the usual sort of thing."

"What about your relationship history before then?" Flanagan asked.

Mrs. Garrick raised her eyebrows. "I don't

see the relevance of that."

"Like I said, the broader picture."

"I had a few boyfriends over the years."

"Serious? Casual? Long term? Flings?"

Mrs. Garrick bristled, folded her arms across her chest. "Both."

"Which was the longest?"

"Three years, on and off."

"Tell me about him."

"Why?"

"The broader picture."

"His name was Malachi. He was a drug user. So was I at the time. Cannabis, speed, MDMA, that sort of thing. Cocaine, sometimes. When he moved on to heroin, that's when I knew I had to leave him." Her features softened, as did her voice, her gaze distant. Then she came back to herself and said, "That's when I cleaned myself up. That's when I found Jesus and turned my life around. Is that enough for you?"

"Malachi. What was his surname?"

"I don't remember."

Flanagan met her gaze. "Yes you do."

"I do, but I'm not going to tell you because it's none of your business."

"Were you ever violent towards Malachi?"

Mrs. Garrick paled. "Excuse me?"

"Were you ever violent towards him?"

Mrs. Garrick shook her head. "That's a

ridiculous question."

"Is it? I thought it worth asking seeing as I was told you were violent towards your husband."

Mrs. Garrick took a step forward. "That's a lie. Who told you that?"

"The police officer in Barcelona who investigated your daughter's death," Flanagan said. "Your husband told him in what I suppose was a moment of weakness."

"I think you should leave now," Mrs. Garrick said. "If you want to ask further questions, it'll be with a lawyer present."

"I haven't had my coffee yet," Flanagan said, indicating the machine, which had ceased gurgling and hissing.

"I'm sorry, you'll have to do without." Mrs. Garrick took the cup from beneath the spout and poured the steaming contents down the sink. "Please leave now."

Flanagan did not move from the stool. "Mrs. Garrick, how did your daughter really die?"

Silence. Mrs. Garrick stared at Flanagan, wide-eyed. Then she threw the empty mug into the sink. Fragments exploded from the bowl.

"Get out of my house," she said. "Get out and don't come back."

"What did you do, Mrs. Garrick?"

"Go," Mrs. Garrick said. "Right now. Leave."

Flanagan stood, packed her notepad and pen away, slung her bag over her shoulder. "Thank you for your time," she said, heading for the kitchen door. "I'll be in touch soon."

As Flanagan walked to her car, Mrs. Garrick slammed the front door behind her. Once behind the wheel, she looked back to the house and saw Mrs. Garrick through the living room window. She had a phone pressed to her ear.

Reverend McKay or Jim Allison, one of the two.

Mrs. Garrick stared back at Flanagan, her anger burning through the glass.

Flanagan gave her a nod, started the car's engine, and pulled away.

30

McKay hung up his cassock and lifted his mobile phone from the desk. He had kept the morning prayer service short, and some of the congregation had seemed confused to be leaving so early. Instead of bidding farewell to the stragglers, he had come straight to the vestry. After a sleepless night, he intended to cross to his house and try for a doze, though he was not optimistic.

What little sleep he'd managed had been riven with dreams of Henry Garrick dragging him to the hell to which he was surely damned. Except McKay didn't believe in hell. But even so, no matter how he protested, Mr. Garrick dragged him there anyway, down into the fire and the tangled screaming souls.

At one point in the night, McKay had gone to the bathroom to relieve his bladder. Washing his hands, he saw a strange and hollow man in the mirror. He remembered that he had neglected to eat again, so he went downstairs and toasted some stale bread, chewed it without tasting, swallowed it without satisfaction. Then he fetched the cigarette packet and lighter from the cutlery drawer and smoked one to the butt before lighting another from its embers.

He had realised then that it was only a matter of time. Roberta would cast him aside now that he had served his purpose, leaving him with the dreams of burning and nothing else. He had wept. Like a child, desperate hacking sobs like he cried when Maggie died.

Let it end, he thought. Just let it end.

Now, as morning light hazed through the small vestry window, he felt little better. But another cigarette would help. Another drive into Moira, to the filling station or the supermarket. Remove the white collar, undo the top button, and he'd be nothing but a man in a black suit.

He switched on the phone, put it in his pocket while it booted up. It was quiet outside now, so he slipped out of the side door, locked it behind him. The phone pinged and vibrated against his thigh. He was about to reach for it when he saw DCI Flanagan leaning against her car. Frozen, he could only watch as she approached.

"Reverend McKay," she said, "can you spare a few minutes?"

As hard as he tried, he could think of no reason why he couldn't. "All right," he said. He considered correcting how she addressed him, but he had grown weary of that. Instead, he unlocked the side door again and led her into the vestry, pulled a chair out from the table. Flanagan sat, and he took the seat opposite.

"I'd thought everything was all wrapped up," he said, watching her take a notebook and pen from her bag.

"More or less," she said. "Just a few loose ends. Have you heard from Mrs. Garrick this morning?"

"No, my phone's been turned off," he said. "I've been busy with the morning service."

Was that surprise on her face? Gone before he could really see it, her expression turned to concern.

"Are you feeling all right? You don't look well."

"Tired," he said. "It's been a difficult week."

"Of course. I'll try to make this quick. Did something happen?"

She brought a finger to her lower lip, mirroring the redness on his.

"Oh, this." His fingertip found the tender spot on his own lip. "Stupid. I was leaning in to get something out of the car, and I misjudged it. So what do you need to know?"

"I wanted to ask about Mr. Garrick's brother, George Garrick."

"George," McKay said, picturing the tall man who looked so much like his brother. "I spotted him at the funeral yesterday, right at the back. That was the first time I'd seen him in a few years. It was a shame what happened."

"And what did happen, to your knowledge?"

"I suppose it's no secret. Not long after Erin died, George . . . touched Mrs. Garrick inappropriately. In their home, while Mr. Garrick was in the other room. I think George had been drinking at the time."

"Did George Garrick ever give you his version of events?"

McKay nodded. "Yes, he came to see me a few days after. He denied it."

"Did you believe him?"

"It wasn't up to me to believe or disbelieve him. It was my job just to listen. Anyway, it was too late by then. Word had gotten around the congregation. He couldn't show his face around here any more."

"You couldn't have supported him?"

"I could, but that would mean turning my back on Mr. and Mrs. Garrick. You understand, a congregation is like a family, a very tight-knit family. And sometimes families split. The tighter they are, the harder the split. Churches sometimes break in two. Even in a small town, you'll get two churches of the same denomination because somewhere along the way there was a split. If I'd stood by George Garrick, this church would have been blown apart. It was a difficult choice, but it was the right one for my congregation."

"Even if George Garrick might have been innocent?"

McKay thought about the cigarettes in his kitchen drawer. "I don't get everything right. Do you?"

She did not drop her gaze. "No. I don't."

"Sorry," he said, looking away. "I didn't mean to be confrontational."

She dismissed his apology with a shake of her head. "You were close to Mr. and Mrs. Garrick."

"That's right."

"More so than others in the congregation."

"I suppose so," McKay said. "Mr. Garrick was very generous in his support of the church. And he was very good to me when my wife died."

"Did he ever speak to you in confidence?"

"Sometimes."

"Did he ever talk to you about his relationship with his wife?"

"Not really. They were very happy together."

"Did he ever indicate that Mrs. Garrick might have been abusive towards him? Violent?"

McKay pictured his own blood on her teeth. Felt her hand at his throat. He had to fight to keep his fingers from going to the red swelling on his lip again.

"No," he said. "Never. Why?"

"Just an avenue I'm exploring. Did he ever show up with any marks or injuries that he couldn't explain?"

"No, not that I can remember."

She turned to a fresh page in her notepad. "Okay. Let's talk about Jim Allison."

McKay felt a strange sensation, like cold sparks running up his spine to his brain. "What about him?"

"What's the nature of his relationship with Mrs. Garrick?"

"What do you mean?"

Flanagan shrugged. "He seems very protective of her. Defensive, even. I wondered exactly how close they are."

The cold sparks turned to hot flashes of anger. "What are you suggesting?" he asked.

"Nothing specific. I don't know them like you do. Have you ever wondered if their relationship went further than friendship?"

No, McKay had never wondered that. Not until now. He clenched his fists under the table and shook his head, no.

"You're certain of that?" Flanagan asked.

"I'm certain," he said, keeping his voice low and calm as he pictured Allison's hands on Roberta's body. "Why, have you seen something? Heard something?"

"No," she said. "But I find it useful to explore all possibilities."

Perhaps he should have felt relief in that, but he didn't.

She closed her notebook. "Okay, I think that's all for now. While I'm here, I wanted to thank you again for the other day. It did help a lot."

He forced a smile. "That's what I'm here for."

"I might come to the service tomorrow morning. See if I can convince the kids to come too. I don't think they've ever seen the inside of a church."

"You'll be very welcome," he said, wishing she would hurry up and leave.

At last, she stood. "Hopefully see you tomorrow, then," she said.

He nodded, stood, and showed her to the door. From the vestry window, he watched her get into her car. She sat there for an agonising time.

"Go," he said to the window. "Just go."

There, her hands moved on the steering wheel and the car moved off, turning towards the gate. He reached into his pocket, retrieved his phone and his keys. He exited through the side door, locked it, and thumbed the phone as he crossed the grounds to his house. The display showed a missed call from Roberta. As he unlocked his front door, he pressed the callback option and put the phone to his ear. It connected as he reached the kitchen, and he listened to the dial tone as he took the cigarettes and lighter from the drawer. By the time the answerphone message played, he had breathed a lungful of tarry smoke.

A cloud of blue billowed around him as he said, "It's me. Flanagan was here. Call me back."

He sat down at the table and finished the cigarette, holding it between quivering fingers. Twenty minutes later, the packet was empty and the phone still silent. McKay returned it to his pocket and lifted his car keys.

31

Flanagan had checked her watch as she returned to the car. Maybe time to meet Alistair and the kids. In the driver's seat, she opened the favourites list on her phone and called her husband. As she listened to the dial tone, she saw McKay through the vestry window, watching her.

A realisation hit her, sure and clear in her mind: Reverend McKay loved Roberta Garrick.

He couldn't hide his shock and anger when she mentioned Jim Allison's name. Jealousy had been clear and plain on his face. Had he ever acted on it? Surely not. Not a man like him. McKay had a decency about him, and not just something she inferred from his vocation and his collar.

Before she could consider it further, Alistair's impatient voice sounded in the phone's earpiece. "Hello? Are you there?"

How long had he been on the line?

"Sorry," she said. "Yes, I'm here, I got distracted. Where are you?"

"In Lisburn, we're just out of the cinema. Will you make the restaurant?"

"I'll be fifteen, twenty minutes. Go ahead and order for me."

"All right," he said.

Flanagan hung up and looked back towards the vestry. McKay still stood there, watching her.

Another idea formed in her mind, clearer, brighter, colder than the first.

Was it you?

No. She looked away and shook her head. She had already reached far enough on this case. Her mind had been slipping into irrationality too often recently. Enough. She turned the key in the ignition and set off, chiding herself for letting her thoughts run away like that. Keep control. Reach within your grasp.

Flanagan turned right out of the gate, towards the far end of Morganstown's main street. As she neared the filling station, without thinking, she slowed her Volkswagen to a halt. She gripped the steering wheel tight.

No, not him. Couldn't be.

A car horn blasted behind her. She flicked the indicator lever and pulled onto the filling station's forecourt, manoeuvred into a parking space by the exit, shut off the engine.

Think about it.

She played out scenarios in her mind. Desires. Impulses. Actions. She sought logic in them, even if — especially if — it was in intent rather than deed. Was there a sequence of events that could fit such an unlikely answer? She closed her eyes and imagined threads intersecting, each a course of action, each intersection a choice made, and the end of every thread led to a dead man surrounded by photographs of his loved ones that he could not see.

"Evidence," she said aloud as she opened her eyes. "There is no evidence."

Forget it, she thought. You're chasing a phantom.

No reason, no logic. Let it go.

Flanagan thought of her husband and her children, that she could be with them now, enjoying them, not sitting here, torturing herself over something far beyond her control. She turned the key in the ignition once more, felt the resonance of the engine starting.

She reversed out of the space, shifted into first, and approached the forecourt's exit. As the car idled and she looked for oncoming traffic, she saw McKay's Ford Fiesta pull out of the church grounds at the far end of the street.

Flanagan knew where he was going: to the Garrick house.

Follow him?

And what would that achieve?

Once more, Flanagan thought of her family, and she pulled out of the forecourt, drove towards Lisburn and her children.

32

McKay rang the bell once more, rapped the door with his knuckles, hard enough to hurt. And again, leaving a trace of red on the wood.

The door opened, Roberta's face in the few inches between it and the frame.

"What are you doing here?" she asked.

"I need to talk to you."

"Now's not a good time," she said.

"I don't care," he said. "We need to talk."

"Not now," she said, her voice hardening.

He pushed the door inward, making her stagger back into the hall.

"What are you doing?" she asked as he walked past her.

He looked into the living room, saw it empty, headed towards the kitchen. There he was. Casually dressed in polo shirt and beige chinos. A mug of something steaming on the island in front of him. Sitting there like he belonged in this house. Like he belonged with her.

"Peter," Jim Allison said. "Is everything all right?"

"Why are you here?" McKay asked.

"Roberta called me," Allison said.

"Why?"

Roberta entered, came to McKay's side. Put a hand on his arm. He shook it away.

"Reverend Peter," she said, "I think you should go home and get some sleep."

"Why did you call him?" he asked.

Allison answered for her. "That police-woman Flanagan called here this morning and questioned Roberta. She's crossed the line into harassment. I'm going to see what can be done about it."

McKay stepped forward and put his hands on the black granite. "Why are you here?"

Allison gave a nervous smile. "I just told you. Roberta was —"

"Why are you here?!"

The shout reverberated off the tiles, made all three of them flinch. Allison raised his hands, palms out.

"Peter, I really think you need to calm yourself down, get some rest. Pardon my language, but you look like shit."

McKay felt his face contort with hatred as he said, "Go fuck yourself."

Allison's mouth dropped open.

McKay turned to Roberta. "I need to talk to you."

"Later," she said, reaching for his arm again. "What you really need is —"

"Now," he said. "We're going to talk now, whether you want to or not."

She went quiet for a moment, her eyes flickering, before she said, "Okay." She turned to Allison. "You go on, Jim. I'll call you later."

Allison shook his head. "No, no, I'm not leaving you alone with him when he's like this."

"It'll be fine," she said. "I'm going to make sure he gets some rest."

"Roberta, no."

McKay flinched at the tenderness in Allison's voice.

"Jim, go," she said. "I can handle this."

"Roberta —"

"Go!"

Allison shook his head, but he stood and reached for the jacket and keys on the island. "I'll call you later," he said as he headed for the door. "And don't worry, I'll deal with Flanagan."

Alone now, McKay turned to her.

"It's over," he said.

"What do you mean?" she asked.

"I'm going to confess," he said.

Roberta stared at him for long seconds before she said, "No you're not. Calm down."

McKay watched her pace the kitchen, arms folded across her chest, and realised that he was indeed calm. For the first time since Mr. Garrick had taken his last guttural snoring breath, McKay felt peace in his heart.

"I am calm," he said, and as much as it shocked him, a smile found its way to his mouth. And a feeling of lightness behind his eyes, and on his shoulders. A terrible weight lifted away so it felt as if his feet hovered an inch above the floor. Heat in his eyes.

He recognised this feeling, a sensation rooted deep in his youth. The euphoria he felt when he first accepted Christ into his heart, when he first felt his sin washed away by the Lord.

I am saved, he thought.

Roberta stopped pacing. "What are you smiling at?"

"I'm saved," he said.

A high laugh escaped him, and he put his hand over his mouth. Roberta watched him, concern on her face.

"You need to get some rest," she said. "Sleep for a couple of hours. Then you'll feel better. You'll see things differently."

"No." He shook his head, the words clarifying his feelings as he spoke. "I don't need to sleep. I need to tell the truth. I need to get this over with."

"You're not in your right mind," she said. "You don't know what you're saying."

"My right mind?" He laughed again. "I haven't been in my right mind since the first time I touched you. And I can't take any more. It's time to stop this."

She walked slowly around the island to him, and he knew that look on her face, the mask she wore. The seductress, Eve with the serpent's whisper in her ear, the taste of apple on her tongue. She came close, spoke softly.

"Just come upstairs and lie down," she said. "I'll lie with you."

She went to put her arms around his neck, lace herself around him like so many times before, but he took her wrists in his hands and lifted them away, held them tight against his chest.

"I see what you are now," he said. "I should have seen it months ago, but I was weak, and you knew it. Just like you knew your husband was weak, when you found him, and you knew you could bleed him dry. Until you were faced with caring for him for the rest of his days, and you couldn't have that, could you? So you came after me. Because I was weak."

She tried to pull her wrists away from him but he held them firm.

"And Jim Allison is weak too, isn't he? What is it you want from him? You've got all the money you could ever want. What can you take from him? Protection? Is that it? You think he can protect you from Flanagan, don't you? Does he know what we did?"

Now she pulled with a strength he didn't know she possessed, wrenched her wrists from his grasp. He saw the rage in her, burning and crackling, barely held in check.

"You've lost your mind," she said.

"Maybe," he said. "Or maybe I've just found it again. Either way, tonight or tomorrow morning, whenever I've got the courage, I'm going to call the police. I'm going to call Flanagan and tell her everything. I just wanted to warn you so you can prepare yourself."

He walked to the kitchen door, but she called after him.

"I'll deny it," she said, closing the distance between them, anger and hate in her eyes. "You go ahead and tell them what you did. But remember, *you* did it. Not me. You have no proof that I knew anything about what you planned to do. After all, you'd been chasing after me, hadn't you? Trying it on with me for the last six months, you were, all the time my poor husband was lying there suffering. You were trying to take advantage of a poor woman coping with a terrible situation."

A grin, familiar to him, stretched her mouth as the lie took form. Close now so he could feel the heat of her. "You tried to exploit me. You tried to exploit my vulner-ability. And when you couldn't, when I wouldn't let you because I loved my hus-band so dearly, you decided to kill him. As far as I'm concerned, that's what happened, and that's exactly how I'll tell it. And there isn't a single piece of evidence to say other-wise."

McKay laughed once more. Not the near hysterical laughter of before, but the calm and easy laugh of a man who knows he's right.

"You don't get it, do you?" he said. "I don't care what you say. I don't care what you do. You can tell them anything you want. All I need is to tell the truth. Nothing else matters."

He walked along the hall to the front door, reached for the handle.

"I'll kill myself," she shouted from the

kitchen doorway, her voice rising with each syllable.

He looked back over his shoulder and said, "I don't care."

She screamed as he closed the door behind him.

33

Flanagan's phone rang as she parked outside the restaurant. A number she didn't know. She should have rejected the call, she knew that, but she didn't.

"Flanagan," she said.

"Good afternoon, Inspector, this is Jim Allison."

She closed her eyes and mouthed a string of the worst curses she could bring to mind. Then she said, "Good afternoon, Mr. Allison, what can I do for you?"

"What can you do for me?" She heard the sneer in his voice, and anger. "What you can do for me is stop harassing my friend Mrs. Garrick."

Flanagan took a slow and deep breath, in and out, willed her temper to be still. "Mr. Allison, it's Saturday, and I'm late for lunch with my family. Do you think we could keep this conversation for Monday morning? I can give you a call, say, ten —"

"That's right, it's Saturday, but you were happy enough to call at Mrs. Garrick's home this morning. And Peter McKay. You've pushed that poor man to breaking point, and you're trying to do the same with Roberta."

Her temper roused whether she wanted it to or not. "What I'm trying to do is my job, and I'd thank you to let me get on with it without interference."

"You might think it's your job to intimidate a grieving woman in her home, but I think otherwise. As an elected representative of this constituency, and a member of the Policing Board, it is my job to protect people from this kind of —"

"Oh, fuck off."

Flanagan listened to the silence, already stinging with regret. She winced and put her hand over her eyes.

"Excuse me?"

I should apologise, she thought. I should beg forgiveness and back off. Even as those ideas moved through her mind, she knew she would ignore them.

"Let me rephrase that," she said. "I would very much appreciate it if you'd save your grandstanding for the Assembly. You might be on the Policing Board, but your job is to tick whatever boxes and sign whatever

279

declarations the civil servants put in front of you, nothing more, nothing less. Some people might be impressed when you start swinging your dick around, but I'm not one of them. Now kindly shove your indignation up your arse while I go and spend a little time with my family. Goodbye."

She hung up before he could get a word out in response, held the phone in her fist.

"Stupid, stupid, stupid," she whispered, shaking her head.

Doesn't matter, she thought. It's done now.

She stowed the phone in her bag, got out of the car, locked it, and made her way to the restaurant. Inside, she craned her neck and stood on tiptoe, scanning the booths full of parents and children, young teens on dates, middle-aged couples looking out of place. There, near the back corner, Alistair and the children. Ruth and Eli staring wide-eyed at the ice cream sundaes the waitress was placing before them; she had a coffee on the tray for Alistair. She went to lift the untouched plate of food, chicken wings and fries, but Flanagan interrupted her.

"That's mine, thanks."

Alistair looked up at the sound of her voice, surprise on his face at first, followed by anger, then a blank coldness that cut her

280

deepest of all.

The waitress smiled and left them. As Flanagan lowered herself into the booth beside Eli, Alistair said, "Hardly worth your while sitting down."

"I can throw this into me while you have your coffee," she said.

"Suit yourself," he said.

"Look, I'm sorry for being late. I couldn't avoid it."

Flanagan felt a faint itch of guilt at the lie as she took a bite of chicken from the bone. There had been a choice: go to see McKay or not. She still couldn't be sure if she'd made the right choice. She supposed she'd find out soon enough.

"So, what did you guys have?" she asked, a cheer in her voice that probably sounded as fake to them as it did to her.

"Burgers," Ruth said.

"Were they any good?"

Ruth shrugged and resumed pushing ice cream around with her spoon. Eli hadn't even acknowledged her presence.

Flanagan put down the chicken, wiped her fingers on her napkin, reached for each of their hands, grasped them tight. "I'm sorry," she said. "Honestly. I'll make it up to you tomorrow, I promise."

"You promise," Ruth echoed, her voice

flat. "You always promise."

Flanagan let go of their hands, brought hers together on the tabletop. She considered arguing, pleading, but knew it was useless. Let them be angry, she thought. They're right to be angry. She ate her food, all four of them silent apart from the clink of spoons on glass.

By the time Flanagan had eaten all she could stomach, which was barely a third of the plate, the children had cleared their bowls and Alistair's cup was empty.

She set down her knife and fork, pushed the plate away. They all looked at her, knowing she meant to speak. She cleared her throat.

"I know this is difficult to understand," she said, "but I have a very important, very difficult job. A lot of people depend on me to do this job. And sometimes that means I can't be around as much as I want to be. I know that's difficult for you, that you think it's not fair, but I can't let those people down."

"But you let us down," Ruth said. "All the time."

Flanagan felt Alistair's eyes on her, gauging her reaction. Don't get defensive, she warned herself. It won't help.

"I know," Flanagan said. "Sometimes I let

you down. And sometimes I let down the people I'm trying to help. But I want to do better, for you and them both."

She reached across the table for Ruth's hand.

"Will you let me try?"

Ruth did not answer, but neither did she pull her hand away. Flanagan was glad of that.

Alistair ran his fingers through Ruth's hair, leaned over and kissed the top of her head. He exchanged a glance with Flanagan, a hint of a smile. Flanagan returned it.

"Doesn't mean I'm not angry," he said.

"I know," she said. "Tomorrow will be better. We'll do something." She reached for her children once more. "Come on, what'll we do tomorrow? What about the zoo? We haven't been in ages."

Ruth shook her head. "I don't like the zoo. The way the elephants walk up and down like they're crazy people. It makes me sad."

"All right, what else?"

Eli spoke for the first time, a smile breaking on his face that lit a flame in Flanagan's heart. "The museum," he said. "The one with the dinosaurs."

"The Ulster Museum," she said. "Good idea. We can go to the park after. What does everyone else think?"

Her phone trilled in her bag before anyone could answer. She squeezed her eyes shut, cursed under her breath. Without looking at Alistair, she fished it from her bag, looked at the screen.

DSI Purdy.

"Shit," she said.

Now she looked to Alistair. With an expression of defeat and a wave of his hand, he indicated, go on, take it. She squeezed her husband's shoulder as she passed on the way to the corridor that led to the toilets. As the door swung closed behind her, she thumbed the green button.

"You know what I'm calling about," Purdy said. It wasn't a question.

"Allison," she said.

"What in the name of Christ did you say to him?"

"We had a disagreement about my methods," she said.

"I'm supposed to be here preparing for my last week in this bloody job, not dealing with your mess."

"Yes, sir," she said. "I'm sorry."

I'm so tired of apologising, she thought, feeling a heavy weariness like sand in her soul.

"Sorry my arse," he said. "Allison tells me

you're harassing his good friend Mrs. Garrick."

"His *very* good friend," she said.

"What's that supposed to mean?"

"Sir, I think you know what it means."

"Watch your mouth, Flanagan."

She bowed her head, covered her eyes
with her palm. "Sorry, sir."

The men's toilet door opened and a tubby
teenager in goth gear stepped past her and
out through the door to the restaurant.

"All right. Whatever you think the relationship is between Jim Allison and Roberta
Garrick, you don't allude to it again without
proof."

"Yes, sir."

"Allison says you insulted him, effed-and-
blinded at him," Purdy said.

"Maybe," Flanagan said. "And I might
have said something about his dick."

"Oh, fuck me pink," Purdy said with a
despairing sigh.

"Is he going to pursue this?"

"He said he'd drop it if you left Mrs. Garrick alone," Purdy said. "I told him that
would be your choice to make."

"Thank you, sir," Flanagan said. "Thank
you."

"It's all right," Purdy said. "Listen, there's
not a thing in the world Jim Allison can do

to stop me drawing my pension in a week. He tries to give me grief in my last few days here, I'll happily tie his bollocks in a knot and whistle as I head out the door. But Flanagan . . . Serena . . . you need to think hard about your future. I don't know if Allison really has the clout to damage your career, but if you push him, I have no doubt he'll try."

Flanagan leaned her shoulder against the wall. "I won't let that stop me any more than you would, sir."

She heard a small laugh in her ear.

"I'd be a liar if I said I wasn't glad to hear that," Purdy said. "But tread carefully. Promise me that."

The tiled wall cooled her forehead. "I don't keep promises," she said.

"What?"

"Nothing, sir. I'll try to keep out of trouble."

"Good," he said. "Take care."

The phone silent in her hand, Flanagan remained against the wall for a minute, fighting the desire to weep for herself. She sniffed, straightened, and left the corridor. Back in the restaurant, the place had quietened, patrons finishing their meals, wait staff clearing the tables after the lunchtime rush.

Flanagan felt sure Alistair and the kids had been at the last booth on the far wall, but wondered if she was mistaken as she approached and found it deserted. Then she saw the empty coffee cup, the glass dishes scraped clean of ice cream, her own plate still two thirds full.

Anger bloomed in her, the urge to cry once again. Then a wash of relief as she saw her husband and children over by the till, coats on, waiting for her. Alistair took his debit card from the machine, placed a ten-pound note on the counter. The waitress thanked him.

As they walked towards the exit together, Flanagan took Ruth's hand in hers. Ruth resisted at first, but Flanagan tightened her fingers. Outside, Ruth said, "I'm too big to hold hands."

"But I'm not," Flanagan said. "Do you want to come home in my car? Girls' club. Let Eli and Daddy go together. They can be the boys' club."

Ruth worked her hand free. "No. I want to go with Daddy."

Flanagan nodded, said, "All right. See you at home."

She held the tears back until she was in her car, the doors locked against the world.

34

McKay spent the rest of the day driving: motorways, country roads, through villages and towns. At some point he realised he had gone as far as the north coast and he pulled into a lay-by to get his bearings. Beyond the rolling countryside, a sliver of grey sea. He checked the map on his phone, saw he was between Ballycastle and Cushendun.

Cushendun, where he and his parents — long gone now — spent summer weekends in a caravan. As a child, he had loved it. The beach there, the thunder of the water. On a clear day, you could see Scotland, sometimes even the white specks of dwellings on the Mull of Kintyre. By the time he was a teenager, he hated it. Weekends of rainy boredom cooped up with his mother and father. By the time he was an adult, of course, he found he loved the place again. Or at least the memory of it. His parents were too elderly and infirm by that time to spend a night in a caravan.

McKay had brought Maggie there not long after they married. They had kissed in the grassy dunes, neither of them brave enough to take it further. Only the once. They never came back, though they talked about it often before she died.

"I miss you," he said aloud.

What would she make of him now? Damned murderer, a monstrous distortion of the man he had been before she fell dying to their kitchen floor.

Only a few miles to Cushendun. He pulled out of the lay-by, turned the car, and headed east.

Twenty minutes and a wrong turn brought him to the small car park on the bay, the mouth of the river on one side, the long golden stretch of sand on the other. He got out of the car, didn't bother to lock it, and walked along the path to the knots of grass and the beach beyond.

The wind came in hard off the water, grey out there, sea and sky meeting at their darkest points. Spray prickled his skin and he tasted salt on his lips. Last time he'd been here, it had been quiet. Now a scattering of tourists wandered from the caves beyond the river along the length of the bay. All brought here by the location being used in a television fantasy programme he'd never seen.

Sand dragged at his shoes as he trudged out towards the water, moving farther away from the car park and the river mouth. Still wearing his black shirt and white collar, he wrapped his jacket tight around himself, but it did little to keep out the wind's bite. Passers-by gave him sideways looks, most of them more appropriately dressed in anoraks and outdoor shoes.

He stopped at the water's edge, the foaming lip of the sea a matter of inches from his feet.

I could just keep walking, he thought. Keep walking until the cold stops the blood in my legs, until the salt water fills my lungs. He thought of the case he'd read about last year, two brothers drowning themselves in the sea farther down the eastern coast. How would it feel, to die like that? He closed his eyes and imagined.

Cold swallowed his feet, and he looked down to see a murky wash lap at his shoes. He should have stepped back, moved clear, but instead he watched the water draw back towards the sea again. Still as the sweeping hills around him, he waited for it to return.

As it did, a large brown dog galloped past, splashing water up as it went. McKay felt it chill his thighs, his belly. He followed the dog — a Weimaraner? — with his gaze as it looped around, back across the sand to its owner, a woman in a red and black coat, the kind they sell in outdoor sports shops alongside camping gear and hiking boots. She patted the back of the dog's neck, and it bounded in circles around her.

McKay realised she was staring back at him. He looked out to sea again, feeling a ridiculous blush on his cheeks.

"You're getting your feet wet," the woman called as she approached.

McKay looked down, feigned surprise, and stepped back.

Close now, she asked, "Are you all right?"

He reached for something to say, but could only look around as if searching for a lost companion.

"Do you need help?" she asked. Closer still, she put her hand on his arm.

Tell her something. "I'm just . . . out for a walk."

She reached for the zip at the neck of her anorak and pulled it down, revealing a grey shirt and a white collar.

"I work for the Big Man too," she said, a smile wide on her mouth. The first real smile McKay had seen in so long he couldn't remember. "Come on, I'll get you a cup of tea."

They sat opposite each other at a picnic table on the grass above the beach. Young men played Gaelic football on a pitch behind them, shouting to each other, the referee's whistle chirping. The dog lay on the ground beside McKay's shoes and socks. Deborah had insisted he take them off.

Reverend Deborah Sansom, rector of three churches in the locality. The scant Protestant population in the area meant her work was spread over the countryside, she explained, as she poured steaming tea from a thermos into a plastic cup.

"Forgive me for saying, but you didn't look like a man at ease with the world when I saw you there."

"I suppose not," McKay said.

"Talk if you feel like talking," she said. "Or just drink your tea."

He reached for the cup and took a mouthful. Sweet and hot enough to leave his tongue tingling. It stung his lower lip.

"Tea it is then," she said.

Deborah Sansom had brown hair streaked with grey, round cheeks reddened by the wind, sparks in her eyes as she smiled.

"I did a terrible thing," McKay said.

"Oh?" The smile dimmed. "Do you want to tell me?"

McKay shook his head.

"Can you put it right?"

"No," he said. "Never."

She raised a finger skyward. "Did the Big Man have anything to say about it when you asked him?"

He shook his head again. "I didn't pray."

"No?"

He took another swig of hot sweet tea and said, "I don't believe any more."

"My goodness," she said. "No wonder you looked like you wanted to throw yourself in. Have you spoken to anyone else about this? Your bishop, maybe?"

"No one."

"When did you lose your faith?"

"A few months ago," he said. He looked up from the cup and into her eyes. "No, not then. Not really. It was ten years ago. When my wife died. It just took all that time to admit it to myself."

"How did she die?"

He told her. The headache, the short walk, the return to find her rigid on the floor.

Deborah reached across the table and took his hand. "I'm sorry. That would make anyone question things, no matter how strong their faith."

She removed her hand, and they both sat quiet for a time, listening to the waves, watching the walkers on the beach.

Eventually, she said, "Look at it."

McKay raised his head, looked out to sea.

"All of it," she said, her free hand sweeping across the horizon, from the sloping hills in the north to the cliffs in the south. "Even today, when it's grim like this, it's still beautiful. I know it's possible all this is an accident. Billions of years of dust aggregating in space until it makes this. Until it makes us. But my goodness, what a sad and lonely thought. That this is just chance. That there's nothing deliberate about us. That we are chaos."

"Chaos," McKay echoed.

"Chaos or faith," she said. "It's one or the other. I know which I prefer."

"It's not a matter of preference," McKay said, already regretting the hardness in his voice. "It's a matter of reality. What's real and what's just a story to cling to."

"You were thinking about suicide when I came along," Deborah said. "Weren't you?"

He couldn't look at her.

"Don't worry, I didn't read your mind. But a person doesn't stand with his feet in the sea if he's not thinking about drowning."

"I wouldn't go through with it," he said.

"Why not?"

"Because I'm a coward."

"I don't think that's true. I think somewhere inside, buried deep, you still believe."

"No," he said. "I don't."

She pointed at the crashing water. "Then go on and do it. If all is chaos, then submit to the chaos. What difference will it make? If we're just random clusters of cells clinging to a rock in space, if that's what you really believe, then why live in pain? Just go and bloody do it. The universe will go on as if you'd never been here."

McKay got to his feet, walked across the grass, feeling each blade beneath his bare soles, between his toes. Do it, he thought. She's right. Nothing matters anyway.

He reached the edge of the grass, the sandy slope down to the beach another footstep away. Just a step. He went no farther. After a while, he turned and went back to the table and sat.

"Glad to have you back," Deborah said. "You didn't get too far, mind you."

He looked her in the eye, challenged her to contradict him. "I told you, I'm a coward."

"Bollocks," she said. "Then we're all cowards."

"I should go," he said.

"Home?"

"I suppose. There's nowhere else."

"Where's home? Where's your church?"

"Morganstown."

"Ah, I know it. I went to a wedding there, oh, must have been twenty years ago. It's a lovely little church. Do me a favour when you get there, will you?"

"What's that?"

"Pray."

"I can't."

She smiled. "Course you can. It's easy. You just go into your church, get down on your knees, close your eyes, and talk to God for a bit. Or if not God, then talk to yourself. Someone. Anyone. Just say it out loud, whatever it is that's eating you up. Do it for me. I gave you that nice cup of tea. You owe me something in return. Make me feel like I did you some good."

McKay stood and said, "I'll think about it."

He bent and picked up his shoes and socks, carried them towards the car park that lay two hundred yards along the beach. After a few paces, he stopped, turned back to her.

"Thank you," he said.

She nodded and waved.

The dog followed him along the grass almost to the end of the beach, an escort, a guardian, until it missed its master. It gave him a nudge on the hand, and he gave it a scratch, then it turned and ran back to where she stood watching.

35

Flanagan sat at the kitchen table, a mostly empty bottle of Shiraz in front of her, a mostly full glass beside that. Her tongue felt gritty from the wine, a pleasing sway behind her eyes. She took another mouthful, swallowed.

Alistair was upstairs with the kids, putting them to bed. She could hear their voices, him ordering them to brush their teeth, them screeching as he tickled them instead of getting them into their pyjamas, the soft murmur as he read them stories. Ruth said she was too old for them now, she only played along for Eli's benefit.

Flanagan smiled, but the smile faded from her mouth, unable to gain purchase there.

She had arrived home not long after them, and everyone had behaved as if nothing was wrong, only that they had entered a world of silence. Alistair had barely looked at her. The children had insisted their father do their bedtime, had given her begrudging kisses goodnight at Alistair's instruction.

Is this really it? Is this how it ends?

Not with an explosive row, nor a discovered affair. No final betrayal to sever them. Just a slow decline of bitter reproaches and fake apologies until there was nothing left but a festering resentment between them all.

Flanagan buried her face in her hands, thought about the cool space of the church, the salve of prayer whether she believed in it or not. She kept her eyes closed, brought her hands together. Formed the words in her mind.

Not like this. Please, not like this. Help me save us. Please, God, I don't want to lose my family. Please tell me what to do. Please show me —

She cried out, raised her head, as glass clinked against glass.

Alistair poured the last of the wine into a fresh glass. "Don't mind, do you?"

Flanagan inhaled, steadied her breathing. "Course not."

"What were you doing?" he asked, taking the seat opposite.

She considered lying, but said, "Praying."

"You?" He smiled, a gentle smile, no mockery in it.

"Yes, me. I've been doing it more often lately. It helps."

"My mother prayed a lot," he said.

"I remember. She swore by it. Said it could cure anything."

He took a sip of wine. "And can it?"

"I don't know what it does," she said. "Maybe nothing. Maybe something. Who knows?"

He gave her a coy look. "Were you praying for us?"

"Yes," she said.

"You think we need praying for?"

"Christ, we need something," she said with a weak laugh.

He smiled then, and she wanted to kiss him.

Want?

Do it.

Flanagan stood, went around the table to him. As he watched, confusion in his eyes, she got down on her knees beside him, took his face in her hands. Brought her mouth to his. He remained still for a few seconds, then he wrapped his arms around her, brought her in close.

"Listen," he said, "what you said earlier, about your work, about trying to do better for everyone. I think it got through to Ruth."

Flanagan sat back, arms still around his

neck. "Oh?"

"She asked me about it upstairs. If what you did really helped people. I told her yes, and she said, well, then that's what Mummy needs to do. And maybe we shouldn't expect to have you all to ourselves."

"And what did you say to that?"

Alistair sighed, rested his forehead against her cheek. "I told her she was a very smart and grown-up girl. That maybe Daddy's been asking too much of Mummy. Maybe Daddy needs to get his head out of his arse and acknowledge the fact that he's not the centre of the universe. Well, I didn't put it like that, exactly, but you get the gist."

"I do." She kissed him once more. "Thank you."

Then her phone vibrated on the table.

Alistair stiffened. She did not pull away. She kissed him harder, feeling his teeth through his lips. The phone vibrated again.

Now she let go, and so did he. She got to her feet, reached for the phone. A mobile number she did not recognise. Alistair started to get up from the chair, but she put a hand on his shoulder, pushed him back down.

"Wait," she said. "Just wait."

She thumbed the green button and brought the phone to her ear.

"DCI Serena Flanagan," she said. "Who is this?"

A pause, then, "Peter McKay. I'm sorry to disturb you on a Saturday night."

"Yes," she said, not allowing him an acceptance of his apology.

"I need to talk to you."

She hesitated, looked down at Alistair. "I'm sorry, now's not a good time."

"It's important. Can you come to the church?"

His voice sounded thin and far away, as if a shadow of a man spoke in his place.

Alistair went to say something, but she put her fingertips on his lips.

"No, I can't, I'm sorry. I've had a glass of wine, so I can't drive."

"I can't do it over the phone," McKay said. "Can I come to you?"

"No," Flanagan said. "I'm sorry, really, but not right now, not tonight. The morning. I can come to you first thing in the morning, before your service."

Silence as he considered. "All right," he said. "The morning. Eight-thirty?"

"The morning," Flanagan said, looking to Alistair, her eyebrows raised. "Eight-thirty?"

Alistair nodded his assent.

"Yes, eight-thirty."

"Okay," McKay said. "Thank you."

She hung up and dropped her phone to the table. Alistair drew her down to him, sat her on his lap as if they were a boy and girl, still in love with the joyful newness of it all.

He kissed her and said, "Thank you."

Flanagan returned the kiss and tried not to think of Reverend McKay and the terrible things he knew.

36

McKay placed the phone on the passenger seat beside him. Tomorrow. He could tell her tomorrow. One more night wouldn't change things. He got out of the car into the darkness outside his house, the keys in his hand. The glass of the front door showed the black inside there, that cold and hollow house, where his wife had died and he had years later betrayed her with a monster dressed as a woman.

He looked across the grounds to the church, a spired silhouette against the dark blue. A beautiful building, it really was. He remembered when he had first inherited this parish. He and Maggie had sat inside on that first night, the building dark around them, street and moonlight illuminating the stained glass, making strange shadows. They had embraced and thanked God together.

Do it for me, the woman had said.

No, he thought. I'll do it for Maggie.

He dropped his house keys back into his pocket and found the long spindly keys for the church. His fingers wrapped around them as he crossed to the building, feeling for the familiar lines of the vestry key. He found it by the time he reached the door and let himself inside. Dark in here, a weak orange sheen from the street lights outside. The burglar alarm buzzed until he entered the code: 1606, Maggie's birthday. He found the small desktop lamp, flicked it on. As he passed the open closet he brushed his cassock and surplice with his fingertips, coarse black fabric and smooth white silk.

Out into the church where the stained-glass windows rose above and looked like angels come to observe his hypocrisy. Weariness crept into his arms and legs as he crossed in front of the pulpit and into the aisle.

He chose a pew three rows back, slid down and into the hard wooden seat. Rested his forearms on the back of the pew in front. Lowered his knees onto the padded bench. Clasped his hands together. Closed his eyes.

"Maggie," he said. "Maggie, I'm sorry. I don't know what I've become. I'm not who I used to be before you left me. I've changed. Everything's changed. You would hate me. No. You never hated anybody. But you could never love me. Not the way I am now. I betrayed you. I turned your picture away so you wouldn't see what I did. I didn't want you to see me with her.

"Oh, Maggie, I've done an awful thing. I've done a thing so awful I'm glad you're not alive to see it. Do you understand? Do you see what I did to myself? I made myself glad you died."

He wept then. Hard choking sobs trapped his voice in his throat. He swallowed, forced the tears back, the words out.

"I want you back," he said. "I prayed for you not to die and you died anyway. And now I want you back. I want everything back like before. I know it's not possible, it'll never be, but that's what I want. I want it so badly it's been killing me all these years. And God, I'm so angry at You. You took her from me for no reason at all, You took her just because You could and I'm so fucking angry and I hate You, God, I fucking hate You for doing that to me, I fucking hate You, I hate You, and I want her back, please give her back."

A movement in the darkness by the vestry startled him.

"She's gone," a voice said. "There is no giving back."

He got to his feet and said, "Come out

306

where I can see you."

She moved into the dim light. Roberta, dressed in a hooded top and jeans.

"What do you want?" he asked.

"To talk," she said.

A quiver in her voice, as if she held back tears.

"We've nothing to talk about," he said. "Go home."

"Please," she said. "I've got no one else."

He stepped out of the pew and into the aisle, but went no closer to her. "You never really needed anyone else, did you? Not unless you had some use for them. Now go."

"I'm going to kill myself," she said.

"No, you're not."

"I am. And I want to do it here. Before God."

"You don't believe in God," he said.

"Do you?" she asked.

He went to speak, but realised he did not know the answer to that question. This morning he had certainty, absolute faith in his disbelief. Now the certainty crumbled.

"Everyone believes," she said. "Even if they say they don't, there's always that idea inside them. Maybe they're wrong. Well, maybe I'm wrong. So I want to do it here."

"Enough," he said, taking a step forward. "This won't work on me. Not any more."

"I know how to do it," she said.

She raised her hands, and for the first time he saw that she held a belt between them. His belt, the one from the waist of his cassock. Two inches in breadth, thick coarse material, a plain metal buckle at one end. She had fashioned the other end into a noose.

"It shouldn't hurt too much if I do it right," she said, a strange calm to her voice now. "I just put the buckle over a door and close it. Put this end around my neck and sit down. Simple as that."

"You won't," he said, feeling his anger fade. "And you certainly won't do it here."

She moved towards the top of the aisle. "All you have to do is walk out. You don't have to have any part in it. I can manage by myself."

McKay knew his rage should have burned bright, he knew he should have dragged her by the arm, thrown her out of the church. But instead of anger, he felt something else, something familiar yet strange to him.

Compassion, if he had to put a name to it.

She's right, he thought. Deep down, everyone believes. And I believe.

The urge to weep came upon him once more, but he resisted it. The urge to pray surged in its place. He stepped towards her.

"You're confused," he said. "You're angry. You're afraid. I know how that feels."

She shook her head. "You don't know how I feel."

"Maybe not." He came close, close enough to see the glittering in her eyes. "But God knows. Why don't you pray with me?"

She turned away, but he stepped around her, wouldn't let her avoid his gaze. Her mouth opened and closed, her eyelids flickered.

"Yes," she said. "I'd like that."

McKay lowered himself to his knees. "Then let's do it."

She nodded and said, "All right."

Then he saw the movement of her hands, felt the coarse cloth slip across his nose and cheeks and lips, felt the belt settle around his neck.

Quick, so quick he couldn't get his fingers between the belt and his throat, she yanked the noose tight. As he grabbed at the belt, she slipped behind him, pulled hard, taking him off his knees. His heels kicked at the floor, the back of his head cracked on the tile. Pressure inside his skull, in his ears, his temples.

She hauled him across the smooth tiles, crying out at the effort. His jacket whispered on the sheen of the floor as he opened and closed his mouth, trying to vent a scream that could not escape his chest. As she grunted and dragged him across the threshold of the vestry, in the dim light of the lamp, he caught a glimpse of her hands and saw she wore the same surgical gloves as he had the night he killed her husband.

Amid the crushing pressure in his head, through the clamour of his fear, a thought speared into his mind: scratch her. Get some trace of her under his nails. Get it for the police to find. He reached back over his head, but she kept her hands out of his reach.

She stopped inside the vestry, kicked the door over. Then she planted both her feet firm on the floor, tightened her grip on the belt, and hoisted him up by his neck. Somewhere through the storm behind his eyes, he heard her growl. Pain as the fabric cut into his skin, constricted his throat. He scrambled to get to his feet, swung his arms in wild arcs, trying to get hold of her, get hold of the belt, anything at all.

She gave an animal roar as she threw herself towards the door, dragging him staggering after. Up and up, she pulled up, he could see her arms stretching up, pushing back. She howled and wrestled, and for a moment his heels left the floor.

Then the door slammed shut behind him, the handle digging into the small of his back, and she stepped away. Feeling the noose loosen a fraction, he lunged forward, but the belt tightened again, yanked him back against the door. He realised she had fed the buckle over the top, closed the door, trapping it in place.

She stared at him, wide-eyed, her face burning red, panting as he tried to dig his fingertips between the belt and his throat. Then she raised the hood over her head, dropped to her knees, and reached for his ankles. The noose tightened, harder than before, as she pulled his feet from under him, held his ankles in front of her. The belt pulled tighter still, and the storm inside his head swelled into a hurricane. He reached behind to the small of his back, his fingers trying for the door handle, but the weight of his body kept the door closed. He grabbed for her, but his fingers swiped at the clear air between them. His legs kicked of their own accord, but she held her grip firm on his ankles.

Roaring, roaring, roaring between his ears. The pressure behind his eyes like a balloon inside his skull. Bursts of black in his vision. He watched her through a shrinking funnel of light, the wildness of her, and she opened her mouth and sparks flew from it and from her eyes and lightning all around her and darkness eating at the edges of everything and all he could think was Maggie, Maggie, forgive me, Maggie . . .

37

Roberta Garrick held on tight to his ankles long after he'd stopped writhing and twitching, even as the foul odour of his body's expulsions made her gag. Each ragged inhalation brought the smell into her lungs, and she coughed each breath out until she grew light-headed and almost fell. But still she held on.

Eventually, she let go. One easy movement, she opened her fingers, and his body dropped, his back thudding into the door. She watched him for a while, as if the blood would return to his brain, the air to his chest. But he was gone. At last, she stood upright. She rotated her shoulders and cried out as a dagger of pain shot into her neck from the right. She brought her left hand to the offended muscle and massaged it as her heart slowed.

It hadn't been so bad. Not really.

The fourth life she had taken, if she

counted her husband's, even though she hadn't actually fed him the morphine herself. The first had been long ago. That other life that seemed so far away now, so distant that she sometimes wondered if it had ever been hers at all. She dreamed about it still, that past version of herself, and she awoke unsure of which life she lived now.

Like that morning when she woke to find Peter in the bed beside her and she didn't know who he was, who she was, and how she came to be there in a stranger's bed. So she had shouted and kicked until he fled, and then she remembered she was Roberta Garrick and he was Peter McKay, the man who killed her husband for her.

A sense of peace settled over her, a sense of having addressed the problems at hand. Now she could proceed unburdened by Peter McKay and his needy whining. She had intended to distance herself from him, in fact had begun to do so, but perhaps this was better. A clean break, over and done with.

Roberta surveyed the room, made sure she'd left nothing of herself behind. Satisfied, she exited the vestry through the side door and went to the car she had borrowed from the dealership. A twelve-year-old Citroën, taken from a customer for a couple of hundred pounds as a token part exchange on a newer vehicle, stored at the rear of her dead husband's dealership ready to be taken to a scrapyard. An unremarkable car, one that would draw no attention on the road.

She opened the passenger door, reached inside for the plastic bag she'd stowed in the footwell, sending ripples of pain through her shoulders and back. The bag's contents clinked and rattled as she lifted it and brought it back to the vestry. There, she opened it and set the ceramic pestle and mortar on the desk beneath the lamp. She bundled up the bag and stuffed it into the pocket of the hooded top she had bought in a charity shop in Lisburn.

Roberta closed the vestry's outer door behind her, went to the car, got in, and turned the ignition. The engine whirred and coughed but did not start.

"Shit," she said.

Again. More whirring and coughing, and a hard grinding.

"Come on," she said.

One more time, and as the engine rattled, she dabbed the accelerator pedal to feed it a little more petrol. The car juddered around her as the engine finally clattered into life. Morganstown's main street remained as dark and quiet as when she'd arrived here fifteen minutes ago. She eased the Citroën out onto the road, kept the acceleration light, not wishing the engine to grumble too loudly as she left the village. The back roads stretched black and empty ahead. She took the single-track lanes wherever possible, doubling the length of her journey back to Garrick Motors, but the reduced risk of meeting a police car was worth the extra time. Patrol cars had all sorts of technology now, she'd seen it on television; they had computers that could read number plates and trigger an alert if the car lacked insurance or road tax.

A flash of red on the narrow road in front of her, and by instinct her right foot went to the brake pedal, stamped hard. The car shook and hunkered down as it slowed, the spongy brakes gripping as hard as their wear would allow. She hissed through gritted teeth as the wheels skidded, the near-bald tyres barely keeping hold of the tarmac. When the Citroën finally halted, she watched the road to see what had appeared in her path.

A fox sprinted away from the front of the car — she must have been inches from crushing it — and dived into the hedgerow.

A deep laugh erupted from her belly and she covered her mouth with her hand.

I killed a man, she thought, and I saved a fox.

No, not funny. It was good she hadn't hit the animal. Someone at the dealership would have noticed the damage to the car, the blood, the fur. Someone would have asked questions. Someone would suspect the Citroën had been taken from the rear yard. There were no cameras back there, but still, she could not have it known that the car had been used for anything more than gathering rust and waiting for transport to the breakers.

She set off once more. Not far now. Within ten minutes she had pulled up at the back of the dealership property and opened the gate; she had left the padlock undone when she'd swapped cars earlier in the evening. She moved the Citroën inside, reversed it into the space where she'd found it, though turning her head to look through the rear window caused a spasm in the muscles of her right shoulder. The door to the back shed where the scrap car keys were kept was seldom locked; she had done this many times before. She dropped the keys into the Tupperware tub where she'd found them among the half-dozen other sets, pulled the shed door closed, and went to her Mini Cooper.

As she drove away from the locked gates, back towards her house — *her* house now, not her husband's — she began to laugh again. A joyous laugh, like when she was a girl chasing chickens across her grandfather's yard.

It's all done now, she thought. Every detail squared away. Free of them all, every hand that had ever dragged at her heels.

All except Jim Allison. But he knew nothing, and she'd freeze him out soon enough. Take it slower than she had with Peter, let him down easier. She'd learned from that mistake.

And the policewoman. Flanagan could yet cause her more problems, but nothing Roberta couldn't cope with. If the ideas she had planted in Jim's mind took root, the next few days would be difficult for Flanagan.

By the time Roberta had returned home, driven the Mini into the garage and entered the house, that feeling of peace had come back. Deeper than before, more complete. She ran a bath with a generous dose of soothing bubbles, soaked herself until the water cooled and her muscles tingled. Then she went to bed and slept a solid black sleep until the telephone woke her the next morning.

38

Alistair was still asleep in bed when Flanagan left the house. They had made love last night, and it had been good. Relaxed, easy, nothing begrudged, nothing withheld. As she had lain awake in the dark, she had wondered at how within a couple of hours she had gone from feeling sure their marriage was over to a sense that it had a lifetime left to grow.

She had looked in on the children before she left; they both dozed on, oblivious to her watching from their doorways. She had resisted the urge to sneak in and steal a kiss for fear of waking them.

A warm autumn sun hung low over the trees as she approached Morganstown. Early morning shoppers parked their cars in the filling station forecourt to buy the Sunday papers. Flanagan made a mental note to drop in on the way back, buy an *Observer* and a *Times,* maybe the makings of a fried breakfast for everybody. As she neared the church, her mind was more focused on whether or not she had the ingredients for eggs Benedict than on whatever had been so urgent for Reverend McKay to have called last night.

She parked her Volkswagen next to McKay's Ford and got out. A strange quiet about the place, she thought. Even before she knocked on the front door, she was certain no one would answer. After a wait of a minute or so, and a second knock, she looked across to the church. Maybe he was in there, getting ready for the morning's service. The front doors had been closed as she entered the car park, but perhaps he didn't open them until he was ready for the congregation.

Flanagan walked towards the side door, and as she came close she noticed the lamplight through the small window. She knocked on the door, listened for a response. When none came, she tried the handle. The door opened inward.

She saw the bright red ceramic pestle and mortar by the lamp first of all, had only a moment to wonder why such things were sitting there before she looked towards the door leading to the church. Then the smell hit her.

"Oh Christ," she said, her hand reflexively going to her mouth and nose.

She saw McKay there, his head at an unnatural angle, legs splayed in front of him, arms loose at his sides, torso suspended above the floor.

"Oh no," she said.

Flanagan grabbed her phone from her bag and dialled.

DSI Purdy arrived last, pushing his way through the crowd that had gathered at the church gates. A pair of uniformed constables stayed between the people and the church, but the crowd seemed content to watch, concern on their faces. Members of the congregation, most of them, arriving for their Sunday service to find a police line they could not cross. Flanagan recognised some of the faces, saw tears on many.

"Dr. Barr here yet?" Purdy asked as he approached.

"He's in there now," Flanagan said, nodding towards the vestry. Flashes of light burst from inside as the photographer recorded the scene.

Light drops of rain spotted Flanagan's skin, but she still had to shield her eyes against the sun. A rainbow arced above the buildings opposite.

"Tell me what you know so far," Purdy said.

She looked to the ground, felt it drag her down, felt like she wanted to lie there and let the tarmac swallow her whole.

"I found him hanged just after eight-thirty," Flanagan said. "A black belt over the door. There's a belt missing from the cassock that's hanging up in the closet, so that must be it. No immediate sign of anyone else having been here. Everything points to a suicide."

"Just like last week," Purdy said.

"Yes, on the face of it. But there's something else." She indicated the window, the lamp still glowing beyond the glass. "There's a pestle and mortar sitting there, beneath that light."

"A pestle and mortar?"

"I haven't touched it — no one has — but I could see a residue of white powder in the bowl."

"Morphine," Purdy said.

"I'm guessing so," Flanagan said. "Tests will confirm."

"Jesus. So it was him killed Garrick. He couldn't hack it, so he leaves the evidence out and does himself in. Is that how you see it?"

"I'd say that's how I'm *supposed* to see

it," she said.

Purdy kept his gaze hard on Flanagan. "Go on."

"It's too neat," she said. "Too easy. A week I've been chasing after this, and all of a sudden it's handed to me on a plate. I don't buy it."

Purdy looked back to the crowd at the gate. He sucked his teeth, tapped his foot, then turned back to Flanagan. "Well, maybe you *should* buy it."

She squinted at him, the sun bright behind him. "Sir?"

"You've had an answer handed to you," he said, his voice lowered. "Maybe it's time you just took it and moved on."

"Sir, no, I —"

"Let me finish," he said, raising his hands to quiet her. "You've been grabbing at threads through this whole case, trying to find something other than what was staring you in the face. I'm not saying your suspicions were wrong, we may never know what the truth is, but just think about how much harder you want to push at this. Look at it this way: you suspected this was murder from the start and it looks like you've been proven right. You didn't get the person you wanted for it, I understand that, but maybe you should accept this as a break and have it over and done with."

Flanagan felt heat in her eyes, shook her head.

"No," she said. "I can't. I just can't. I know this is a set-up, and you know it too."

"I don't know any such —"

"Sir, with respect, you haven't been talking with Reverend McKay or Mrs. Garrick. You haven't looked into their eyes like I have. And there's something else."

"What?"

Flanagan hesitated, then said, "He called me last night."

Purdy raised his eyebrows, pointed his thumb towards the vestry.

"Yes," she said. "Around nine. He asked me to come over, he needed to talk to me. I said I couldn't. He offered to come to me, and I refused."

Purdy sighed. "I know where you're going with this, and you're wrong."

She kept her voice low, but anger pushed the words out — anger at herself, jagged and bitter. "I'm not wrong. If I'd gone to him, if I'd let him come to me, he'd still be alive. Whether he killed himself, or somebody else did it, it wouldn't have happened if I'd listened to whatever it was he needed to tell me."

"Stop it," Purdy said, pointing a finger at

her, inches from her face. "Fucking stop it. It's bad enough you're looking for someone else to blame for that man's death, let alone yourself. Whatever brought McKay to suicide had nothing to do with you, and I don't want to hear another word on that. Clear?"

Flanagan didn't answer. Clouds obscured the sun, and the rain thickened. Drops gathered on Purdy's glasses.

"Now, I need you to be careful," he said. "Something's brewing elsewhere."

"Sir?"

"I got collared by a journalist on the way in, something about allegations made by Jim Allison. Whether it's to do with what happened yesterday, I don't know, but he's been shooting his mouth off to the press. Watch your step."

"Yes, sir."

He pointed to her car, still parked by McKay's house. "Now go on, get out of the rain."

Flanagan nodded and turned towards the Volkswagen. She walked with her head down, hearing the murmurs of the crowd.

"Why couldn't you have left them alone?" a voice called.

She stopped, turned her head to the gates. An elderly woman called again. "Why did you hound them like that? Now look what you've done."

Flanagan stared for a moment, confused, then resumed the short walk to her car. Inside, rain sounding on the roof, she put her head in her hands and prayed.

39

Roberta Garrick watched the local news bulletin on the small flat screen television in her kitchen, the sound muted, the coffee machine gurgling and hissing. A long shot of the church, taken from the village side, with the rear of Peter's house closer to the camera. Police officers milling around, some wearing forensic overalls. Then a photograph of her and her husband at a Christmas get-together.

She reached for the remote control and turned the volume up. The reporter spoke in voiceover as the photograph zoomed in to fill the screen.

". . . local MLA Jim Allison, a close friend of both the deceased men, had this to say about the police investigation so far."

And there was Jim, the church farther in the background, the hubbub going on behind him, sunshine making him squint. He wore his Sunday suit and a serious face.

"I have been in touch with the Assistant Chief Constable and expressed my disgust at the treatment meted out to both Mrs. Garrick and Reverend Peter McKay over the last week."

Strange how his voice became nasal and pinched when he spoke in public, not like when he whispered and moaned into her ear in the back of his Range Rover.

"Specifically, Detective Chief Inspector Serena Flanagan has subjected both of my good friends to a week of abuse since Mr. Garrick took his own life. Mrs. Garrick has suffered enough tragedy over the last few years without being hounded by a police officer, particularly when the coroner has unequivocally ruled Mr. Garrick's death a suicide. Likewise, Reverend McKay, having just lost a very dear friend, has been constantly intimidated by DCI Flanagan."

Cut to a shot, zoomed in from some distance, of Flanagan outside the church, a taller man leaning over her, a heated discussion, the man's finger in her face.

Cut back to Jim Allison, nodding to emphasise each point.

"I have absolutely no doubt that this police harassment has played at least some part in driving Reverend McKay to an apparent suicide. The Assistant Chief Constable has assured me he will look into this matter, and believe me, I will hold him to that promise."

Cut to the reporter, an earnest young man with shaving rash on his neck, hunched against a shower of rain.

"Detectives have not as yet confirmed the sudden death of Reverend Peter McKay as a suicide, though that is the view of most of the people I've spoken to this morning. As for Jim Allison's allegations of harassment, the PSNI have declined to comment, saying to do so would be unhelpful at this stage of the investigation."

Back to the studio, and the news bulletin switched to a story about a factory closure. Roberta turned the television off and waited for the coffee machine to finish. She winced at the pain between her neck and shoulders. Stabbing spasms had been nagging her since she woke, and the muscles of her upper back felt stretched and quivery. She was in excellent shape, made good use of the gym upstairs, but still, dragging Peter across the church floor had been a strain.

No mention of the pestle and mortar. The police hadn't let that detail slip yet; Jim Allison still believed her husband's death to be suicide. Let him go on thinking it, and everyone else, until the police made it known. His railing against Flanagan and the PSNI would come back to haunt him when he was proven wrong, but the short-term damage to Flanagan was more than worth it.

It had been a week of terrors and triumphs. Certain one moment that she had let one small thread slip her grasp, enough to unravel everything; the next moment, confident the way ahead had cleared. And in between those moments a giddy shrieking inside her mind, a feeling of being adrift and lost. The sense that she would never regain control. But those moments passed too, only to return again and again as her thoughts cycled between the best and worst of all things.

She knew what she needed now: stability and peace. The space to calm down, to find her balance. Then she could get on with enjoying the life she had worked so long and hard at crafting for herself. All she had to do was get through these next few days and all would be as she desired.

Patience and a steady hand, that was all.

Roberta went to the coffee machine, lifted the cup from beneath the spout, and the other from the worktop. She carried both, steam and dark aroma rising from the frothy liquid, out of the kitchen and up the stairs to the open door of her bedroom.

Jim waited there, sitting on the edge of the bed, hands clasped together in front of his mouth. He had put his trousers back on, the belt still hanging loose, the flab of his belly spilling onto his lap.

He didn't look at her, even as she held a cup in front of his eyes. He took it, but did not drink. She sat on the chair in the corner, the one where Harry had draped his clothes every night, back when he had been able to dress himself.

"What?" she asked.

Jim stared at the carpet, his toes curling and gripping the deep pile. "We shouldn't have done that," he said.

"Of course we should," she said.

"Harry's only just in his grave, now Peter. And we're . . ."

He turned his head, looked at the scattered sheets.

"Fucking," Roberta said.

Jim looked at her now, shocked at the word he'd been too afraid to speak for himself. But he dropped his gaze almost as soon as it met hers.

"It's not right," he said. "It's too soon."

"Nonsense," she said. She blew on her coffee, felt the heat on her lips. Tasted him. "It's been more than a year. You think it was all right to fuck your friend's wife while he was still alive, but not once he's dead? What's the difference? Apart from being able to do it in a bed instead of the back of your car."

"It's not right," he said again. "It's just not."

Roberta set her cup on the floor, stood, crossed to the bed. She took the cup from his hand, set it on the bedside table. Then she put her hand on his bare chest, eased him back onto the mattress. She climbed onto him, straddled him, and with her hands she pinned his wrists down behind his head. She leaned down, her mouth to his ear.

"It's not right," she said. "And it's not wrong. It just is. Life becomes so much easier when you let go of right and wrong."

The tip of her tongue traced the shape of his ear. He moaned as his hips rose to her.

"Believe me," she said. "I know."

40

DSI Purdy had sent Flanagan home half an hour after he'd arrived at the scene. No explanation, only that he would call by and see her later. Regret had been clear on his face, and she knew the order had come from above.

She turned on the radio as she drove the short distance to her house, tuned it to BBC Radio Ulster. The news started as she pulled her car into the driveway. She drove around to the rear of the house, shut off the engine, but kept the key in the ignition so she could listen.

Reverend McKay's death was the lead item, but no mention of the pestle and mortar. A straightforward suicide, according to sources. Flanagan knew the 'sources' were members of the congregation who had gathered outside the church and that they knew nothing of what had occurred inside.

Alistair appeared at the kitchen window,

waved to her. She returned the gesture, then raised a finger, mouthed the words, "One minute."

He nodded and disappeared from view.

She listened to the rest of the report, unsurprised by any of it until Jim Allison said his piece. Harassment, he said, intimidated. Flanagan flinched at the words, balled her hands into fists. She thumped the power button on the radio with the heel of her hand.

"Arsehole," she said. "Fucking arsehole."

She stayed there in the driver's seat until the anger had ebbed enough for her to speak without a tremor in her voice. No need for the kids to see the rage on her, not with how stretched and thin everything had become in recent days.

Alistair opened the back door as she got out of the car. He put an arm around her waist, kissed her cheek as she crossed the threshold, gave her a look that said she didn't need to explain. She loved him then as much as she ever had, and she entered into the warm scents of the meal he'd been preparing.

"Where are they?" she asked, looking towards the hall.

"Eli's on his PlayStation," Alistair said, "Ruth's up in her room reading."

"So we've got a minute to ourselves," Flanagan said.

Alistair smiled and took her in his arms. They stayed like that, holding each other until she said, "A good man died last night."

"A friend?" he asked.

Flanagan thought about it for a moment before saying, "Yes. Yes, he was."

The bubbling and hissing of a pot boiling over pulled Alistair away. She watched as he lowered the heat under the pot, stirred another, peered inside the oven.

"Are we going to be all right?" she asked.

He closed the oven door and turned back to her. "I don't know," he said. "I hope so."

Two hours later, the children cleared their bowls of dessert and Flanagan gathered up the rest of the dishes. It had been a good meal, no brittle borders between them at the table. Just a family enjoying a Sunday lunch, and Flanagan wished she could drown out the whispering worry that lingered in her mind, along with the pangs of sorrow for Peter McKay.

The doorbell rang as she closed the dishwasher. She looked to Alistair, and he said, "Go on, I'll clear up."

DSI Purdy stood on the doorstep with his hands in his pockets, a frown on his face. Without a word, she showed him into the small downstairs office. Booms, thuds and shrieks from whatever game Eli was playing in the next room. Flanagan sat at the desk beneath the window while Purdy squeezed his bulk into the old wicker chair in the corner.

"You know what I'm going to tell you," Purdy said.

Flanagan nodded. "Who's taking over?" she asked.

"DCI Conn," he said.

Flanagan gave a hard laugh. "Christ, he'll love that. He'll take every chance he can to shit all over me after the Walker case."

A year ago she had humiliated Conn by pulling a case from under him, proving he had it all wrong. They hadn't spoken since.

"It wasn't my choice," Purdy said. "The ACC chose him. Either way, you knew it'd be taken from you."

"I know," she said. "But him."

"Listen, whatever Conn does with it from here on, the ACC knows you were right all along about it not being a simple suicide. If it wasn't for you, this would've been wrapped up four days ago and the truth would never have come out. I'll be reminding Conn of that, and the ACC."

"But the truth hasn't come out," Flanagan said. "Not all of it. He didn't act on his own. Roberta Garrick has to be interrogated."

"That'll be Conn's decision to make," Purdy said.

"Can I offer to assist?" Flanagan asked.

Now Purdy laughed. "Do you think Conn will have that?"

She shook her head. "No, I suppose not."

"Well, then. First thing tomorrow morning, pack up everything you have on the case and give it to me to pass on. After that's done, why don't you take a couple of days off?"

She considered it for a moment. "No, moping around here won't do me any good. Give me some grunt work to do, anything to keep me occupied."

"There's always plenty of that lying around." He smiled, and she returned the gesture, albeit with no feeling behind it.

"You know," Purdy said, "it's all for the best. I'll be glad for this to be wrapped up. I don't want to leave any loose ends when I go at the end of the week."

"But you'll know that woman got away with it," Flanagan said.

"I don't know any such thing," Purdy said, his voice hardening. "Besides, remember where we are. This is Northern Ireland. How many killers have we got on our streets

— people you and I know have blood on their hands — that are walking around free, knowing they'll never see the inside of a cell? Even if I thought Roberta Garrick had got away with murder, she'd be at the end of a very long list."

Flanagan had no comeback for that. She offered him a tea or a coffee, but he declined, said he was needed back at the scene.

"I'll see myself out," he said, getting up. He stopped in the doorway and said, "Don't dwell on this. You'll drive yourself crazy."

"I'll try," she said, knowing he didn't believe her.

"Take care."

He closed the door behind him. From her seat by the window she heard his car door open and close, his engine starting, the tyres on the driveway.

"Shit," she said.

A knock on the door, then Alistair entered. He carried a fizzing glass of gin and tonic, a wedge of lime trapped among the ice, and a pale ale for himself. She gratefully took the glass from his hand, had a sip, savoured the juniper and lime taste, the hard crisp cold of it. He'd made it strong, and she was glad.

"Thank you," she said.

Alistair took her mobile phone from his pocket; she'd left it on the kitchen table.

"Sounds like there was a text for you," he said, handing it to her.

Flanagan entered her passcode and saw Miriam McCreesh's name. She cursed herself for neglecting yet again to reply to Friday's message. The text read: *I see from the news that you've got your hands full. Might see you tomorrow. Catch up then.*

But Flanagan wouldn't see Dr. McCreesh tomorrow. DCI Brian Conn would stand watch as the pathologist cut Peter McKay open on the cold steel table. That thought, the relief of not having to endure the post-mortem clashing with the regret at not seeing McCreesh, dissuaded her from replying now. She tossed her phone onto the desk and took another deep swallow from her glass.

Alistair perched on the edge of the desk, swigged his ale. She had discussed little of the case with him, given how seldom they'd talked at all in recent weeks, but he knew enough to understand things weren't good if Purdy had called to the house.

"End of the world?" he asked.

"Probably not," Flanagan said. "Just feels like it."

He put a hand on her shoulder, squeezed, took it away.

They sat and drank together without

speaking. She thought of the turmoil of the last couple of months, how much her job had cost her, what it cost her family. And yet it came to this. No one saved, no justice served. Another dead man and a hollow feeling in her gut.

Flanagan leaned into Alistair, her head resting against his side, and he put his arm around her.

"Let's get drunk," she said.

"We've both got work tomorrow," he said.

"So? Wouldn't be the first time either of us went in with a hangover."

"What about the kids?"

"They can fend for themselves. He's got his games, she's got her books. I'll throw a ham sandwich at them at some point."

He smiled and said, "All right."

41

Roberta Garrick was not surprised when the police officers called at her home that evening, only that it had taken so long. She recognised the male as she watched him approach through her living room window. He had been with Flanagan, seemed to be an assistant of some kind, but she couldn't recall his name. A younger policewoman followed him, a uniformed officer, sturdy, broad at the hips, but pretty enough in her own way. Roberta Garrick always noticed these things.

"Answer the door, would you?" she said.

Jim had been dozing on the couch, had not heard the police car pull up to the house.

"Hm?" He blinked at her like a slow child asked to solve an equation.

"Get the door," she said. "Please."

Jim looked out to the hall, confusion still lingering on his face. Then the doorbell rang, and he said, "Oh."

He got to his feet, tucked his shirt into his trousers, smoothed and straightened himself as he went to the hall. Roberta listened to the murmur of voices, then Jim returned, the two young officers following.

"Roberta," Jim said, "Detective Sergeant Murray needs a word."

"What can I do for you, Sergeant?" she asked.

Murray clasped his hands together as he spoke, an act of supplication. "There's been a significant development in the case of your husband's death," he said.

"Oh?" She raised her eyebrows, felt the worry on her face like she'd slipped on a mask.

Murray indicated the couch. "Maybe you should take a seat."

She went to the couch, sat down, reached a hand out towards Jim. "Can Jim stay?"

"Of course," Murray said.

Jim took her hand and sat down next to her, a good family friend offering comfort and support. Murray sat in the armchair opposite, where DCI Flanagan had sat almost a week before. The uniformed policewoman remained standing near the door. Murray hadn't bothered to introduce her.

The sergeant sat forward, his hands

clasped together once more, as if praying. "Mrs. Garrick, I have to warn you, what I'm about to tell you will be upsetting."

She blinked, searched for that feeling inside, the one she used to summon tears. There, there it was. She blinked again, felt the warm wetness in her eyes. Jim squeezed her fingers between his.

"Go on," she said.

"Mrs. Garrick, we have reason to believe your husband's death was not a suicide."

She opened her mouth, inhaled, held her breath. Just long enough. "What do you mean?" she asked in a very small voice.

"We have reason to believe that Mr. Garrick was murdered," Murray said. "More than that, we believe that Reverend McKay might have killed him."

Jim looked from the sergeant to Roberta and back again. "What?"

"No," Roberta said. "That can't be true."

"We have evidence to suggest that's the case," Murray said. "It's early days in the investigation, but right now we're not looking for anyone else in connection with this."

Roberta shook her head. "There must be a mistake."

"Mrs. Garrick, is it possible that Reverend McKay might have been able to take some sachets of morphine granules out of this house?"

"I don't know," she said. "I suppose it's possible. When he came round, he often fed Harry his yogurt with the morphine in it. We kept the sachets by the bed."

Murray wrote something on his notepad. "As you're aware, Reverend McKay committed suicide at some time last night. He used a belt to hang himself from the vestry door."

She pushed the tears out, fished a tissue from her sleeve, dabbed at her cheeks.

"We found a pestle and mortar on the desk in the vestry. It's yet to be confirmed, but there were traces of powder in the mortar that we believe to be crushed morphine granules. We believe that Reverend McKay took some sachets from your home, crushed the contents with the pestle and mortar, then when he came back to your house, he mixed them in with your husband's nightly yogurt."

Roberta began to shake, more tears. "No, no, no," she said. "It can't be true, it can't be."

Murray shuffled forward on his seat. "Where we're struggling, Mrs. Garrick, is the reason. Why would Reverend McKay do this?"

She became still and quiet, staring into space. She felt their gaze on her, their waiting breath, their anticipation. Let them wait.

"Mrs. Garrick?"

What was the threat she'd made to Peter before he left yesterday? What had she said she'd tell the police? Oh, yes. She slowly came back to herself, shaking her head as she did so. "No," she whispered. "That can't be it."

"Anything at all you think of, Mrs. Garrick."

She tilted her head as she spoke, knitted her brow. "There *is* something, but it seems so unlikely."

Murray's voice took on a pleading tone. "Anything at all."

Roberta exhaled, a defeated sigh. "Peter had feelings for me."

She felt a twitch in Jim's fingers and had to suppress a smile.

"Feelings?" Murray echoed.

"I always dismissed it," she said. "He was lonely. I never knew his wife, she died before I became a member of the church, but I know he missed her constantly, even to this day. And he was all on his own, alone in that big house, the rectory. He was always a good friend of ours, but after Harry's accident we became very close. We talked a

345

lot, just me and Peter. I suppose he hadn't had anyone to talk to like that for a long time. And I suppose it became more for him."

Murray asked, "Did he ever make any . . . approaches to you?"

"You mean, physically?"

"Yes."

"No, at least not at first. It started with him telling me how close he felt he'd come to me over those few months. How he wished he could meet someone like me, someone to keep him company. So I tried to talk him into getting out there, meet people outside the congregation, but it didn't seem to do any good. You know, I didn't think much of it at the time, but he would always hold my hands when we prayed. It seemed to be a very intimate thing for him."

Dare she push the lie a little further? Murray and the young policewoman seemed so rapt in her words. One more tiny detail to reel them in.

"Then once," she said, "he tried to kiss me."

Jim let go of her hand.

"And what happened?" Murray asked.

"We were praying, like we always did, and he had my hands held to his chest. I remember I could feel his breath on my skin. Then, as we finished, I opened my eyes, and he was so close. He leaned in and kissed me. I was so shocked, I didn't pull away immediately, but when I realised what was happening, I pushed him back."

"How did he react?"

"I remember his face," Roberta said, warming to the tale, the picture she painted for them. "At first, for a moment, he looked shocked, then angry, then sad. He kept apologising, over and over, and I kept telling him not to worry about it, I understood, he was lonely, and so on. Perhaps I led him on. Maybe I shouldn't have let our relationship get so close."

"How was he after that?" Murray asked. "Did things get back to normal?"

"Yes and no," she said. "He was bashful, timid around me for a week or two, then things seemed to be fine. He still came round to see Harry, to pray with me. Just like before. But there was always this look in his eyes, like there was something going on behind them. And sometimes in church, he seemed to be looking at me in a way he didn't look at the other women. I told myself it was my imagination, but now I'm not so sure. Does any of this help?"

"It helps a lot," Murray said, closing his

notebook. "Would you be prepared to repeat this in a full statement?"

"Yes, if you think it's necessary."

"Good," he said, opening his notebook again. "One thing, though."

An alarm sounded in Roberta's mind. She had made a mistake. But what?

"Given what happened between Reverend McKay and you," he said, "why did you agree to stay at his house after your husband's death?"

She sat quite still, staring into the empty air between the two officers. Think of something. Think.

There. Imperfect, but it would have to do. She let her features harden.

She turned her gaze on Murray. "I had just discovered my husband's dead body," she said. "Forgive me if I wasn't in the most rational state of mind."

Murray looked away. "Of course," he said, a red flush creeping up past his shirt collar. "I think that's all for now."

He stood. Roberta and Jim did the same.

As Murray turned to the door, Roberta said, "Can you please do me a favour?"

"Of course," Murray said.

"Please pass on my apologies and thanks to DCI Flanagan. I was harsh with her. I realise now that she suspected something

348

and was just doing her job. If she hadn't pushed so hard, then the truth might not have come to light. I'm grateful to her. Please tell her that."

Murray nodded. "I will. I'll be in touch over the next day or two."

Jim saw them out while Roberta waited in the living room. She watched them get into the car and pull away. As the car passed through the gate at the end of the drive, she felt a warm satisfaction in her breast. She turned away from the window as Jim returned to the living room.

Without looking at her, he said, "I should go."

"You should," Roberta said. "Your wife will be wondering where you've got to."

"You should have mentioned Peter to them earlier, after Harry died. How he felt about you."

"Should I?"

He still did not meet her gaze. "Maybe if they'd questioned him about it, he might have confessed. He might not have taken his own life."

"Maybe," she said. "Might. I suppose we'll never know."

"If I'd known, I wouldn't have said what I did about DCI Flanagan on the news. I wouldn't have made a fool of myself like that."

"For God's sake, get your head out of your arse, Jim," she said, unable to keep the sneer from her voice.

Now he looked at her. "What?"

She speared him with her gaze, let him have the full force of it. "No one cares what you said. Now go on home, there's a good boy. Don't keep Mrs. Allison waiting."

He left without saying another word.

42

Flanagan sat at her desk in Lisburn station, the lamp on so she could read the local newspaper. Always dark in here, the tiny window that didn't open more than a crack. On a warm day the air grew thick and heavy with heat. Today was cool, but that was about all she had to be glad of.

CLERGYMAN'S SUICIDE LINKED TO MURDER.

A shriek of a headline above a story that relished the details of the case, scant as they were. DCI Conn had given a press conference the previous night; she had watched it on the news that morning as she had an early breakfast. Conn at a desk, flanked by DSI Purdy and DS Murray, PSNI insignia behind them.

A suicide, Conn said, believed to be linked to the death of Henry Garrick six days before. Reverend Peter McKay had been very close to the dead man and his wife.

They were seeking no one else in their inquiries. A few shouted questions from the journalists, most of them dismissed with pat answers, then one about the relationship between the minister and the widow. A flicker on Conn's face was enough.

The story Flanagan now read had taken those points, extrapolated, made insinuations far beyond anything that was in the public domain. 'Sources close to the investigation' suggested that there was an abnormally close tie between Reverend McKay and Mrs. Garrick, and that formed a central pillar of police inquiries.

Purdy had told Flanagan what Mrs. Garrick had said to Murray the previous evening, but she felt certain that Murray would not have spilled to a reporter. More likely, whoever had written the piece had grasped a thread and woven his story from that, citing sources that simply didn't exist.

A brief paragraph stated that local MLA Jim Allison had been publicly critical of her handling of the case. No mention of Flanagan's suspicions of murder being proven correct, or of the statement Allison had issued that morning to apologise for his stance. In fairness, that would have been too late for this edition of the paper, but she doubted that any of the news outlets would bother carrying the apology.

When she'd called into Purdy's office this morning, Flanagan had once again offered to assist Conn through the remainder of the investigation.

"I told you no already," Purdy had said.

She had tried to argue. "But I could save him so much digging, all the work I've already —"

"No," Purdy said, his voice higher and harder. "DCI Conn is going to wrap this thing up, do all the box-ticking. You should be thankful he's saving you from a mountain of paperwork."

She knew then that Purdy just wanted it over and done with, off his desk before his retirement on Friday. The explanation of events that had been presented to him was good enough. She couldn't blame him. There was no evidence of Roberta Garrick's having had a hand in either death. Her suspicions and instincts did not outweigh what was in front of Purdy's nose.

"All I need you to do," Purdy said, "is make sure you have everything gathered and ready to hand over to Conn. And I'd better not get any complaints from him about you sticking your nose in. Understood?"

"Yes, sir," she said.

Now all her work sat in three file boxes

against the far wall while she studied the newspaper piece as if it contained some secret, some new scent for her to track. Nothing but speculation dressed as reportage. As crappy a piece of journalism as she'd ever seen. Salacious and puerile. There, a boxed-out image of Roberta Garrick at her husband's funeral. Flanagan would have been angered at the paper's intrusiveness had it been any other widow at the front of any other funeral procession.

She studied the woman's face, the blankness of it.

Who are you?

The question Flanagan could not escape. She'd been asking it for a week now and had yet to come up with a satisfactory answer. Who is this beautiful woman who appeared in this community seven years ago seeming never to have left a trace elsewhere?

Who are you?

Flanagan set the newspaper aside and once again opened the web browser on her computer. Facebook again. That profile again. This nothing life, this existence of Bible verses and flower arrangements and coffee mornings.

Who are you?

A knock on the door startled her, and she clicked the mouse to close the browser before calling, "Come."

DS Murray entered carrying a manila folder. "Ma'am, these are the bank records. Where do you want them?"

She pointed to the stack of file boxes. "Stick them in there."

Murray crossed to them, lifted the lid of the top box, was about to shove the folder inside.

"Hang on," Flanagan said.

Murray paused, looked at her.

"That's both Mr. and Mrs. Garrick's personal accounts, yes?"

"Yes, ma'am," Murray said. "I went through them like you said, but nothing stood out."

As a matter of course, DSI Purdy had sought authorisation for a RIPA request for access to two years' records of the deceased's and the widow's current and savings accounts. The Regulation of Investigatory Powers Act meant that any such request had to be made by an officer of his rank or higher, but not one directly involved in the case. Signs of financial distress would reinforce the assumption of suicide, but Murray had found they seemed to be comfortably solvent, to say the least.

"Let me have a look," Flanagan said, holding out her hand.

Murray brought the folder over. She took it from him and dropped it onto the desk with a thud.

"There was nothing untoward," Murray repeated. "Not as far as I could see, anyway."

"That's fine," Flanagan said. "I just want to satisfy my curiosity."

She pointedly looked to the door and thanked him. Murray took the hint and left. Alone, she opened the folder, slid out the slab of printed paper.

A current account in each of the Garricks' names, an ISA each, a reserve account for tax, as well as a general savings account belonging to Henry Garrick.

Flanagan hesitated for a moment, wondering what she was doing. What did she hope to find? She put her head in her hands and said, "Give it up." She had nothing to gain from digging a deeper hole for herself. Even so, she turned over a page and began.

She started with the tax-free Individual Savings Accounts. Only a few transactions a year. Into each account had been deposited the maximum annual allowance on the 6th of April for the last two years, and Flanagan assumed every year before that. A string of small monthly additions as the miserable interest accrued. Nothing she didn't expect

356

to see. Next Flanagan looked at Henry Garrick's own savings account. Again, a series of deposits, no withdrawals. A better rate of interest, presumably in return for not touching the balance.

Now the current accounts. Flanagan started with Henry Garrick's, tracing the tip of her pen down the columns of debits and credits.

A modest monthly amount from Garrick Motors Ltd; his salary from the limited company. Flanagan took a highlighter from the penholder on her desk, coloured each deposit a bright yellow. Then she ran a quick tally in her head; as she expected, the rough total came out well below the individual tax-free allowance. Henry Garrick would pay nothing on this money, and any more that was paid as a dividend would be charged at a lower rate. Plus it avoided National Insurance. She took an orange highlighter, found the additional payments into the account from Garrick Motors Ltd. A couple of thousand here, five thousand there. In every case, a dividend would be paid a few days before a larger outlay. A holiday company in one case, a jeweller in another.

Flanagan marvelled at the sums moving back and forth, the thousands of pounds passed around like loose change, felt the sour envy in her belly she'd felt standing in Roberta Garrick's walk-in wardrobe a week ago. She banished the feeling just as she had seven days before.

Despite the apparent excess of Henry Garrick's finances, they had a solid foundation. For every dividend taken, a percentage was also moved to the tax reserve to be paid when Her Majesty's Revenue and Customs came calling for their due. All very sensible and responsible. Taking whatever steps were necessary to minimise the tax obligation, and ensuring there was always enough to cover what couldn't be avoided. Murray had been quite right: no sign of financial distress. Quite the opposite, in fact. Even the monthly tithe to the church was generous, somewhat above the ten per cent convention demanded.

But something caught Flanagan's eye as she ran her finger down the series of orange highlighted dividend payments, turning pages as she went: beginning five months ago — one month after Henry Garrick's car accident — a string of dividend credits followed by payments to another company.

Manx-Hibernian Investments Ltd.

Flanagan made another tally in her head. Not far off one hundred thousand bouncing through the account over less than half a year, even allowing for the percentage that had been set aside for tax. She highlighted the outgoing money in green then turned to Roberta Garrick's current account.

Not dissimilar to her husband's. She took the same salary from the car dealership — she probably had a token title of secretary or treasurer, and probably took over as director after the accident — and the same kinds of dividends. A similar amount to her husband's paid out in tithe to the church. Flanagan took her time, not leaping ahead to the discovery she sought, highlighting the same transactions in the same colours. Then she moved back five months to a substantial dividend payment, £17,500. Two days later the same amount, minus a percentage moved to the tax reserve, paid out to another company.

Manx-Hibernian Investments Ltd.

Flanagan made another total. Just over a hundred thousand. She checked the total she'd scribbled in the top corner of Henry Garrick's account. Almost exactly two hundred thousand going to what appeared to be an account on the Isle of Man.

She lifted the telephone handset and dialled Purdy's extension.

43

Roberta snapped awake, sprawled on top of the sheets. Falling, still falling, she grabbed the edge of the bed to quell the sensation. Her chest heaving, terror ripping through her.

"Oh God," she said. "Oh God."

She did not remember coming upstairs or lying down. She'd watched the news while she ate breakfast and drank coffee. After that? She recalled feeling weary, but not the decision to climb the stairs and sleep.

And what had woken her?

The thin glimmer of a dream remained in her mind. Peter's hands on her, touching her, kneading at her body while his eyes bulged and his face turned purple. The smell of his dying while he still clung to her. Perhaps the dream had scared her awake. She hoped it was that and not the other.

But then she heard it.

The high keening cry. The calling,

Mummy, Mummy, Mummy.

Roberta pulled a pillow over her head, pressed it to her ears, tried to block out the cries. But they cut through, pierced her brain, so high, so loud, always, always, always crying. Never peace, never quiet.

"Stop," she said, her lips pressed against the mattress. "Please stop."

But it did not stop. Calling for her, Mummy, Mummy, Mummy, the name she hated more than any other. Like needles in her skin, burning hot until she screamed into the bed, the pillow still wrapped tight around her head.

Finally, she said, "All right."

She threw the pillow aside and sat upright on the bed. The crying did not abate as she got to her feet, it only intensified, little gasps between each shriek. Roberta went to the double bedroom doors, paused there, knowing the cries would be louder still when she opened them. And they were, so fierce that she had to clasp her hands over her ears.

Out on the landing, the cries echoed through the hallway. She knew the source: the bedroom next to hers, the child's room, where her cot had been, the colourful painted walls, the toys, the drawers and wardrobe full of pretty clothes. The squealing, the Mummy, Mummy, Mummy came from in there.

"All right," Roberta said, unable to hear her own voice above the crying. "All right!"

She threw open the bedroom door, let it swing back and slam against the chest of drawers. No cot, no colourful painted walls, no pretty clothes. The room had long since been redecorated, but no amount of paint or carpeting would quiet the child who still lived here.

"All right, I'll do it," she said.

The crying ceased, and she felt the pressure in her head ease. She took her hands away from her ears.

"I'll do it," she said.

She turned, left the bedroom, and went back to her own. The antique chest, the clean rectangle of wallpaper above it. Roberta went to the chest, opened the top drawer, reached inside. The picture frame cold and hard in her hands. She lifted it up, back to the wall, found the hook, guided the string onto it.

The child stared down at her, that sweet smile on its face, the baby teeth showing. Dimples and blonde curls. The loveliest girl, everyone said, such a wee angel. But they didn't have to listen to it scream, tend to it day and night, feel it bound to her, tying her up, keeping her captive, promising to

362

do so for years to come.

Roberta went to the bed, sat on its edge, keeping her eyes on the photograph. Always watching, it was, always knowing. Even when it was closed in the drawer, it could see.

She closed her eyes, remembered the sensation of thrashing, struggling beneath her hand, and cold, the water up to her chin. Then stillness, a rushing in her ears, then under, tasting salt, then up, screaming help, help me, help my baby . . .

Roberta shivered, opened her eyes, got to her feet. Quiet now. Her bare feet padded across the carpet, out onto the wooden boards of the stairs, down to the kitchen.

Lunch, she thought. What will I have?

44

"Look," Flanagan said, spreading the printed bank records across Purdy's desk.

"What?" Purdy said.

He sat in his chair, Flanagan standing at his side, leaning over the sheets of paper.

"This," she said, pointing to the first orange highlighted debit, then the green highlighted credit above it. "And this."

"Money going in and out," Purdy said. "So what? They had plenty of it to throw around, didn't they?"

"But look," Flanagan said, pointing at another credit, another debit. "These start three weeks after Henry Garrick has his car accident. Dividends from the company coming in then going straight out again. I make it two hundred grand in total over a space of five months. All going to this Isle of Man investment fund."

"So?" Purdy asked. "It's a tax dodge. All these rich bastards are at it. It's a shitty

364

move, but there's nothing illegal about it."

"But don't you see?" She stabbed at more debits. "The tax has already been set aside. There's nothing to be dodged. I checked with HMRC, and the percentage due on these dividends matches what was moved to the reserve account. Why would you set up a tax dodge when you've already put aside the tax to be paid?"

Purdy was silent for a few moments, then said, "Maybe it's just some savings being put away."

"There are plenty of savings accounts they could use without going to the Isle of Man. Look, they've got three or four already. Why have this?"

Purdy shook his head. "I still don't see what you're getting at. Why would Roberta Garrick need to spirit away two hundred grand? She's got ten times that in assets as it stands, plus the money the dealership brings in, and the stock they're holding. There's no need for her to move money away; she's already set up for life."

"That's right," Flanagan said. "She's got all the money she could ever need, and the lifestyle to go with it. But what if she needs to run? What if she was planning all this five months ago, what if she needed enough put away in case something went wrong?"

"An escape fund?" Purdy said.

"Exactly. Two hundred thousand would be enough for her to make a start somewhere else if she couldn't stay here. Maybe she thinks having this money in the Isle of Man gives her some protection. Particularly if it's been bouncing from there to somewhere else. If we can see where the money goes from there, we might be able to figure out what she was planning."

Purdy sat silent for a moment as he thought, then he shook his head. "No," he said. "I don't buy it."

"Get a RIPA order, sir, get access to the Isle of Man account. Then we'll know for sure."

"I can't get the order, I'm still involved in the case. It has to come from a superintendent who's not attached to the investigation."

"McFadden," Flanagan said. "He can do it. I can put the request in today."

"No, you can't," Purdy said. "It's not your case."

"Then you ask him."

"He'll want to know on whose behalf. When I tell him it's for you, he'll refuse it. And he'll bloody well be right, too. This is none of your concern. If Conn wants to make the request, that'll be up to him."

366

"For fuck's sake." Flanagan slapped the desk, walked around it. "I know there's something there, and you know it too."

"Flanagan —"

She paced a circle around the office. "You just can't be bothered with it, can you? It's one more headache you can do without in your last week, isn't that right?"

"Flanagan —"

"You've got an easy answer, and you're going to let Conn tidy it all up, just so you —"

Purdy shot to his feet. "DCI Flanagan, shut your mouth!"

The ferocity of his voice stopped her pacing. She froze, staring at him.

"Just who the fuck do you think you're talking to?"

"Sir, I —"

"Don't you dare talk to me like that," Purdy said, his cheeks florid. "A week from now, when I'm out of this shitty job, you can talk to me however you want. But this week, now, you will address me with respect. Do I make myself clear?"

Flanagan looked to the floor. "Yes, sir. I apologise, sir."

He nodded and said, "Get out."

She approached the desk, went to gather up the sheets of bank records.

"Leave them," Purdy said. "I'll let Conn go through it all. If he thinks it's worth following up on, he can. I won't say you've been chasing it. He'll not bother his arse if your name comes into it."

"Thank you, sir," she said.

"All right," he said. "Go and do something useful."

Flanagan waited in the reception area of the General of Register Office.

Something useful, Purdy had said. She had gone back to her office and tried to apply herself to the reports being readied for the Public Prosecution Service, but her mind would not leave Roberta Garrick and the dead she had left in her wake. The Manx-Hibernian account still nagged at her. She wasted more time googling the investment firm, scouring social media, none of it leading anywhere.

There was still one thing, though.

So Flanagan had driven to Belfast city centre, parked, walked to the General of Register Office, and presented her warrant card. She had given Roberta Garrick's full name, place and date of birth, then taken a seat to wait.

Less than ten minutes passed before the clerk came back with a C4-sized envelope.

Flanagan thanked him and left the building, walked the five minutes back to her car, behind the Central Library. Huddles of redbrick buildings hemming in narrow streets, once bustling with industry, now mostly abandoned, some in redevelopment.

Once in the driver's seat, she checked the rear-view mirror.

Two young men, baseball caps, hoodies, tracksuit bottoms.

She locked the doors. Hijackings had become commonplace in the city, young thugs taking cars — usually from women — simply to race them around the estates before burning them out on some patch of waste ground.

Flanagan turned her attention back to the envelope and slid out the A4 sheet of pink and purple within. She studied the birth certificate. All was in order. Born Roberta Bailey in Magherafelt Hospital, 15th July 1980. The mother, Maisie Bailey, née Russell, the father Derek Bailey. Nothing untoward.

She glanced back to the rear-view mirror. The two young men separated, each approaching at either side of the row of parked cars behind her. She looked in her side mirrors, made eye contact with one of them. He didn't look away.

Flanagan set the envelope and the birth certificate on the passenger seat. Her right hand unclipped her holster, the other took her mobile phone from her bag. She dialled DS Murray's number, brought the phone to her ear.

The young men reached the car, and they each tried the door handles. The one at the driver's side tapped the window with the blade of a knife. Flanagan drew her Glock 17, let him see it. She smiled as he sprinted away towards the city centre, his friend still at the other side of the car, staring after him. He looked down into the car, saw the pistol, and followed the other, the soles of his trainers blurring as he ran.

Murray answered, and Flanagan holstered her weapon.

"Are you at your desk?" she asked.

"Give me a second, ma'am." A few seconds of rustling and fumbling. "I am now. What do you need?"

"Call up the electoral register," she said.

She listened to a minute's worth of mouse-clicking and key-tapping, along with a few muttered curses, before Murray said, "Right, got it."

"Bailey, Derek," she said, "and Bailey, Maisie. Magherafelt area."

More key-tapping, then a pause. "Bailey,"

Murray said. "That's Roberta Garrick's maiden name."

"That's right," Flanagan said.

"This is DCI Conn's case," Murray said. "I'm not sure I should be doing this for you, ma'am."

"I won't tell if you don't," Flanagan said.

Another pause, then the key-tapping resumed. "All right," he said, "I've got an address in Moneymore. Are you ready?"

Flanagan pulled the notepad and pen from her bag, juggled them and the phone as she got the cap off the pen and found a new page to write on. "Go ahead," she said, and wrote down the house number, the road, the postcode.

When she thanked him, Murray asked, "What's going on, ma'am?"

"Nothing for you to worry about," Flanagan said as she started her engine.

45

The police arrived at Roberta Garrick's home at five in the afternoon. A small group of them led by a middle-aged man who introduced himself as DCI Brian Conn.

"Where's DCI Flanagan?" Roberta had asked.

"She's no longer working on this case," Conn had said, and she could see that he suppressed a smirk. In truth, she had to do the same.

The scene of her husband's death had to be reopened, Conn told her, and a cursory search undertaken. He hoped she would understand, and apologised for the intrusion. She had graciously offered to make tea for Conn and the three other officers, and they accepted.

Murray was not among them, she noted. A pity, she thought. Murray was much easier on the eye than the group Conn brought with him.

Now they worked in the rear reception room where the hospital bed remained. She heard grumbling about the futility of the search, particularly as she'd had the cleaner in since last week. Surely nothing useful could be found. Look anyway, Conn instructed.

Roberta listened with one ear as she watched the evening news. She had watched a lot of news in recent days; it was becoming a habit, adding punctuation to her routine. The newsreaders had become familiar, their names, their mannerisms, their turns of phrase. On a few occasions she had caught herself mimicking the female presenters, the tilt of their head, the pitch of their voice, the shape of their mouth. An old habit from her childhood, distant as that now seemed, the taking on of others' tics and quirks.

On the television, Peter's house appeared, and the church. Police officers wandering in and out. Just like here, she thought, as she heard two pairs of shoes climb her stairs. Searching the bedroom next. It didn't matter. They would find nothing there. Everything she had worth hiding was nowhere near this house.

The television caught her attention again.

"George," she said as her brother-in-law

filled the screen with his loping frame and country-handsome face. She had spotted him at the funeral, lurking at the back, keeping his head down. She had pretended not to see him. Not that she cared, anyway.

The reporter caught George on the doorstep of some shabby terraced house — his home, presumably, since his wife had kicked him out — and questioned him about his brother's possible murder.

"I don't know what I can say," George mumbled in that blunt-edged country way of his. "I don't think we'll ever get to the truth of it. There's more to this than will ever come out, but that'll be up to the police, and them that knows what really happened. And them that does know, I hope their conscience will guide them. If it doesn't, then I pity them."

He glanced at the camera lens, and Roberta knew he spoke to her.

"They'll have to live with this and everything else that's gone on. I don't think they'll have a peaceful night's sleep as long as they live. And I know I couldn't live too long with that hanging over me. That's all I have to say."

The report cut back to the studio, and she threw the remote control at the screen, making it flicker.

"Fuck you," she said. "Fuck you."

"Is everything all right, Mrs. Garrick?"

She spun to the voice. DCI Conn in the kitchen doorway, concern on his face.

"Fine," she said, offering a regretful smile. "It's fine. It's been a difficult time, that's all."

He nodded and said, "Of course."

She went to the door, closed it behind him as he left. Alone now, she rested her forehead against the cool wood. No good. This wouldn't do at all. She was nearly through it, almost out the other side. All she had to do was keep control.

Her hand shot to her mouth, stifling a cry, as her mobile phone trilled and vibrated on the granite worktop. She went to it, saw the number, thumbed the green icon.

"Jim," she said.

"Roberta," he said.

Then nothing. She could picture him at the other end, mouth moving like a goldfish as he reached for the words.

"Say what you want to say."

"I just . . ."

"Come on," she said, her patience flaking away.

"I don't think we should see each other any more," he said.

She smiled. "I think you're probably right."

"I want you to stay away from me," he said.

"That won't be a problem."

"I mean it," he said. "Stay away. I've deleted all those photographs. Don't send any more. Don't call me. If you do, I'll . . ."

"You'll what?"

Call the police, she thought. It was clear he suspected, but he was too much of a coward to do anything about it. A weak man, even weaker than Peter had been, weaker still than her dead husband.

"Nothing," he said.

"That's right," she said. "You'll do nothing. That'd be better for everybody, don't you think?"

"Just keep away from me," he said, and the phone died.

46

Flanagan followed the satnav's directions, skirting the town of Magherafelt, heading south towards the village of Moneymore. A long steep descent down a hill, pastureland all around, deep greens and cattle and sheep. The smell of the countryside, thick and heavy in the air. She passed a tractor coming the other way, towing a slurry tank, slow on the incline, half a mile of traffic backed up behind it. Drivers with angry faces, impatient for the tractor to pull in and let them past.

A thirty-mile-per-hour limit sign as she entered the village. She slowed the Volkswagen, shifted down to fourth gear, noted the newbuild houses climbing the hillside to her left, older dwellings to her right. A busy filling station that doubled as a supermarket. A sweeping bend and a small roundabout brought her into the heart of Moneymore. A typical Ulster plantation village, lacking the quaint charm of an English equivalent but pleasant in its own way. Austere functional buildings, painted rendering rather than attractive stonework, bunting and Union flags still lingering from the dying summer's marching season.

She followed the road through a sharp bend, passing an Orange Hall and a Presbyterian church, obeyed the satnav's command to go straight on, the signs guiding her in the direction of Cookstown. A quarter mile outside the village, the satnav told her to take the next right, a narrow lane, its junction barely visible until she was on top of it.

Another quarter mile, and the Baileys' house was up ahead, on the apex of a bend. A large open gate leading to a modest bungalow set in half an acre of well-tended lawns and outbuildings. As she steered onto the short driveway, she saw a chicken pen to the rear of the house. Somewhere at the back, a dog barked at her arrival.

Flanagan shut off the engine and checked her mobile phone. No signal out here. She had intended on texting Alistair to apologise for missing dinner, but that would have to wait.

As she got out of the car, the front door opened, and a white-haired man stared out

378

at her. Mid sixties, she thought, neatly dressed, wearing a tie for no apparent reason in the way that country Protestant men did.

"How're ye," he said, a wary look on his face.

"Good evening," Flanagan said with as friendly a smile as she could manage. "Are you Mr. Bailey?"

"Aye," he said, giving a single nod, his expression impassive.

Flanagan wondered had he been a reservist, a part-time soldier or policeman; many of his generation had been during the Troubles. Not very long ago, a strange car pulling up at a reservist's home meant danger, shots fired through windows, doors broken down, men killed in front of their children. He said nothing more and remained watchful.

She reached into her bag, produced her wallet and the warrant card within, brought it to his doorstep. With quick blue eyes, he read it as she spoke.

"I'm sorry to disturb you, Mr. Bailey," she said. "I'm Detective Chief Inspector Serena Flanagan, based at Lisburn. You can call to verify, if you'd like."

She hoped he wouldn't. No one knew she had come here, and Purdy would rip her to shreds if he found out.

"That's all right," he said, looking from the card to her face, a flicker of worry in his eyes now. "Is there something wrong?"

"Nothing for you to be concerned about," she said. "I wanted to have a word with you and Mrs. Bailey about your daughter, Roberta."

"Roberta?" he asked, his brow creased.

"Yes, if you can spare a few minutes."

He stepped back, opened the door fully. "You'd better come in."

"Thank you," Flanagan said as she entered.

Mr. Bailey reached behind the open door, lifted the double-barrelled shotgun he had propped there and put it into a closet. "I've got a licence for it," he said. "There's still some bad boys about the country. Maisie's just doing the dishes. Go on in the living room and I'll get her."

Flanagan heard water running, the clatter of cutlery. The house smelled of beef and potatoes and boiled vegetables, warm homey scents that sparked a memory of her grandmother, even though she barely remembered what Granny Jane looked like.

She thanked Mr. Bailey once more and walked through the open door into the living room where a log burned red and grey

380

in the hearth. A plush three-piece suite, small bookcases, a china cabinet, figurines, brassware. A carved wooden elephant on a sideboard.

On the mantelpiece above the fire, a framed photograph of a young girl, fiery red hair, pretty, someday beautiful. A school portrait, and Flanagan imagined the young Roberta Bailey, the first flush of puberty about her, sitting for a photographer in an echoing assembly hall while a line of children waited their turn.

She turned a circle, looking for more pictures. There were a few, all of her as a youngster, smiling. A little girl who was loved.

What happened to you? Flanagan thought. What went wrong?

Mr. Bailey entered, followed by his wife, a sturdy woman showing little sign of going grey, still more copper in her hair than silver. A redhead like her daughter. High cheekbones like Roberta's, but the face rounded with age. She dried her hands on a towel and tucked it into the pocket on the front of her apron.

"Hello," Mrs. Bailey said. "Would you take a cup of tea?"

"No, thank you," Flanagan said. "I don't want to use up any more of your time than

I have to. Do you mind if I sit down?"

"Not at all," Mrs. Bailey said. "Go ahead."

Flanagan took the armchair, and the Baileys sat on the couch, both watching her with a mix of curiosity and worry. She readied her notebook and pen.

"As I said, I wanted to ask you about your daughter, if you don't mind."

The Baileys looked at each other, then back to Flanagan.

"Ask away," Mr. Bailey said, that knot of caution still on his brow.

"She was a pretty girl," Flanagan said, indicating the picture over the fireplace.

"Aye, she was," Mrs. Bailey said, a sadness in her voice. "She was gorgeous."

"How was she as a girl?" Flanagan asked. "Was she well-behaved or did she give you any trouble? Was she sociable? Was she shy?"

"She was a good girl," Mrs. Bailey said. "She was a wee bit shy, I suppose, but she had plenty of friends. The teachers always liked her at school. She loved school, so she did."

"So never any problems," Flanagan said.

"No, never."

"I'm curious, then, what happened later on? Why did she become estranged from you?"

Mr. and Mrs. Bailey looked at each other

again, then back to Flanagan.

"What do you mean?" Mr. Bailey asked.

"I know there was a falling out when she was older," Flanagan said. "That she got into some trouble later on. Can you tell me about that?"

They stared at her. Tears welled in Mrs. Bailey's eyes.

"I'm sorry," Mr. Bailey said. "You've made a mistake."

"I don't understand," Flanagan said.

"Our Roberta's dead," he said, a waver in his voice. "She died in March 1993. Meningitis. Two other children at her school died around the same time."

Flanagan's skin prickled. Her mouth dried.

"I'm very sorry to hear that," she said. "You're right. I must have made a mistake. I'm sorry to have bothered you."

She reached for her mobile phone, saw there was still no signal.

"If it's not too much trouble," she said, "do you think I could use your landline?"

47

"This is good coffee," DCI Conn said, raising his cup to her.

Roberta smiled and said, "I can't take credit. The machine did the work."

"Still, it's very good," Conn said. "Thank you."

He took a sip and set the cup on the black granite. She sat opposite, on the other side of the island, nursing her own cup. Conn looked tired, stubble darkening his jawline. The other police officers had left more than an hour ago, but he had remained, going through the wardrobe and drawers in the back room, looking for God knows what.

He was a tall man, not bad looking, though he had a meanness about him. The kind of man who enjoyed petty victories, held on to anger at every small defeat. She could read men that way, always had done, a talent she'd developed when she was barely a teenager. How easy it had been to manipulate the boys with their crude and simple impulses. And they never grew out of it. They never learned to let their brains do their thinking. Even the smartest of them. When everything was stripped away, they were all the same, from the highest to the lowest, animals whose sole drive was to rut with her.

And here she was, alone with this man. He wore a wedding band, but she had noted how he toyed with it, sliding it from knuckle to knuckle. And how he glanced at her body, thinking himself sly and unnoticed. It would be so easy to take him, just move closer, fingertips, delicate butterfly touches, let him feel the heat of her.

"Is something wrong?" he asked.

She snapped back into the moment. "I'm sorry?"

"You were smiling," he said.

"Was I?" She let the smile spread, felt it light up her face. He couldn't help but reflect it back to her. "I was just thinking about something," she said.

"What?"

"Oh, nothing. Just a memory."

He nodded, smiled once more, and took another sip of coffee.

"You've been very kind," she said. "I hardly knew you were here today. Very professional. Not like that Flanagan woman."

Conn cleared his throat. "Well, she has her own way of doing things."

Roberta saw the way he bristled at the name, the tightening of his jaw. She caught a scent, followed it.

"She was so . . . hard," she said. "Do you know what I mean? And rude. What's the word? Abrasive? Yes, abrasive, that's it."

He gave a shallow smile, looked at her, looked away. "I can't really comment."

She saw the angle, honed in on it.

"Call me old-fashioned," she said, "but women in jobs like that. They overcompensate, don't you think? They think they have to out-man the men. It makes them bitchy and mean, doesn't it?"

He shrugged, laughed, raised his hands in a motion of surrender. "If I said that out loud to anyone, they'd have me off on one of those equality awareness courses."

Got him, she thought.

"I'm glad you've taken over," she said. "I feel better having you around, Brian. Can I call you Brian?"

She reached across the worktop, almost let her fingertips brush his.

"I suppose," he said, his cheeks reddening, his eyes flicking to her and away, over and over.

Like a schoolboy, she thought. So easy.

Reel him in or let him go?

Conn's mobile phone chimed, making the decision for her. What might have been relief broke on his face as he reached for his breast pocket. He looked at the display and said, "Sorry, I have to take this."

"Of course," she said as she drew her hand back to her side of the island.

He brought the phone to his ear and said, "DCI Conn."

She heard a metallic voice, words she could not discern.

"Yes, I'm at the Garrick house now."

His features slackened. He looked at her, eyes blank, then looked away again.

"I understand," he said. "Give me twenty minutes, half an hour."

When he hung up, she asked, "Is everything all right?"

He lowered himself from the stool, slipped the phone back into his pocket. "Fine, fine," he said. "They need me over at the church is all. There's something they need me to see. Thank you for the coffee. I can let myself out."

"You're welcome," she said as he hurried out of the kitchen.

She listened to the front door open and

close, the bark and rumble of an engine. As it faded, a cold finger touched her heart.

"No," she said. "It's nothing."

Yet the chill remained. A warm bath would help. Yes, she thought, a soak to wash the day away. She finished her coffee, set the two cups in the sink, and made her way upstairs. In the master bathroom, she plugged the tub, turned on both taps, adjusted until the temperature was just so. Added a generous dose of bubble bath.

She went to her bedroom, into the walk-in wardrobe, and selected a nightdress and gown, brought them out and laid them on the bed. As she set about unbuttoning her blouse, she glanced up at the wall over the antique dresser.

The child stared back down at her.

Roberta crossed the room, took the picture from its hook. She opened the dresser's top drawer, placed the picture inside, and slid it closed again. Her hand against the wood, she held the drawer in place as if the image of the child might try to climb out again.

"Now be quiet," she said.

48

Flanagan knocked on Purdy's office door and entered without waiting for an invitation. She found Conn pacing the floor, Purdy sitting behind his desk. DS Murray sat in the corner, his arms folded across his chest. They all looked to her as she closed the door behind her.

"When do we bring her in?" Flanagan asked.

Conn and Purdy exchanged a glance.

"Not tonight," Purdy said.

"Why not?"

"All we have right now is the suspicion — suspicion, mind — of identity theft. The best we could do is some sort of fraud, and even that isn't straightforward."

Flanagan approached the desk. "She's been ghosting for years. Surely that's enough to arrest her on."

"In itself, yes," Purdy said. "But is that really all you want her for? Ghosting on its own will be a minor offence. It's what she did with the identity that counts, not just that she's used it."

"So what do we do?" Flanagan asked.

"We wait," Purdy said. "First of all, we need to find out who she really is. Let's hope that Isle of Man account can tell us something. If there's a name attached, we reference that back to the credit reference agency, find any other accounts connected to it. We'll have to go through the Attorney General's Office, but we should have that information some time tomorrow morning, maybe afternoon, and young Murray here will go through it. Then we can look at her history under the fake identity. Any bank account she has in the name Roberta Bailey or Garrick is a financial fraud, even more serious if she's taken out a credit card or a loan."

"Come on," Flanagan said, "we're not taking her for credit card fraud. Two people have died."

Now Conn spoke, raising himself to his full height. "Hang on a minute. *We're* not taking her for anything. This is my case. Any involvement you have from here on will be simply as a courtesy for your work up to now."

"Oh, fuck off," Flanagan said. "If I hadn't

kept digging, you'd be wrapping it all up now with no idea she wasn't who she said she was."

"I'd have found out," Conn said. "Sooner or later."

"Bollocks." She turned back to Purdy. "Sir, I request that you speak with the Assistant Chief Constable and ask that this case be reassigned to me."

"No," Purdy said, shaking his head. "Not going to happen."

"Sir, please, I —"

"I said no, and that's final." He raised a finger before she could protest again. "But I'm not freezing you out. You will provide any assistance needed to DCI Conn, and I will personally make sure the ACC and the Chief Constable know how much you contributed to the investigation. If that's not good enough for you, then you're welcome to step aside."

Conn put his hands on his hips, placed his body between Flanagan and Purdy. "Sir, with respect, I don't need any further assistance from DCI Flanagan. I have all the materials I need, and I feel DCI Flanagan would be more hindrance than help at this stage."

Purdy gave him a withering stare. "DCI Conn, Brian, listen very carefully. Are you listening?"

Conn swallowed and said, "Yes, sir."

"Don't be a dick. I'm offering a workable compromise. For Christ's sake, show some intelligence and take it."

Conn took a step back. Flanagan noticed the flush on his cheeks. Murray put a hand over his mouth to hide a smirk.

"Yes, sir," Conn said.

"Good," Purdy said, nodding. "Now, I want the three of you to bugger off home, get some sleep. We'll have the new information by late morning, and I expect you to come up with a plan of action between you. A way to prove she killed those men. Get whatever you can on this woman, whoever she is, and bring her down. I want her in custody by tomorrow evening, the day after, at the latest. With any luck we'll get a confession out of her, but only if you have enough evidence to put in front of her. I want nothing done half-assed, no acting on nothing more than a feeling." He pointed at Conn and Flanagan in turn on those points. "Understood? Now piss off, the lot of you."

Flanagan, Conn and Murray left the office without speaking. Out in the corridor, Purdy's door closed, Flanagan and Murray held back while Conn strode towards the stairs.

"He'll try to freeze me out," Flanagan said. "I'll need you to keep me up to speed. Tell me what he won't. Okay?"

"Yes, ma'am," Murray said.

She put a hand on his arm, squeezed, a gesture of thanks, and left him there.

Flanagan slept poorly that night. The children were in bed by the time she got home, the dinner things cleared away, Alistair once again sitting at the kitchen table working through a stack of essays. She took the plate of food he'd left in the fridge for her, blasted it in the microwave, and ate it opposite him. They said nothing beyond the greetings they'd exchanged when she came in.

His nightmares woke him in the small hours, and she pretended to be asleep as he climbed out of bed and left the room. She rode the waves of the soft burble from the television downstairs, in and out of sleep, dreams and disorientation, spectres and shadows in the darkness. Eventually she gave in and reached for the lamp on the bedside table.

Still scared of the dark. Strange how the fear grew when she felt under pressure, became less containable. She pulled the duvet up to her chin, closed her eyes, and tried to find the rhythm of the waves once more.

In the morning, Alistair and the kids had only started breakfast when Flanagan left for the station. She arrived a few minutes after eight and went straight to the temporary office that had been allocated to Conn. He and Murray sat there, each hunched over a computer.

"Nothing yet," Conn said. "I'll call you when we've got what we need."

"I can stay," she said. "Help go through whatever you get."

"That won't be necessary. I'll call you when I need you."

Murray looked up from his computer, met her gaze, then looked away again.

"All right," Flanagan said. "I'll be waiting."

So she waited. Nine o'clock passed, ten, eleven, then twelve. She tried to fill her time by working through the mound of Public Prosecution Service files Purdy had asked her to review, but her concentration lagged. Every time the phone on her desk rang, or her mobile, she grabbed at it, hoping and expecting. Every time she was disappointed.

As the minute hand on her watch dragged close to the six, her mobile rang once more. She looked at the display. DS Murray.

"Yes?" she said.

"Ma'am, can you come to DCI Conn's

office right now?"

"Yes," she said, and hung up without waiting for a reply.

She knocked on Conn's door less than a minute later. Murray opened it, and she looked past him to see he was alone.

"Where's Conn?" she asked.

Murray stepped back to let her enter. "He went out. That's why I needed you to come now, while he was gone."

Flanagan noticed the printouts spread across the two desks. "What's happening?"

"DCI Conn didn't want you to be told anything, but I thought I should let you know. I'm aware I've gone against his instruction."

"It's all right," she said, walking to the other side of Conn's desk. "What've you got?"

Murray came to her side, sorted two pages from the rest. "The Isle of Man account has money moving out as soon as it goes in, same as both the Garrick accounts. It only goes out to one account."

He pointed to eight digits that appeared several times, months apart. Then he reached for another set of pages.

"The account belongs to a Hannah Mackenzie. I've got the info from the credit reference company. Date of birth is 29th of

April 1978. Two years older than Roberta Garrick. The address is in Ballinroy, an estate off the Airport Road, between Glenavy and Nutt's Corner. She's had that house at least six years, as far back as the credit report will show. I'd guess it's a private rental, not social housing, or maybe she owns it, given the money she has access to. There's another bank account attached to that name, and a credit card. The card hasn't ever been used. I'm waiting for more coming through on the financial side. I checked with the DVA, and there's a driving licence under that name and address, but no insurance. The licence was last renewed five years ago. There's a British passport, renewed three years ago, and I'm waiting to hear about an Irish passport."

"Okay," Flanagan said. "So you reckon this is her?"

"Ma'am, there's more."

He reached for the computer mouse, moved it to wake up the machine. The monitor flickered and an image of a young woman appeared, red-haired, bright-eyed. A mug shot, the flat lighting, the blank background. But it was her, no question.

"Tell me," Flanagan said.

"Hannah Mackenzie was convicted in 1997, when she was nineteen, of the manslaughter of another young woman, a friend of hers. She was sentenced to seven years in Hydebank, served five, got out in 2002."

"Jesus," Flanagan said. "And Conn knows all this?"

"Yes, ma'am."

"That bastard was supposed to let me know as soon as he had anything."

"Ma'am, can I speak freely?"

"Yes," Flanagan said.

"DCI Conn is a complete prick," Murray said. "I wanted to call you as soon as the Isle of Man account came in, but he wouldn't let me. He'd kill me if he knew I'd gone behind his back."

"You did the right thing." She put a hand on his shoulder for reassurance. "Where is he now?"

"He's with DSI Purdy," Murray said. "He wants to mount an arrest operation this afternoon, but he doesn't want you involved. I tried to argue, but he wouldn't have it."

He had barely finished the sentence when Flanagan ran out of the room and into the corridor. One floor up to Purdy's office, she was breathless when she hammered the door with her fist, then shouldered it open.

Purdy and Conn looked up from either side of the desk. Sergeant Beattie from E Department, Special Operations Branch, kitted out in tactical gear, stood over both of them.

"Flanagan," Purdy began.

She cut him off. "What's happening?"

"Sit down," Purdy said.

"I'd rather stand, sir. What's happening?"

"Sit down," he repeated, his voice hardening.

Flanagan moved the free chair a few inches farther away from Conn and did as she was told. "Sir, please tell me what's going on."

"I was going to call you when things were a bit more solid," Purdy said, "but now you're here, I might as well fill you in. We're planning an arrest operation for this afternoon. Four-thirty, to be exact. DCI Conn and I will make the arrest with the support of Sergeant Beattie's team."

Fury, fury, white hot inside her. Keep it inside, bury it.

"What about me?" she said.

"You won't be involved."

"Why not?"

"It's the ACC's shout. He reckons you've been too personally involved in this case, that your judgement is clouded."

"Bullshit. I'm not —"

"I agree with him," Purdy said. "You're out, that's all."

"Sir, I —"

"I'm not arguing with you, Flanagan. The decision's been made."

Purdy stared her down, dared her to speak. Instead, she closed her eyes and nodded as she fought to steady her breathing. Grinding pain in her teeth from clenching her jaw. She forced her teeth apart, bit her tongue until the sting pierced her mind, bringing clarity with it.

Purdy's features softened. "If it makes any odds, I'll personally make sure that everyone, right up to the Chief Constable, the press, everyone, knows you drove the case this far, that DCI Conn here only came in to finish the job."

Conn spoke up. "That's hardly fair, sir."

"Tough shit," Purdy said. "When it's all over and you're speaking to the press, you'll give DCI Flanagan due credit for her part in the investigation. Understood?"

Conn's lips thinned. "Yes, sir."

"Good." Purdy turned back to Flanagan. "If you want to make yourself useful, you and Murray head over to this house in Ballinroy. I'll make sure you're cleared to force entry if need be. See if there's anything there to back up the identity fraud. I'll call when I've got the RIPA forms back. Good enough?"

399

Flanagan exhaled, slumped in the chair. "No, sir, but it'll have to do."

"All right. Now go and get Murray, get yourselves ready to roll."

"Sir," she said as she stood.

In the corridor, after she'd closed the door between her and the officers, Flanagan bit her knuckle to stifle the anger.

49

Once more, Roberta Garrick was woken from sleep by crying. She sat upright on the bed, the cardigan she'd draped over herself falling away. Her heart thudded heavy in her chest, her breath coming in sharp swallows. While she napped she had dreamed of the child dragging her down with it, its small hands clinging and clawing. Under the salt water, waves washing over both of them, it still cried, the shrieks cutting like blades.

Awake now, she said, "Shut up."

But the crying went on.

"Shut up." Louder this time, the edge of her voice sharpened.

And still it cried.

Cold, suddenly, Roberta reached for her cardigan and slipped off the bed. She walked towards the chest of drawers.

"All right," she said, "just be quiet."

She opened the drawer, lifted the framed

photograph out. As she reached up to the hook on the wall, a movement caught her eye, a white flash reflected on the glass. She turned to the window, saw it again, a brilliant white form racing along the lane that flanked her property. Then it was gone behind the small wood that bordered the rear of the garden.

A clamour in her head, like a bell ringing, beware, beware.

Then another white shape moved along the lane, not so quick, and this time she knew what it was: a police Land Rover, painted white with garish blue and yellow stripes on its side. Again, she lost it behind the trees, but she could see that it had been slowing.

The baby had ceased its wailing. Now there was only the hammering of her heart, the thunder of blood in her ears.

Roberta slipped out of her bedroom, the photograph still in her hand, and crossed the landing to the guest room with a window overlooking the front lawn. She kept to the wall as she moved to the glass, the voile curtain misting everything beyond. The sheer material brushed her cheeks. She parted the curtains with one finger, nothing more than a sliver for her eye to peer through.

Nothing. She could see nothing.

Look, look, look. Are they coming?

Are they coming for me?

There. Adrenalin hit her system the moment she saw it. The bright white and yellow and blue of another marked police Land Rover, this one not moving. Flashes of paintwork visible through the hedgerow. Barely a glimpse, but it was there.

Yes, they have come for me.

Now the baby's wailing cut through the noise in her head and she threw the photograph against the far wall, glass shattering, and then silence.

Run, she thought. Run now.

Her bare feet slapped on the floor as she sprinted to the master bedroom, dug in the drawers for socks, then in the wardrobe for trainers. She had minutes at most, maybe seconds. She pulled a sliver of glass from her heel, ignored the sting. The socks on, then the shoes. Out of the room, down the stairs, to the kitchen. Harry's old coat hung in the utility room, dark green, a hood. She grabbed it, pulled it on, put her hand in the pocket, felt the padlock keys she kept there. Unlocked the back door, threw the house keys to the floor, she'd never need them again.

Fast across the landscaped garden to the

cluster of trees that bordered it and the fields beyond. In the shadows of the balding branches, the chest-high fence that marked the edge of the property. Up and over, she fell on the other side, landed hard on her shoulder. In a crouching run, she went to the far edge of the small wood, looked up, over to the lane that cut down to the far side of the house. Through the hedgerow and branches she saw another Land Rover, saw its passenger door open.

The gate into the next field only ten yards away, to her left. Up on her feet, another crouching run, and she was over it. Cows watched as she moved along the line of trees and barbed wire, peering through the gaps as four — no, five — policemen entered the other field and trudged towards the trees at the rear of her house. She paused and watched them enter the wood she had left moments before.

What had happened? What had they discovered? It didn't matter now. All she could do was run. She got moving, keeping to the treeline, towards the church steeple in the distance.

Roberta arrived at the rear of the dealership half an hour later, her feet heavy with mud, scratches on her cheeks from the low branches and thorns. She looked both ways as she crossed the narrow lane to the gate. Reaching inside the hole in the gate, she found the padlock undone, as she'd expected. She pulled back the bar and pushed the gate open, latched it to the wall.

Young Tommy McCready stood at the door of the back shed, watching her, his hands in the pockets of his oil-stained overalls. Concern sharpened his features.

"You all right, Mrs. Garrick?" he called.

She marched towards him. "I'm fine. I need one of the cars." She scanned the line of vehicles. The Citroën she'd taken two nights ago still sat closest to the gate. "That one," she said, pointing.

Tommy stepped aside as she reached the shed, allowed her to enter.

"I don't know if you can just take it," he said. "You don't have trade insurance, do you?"

"Doesn't matter," she said.

"If the peelers stop you, you'll get points," he said.

"Doesn't matter," she said as she lifted the plastic tub of loose car keys and emptied them onto the desk. She spread them out with her fingers, looking for the Citroën logo.

Tommy shifted his weight from foot to

foot, scratching at his head with oily fingers.

"Here, I'll go and get John-Joe."

John-Joe Malone, the grubby workshop manager who picked his nose with oily fingers while he eyed her up every time she visited the dealership.

"You don't need to," she said. "Where's the key to the fucking Citroën?"

"It's going to be scrapped tomorrow," Tommy said. "Look, hang on, I'm going to get John-Joe."

He turned to go, but she grabbed his arm with her left hand. "Just tell me where the key to the Citroën is."

"It's there," he said, pointing to the wall, a row of hooks with the words FOR SCRAP in a childish hand above them. There, on its own, the key.

He pulled his arm from her grasp, said, "I'm getting John-Joe."

"Yes, go and get him," she said. "Go now."

He kept her in sight as he backed towards the workshop door.

She heard him calling his boss as she grabbed the key. She saw John-Joe and Tommy in the rear-view mirror as she pulled out of the yard, staring after her.

50

As Murray steered his 1-Series BMW around the Moira roundabout, Flanagan noted the distance from there to the Ballinroy estate. Roberta Garrick — Hannah Mackenzie — lived only a few minutes from the junction, and another twenty would bring her to Ballinroy. Fifteen from Ballinroy to the International Airport.

"Perfect," Flanagan said.

"Ma'am?" Murray asked as he exited the roundabout onto the Glenavy Road, the filling station and café of Glenavy Services half a mile ahead.

"Ballinroy," she said. "It's perfect for her. She can get there in less than half an hour when she has to pick up mail or whatever, and it's only a few miles more to the airport if she needs to get out in a hurry."

"It's a rough estate," Murray said. "Old Housing Executive houses, most of them bought up by investors and rented out to migrant workers. After the property crash, a lot of them were left to rot. There's been problems with over-occupation, the landlords shoving in as many people as can sleep in shifts."

Flanagan had heard and seen similar around the country. Young men and women from all over Europe, and further afield, desperate for a better existence, exploited by landlords and gangmasters.

"One part of the estate — the side farthest from the airport road — is still local people, loyalists, and they don't like the new arrivals. I spoke to an old mate of mine who's stationed near there. He's been called out more times than he can remember. One side always fighting with the other or between themselves."

"She doesn't have to live there," Flanagan said. "If there are a lot of people coming and going, that'd suit her better. Easier to slip in and out without anyone paying attention."

The road stretched ahead, long straights, sweeping bends, few roadside houses. Twice they were caught behind tractors, unable to pass until the tractor pulled off into a side road. Before long, Flanagan saw a cluster of homes to the left, a quarter mile ahead. She had driven past this estate dozens of times

408

on her way to the airport but had never given a thought to the condition of the houses or who lived here.

Murray flicked the indicator lever and slowed the car as he approached the turn. He pulled in, reducing the speed to a walking pace, and glanced at the map on the BMW's touchscreen. An arrow showed their direction of travel, a chequered flag their destination.

"Just up here and around to the right," he said.

The houses stood in semi-detached pairs, each block of two separated from the next by an alley, or in terraces of half a dozen. Made with dull beige brick, wooden boards beneath the windows, wire fences suspended between concrete posts to mark out the gardens. None of the houses had garages, and cars were parked bumper to bumper on the pavements leaving barely enough room for Murray to steer his way through. The rags of a Union flag fluttered on a lamp post. The gable wall of one terrace bore the words NO FOREIGNERS NO TAIGS in two-foot-high red painted letters. This place rang with the kind of hatred that only poverty fosters.

"Here," Murray said as they neared the end of a row of semi-detached homes.

"Number thirty-six."

With no room to park in front of the house, he pulled around the corner, put two wheels on the patch of stubbly grass and shut off the engine. Flanagan cursed as she stepped out onto the soft ground, narrowly avoiding a mound of dog excrement. Murray thumbed the key to lock the car. He loved the little BMW in the way a child loves a puppy. Cute in a child, slightly pathetic in a grown man. She let him lead her around to the front of the house, a small crowbar in his hand. Single-glazed, paint peeling from the door and window frames, the small patch of garden knee-high with grass and weeds, the chain-link fence long gone.

"This isn't the kind of living Mrs. Garrick is accustomed to," Murray said.

"Mrs. Garrick isn't real," Flanagan said. "Hannah Mackenzie lives here."

A rusted iron gate hung between two concrete posts, serving no purpose that Flanagan could see. She stepped around it onto the cement path and walked towards the house. A step up to the door, and the alley beside it. She cupped her eyes with her hands and peered through the frosted glass by the door into the hall. Nothing to see, only vague shapes and shadows. Her

410

footsteps echoed in between the walls as she walked through the alley, avoiding the puddle from a blocked drain, towards a pair of wooden gates to the rear, each leading to the backyards on either side.

Somewhere to the rear, a dog objected to their presence, its barks high with alarm.

The gate belonging to number thirty-six hung loose on its hinges, the wood rotten and crumbling. It dragged on the cement as Flanagan pushed it inward, leaving fragments and a smear of algae and dirt. A paved yard beyond, grass growing in the cracks, a row of bins against the back wall. Green clung in flakes to the bare wood of the back door, two panes of mesh safety glass. A small square kitchen inside, decades-old fittings, a freestanding electric cooker. A space where a fridge had once been.

Murray picked at the door with his thumbnail, the wood splitting and splintering.

"Rotten," he said.

"Go ahead," Flanagan said.

He wedged the crowbar's blade between the door and its frame, rocked it back and forth, applying more weight as it burrowed in, until Flanagan heard a dull crack.

"Almost there," Murray said.

Flanagan startled at the sound of a bolt

411

sliding. She spun on her heels and saw the gate on the other side of the alley ease open. A small man with black hair peered out at them. Flanagan reached into her bag, showed her warrant card. The gate slammed shut, the bolt slid back. None of his concern. A perfect place to hide in plain sight.

Murray grunted with effort, another crack, sharper this time, and the door swung inward. Musty odours drifted out to them. The stale smells of a house that had not been a home for many years. Dust everywhere. Spiderwebs in the corners, the carcasses of flies tangled in them, or lying loose on the surfaces. Just inside the doorway, a space where a washing machine had once stood, the hoses hanging from the pipes to the rear, the withered remains of a mouse curled on the floor.

"Lovely," Murray said.

Flanagan stepped past him, her shoes clicking on the worn linoleum. Murray pushed the door to behind him, followed her into the hall. A concrete floor, patches of carpet liner still stubbornly glued to it. A cupboard under the stairs.

She put her fingertips against the door to the living room, pushed it open.

"Fuck me," Murray said.

Flanagan said nothing.

Thin curtains drawn across the window coloured everything in dim oranges and reds. Dozens, perhaps hundreds of photographs lined the far wall, some framed pictures perched on the mantelpiece above the tiled fireplace. Boys and girls, men and women, all of them with a familiar figure, holding her, smiling with her, dancing with her. Roberta Garrick, Hannah Mackenzie, whoever she really was, young and pretty and bright-eyed. Among the photographs were printed pages, letters and forms. From her place on the threshold, Flanagan recognised one of them as an exam certificate. She stepped forward to look at it, a list of eight GCSE results, As and Bs. Another certificate showing three A-level passes.

A letter of offer from a university. A birthday card to Hannah, with all my love, Granny, a ten-pound note still clipped inside. Boxes all around the floor full of books, letters in envelopes, old cassettes and VHS tapes, ornaments, the kind of worthless bric-a-brac that meant the world to a young woman.

Flanagan turned in a circle, seeing Hannah Mackenzie's life crammed into this room, her entire existence stowed away for safe keeping. A shrine to the girl left behind. She stopped when she saw the writing scrawled on the wall facing the window. Rows and rows of neat script, arranged in columns, broken up by slashes through the letters, sentences crossed out, words obliterated.

She reached for the light switch, ignited the bare bulb above their heads, then stepped closer to the wall until she could make out the writing. Flanagan took in snatches of it, lucid phrases and rambling ideas colliding against the faded flowers of the wallpaper.

I know she hated me so that's why I
    pushed her . . .
It's broken I broke it never put it back
    together now . . .
Can't stop the crying even when I put her
    back on the wall again . . .

"What is this?" Murray asked, his voice low.

"It's where she keeps her madness," Flanagan said.

They stood in silence, turning in circles, the ghosts of Hannah Mackenzie glaring at them from the walls. Eventually, Murray spoke.

"Ma'am, we should call DSI Purdy. Get a proper team up here."

Flanagan nodded. "You're right. Let's clear out. We'll wait in the car."

Murray was on his way back to the kitchen before she finished speaking. She switched off the light and followed him out into the yard, through the gate and into the alley. A thought occurred to her, and she stopped.

"Go on," she said. "I'll be out in a minute. I just want to check something."

He turned and looked at her, then to the house, before saying, "Okay."

Flanagan watched him leave the alley and pick his way through the overgrown grass before she went back to the rear of the house and pushed the door open once more. That musty smell again, and something else, something she hadn't noticed before. Something low and bitter.

She walked through the kitchen and into the hall, where she stopped at the cupboard beneath the stairs. A small door, waist-high, with a plain plastic handle. She crouched down and pulled it open. Inside, an old-fashioned safe with a dial combination lock. She brushed the scarred surface with her fingertips, felt the cold steel, reached inside, tried to move it. Too heavy.

"What are you hiding?" Flanagan asked the air, knowing full well the answer.

Everything in the other room was a me-

mento, a story of a past life. But in here was the proof. In here was whatever Roberta Garrick needed to become Hannah Mackenzie once more.

"Got you," Flanagan said.

She gasped at the sound of the iron gate opening outside, the metallic clank as it closed again. Murray? What had he come back for? The place gave him the creeps, obviously, and he had been glad to leave. She stood upright and looked towards the frosted glass of the door.

A form grew and solidified as it approached. Hooded and dark. Then hands reached up and pulled the hood away.

Red hair blazing through the glass, Roberta Garrick come to take back her true name.

51

Roberta Garrick turned the key in the lock, pushed the door open. As Hannah Mackenzie, she had rented a house on the same street, and kept it after she had changed and married Harry. Then this place came up for sale, priced at a pittance due to the property crash and its poor condition, so she had paid cash and said nothing to her new husband.

She breathed in the air, the stale smell she had grown to love.

Except it wasn't stale.

Not as stale as it should be. The air had a cool freshness about it, she could taste it, as if a window had been left open. She paused in the doorway, holding her breath, listening.

If they had come for her, could they also have found this place? Did they know about Hannah Mackenzie? Had they come looking for the woman who lived in this house?

"Stop it," she said aloud.

Panic had been threatening to break free ever since she had fled across the fields, and she had kept it in check all this time. She would not let it take her now. Paranoia crept alongside the panic, but it was more slippery, harder to hold. It now whispered in her mind, told her to turn around, get back in the car and go.

Go where?

Without the contents of the safe, she could go nowhere. Fear be damned, there was no choice. She stepped inside, closed the front door behind her. Her shoes, still muddy from the fields, left dark prints on the concrete floor as she moved along the hall.

The living room door stood open, the kitchen door closed over. Had she left them that way? She dredged her memory; it had been only three days since she had been here to retrieve the pestle and mortar. She seldom left long between visits.

Over the month leading up to Harry's death, she had come to this house more frequently, sometimes spending the night. She had waited for his dose of morphine to shut him down, then she drove to the dealership, took one of the scrap cars, and drove to Ballinroy. Here, the dreadful effort

418

of being Roberta Garrick was left outside. Here, she slept soundly on the mattress upstairs. She always woke in time to drive back to Morganstown, swap cars, and get home to serve Harry's breakfast.

Sometimes, but not often, she woke in the night, sprawled on the mattress, cold and frightened. She lay in the dark, quiet as the dead, and listened. Sometimes she heard Roberta Garrick outside, trying to get in. Scratching at the doors and windows, seeking entry so that she could eat Hannah Mackenzie whole.

But not often.

The living room open, the kitchen closed. Had it been so the last time? Didn't matter. She needed to empty the safe, that was all.

Roberta got to her knees in front of the cupboard, opened it, revealing the safe she had found on a second-hand goods website. She remembered the man who delivered it here six years ago, how he struggled to move it with the hand truck, how he grumbled when she asked him to bring it inside and put it in the cupboard.

The dial clicked as she turned it, listening to the tumblers fall into place. Then the door wheezed open half an inch, and she pulled it the rest of the way. Inside, on the top shelf, one thousand pounds in sterling,

another two thousand in euros, and passports in the name of Hannah Mackenzie,
one British, one Irish. On the lower shelf, a
birth certificate, an envelope full of bank
statements, one debit and one credit card.

Everything Hannah Mackenzie needed to
get out, get away, start again. Maybe even
find another dead girl whose life was lying
around waiting to be picked up and used
again.

Twelve years ago, Hannah Mackenzie had
been shocked at how simple it was to
become Roberta Bailey. Death and birth
records were easily searchable, and not
cross-referenced. She had gone to the
library and checked old editions of local
newspapers to find any deaths of young girls
around a decade or so before. It didn't take
long to find the headlines about a meningitis
outbreak in the Magherafelt area. One of
the victims a twelve-year-old girl, an only
child, taken so tragically young. Red hair,
just like hers. Pretty, just like her. Hannah
Mackenzie simply paid for a copy of
Roberta Bailey's birth certificate, and the
rest was easy.

The new life she had manufactured for
herself had, for a time, been glorious. Harry
had not been hard to find. The dating
website was full of lonely men with money

to spend, and she had gone on several dates. But Harry was the best of them all; not only the wealthiest, but the most willing to be drawn in by her. The religion part had been easy, seeing as her mother had made her go to church and Sunday school every weekend, just to get her out of the house. She bluffed what she couldn't remember, and Harry was swept away by her, this young attractive Christian woman.

That life only began to crack when the child took root in her belly.

She didn't want to think about that. Instead, she concentrated on gathering up what she needed, stuffing rolls of cash into her coat pockets, slipping passports and documents into the envelope with the bank statements.

Not far to Antrim from here, and the outlet mall, a complex of shops selling discounted brands. Buy a few changes of cheap clothes and a small carry-on bag, along with a prepaid mobile phone. Call an airline, get a ticket to anywhere so long as it was out of this country. She could find a guesthouse for tonight if need be. This time tomorrow, she would be somewhere far away, somewhere warm where no one knew what Hannah Mackenzie or Roberta Garrick had done, those wicked sisters with their poisonous sins.

She pushed the safe door closed and spun the dial. Done. Time to go.

As she withdrew her hand, she felt air move across the back of it, cool on her skin. She turned her head towards the kitchen door. Again, a draught.

A strange calm settled on her then. The panic should have torn itself loose, crashing through her mind. She should have sprinted for the front door, out to the car, and away. Instead, she got to her feet and reached for the kitchen door handle.

52

Flanagan stood wedged into the space between the door and the end of the row of high- and low-level cupboards, the edge of the tiled worktop digging into her hip. Perhaps she should have made for the back door, but she could not do so in silence. Roberta, Hannah, whoever the hell she was, would have heard the door creak open and would have either attacked or fled.

But what to do?

She had listened to the woman on the other side of the door, heard the clicks of the combination lock, the rustling of paper, then the clank as the safe closed once more. Then deep silence. Why didn't Roberta go? Just turn around, go back out and drive away? Flanagan and Murray could find her, follow her. It was almost certain she would head north towards the airport. But she did not go. Flanagan pictured her on the other side of the door, listening as Flanagan listened.

Slowly, Flanagan let her fingers creep towards the holster attached to her waistband. She undid the catch, eased her Glock 17 from the leather, brought it up to her other hand. No round in the chamber. She could not risk racking the slide, the snick-click sounding like a thunderclap in the quiet.

The door handle moved, the springs of its mechanism creaking. Flanagan held her breath, pressed herself deeper into the space. The handle depressed, the door opened, cracking from its hinges. She felt the door against her shoulder. In the window, her faint reflection, and that of Roberta Garrick, separated by a barrier of white-painted wood.

53

Roberta looked into the kitchen, saw the source of the breeze: the back door open, its frame split at the lock. Cool air on her face.

Who had been here? And when?

Perhaps a burglary, some intruder hoping for an easy haul. They would have been disappointed, the only thing here a safe they couldn't open and would have struggled to move.

But no. Too great a coincidence.

It had been the police. Had to be. So they had traced Hannah Mackenzie to this house. How? The only thing that linked Roberta to Hannah was a payment bounced through the Isle of Man account, and the accountant had assured her that it was in a separate jurisdiction, one that was known for its financial discretion, and no UK authority could touch it. What if he had been wrong? Freddie Boland had been her

425

husband's accountant for years, and she had always had a low opinion of him, but surely he couldn't get something like that wrong?

She would have cursed him, but it didn't matter now. The police had been here, and the passports and documents were now useless to her. The only remaining option was to head for the border, use the cash to buy some time until she could figure out what to do next.

She was about to close the door, head for the car and get out of here, when she noticed her reflection in the window, silhouetted by the light from the hall. Hannah Mackenzie's reflection. Roberta Garrick's reflection. The lives of both of those women had now ended, and she felt a pang of mourning for them both.

Move, she thought. Get out. Find a new woman to be.

Then she noticed the other reflection, faint next to hers.

A woman on the other side of the door.

For a wild moment, she thought it was another her, Roberta and Hannah separated, standing side by side. As panic flared in her breast, she stared, forced her eyes to focus on the faint form.

Then she knew, and the panic turned to scorching rage.

54

Flanagan stared at the ghosts on the glass, met Roberta's reflected eyes, thought: she sees me.

They both stood still and quiet, not a breath between them, watching, watching, watching.

Slowly, so slowly, Flanagan raised her left hand up to the pistol held in her right, gripped the slide assembly, silently counted to three, then pulled it back, released it.

She didn't see Roberta move, only felt her weight on the other side of the door as she slammed her body against it and into Flanagan. The door drove Flanagan's hip into the edge of the worktop, and the side of her head into the upper cabinet. Hot and heavy pain burst behind her eyes, she saw the room turn as if upended. A warm trickle over her ear. Her knees gave way, but she caught herself with an arm on the worktop.

A moment to swallow a breath, then

Roberta screamed and rammed the door into her once more, the weight of it now trapping Flanagan's chest between the wood, crushing all air from her lungs. She fell, her right hand striking the linoleum first, the pistol clattering from her grasp, then her chest and chin, sending more black stars to dance in her vision.

The pistol, get the pistol.

She tried to get to her hands and knees, but her lungs shrieked for air, her diaphragm flexed and spasmed. The Glock remained three feet beyond her reach, and she crawled on her belly towards it, but Roberta fell on her back, put a knee between her shoulders. Flanagan croaked, a string of spit flowing from her mouth.

Air, air, please God, I need air.

Roberta drove her fist into the side of Flanagan's head, and Flanagan heard a crunch and a cry of pain before everything went grey for a moment. Another cry, and Flanagan knew something had broken in Roberta's hand. She turned her head, tried to shift her weight, but Roberta's forearm dropped onto her cheek, slammed her head against the floor, and once more she lost the edge of her consciousness to the grey.

Then the weight left her back, and she felt she could float there an inch from the floor, and she saw Roberta scramble to the pistol, grab it with her left hand, heard the bark of its discharge as her finger found the trigger, sending a bullet into the wall. Roberta gasped and dropped it again, the empty cartridge jangling across the floor. Flanagan squirmed towards the pistol, her ears ringing with the shot, but Roberta retrieved it, crawled to the other side of the kitchen.

Blood pooled on the linoleum beneath Flanagan's chin. Her mouth filled with hot pennies. A stream of it around her ear. She tried to inhale, choked on it, coughed a spray across the floor. Then she vomited, her gut convulsing, the grey flooding in, and now she wanted to sleep. Roll away from the foulness she lay in, close her eyes, let the darkness take her.

Concussion, I've got concussion. Stay awake.

Flanagan forced her gaze upwards and saw Roberta hunkered against the wall, cradling her right hand in her lap, the pistol held loose in her left. Roberta raised the Glock, her hand trembling. She pushed up with her legs, her back sliding on the tiled wall. The Glock's muzzle twitched in Flanagan's vision. Roberta brought up her right hand, already swelling around the break, and steadied her left wrist against her fore-arm.

"Don't," Flanagan said.

She saw the muzzle flash, felt the pressure in her ears, and linoleum and concrete exploded inches from her face. Somehow she found the strength to roll to the side, her back hitting the cupboards as another boom hit her ears, another burst of concrete.

Stop, she wanted to shout, stop, let me see my children again.

She opened her mouth, found a gasp of air, heard the crashing of wood through the high whine, saw the gate through the back door, saw it slam against the wall, teetering loose from its hinges. Murray there, his weapon up and ready, peering into the dim-ness of the kitchen.

Roberta saw him too, swung her left hand around, pulled the trigger once, twice, three times, the glass spidering, fragments hang-ing from the wire mesh, spent cartridges falling to the floor. Flanagan saw Murray duck back into the alley, his head down. Roberta sank back into the corner where the worktop met the wall. Her back against the cupboard doors, Flanagan smelled cordite and vomit, and her stomach threat-ened to revolt again.

Murray edged back to the door, then

dipped away again as two more shots cracked and boomed. Flanagan got to her knees, but Roberta turned her jittering aim back to her, and Flanagan raised her hands, knew beyond all certainty that Roberta would not miss this time.

Another shot, but from outside, and the cupboard door closest to Roberta's head splintered. She turned back, fired again and again, hitting nothing but glass and air, Murray taking shelter once more.

Flanagan crawled back towards the kitchen door, keeping her eyes on Roberta. She threw herself through, catching a glimpse of Roberta turning back to her, heard an animal scream, a shot, felt wood splinters scatter above her head. She got to her hands and knees again and crawled into the living room, turned on her back, kicked the door closed, put her feet against it.

"Bitch!" The voice high and fractured on the other side of the door. "Fucking bitch!"

The door pushed against Flanagan's feet, and she pushed back.

Crack, crack, crack, three splintered holes in the door, three explosions of plaster dust, photographs falling from the wall. Then another shot from farther back, Murray, coming after her. And running footsteps, the front door opening, slamming closed again.

Flanagan got up on her knees, grabbed the door handle, hauled herself to her feet, opened it as Murray emerged from the kitchen, his pistol smoking.

"After . . ." Not enough air to finish the command, Flanagan pointed at the front door.

Murray sprinted for it, open, through, out onto the street. Flanagan heard the spinning tyres, a metallic thud as Roberta's car hit another, then the engine roaring and fading. She staggered to the front of the house, tried to tell Murray to get his car, but her lungs would not allow it. He understood anyway, ran to the side of the house where he had parked.

Flanagan lurched along the path, stopped to throw up once more, wiped blood and vomit on her sleeve. She followed Murray to the corner, and he reversed to meet her. He spoke as she collapsed into the passenger seat, but she couldn't hear him above the whine in her ears and the roar in her skull.

The car launched forward as she closed the door, and through the chaos in her mind she wondered why Murray drove this way. Seconds later she understood as he followed a curving lane that looped back to the main road. They rounded the bend in time to see a wreck of a Citroën pull out of the junction, causing another car to swerve.

The Citroën went right, not left. "Not . . . going for the . . . the airport," Flanagan said, squeezing the words between shallow gasps.

"She's heading back to Moira," Murray said. "The airport's no good to her now. She's going to try for the border."

He flicked on the car's hazard lights. His own personal vehicle, the BMW was not equipped with blues or a siren. He accelerated out of the junction, two cars between them and Roberta.

Flanagan slumped back in the seat, fighting nausea. "Just . . . keep her in sight. Not a . . . pursuit."

Roberta's Citroën edged to the centre of the road as she searched for a gap to overtake the car in front of her.

"Get Pu . . . Purdy on the phone. Tell him . . . she's coming back their way. Head her off."

Murray kept one hand on the wheel as he fished his mobile phone from his pocket, the call connecting over the car's Bluetooth system. Flanagan wound the window down, let the rush of cold air blast the fog from her mind, willed herself not to throw up over Murray's upholstery.

Ahead, Roberta Garrick, Hannah Mackenzie, the animal, veered between cars, nothing but death in front of her.

"I won't let her die," Flanagan said.

Murray glanced at her. "What?"

Purdy's voice barked over the car's speakers before Flanagan could say it again.

55

Roberta Garrick glanced in the rear-view mirror.

Yes, Roberta Garrick. Hannah Mackenzie remained back in that house, a ghost to haunt it for as long as it stood. Hannah Mackenzie was gone, and Roberta Garrick was here, looking in this mirror. She craned her neck, saw her own eyes, wild and wide. Then the road behind her.

The white BMW still there, but hanging back. She hadn't seen them get into that car, but it had followed her out of the junction. It had to be them. So why didn't they chase her?

The gun lay on the passenger seat, a faint pale ribbon of smoke still coming from the muzzle, filling the car with its acrid smell. She didn't know how many bullets it held, how many were left. She kept her left hand on the wheel, her right forearm holding it steady when she needed to change gear.

The end of the world, she thought.

This morning it seemed as if everything was on track, her future secured. And then, in less than two hours, it had all burned to the ground. She would die today, there was no doubt of that. It was only a matter of how and when. How much pain could she endure in the act? All the pain in world. She could take every burning drop of it.

The car drifted to the centre of the road, forcing the oncoming traffic to move to the hard shoulder. Horns blared, but she could barely hear them. One jerk of the wheel, and she could meet one of the cars head on. Or she could lift the gun from the passenger seat, put it to her temple, or into her mouth.

"Not yet," she said.

Roberta Garrick — and that was her name, she was almost certain — began to cry. A desperate keening. She wished to take it all back, to start again. The same way she'd felt when that other her, Hannah, after that drunken night at the Students' Union bar when she had pushed her housemate down the stairs, after she'd stood and watched the girl bounce down the steps, arms flailing, and the snap of her neck as she hit the floor. Back then, Hannah, sober in a cell, had cried and begged God to take

436

today, wipe it out, and make it yesterday.

She wanted that now. The past hours to be erased, the clock to be reset to midnight. And that could not be, so tears were all she had. Had her rational mind been in control, she might have been conscious that she wept not out of remorse for her sins, but out of fear for herself. She did not want death, but it wanted her, and it would have its due.

Another pealing of car horns as she drifted once more, her vision blurred, the road ahead a streak of grey cutting through green. She wiped her eyes on her right sleeve, blinked them clear. She saw the BMW in the mirror, still keeping its distance. How long had she been driving? And where to? She knew she was headed back to the Moira roundabout. There was no chance she would make the border, and even if she could, it wouldn't help.

Home, she thought. I'm going home. To my beautiful house and the beautiful gardens and all the beautiful things that I worked so hard for. The home in which my beloved husband took his own life after months of suffering. I'm going home, and I'm going to lie down on my bed, and I'm going to put the muzzle of this gun to my temple and squeeze the trigger.

The decision made, she felt better. She pressed the accelerator with her foot and passed another two cars, thinking of that fiery bloom inside her skull, the comet trail of the bullet through her head.

56

"Stay back," Purdy said, his voice crackling through the speakers. "Don't make her panic and hurt anyone else. We'll close everything but the Glenavy side of the roundabout, so if she enters it, she won't get out of it again."

"She might not go that far," Flanagan said.

"Maybe, but it's the best guess right now. A pursuit car is heading your way, but I don't know if it'll reach you in time. Stay on the line, I'm going to patch in Command."

Flanagan's head had cleared a little, but the movement of the car, the sway as it pulled out and past other vehicles, churned her stomach. She watched road signs as she listened to the dial tone.

A young woman's voice said, "This is Command, go ahead."

"Glenavy Road," Flanagan said. "A26, we're just coming up to Hammonds Road, heading south, speed seventy miles per hour. Target is approximately one hundred yards ahead, two cars between us. Will update."

"Pursuit car and support should join you at Glenavy Services. Helicopter in the air in five minutes."

"Understood," Flanagan said.

A road sign said one mile to the roundabout. If Roberta intended to get off the main road, she'd need to do it soon. Only a few more turn-offs before the roundabout. They reached the brow of a hill and the long incline on the other side. Glenavy Services at the bottom of the dip, the railway bridge beyond. The Enterprise train crossed it on its way to Belfast.

Flanagan strained her eyes, looking for the marked cars that should have been waiting at the service exit. There, she could make out the bright blues and yellows. She nudged Murray's arm.

"Get moving," she said.

"Yes, ma'am," Murray said, shifting down a gear and stepping on the accelerator.

He hit the button to activate his hazard lights and eased out into the centre of the road. Flanagan felt the BMW's engine thrum as the acceleration pushed her back into the seat. Only a small number of oncoming drivers, who hit their horns and flashed their lights as they had to swerve onto the hard shoulder. No more ahead. Flanagan understood the traffic had now been stopped at the roundabout, no more coming this way. They passed the first car between them and the Citroën, got an angry look from the driver. Flanagan held her warrant card up to the window, but it didn't seem to placate him. The second car edged over to the hard shoulder to make room, and Flanagan waved thanks on the way past.

"Now slow down," Flanagan said. "Leave space for the pursuit car to get in."

Murray eased off the accelerator. Flanagan saw smoke plume from the Citroën's exhaust; Roberta had seen them close the gap and was speeding up.

Up ahead, the pursuit car, a Škoda Octavia VRS, nosed out of the junction. The Citroën wavered as Roberta saw it. She braked for a moment, then accelerated again. The Škoda shot out of the Services exit as she passed, building speed so fast she couldn't create a gap between them. The support car went to follow, but Murray leaned on his horn, and the driver held back to let them take the place behind the pursuit car.

"We're behind the pursuit car now," Flanagan said.

"Understood," came the voice from Command.

Once the support car had slotted in behind Murray's BMW, it slowed to a crawl, forcing the traffic behind to keep back. As the trees in the roundabout's centre island came into view, so did a string of slow-moving cars at the entrance to the roundabout. Flanagan saw a pair of uniformed officers in fluorescent jackets pointing them in the direction of the motorway exit. They intended to close the exit before Roberta's car got there, trap her like a fly in a jar.

The evening sky dimmed, cloud thick and grey above.

Let them take you, Flanagan thought. Don't fight.

But she knew there would be no easy end to this.

57

Roberta wept when she saw the police car edging its way out of the junction. Adrenalin had been raging through her system ever since she found Flanagan in the house, and now it needed its release.

This is it, she thought. This is the end.

Not yet. She could still fight.

She stood on the Citroën's accelerator, and its engine moaned under the pressure. The speedometer needle crawled higher, the little car already running at its limits. Wisps of smoke trickled from the sides of the bonnet, whipped away by the wind.

Up ahead, a line of traffic queuing to enter the roundabout. Nothing coming from the other way. Then she understood: they had closed the entries and exits.

"Fuck," she said, her face wet with tears. "Fuck, fuck."

Roberta jerked the steering wheel to the right, onto the other side of the road, heading the wrong way to the roundabout's exit, keeping her foot planted. She glanced in the mirror, saw the police car and the BMW had followed her move. So had the other police; they'd left this exit open, anticipating that she'd come this way. A marked Land Rover waited by the exit, reversed in to block it as soon as she and the two cars in pursuit had passed through.

She did not slow as the Citroën's tyres scrabbled for grip, the car leaning as she steered the wrong way around the curve, then onto the elevated straight section that led to the Moira exit. She glimpsed the line of cars on the ramp leading off the motorway's northbound lane, held back by another Land Rover. Uniformed officers everywhere.

"Fuck," she said.

The marked car accelerated past her on the inside, its engine roaring, then pulled in front of her. She jerked her steering wheel left and right, but there was nowhere to go. The white BMW pulled up close behind her, and the convoy slowed as it rounded the eastern end of the roundabout, then onto the straight leading back to the western end.

Two Land Rovers blocked the road ahead completely. Trapped. She was trapped.

One thing left to do.

Roberta closed her eyes. Slammed her foot hard on the accelerator pedal. Hauled the steering wheel to the right. Readied herself for the impact and the fall.

The crash came, and she was thrown against the steering wheel, feeling it punch her chest. No airbag, her torso took the full force of it. But no fall. She had expected the car to plough through the fence and plummet to the motorway below, but it had merely buckled the metal.

She pushed herself off the steering wheel, howled at the pain, then groaned as she realised she had broken something inside. Her vision cleared, and through the smoke and steam she saw that the BMW and the marked car had stopped twenty yards ahead, in front of the Land Rovers that blocked the road. A few blurred figures emerged from the cars.

Roberta reached for the pistol on the passenger seat, found it wasn't there. She blinked smoke out of her eyes, coughed, screamed at the pain. Her hand explored the seat, under it, down the sides. The gun had slid off in the impact, bounced away somewhere in the recesses. It didn't matter now. What good would it do her?

She tried the driver's door handle, but the

445

door wouldn't budge, jammed in place. Despite the pain, she leaned over to the passenger side, pulled the handle, let the door swing open. She hauled herself across, pausing to cry out at the grinding of whatever had fractured in her chest, her broken right hand clutched to her belly. The ground slammed into her left shoulder as she fell out, and she lay for a few seconds, glorying in the pain and the sudden clarity it brought.

"Don't move!"

She craned her neck to see who had shouted at her. A woman's voice. She could barely hear it above the whine and clamour inside her head. Flanagan, maybe? There she was, behind the BMW, along with a line of other officers. Weapons pointed at her.

"Put the weapon down!"

"I don't . . . I . . ."

She didn't have the breath to push the words out. Somehow, she got her knees under her, and her left hand, then her feet. Upright, she raised her good hand, showed them it was empty, her right still held tight to her stomach.

"Drop the weapon!"

She tried to lift her right hand, but a sun burned there, too heavy for her to lift.

"I don't have it," she said, but she heard

her own voice as a rumble inside her head and throat. "Don't have it," she said again.

Pretend you do, she thought. Pretend you're going to shoot them, and they'll shoot you. And then it'll be over.

She smiled and pointed her left hand at them, made the fingers into a gun, moved her thumb to mime the hammer fall. Then she laughed at the foolishness of it, and howled at the pain it brought.

Flanagan moved from behind the BMW. Someone, that nice young policeman whose name Roberta could not recall, tried to stop her, but Flanagan shook him off and kept coming.

Roberta looked to her right, saw the traffic backed up on the slip road down to the motorway beneath, the cars slow on the inside lane, quicker on the outside, all heading away towards the city to the north-east. The idea presented itself clear and simple to her. So she acted on it.

She walked the few steps to the metal railing covered in blistered blue paint. One hand useless, the other grasping, she pulled herself up on it, screamed at the fresh surge of pain from her chest.

I don't have the strength, she thought.

Yes you do.

She hauled her left leg over, then her right.

Somewhere very far away she heard Serena Flanagan shout, no, no, no, but she ignored the frantic voice as she found the concrete ledge with her toes. Her chest to the railing, her back to the wind, she saw Flanagan coming in a lopsided, limping run, Murray sprinting behind her, more officers following.

Roberta's eyes met Flanagan's, and she gave her a smile.

Then she let go.

58

Flanagan ignored the pain, the nausea, the drifting of the world on its axis, and threw herself towards the railing, her hands out-stretched. The fingers of her left hand snatched at the fabric of the coat, took hold, her other hand reaching farther. Then Roberta's weight jerked her forward, and her body slammed into the railing, her shoulder shrieking at the strain. As her feet left the ground, she got her right hand under Roberta's arm, pulled with everything she had.

Her legs kicked at the air as her chest slid over the top of the railing. Roberta writhed in her grasp. Flanagan pushed her foot through the gap in the railing, hooked it there, tried to stop the steady slide over the top.

"Let me go," Roberta screamed, her mouth inches from Flanagan's ear.

"No," Flanagan hissed. "You don't get to die."

Roberta wedged the soles of her feet against the concrete ledge, pushed, pulled Flanagan until the top of the railing dug into her stomach. She screamed, hooked her other foot into a gap.

"Then you can come with me," Roberta said, and she jerked her body from one side to the other.

Footsteps behind. Flanagan turned her head, saw Murray and two uniforms, shouted at them to help. She closed her eyes as her feet began to slip, her own weight beginning to carry her forward, out over the edge.

"You don't get to die," she said again.

Then strong arms around and over her, hauling her back.

"Don't let her fall!" she shouted, her hands digging into the fabric of Roberta's coat, her fingernails bending and tearing.

More footsteps, more arms and hands.

"Get her, don't let her fall!"

The fabric slipped from Flanagan's fingers and she was weightless, tumbling back, the road hitting her shoulders hard. She heard a scream, waited for the shrieking of tyres, the sound of a car hitting flesh and bone.

But it never came.

Instead, Flanagan heard another body hit the ground beside hers, followed by a cry of pain and despair and anger. She turned her head, saw Roberta Garrick, Hannah Mackenzie, face down, staring back at her, pure fiery hate in her eyes.

"You don't get to die," Flanagan said.

59

They kept her in a side ward, away from the good people. Four beds in this room, all empty. A laminated sign taped to the door said ORTHOPAEDIC CLINIC. Bustle beyond the door, voices and footsteps. Somewhere out there an old man shouted incoherent rants between cries of pain.

Roberta had not cried out when the doctor set her hand. Instead, she bit down hard until the muscles either side of her jaw ached with the effort. The young doctor had inserted a needle between her third and fourth fingers, and again in her wrist, and a vague numbness followed. But not enough to blank out the pain as he realigned the bones.

She had cracked a rib, he said, looking at the X-ray clipped to a light box. He had been nervous in the company of the police officers, unable to look her in the eye. Afraid of her. She had smiled for him, parted her lips, let him see the tip of her tongue. But the fear did not leave him, because he knew what she was. They all did.

Now the nice policeman, Detective Sergeant Murray, dozed in a chair in the corner of the side ward while two uniformed officers sat in silence by the door. Pale dawn light through the windows. The cast felt clumsy and heavy on her hand, the skin beneath itching. Strapping around her chest made it impossible to take more than shallow breaths.

The anaesthetic in her hand had long since worn off, but she could endure the pain. It wouldn't be for long, anyway. She'd be left alone sooner or later, and she had no intention of going back to prison. A belt, a length of material, a sharp edge. She had studied these things, the methods, over many months. All she needed was the opportunity.

A little after seven in the morning, going by the clock on the wall, DCI Serena Flanagan entered the ward. Swelling on her lip, a gauze pad on her temple. Murray jerked awake, cleared his throat, sat upright. Flanagan came to the bed beside Roberta's, sat on its edge.

She pointed to the side of her head, said, "Three stitches, in case you're wondering."

"I wasn't," Roberta said.

"We'll be leaving soon," Flanagan said. "The Serious Crime Suite in Antrim. We'll make sure it's a ligature-free cell. We won't give you the chance."

Roberta smiled at Flanagan's perceptiveness. "I'll find a way. I tend to get what I want."

"I know you'll try," Flanagan said. "You'll be in DCI Conn's custody for the journey. This is still his case. But I wanted to ask you something before you go."

Roberta waited, still smiling.

"Did you kill your daughter?"

She felt the smile leave her mouth like dust blown from glass. Closed her eyes, opened them again, stared at the fluorescent light above her.

"Yes, I did," she said.

A crackle went through the room, a lightning arc between the men, but not between Flanagan and Roberta. There were no secrets between them; perhaps there had never been, right from the start.

"Tell me," Flanagan said.

"Do you really want to know?"

"No, I don't. Tell me anyway."

Roberta took a breath, turned her eyes to Flanagan, and began.

"The pregnancy was unplanned. I never

wanted a child. I had everything I wanted. What did I need a baby for? Harry knew I was pregnant before I did. He said I'd changed, something was different. My period was late, but I didn't think it was that, not a baby. I ignored him, and another week went by with no period, then another. Then he brought home one of those testing sticks. And there it was, a little blue cross.

"If I could have, I would have got rid of it. Flown to England, if I had to. But there was no way to get past Harry. He was so happy. He'd told everyone almost as soon as the test was done, so there was no getting out of it, unless I had some sort of accident. And I did try. All I did was make myself sick.

"Then the baby came — I had a Caesarean — and everyone around us was so delighted and all I wanted to do was throw it out of a window. But I played my part. I fed it, I looked after it, and it grew. I suppose I liked it well enough, but what about me? It was constant, not a second to breathe. My life had gone. Harry was no use, he thought it was a woman's job to look after it. He just played with it now and again. And his brother and that horrible little wife of his, always hanging around. I hadn't worked so hard for this life to lose it to a baby. I stood it for almost two years, two years of my life soaked up by this little creature that wasn't even really mine."

Flanagan cocked her head to the side. "Not yours?"

"Who gave birth to it? Was it really me? It never felt like it came from my body, even after they cut it out of me. Anyway, I persuaded Harry to take a week off work and take us to Barcelona. We rented an apartment in Poblenou. Do you know Barcelona?"

Flanagan shook her head.

"It's beautiful in Poblenou, not so many tourists. Our apartment was on the Rambla there, just a stone's throw from the beach. Every evening when Harry went to sleep, and the baby, I went and sat out on the balcony and just watched people pass by. It was lovely.

"Then one day the three of us went to the beach. Harry didn't want to go in the water, so I left the baby with him and went swimming by myself. I'm a good swimmer, did you know? I always have been. When I came out, Harry asked me, why don't you take the baby in for a while? It had one of those special nappies on, the ones for swimming. So I carried it out, up to my waist, then a bit farther.

"I remember it was shivering, saying cold, cold. So I walked out a bit farther, till the water was up to my chest. That lovely feeling when the waves lift you off your feet. Then a bit farther again, and I felt the drop beneath my feet. Not much, but enough that I couldn't stand with my head above water.

"You know, I didn't plan anything. It's not like I set out to do it. I remember suddenly seeing it, all those years stretched out in front of me, raising it, sending it to school, all the times it would get sick, and I'd have to clean it up, years and years before I could get my life back. So I knew what to do."

A pause, then in a very small voice, Flanagan asked, "What did you do?"

"I held it under. One hand on the back of its neck, paddling with the other, kicking with my feet. It was hard to do. Physically, I mean. I struggled to keep my mouth and nose out of the water. I started to get a little afraid, especially when it started thrashing around. Then it stopped, and I let go."

Roberta remembered the sensation of floating in the water, lifted and dropped by the waves, her right hand beneath the surface, so terribly empty. A few seconds of elation.

"And then I realised what I'd done," she

457

said. "I realised I shouldn't have. I wanted to take it back. I thought maybe I could save it. I suppose I panicked a little. So I dived under with my eyes open — you can keep your eyes open in seawater, it doesn't hurt — and I could just make it out, drifting near the bottom. I swam down and tried to get hold of it, but I needed air, so I had to go back up. That was when I called for help. I went under again, but it had drifted farther away, and I had to stay under longer. I breathed water. It hurt. Everything went black. Next thing I remember is lying in the sand, vomiting salt water. And that's all."

Quiet for a long time, not even the sound of breathing. Roberta wondered if she should have felt some sort of relief from telling it all, but there was none. Same as before. A hollow place where she supposed her guilt should have been.

Eventually, Flanagan slid off the bed, stood upright, and said, "Okay, let's go. Get up."

Roberta reached out her left hand. "Please."

Flanagan took her hand, helped her sit upright. Then Roberta lowered her feet to the floor, straightened, and faced the police-woman. It hadn't occurred to her before now, but she stood a good couple of inches taller than Flanagan. The policewoman seemed so small now, so tired.

When Roberta opened her mouth to say she hoped Flanagan would get some rest, the fist shot up, caught the underside of her jaw, and the floor tilted beneath her feet. She fell back on the bed, her mouth filling with blood from the bite in her tongue. Then Flanagan's hand was on her throat, the policewoman's weight on her chest, and the pain, oh the pain.

"It was a she," Flanagan said, her teeth flashing. "Her name was Erin."

Roberta wanted to scream, but she couldn't draw breath, and pressure swelled in her head as the fingers tightened beneath her jaw. Flanagan's nose inches from hers, Roberta saw her mouth work, the lips part, then felt the hot saliva as Flanagan spat in her face.

Murray grabbed Flanagan by the shoulders, pulled her away, the hand slipping from Roberta's throat.

60

Alistair slipped a hand around Flanagan's waist, and they leaned into each other as the waiter led them to the restaurant's back room. Deep and rich aromas drifted through the place, turmeric, cardamom, garlic, fresh baked bread. Diners ate tandoori chicken, bhunas, saags. The sights and smells made Flanagan's stomach growl, the first real appetite she had felt in almost two weeks.

She had called Miriam McCreesh that morning, and they'd had a long talk. Flanagan had apologised at least three times for not being in touch, but McCreesh had brushed it off each time. She knew the demands of this life. After the call, Flanagan had locked her office door and kneeled beneath the window. She prayed thanks for her blessings, for her family, for her own health, and for Reverend Peter McKay's soul. A female minister from the north-east coast had given a statement, said she'd met

McKay on the beach at Cushendun. They'd talked about faith and prayer, and Flanagan hoped it had done McKay some good.

Flanagan took a half day, went home at two o'clock, and luxuriated in the rituals of getting ready to go out. It seemed an age since she and Alistair had gone anywhere as a couple, so long a time that she didn't dare count the months.

They arrived early, and DSI Purdy and his wife were the only ones waiting in the private room. Purdy already had an empty bottle of Cobra beer in front of him, and was working on the second, his arm draped around his wife's shoulder.

He stood as Flanagan and Alistair entered. He shook Alistair's hand, then wrapped his arms around Flanagan, tight, squeezing the air out of her.

"Thanks for coming, love," he said before planting a kiss on her cheek.

"Love?" Flanagan said, leaning back.

He grinned. "As of five o'clock this evening, I am no longer your boss, and I can call you love if I want. And I can give you a kiss if I want, so here's another one."

She giggled and accepted the gesture, smelled the booze on him. "Jesus, when did you start?"

"One minute past five," he said, his smile

461

beaming. Flanagan couldn't help but reflect it back to him.

They took their seats, Purdy insisting that Flanagan sit beside him. His wife didn't seem to mind; she was every bit as merry as her husband.

"She's confessed everything," he said.

Flanagan didn't need to ask whom he meant. "Her husband? And Reverend McKay?"

"That's right," Purdy said. "She started an affair with McKay not long after the husband had the car accident. He was weak, and she knew she could manipulate him. She convinced him to slip Mr. Garrick the overdose, thinking she could break it off with him after and he'd be too scared to say anything. But you messed it up for her, talking to McKay the way you did. He was ready to tell you everything, so she did him in."

Flanagan pictured the last time she'd seen McKay, watching her drive away from the church, the look of a lost and desperate man. A man who would still be alive if she'd only gone to him when he asked.

"I know what you're thinking," Purdy said. "Stop it. You'd no way of knowing what was going to happen. Roberta Gar— sorry, Hannah Mackenzie killed that man. It was

nobody's fault but hers. If you keep thinking different, you'll tear yourself to pieces."

Flanagan shook her head. "I know, but I
—"

"Stop it," Purdy said. "That's an order."

She allowed him a hint of a smile. "I
thought you weren't my boss any more."

"I came out of retirement, there, just for a
minute."

The room began to fill, and Purdy's attention turned to the other guests. Alistair
wrapped his fingers around Flanagan's.
With his free hand, he adjusted her hair,
hid the cluster of stitches and the coin-sized
shaved patch. She kissed him for the kind-
ness of the gesture.

Food came and went, beer and wine,
stories told and retold.

Amid the chatter, Flanagan put her arm
around her husband, brought her lips to his
ear and said, "We're going to be all right,
aren't we?"

Alistair kissed her neck, sending sparks
down her spine. His breath warm on her
ear as he said, "Yes, we are."

ACKNOWLEDGEMENTS

I am indebted to all who have helped me get this story out of my head and onto the page:

My agents Nat Sobel and Judith Weber who help me navigate these often-turbulent waters, and all at Sobel Weber Associates. And also Caspian Dennis, who listens to me moan more than anyone should have to, and all at Abner Stein.

My editors Geoff Mulligan, Alison Hennessey and Juliet Grames, who help turn my sow's ears into something resembling silk purses. And all at Vintage Books and Soho Press, especially Bronwen Hruska and Paul Oliver.

A special thank you to Canon John Mc-Kegney. This novel began life as a short story written for radio, and John's kind words about that piece helped encourage me to expand it into a book. Later on, John kindly provided me with tremendous insights into the workings of a church and the life of a clergyman. Any inaccuracies in the depiction are entirely mine.

I am deeply grateful to my local libraries for providing a quiet haven in which to write, and to all the bookstores who continue to fight the good fight. And to my friends in all corners of the crime fiction community.

Thanks to my friends and wider family for the constant support; it's always appreciated.

Finally, and most of all, I owe this book and my remaining sanity to my family: Issy and Ezra, and especially Jo, who has given me so much time and space and support, even when I least deserved it, and also proved an invaluable sounding board.

The employees of Thorndike Press hope you have enjoyed this Large Print book. All our Thorndike, Wheeler, and Kennebec Large Print titles are designed for easy reading, and all our books are made to last. Other Thorndike Press Large Print books are available at your library, through selected bookstores, or directly from us.

For information about titles, please call:
  (800) 223-1244

or visit our Web site at:
  http://gale.cengage.com/thorndike

To share your comments, please write:
  Publisher
  Thorndike Press
  10 Water St., Suite 310
  Waterville, ME 04901